# Inherit the Bones

# Inherit the Bones

## Emily Littlejohn

MINOTAUR BOOKS
NEW YORK

INHERIT THE BONES. Copyright © 2016 by Emily Littlejohn. All rights reserved. Printed in the United States of America. For information, address St. Martin's Press, 175 Fifth Avenue, New York, N.Y. 10010.

www.minotaurbooks.com

The Library of Congress Cataloging-in-Publication Data is available upon request.

ISBN 978-1-250-08939-7 (hardcover)
ISBN 978-1-250-08940-3 (e-book)

Our books may be purchased in bulk for promotional, educational, or business use. Please contact your local bookseller or the Macmillan Corporate and Premium Sales Department at (800) 221-7945, extension 5442, or by e-mail at MacmillanSpecialMarkets@macmillan.com.

First Edition: November 2016

10 9 8 7 6 5 4 3 2 1

For my parents,

who made everything possible

# Acknowledgments

This book would not have been written without the help of a great many people. David Neal and Ana Cabrales were my earliest readers, and their hunger for more chapters propelled me forward when I needed it most. Patricia Hackett, William Lindenmuth, Kelda Neely, and Kathy Littlejohn offered suggestions that strengthened the story. Pam Ahearn and Elizabeth Lacks—you have truly changed my life. Don Sells, you told me once that you could see me as a writer. Here's to offhand comments on cold Oxford days. Mom, Carrie, Kathy, Matt, Jim, and Jill, your support means the world to me. And to my dear husband, Christopher, you are simply the best. I love you more.

# Inherit the Bones

# Chapter one

In my dreams, the dead can speak. They call to me, in whispers and murmurs, and I greet them by name, like old friends. Tommy and little Andrew. They seem to smile in return but this is merely my imagination; I have no way of knowing what their smiles looked like. I've seen photographs, faded black-and-white images, but the pictures are out of focus, and a smile is more than the hazy marriage of lips and teeth.

A smile is the dancing in the eyes, the joy in the face.

When I wake, exquisite sadness overwhelms me for these two souls, whose lives ended in violence thirty years ago. I rise and begin my day, and still, I hear them whisper.

*We are the dead*, they chant. *Do not forget us.*

# Chapter Two

I knelt at the clown's head. His grin, a scarlet smear, stretched across greasy stage makeup and then angled up toward a wig, electric orange and kinky. He lay on his back, hands at his sides, palms open. Under the portable LED lights we'd set up, the reds and yellows in his checkered shirt took on a fiery glow, as though the fabric was illuminated from somewhere deep inside the boy's chest.

Inside the tent, the air was still and smelled of stale popcorn and manure and blood. Shadows and gloom filled areas in the space that the LED lights could not reach, would not reach, without a powerful generator.

Outside the tent, it was a hot, dry August day. We'd seen ninety-five on the thermometer before noon. Over the Rockies, clouds like cotton balls dotted the blue skies, cream-colored puffs that teased our parched forests. A few miles from the fairgrounds, popular trails were crawling with hikers and dogs, their enthusiastic paces slowed only by toddling children and overindulgent parents, all oblivious to the newest spectacle at the Fellini Brothers' Circus.

Heaven outside.

Hell inside.

"Coulrophobia."

I squinted up. Chief of Police Angel Chavez stood a few feet from the body, careful to keep his loafers out of the blood that had pooled and thickened beneath the clown. The shoes were brown and Italian and out of place among the horseshit and dust.

The chief looked down at me and sighed.

"Fear of clowns. Coulrophobia. Lisa lost her fourth-grade spelling bee on that word. I had to listen to her recite it for weeks after. C-O-U-L-R-O-P-H-O-B-I-A," Chavez said.

I smiled. "How'd she spell it?"

"Two *o*'s instead of the *o* and *u*. Who's the clown, Gemma?"

"His name is Reed Tolliver. The general manager for Fellini's, a guy named Joseph Fatone, gave us the ID. Caucasian male, nineteen years old. The injury begins here," I said, and flashed my penlight at the gaping tear under the clown's left ear.

The wound traversed the poor kid's entire throat, carving a jagged canyon across what had once been a smooth surface of flesh. Reed Tolliver's eyes were open and when the beam from my penlight caught them, I was struck again by their icy blue color. An arctic shade so pale it looked unreal, like those contact lenses people wear at Halloween.

Chief Chavez sighed again. "Other than the woman who found him, has anyone else been in?"

I stood, twisted to the side and cracked my spine, and shook my head.

A fairground worker had discovered the body two hours earlier. Searching for a box of raffle tickets, she entered the tented storage space and moved through a dimly lit maze of junk and trash: ropes and canvases, signs, nails, empty containers, wadded up fast-food wrappers, crushed soda and beer cans. She found the tickets, turned to leave, and saw the body.

I arrived ten minutes after the call came in; the crime scene techs fifteen minutes later.

Chavez rubbed at the stubble on his chin. These days, the tiny hairs were coming in more gray than black. "What else do we know?"

Fatone, the general manager, had given me little information. He got sick after identifying the body, throwing up all over the front of his polo shirt. I couldn't handle the smell of the vomit and I let him leave the tent without a full interview.

"Tolliver shows up in Cincinnati two years ago, begging for a job, says he has theater experience. Fatone claims he never takes on kids, but Tolliver had ID and was a few months shy of his eighteenth birthday, and they'd just had a clown quit, so . . ."

"Bullshit. Half these employees are probably underage," Chavez replied.

I thought about the young men and women milling about outside the tent and decided the chief was right. Most of them didn't look a day over eighteen. It would be easy for a street kid to fall in with the troupe and find a place for himself. And it would be even easier for the circus to pay a kid less than what they'd pay a migrant worker.

It was what you might call a win-win situation.

"Any family?" Chavez asked.

I shrugged. "Fatone was under the impression Tolliver was a foster kid. At least, he says, there was never any mention of family."

The chief squatted by the clown's feet and studied the body. When he stood, his knees creaked and popped. "Jesus. Wait until the press gets word. And the mayor . . . he's going to be in my ass tighter than Santa Claus in a damn chimney."

I winced at the image.

"Doesn't Bellington have enough to do without getting in our way? You can't tell me he's got room on his plate, between chemo treatments, running this town, and keeping his fingers in the pie that is Washington. Christ, he nearly ran the whole operation on that home invasion case a few months back. And that was before he got sick."

Chavez pointed an index finger at my face and gave me the look. "You just remember, the man's got eyes and ears all over this valley. The murder of this kid, here at our fairgrounds? It just became your only priority. This sort of thing doesn't happen here."

"Not recently, at least," I said under my breath.

I was pleased to be the lead on this, but I didn't relish the thought of the mayor breathing down my neck every step of the way. Terence Bellington had run his campaign on a sort of idealized return to the 1950s, where family dinners are the norm and neighbors watch out for one another. He thought if things were right with your family then that would translate to the community at large.

Family was everything to him. It was like the Sopranos, or the Medicis, without all the blood and art. I found the man out of touch with reality. In this day and age, the aftershocks of the Great Recession were still being felt. Families were lucky to put dinner on the table and have homes next door with neighbors still in them.

But I kept my mouth shut. Chavez and the mayor had a long history, of which I knew just enough to not want to know more.

I also knew Bellington was a man still grieving the loss of his only son, Nicholas. While hiking with a group of local teenagers, sixteen-year-old Nicky had slipped and fallen off a cliff, high above the raging Arkansas River. His body was never recovered and the mayor and his wife were left to bury an empty casket in a plot they'd bought for themselves.

That kind of loss was hard to come back from. I imagined that kind of grief lasted forever.

The chief lowered his finger from my face to my belly. "How are you feeling?"

I looked down and felt the spark of surprise that hit me every time I saw the expanding dome under my breasts. I was six months' pregnant. A girl, if the sonogram didn't screw up and hide a tiny penis in the shadowy, gray imagery.

We called her the Peanut.

"I still can't figure out why they call it morning sickness when you're puking every hour of the day, but I seem to be over the worst of it. Now I've just got this backache that keeps me up at night."

In truth, I was happy to trade the vomiting for the aches in my lower spine. I could work through pain; I couldn't work through near constant runs to the bathroom . . . or sink . . . or whatever handy receptacle was available.

Chavez grimaced and touched a knuckle to the small of his own back. He'd been through this with his wife, a sturdy Jamaican woman who'd delivered naturally, and at home, four children in the last ten years. There were rumors she wanted more kids but Angel Chavez had put his foot down, crying he couldn't survive one more labor.

"Are you up for this, Gemma? I can talk to Finn. You could take it easy and work on some traffic cases . . ." he trailed off.

I knew he was weighing my skills against the political shit storm we'd hit if we didn't wrap this up nice and neat for Mayor Bellington. There hadn't been an unsolved murder in Cedar Valley in thirty years. Bellington's cronies in the city council would find a way to spin this. Traveling circus, seedy fairgrounds. This wasn't the Cedar Valley way; this was the Outside World Way.

I was happy to take the challenge. While the scene was messy, the motives could only be so many. My money was on a love triangle; the circus seemed ripe with young things used to hard living.

"No way. My call, my case," I said. "I'm fine."

Chavez nodded and walked off. He left through a flap at the far end of the tented space. A cracked and peeling leather strap held the coarse canvas open, allowing one long narrow triangle of sunlight to shine through. Dust floated in the light, sparkly and pretty.

I longed to walk the twenty or thirty feet and step out into the fresh air, but I wasn't done with Reed Tolliver yet. I grabbed my two-way and called in the medical examiner.

Dr. Ravi Hussen had waited patiently outside while we roped off the crime scene and marked the ground with dozens of tiny colored flags and pins. The CSI team would continue working the scene long after Ravi left with the body. The detail guys handle the minutiae, while Dr. Death woos secrets from the dead. I just try to put it all together and chase down the killer.

She ducked into the tent, pristine in spotless pants, blouse, and heels, a black leather medical bag in the crook of her arm. Behind her were two attendants, Lars and Jeff. Brothers, they wore pale blue jumpsuits with the words "Coroner's Office" stitched across the breast in fine, red cursive print. They moved in silent tandem, a gurney between them.

Ravi pulled out latex gloves as she approached, snapping them on with an efficiency that said she had done this sort of thing countless times before. Too many times, it seemed; she swore as she took in the blood, and the body.

"He's just a kid," Ravi said. "He's what, sixteen? Seventeen?"

I patted her shoulder. "Nineteen. His name's Reed Tolliver. I'll meet you at the morgue. I'm going to stop by the station and run some reports and grab a sandwich. Do you want anything?"

Ravi Hussen shook her head. She motioned to Lars and Jeff. Silently, Lars prepared the gurney as Jeff unfolded a black body bag. He paused to pop a peppermint in his mouth and sucked on it with a steady, squelching sound.

Ravi squatted and pulled a large flashlight out of her medical bag. She said, "I just ate. Some concession guy out there gave me a free hot dog. No mustard, though. Jiminy Cricket, it looks like our killer used a butter knife. This is an incredibly jagged cut, Gemma, did you notice?"

I squatted beside her and paired the weak, narrow beam of my penlight with her more powerful torch. Peering closely, I tried to ignore the blood and gore and focus instead on the edges of flesh. I had seen enough knife injuries to agree with the medical examiner; the skin looked torn, not sliced.

"I'll know more when I get him in the lab, but I can tell you right now, this was not any kind of flat blade. I don't even think a hunting knife would leave this kind of damage," Ravi said. She gently touched the crimson pool below the body, her gloved fingertip sinking into the blood and dirt and dust. "Your killer would have been absolutely soaked in this boy's blood."

"How did he manage to leave without anyone seeing him? It's the middle of the damn day. There's a hundred people out there," I said. I stood, my knees screaming.

Ravi stood, too, and shrugged. "That's your area of expertise, not mine."

"I can tell you this much. The blood, the destruction on another human being, it reeks of rage. Yet no one saw a thing. That takes cold, calculated planning. Our guy caught Reed Tolliver alone. He had an escape route. He probably brought the murder weapon with him, whatever it turns out to be. What could this poor kid have done in his nineteen years to make someone kill him?" I asked.

"'There are more things in heaven and earth, Horatio, than are dreamt of in your philosophy,'" Ravi quoted with a grim smile. "Shakespeare wasn't talking about murder but I think he knew a thing or two about the mysteries of our motivations."

Her quote hung in the air over Tolliver's body, an invisible shroud. It contained my question, and a killer's answers, all the thoughts and feelings and ultimate, final action that led to one person taking the life of another.

# Chapter Three

I made a fresh pot of decaf back at the station and two turkey sand-wiches on rye with mayo, mustard, Swiss cheese, lettuce, tomato, and red onions. I added a couple of dill pickles for good measure and a stale-looking chocolate-chip cookie I found tucked behind some cans of soup in the pantry. Balancing the full plate and a cup of coffee, I slowly maneuvered to my desk in the back corner. A low whistle filled the room and I turned to see a handful of cops watching me.

Phineas Nowlin leaned back in his chair and crossed his arms. "Holy shit, Gemma. Are you growing a grizzly in there?"

"Screw you, Finn. I'm starving."

He grinned and something about the way his jaw jutted for-ward, coupled with his gleaming white incisors, gave him a posi-tively wolfish appearance. I could summarize what I knew of Finn in three important points: experienced cop; lousy boyfriend; gen-eral pain in the butt. We'd never dated but I had seen enough of the wreckage he tended to leave behind to feel I had a good grasp on his love life, good enough to apply the "lousy" to the boyfriend.

I gave him the finger and ignored the other cops' laughter as I scarfed down the first sandwich. I slowed a bit on the second, chewing each bite thoroughly. By the time I finished eating the pickles, the room was absolutely silent.

I smiled when I saw the four of them still watching me, their jaws open.

"Do you think one of you could grab me a bag of chips from

the vending machine?" I asked sweetly. Sam Birdshead, the new-est, and youngest, member of our small police department, gulped and nodded. He was almost out of the door when I called to him.

"Sam? Not the Doritos, hon."

"Christ. Your ass is going to be bigger than a house by the time this baby's born," Finn said. "Don't you want to maintain your fig-ure? Maybe get Brody to put a ring on it after all?"

He slid his lanky body out of his chair and joined me at my desk. He sat on the edge of it and as I looked at the manicured black eyebrows that framed his baby blue eyes, groomed as care-fully and obsessively as a woman's, I felt the first ache of acid re-flux flood my chest.

"You know, that kind of language could be considered sexual harassment in many work places," I told him. "But I'll forgive you, I know you haven't been laid in what? Six months? Seven?"

I picked up the last pickle and bit it in half as the grin fell off his face. He stalked back to his desk. Hitting below the belt wasn't my usual style but Finn brought out the worst in me. Part of it had to do with the fact that at his core, Finn was actually more than a decent cop. He was a damn good one. But he didn't know when to shut up and he walked a moral line that weaved a little too much for my taste. I saw a boatload of talent slowly going to waste.

If I was honest with myself, though, which I try to be, what really bothered me the most about Finn was the power he had over my future.

A few months back, he'd almost cost me my job.

We were partners on a home invasion case, high up in the mountains above Cedar Valley, in a subdivision where houses started in the low seven-figures, and four and five-car garages were the norm, not the exception. It was a burglary that went south when the homeowner pulled a knife; not a great idea when the bad guys have guns. The wife and son managed to escape but the six-year-old daughter was shot and killed by a stray bullet. The bad guys were not especially bright and they were caught a few days later.

There were problems from the start, though, with the whole

case. There was a jurisdiction question, as the property line of the house butted up against Avondale County, where the cops are hungry for action. They were first on the scene and one of them, a real sweetheart from Butte, Montana, found cocaine in the master bathroom. He called in his brother, a DEA agent, and by the time Finn and I arrived on the scene, it was chaos. It didn't help matters that the homeowner was a former Cedar Valley City Council member, close to Mayor Bellington. The wife blamed the coke on a foreign housekeeper long since fired. Other things, important things, began to get covered up.

There was enormous pressure to close the case. In the chaos, though, the evidence collection had been shoddy. It wasn't any one person's fault, just the way things go when you've got three agencies duking it out at a crime scene. Just when it looked like the case would be dismissed, new evidence appeared. I couldn't prove it, but I was certain the prosecutor and Finn colluded together to ensure a conviction. Finn took an enormous risk, both for him and for me; had he gone down on charges of planting evidence, as his partner I'd have gone down with him.

Justice was served but the law was twisted and I was reminded of an important lesson, one that I'd seen time and again but never at such risk to my own career. At the end of the day, no one really cares how you put the bad guys away, as long as you get it done. I hated knowing that at any time, on any case, Finn's actions might blow up in our faces. That's the thing about partners; you hold each other's lives in your hands.

I hit the power button on my PC and waited for it to boot up. Before I headed to the morgue to observe the autopsy, I wanted to write up some notes while the crime scene was still fresh in my mind.

Sam Birdshead returned with my chips and he tossed them to me, then sat down and took out his steno notebook. Sam had only been with us a few weeks, a rookie from Denver, fresh meat. He was better than an intern because we didn't have to shield anything from him and he was willing to do the grunt work, the odd jobs and the messy stuff. We took turns babysitting him. This first year was critical to the success or failure he would have as a cop. Sam was a quick study. If I could minimize his time with Finn Nowlin, he might have a chance of becoming a halfway decent officer.

I logged into my desktop and waited for the half-dozen programs to load. Out of the corner of my eye, I saw Sam eyeing the wooden shelves that lined the wall behind me. They sagged with half a dozen large binders, each stuffed to capacity with documents and photographs and topographical maps, and I knew what the next words out of his mouth would be.

"Are those the Woodsman books?" he asked.

Nodding, I opened the word processing program and created a new file. I named it "RTolliver" and added a subtitle with the date and time. The document that popped up stared at me, blank and empty and waiting to be filled with the sad details of Reed Tolliver's final moments.

"Mind if I take a look?" Sam said. Without waiting for a reply, he reached around me and took the top binder, thick and black like the other standard-issue casebooks we bought wholesale from a distributer out west. The department had been buying them for years. Decades.

I didn't fault Sam's curiosity; he hadn't grown up around here.

When tragedy strikes a small town, it leaves a scar that never heals. Months and years may pass and the scar may fade, but it never goes away. It becomes a part of the town, marking it as different, a permanent reminder of what may have been, what could have been.

The Woodsman murders were as much a part of Cedar Valley's culture as the ski chalets and hiking trails. You couldn't go a dozen steps in town without seeing the tattered remains of posters, battered all these years by wind and rain and snow and time. Mostly time.

A few of the posters were still intact, the black headline of "Missing" faded to pale gray, the pictures of the children blurred together so that you couldn't tell who was who anymore. They were simply the McKenzie boys, which makes them sound as though they were a singing group from the '50s, except of course they weren't.

They were Tommy and Andrew McKenzie.

They were cousins, two years apart, with pale hair. They liked chocolate ice cream and Matchbox cars. They rode bikes along the river and chased rabbits with BB guns. They disappeared in the summer of 1985.

Most of what remained of the posters were small corners and narrow strips of paper, the glue and tape pressed so hard to the telephone poles and storefront windows you could feel the panic and urgency with which they had been plastered up.

The disappearance and murder of the McKenzie boys defined Cedar Valley in a way that is hard to explain to an outsider. Perhaps it was the fact that children were involved; maybe it was the fact that the murders were never solved. Unanswered questions take root in people's hearts and burrow in, rearing their heads up every so often.

You go on, but you don't forget. Ever.

It happened with the McKenzie boys and it happened again, twenty-seven years later, with the death of Nicky Bellington. Nicky was a little different; there was no crime, no blame to place on someone. He was there one minute and the next he was gone, a quick slip followed by a long fall. But for the mayor, and his family, it was a fact they lived with every day; them, and countless others whose lives have been torn apart in a single moment.

# Chapter Four

I typed my notes, describing the awful scene inside the circus tent. I let the images of the dust and the dirt on the ground wash over me, the way they swirled around the dead clown like finger paintings. The acrid, ripe stench of fresh manure and heavy sweat that could mean only one thing: farm animal.

The way the air tasted of copper when I inhaled.

Nine times out of ten, the sensory details like this didn't matter. But the tenth time, the time when your early notes record a faint trace of almonds in the air, or the fact that you noted a pair of gleaming, oily-looking shoes tossed together with a dozen battered and dirty pairs . . . you just never know what, days or weeks down the road, will break a case wide open.

And so you notice and record everything.

At my side, Sam Birdshead was quiet; he'd stopped on the first page of the Woodsman murder book. After four years with the binders, files, and folders, I knew them by heart.

I knew what caught his attention: a photograph, shot on an old Polaroid camera.

Taken quickly, the picture is nonetheless striking in its composition. The object in the foreground is small, weighing less than two pounds. The background is snow and forest and boulders. The snow is a white so bright that it mutes the greens and browns of the forest into a murky blend, that is broken only by the speckled boulders that stand like sentinels, and by the small skull, its jaw open in an obscene grin.

It was frigid that day.

Brody and I stuffed our backpacks with fleece jackets and thermoses of hot coffee. At the last second, I'd thrown in a small flask of whiskey and my old Polaroid. The skies were blue, the true blue of a sunny Colorado winter day, and clear, without the cloud cover that might have warmed us.

We loaded up our skis and gear and were at the trailhead within thirty minutes. It was our second date and Brody led me off the trail and into the deep fresh powder of the backcountry.

After an hour of hard skiing, we peeled off our outer layers and scrambled up a boulder and rested at the top, puffy jackets spread under our butts to prevent the cold of the stone from seeping through our ski pants. He kissed me, very gently, and told me he'd wanted to do that for months. His mouth was warm and I kissed him back with an urgency I didn't know I felt. We talked between kisses and I fooled around with his camera, and he teased me for using an old Polaroid.

I still have the picture I took of him that day, his dark hair wavy from sweat and his beautiful hazel eyes obscured by sunglasses. He is standing on the boulder, posed, an elbow on his knee, his chin resting on his fist. Then he took a shot of us together, his long arm holding the camera out as far as he could.

We look happy, the way couples do, when they still think their mate can do no wrong.

After a while, I left him on the boulder and trekked a few hundred meters into the woods to find a place to pee. On a hill that sloped gently down, I grabbed hold of a pine limb to balance. I squatted and did my business. When I was done, I stood and struggled a moment with my ski pants. The tiny catch on the zipper was stuck and it took a few curses and tugs until finally the metal teeth caught.

To this day, I don't know what made me look to my right.

The forest was quiet with the stillness that blankets an open space after a heavy snow. There was nothing to catch my eye or my ear: no tan flash of deer, no witchlike crow's cackle.

I was eager to get back to Brody and hit the trails before it got dark, but I turned and looked and my life changed forever.

It could so easily have been an elk or deer bone. I had seen hundreds of them over the years, scattered across meadows, half buried in the vines and pine needle carpets of the forests that dot the Rocky Mountains. But this bone had an angle and curve to it that struck at something primal in me.

I took one step forward, and then another. When I was five feet away, I stopped and pulled out my safety whistle, one of a pair that Brody insisted we carry around our necks in the backcountry. I blew once, then twice more.

I stood and waited and stared at the human skull until he reached me.


"So you took this?" Sam Birdshead asked, turning the scrapbook around to show me the image, an image I'd be able to describe in perfect detail until the day I die.

I nodded. We took the picture and used Brody's GPS to calibrate our location. Then we skied like hell back to the car and drove straight to the police department. I had only been on the job a year, but Chief Chavez was no fool. He took our story seriously. Could be an old hunter, some drunken deerstalker who'd taken a fall, he said.

I knew there was a part of him that didn't believe it was a hunter.

Sam flipped through the album. I wanted to tell him to slow down, to take in the details and minutiae, but I held my tongue. He'd either get it, or he wouldn't. As we liked to say around the station, cops aren't made, they're born.

I glanced at the clock and swore. My notes would have to wait; I needed to get to the morgue to witness the preliminary stages of the autopsy. It wasn't standard operating procedure for the state, but for homicides, Ravi Hussen insisted on a police presence in the room. She said it was easier to engage in dialogue as she went along, instead of presenting a formal report to the police department post-autopsy.

Cedar Valley had so few homicides, none of us minded sitting in on the autopsies.

"Sam, tell you what. Come with me to the morgue and I'll get you up to speed on the Woodsman murders," I said.

I grabbed my bag and took the case file from Sam's hand before he could object.

Sam gulped. He hadn't been in the Death Room yet.

"C'mon, it doesn't hurt. I promise. Anyway, you can't let a pregnant lady go alone. What will the rest of the guys think?" I asked him.

Sam looked around at the other cops, all of whom were suddenly engrossed in their computers or on the phone. He sighed and slammed his department-issue hat on his head.

"Yes, ma'am. Lead the way."

# Chapter Five

Cedar Valley is a bit of a misnomer. We've got cedars and there is a valley, but the two don't meet until the valley funnels its way into the base of Mount James, five miles outside of town. There, the cedars have invaded what was once native prairie land. In town, the flora is mostly pines, aspens, and birch trees. Mount James is just shy of 14,000 feet. There are fifty-three 14'ers in the state and less than two hundred feet kept us off that list. In any case, Mount James towers over the valley and the town. The peak casts a long shadow that touches everything in town eventually, much like Stanley James Wanamaker, who it is named for, did when he ran the mining of silver in these mountains in the 1800s.

It was late afternoon. The Jeep was hot and we got the windows down quickly. I was born in Cedar Valley, and twenty-nine summers in Colorado told me it would stay warm until about seven, when the mountain breezes would dance into the valley and cool things off in a hurry.

Sweat trickled down the back of my neck and I cursed the county. They hadn't replaced our vehicles in ten years. I fiddled with the air-conditioning knob but the whispers that seeped through the dusty vents were just as warm as the air outside, so I balanced the steering wheel with my knee and pulled my dark hair up into a ponytail.

The morgue was a ten-minute drive from the police department. I talked fast and drove slow. "Sam, what do you know about the Woodsman murders?"

He fiddled with the notebook in his lap. When his hands moved, the heavy silver ring on his right hand caught the sunlight and winked back at me. "Well, let's see. It was what, thirty years ago?"

I nodded.

"And, um, okay, it was thirty years ago and two kids went missing, two boys, right? Cousins?"

I nodded again. Cedar Valley has always been a small mountain town. Up until the mid-nineties, railroad tracks literally divided the town in two. Tommy McKenzie lived in a sprawling country home with his wealthy parents. His father's brother hadn't been so lucky in business; Andrew and his parents lived in a house on the other side of the tracks. It was run-down, poorly insulated, with frequent flooding.

"Right. So, the kids went missing and nobody ever knew what happened to them. It was the hottest summer on record," Sam continued, gaining confidence. "Folks searched day and night for weeks, dredging up ponds and checking every mining shaft and cabin in a hundred-mile radius."

"The papers called them the McKenzie Boys. They disappeared on July 3, 1985, sometime between leaving school and dinnertime. They got off the bus together at Parker and Tremont and that was the last time anyone remembers seeing them. Some said maybe they were runaways, but I think most people, deep down, believed they'd been taken. I was born a year later, by the way, right there, at Memorial General," I said, pointing at the hospital as we drove past. "The case was big news, even the national press picked it up. It was a bad summer all around. In August, a woman's body was found downriver, snagged in some reeds. She'd been strangled. And the mayor at the time, Silas Nyquist, he died of a sudden heart attack a few weeks after that."

Sam twisted the silver ring on his finger. He said, "And they never made a connection, huh, between the woman in the river and the missing boys?"

I shook my head. "They tried. The woman was assaulted,

strangled. The boys were simply gone. And by simply—of course, I don't mean simply. I just mean it was hard to draw a line from missing children and the murder of a young woman. You studied psych, didn't you, at the academy? The two cases present different M.O.'s, different styles. Kidnapping is a lot of work. The killer went to great trouble to hide the boys' bodies. Rose—the woman in the river—she was dumped there after he was done with her. If it was the same guy, why not bury her where he buried the boys?"

Sam pondered this for a moment. "Maybe the perp started small, with the kids, then moved on to murder? Not a total stretch, given what we know became of the McKenzie boys."

I smiled at his use of "perp." He was fitting right in.

He continued. "And to think, that whole time, the bodies were just a few miles away."

I nodded. "The skull was the only bone we saw at first, but later, after the other skeleton was found, Brody and I both admitted we had thought right away the skull might belong to one of the boys. The bones were old, but not that old. And that skull, well, the skull was small, too small to be an adult."

Sam nodded, deep in thought. His hands were quiet now, stilled by curiosity. I slowed the Jeep to let a young woman with dreadlocks the color of pennies wrestle a stroller up and over the curb. As I continued down Main Street, I glanced in the rearview mirror and saw she had stopped to adjust a wheel on the stroller, her copper coils touching the ground as her head bent this way and that.

Sam asked, "When were the other bones found?"

"We skied back the next morning, Brody and I and the chief and a couple of crime scene technicians. They brought hounds and right away, the dogs sniffed out the other grave. The children were buried deep, but not deep enough. Chavez has always suspected animals, maybe a coyote, dug up that first skull, and after that, well, it was only a matter of time."

Four years ago. It could have been yesterday.

"It was my first big case as a cop. Still is my biggest case, for that matter."

Sam gave me a look that I couldn't interpret. I thought it was sympathy but when he spoke I decided he pitied me and I thought that tragedies are like rocks thrown in a lake, creating ripples that never hit shore; they just go on.

Sam said, "Some of the guys, they say you dream about them? The kids?"

In a moment of weakness, nearly two years ago, I told Chief Angel Chavez about my dreams. Rather, my nightmares. He insisted I see a therapist, and I did, and the dreams stopped after a couple of intense months of weekly meetings and detailed journal writing.

I wondered what the good Dr. Pabst would say if he knew the dreams had started again.

I said, "Yes, I dream about them. They were just kids. They didn't deserve what happened to them. And for thirty years, they've been waiting for justice."

Sam Birdshead looked out the passenger window at the old Victorian homes that dotted the street, each one adorned like a wedding cake with square layers and extravagant curls and fancy little eaves and nooks. The front porches were overrun with flower boxes bursting with violent splashes of color; in the yards, the grass was neat and tended, the weeds few if any. We were on the north end of town, the rich end.

The side of town Tommy called home thirty years ago.

Sam said, "We have an old tribal saying that goes something like 'all dreams spin out from the same web.'"

I waited for him to continue, but when he spoke next he asked, "Do you think he's still out there?"

"Who? The Woodsman?"

Sam nodded.

"I don't know. After we found the bodies, we had every expert you could think of come in. There are a few things everyone agrees on. The Woodsman was strong and tall; Tommy was a big kid and whoever took him down had to be bigger. The Woodsman was probably not younger than sixteen, and not older than fifty. The terrain in the woods is rough. There's no vehicle access. He had to be fit enough to drag or carry the bodies. If he's still alive, he's anywhere from mid-forties to eighty. Hell, he could be dead."

The sun ducked behind a single cloud in the sky and for a moment, the sudden shadow caught me at just the right angle and blinded me. I pulled off my sunglasses and blinked, and continued. The roads were clear; we had hit the sweet spot just after school lets out and just before the end-of-day traffic.

Sam said, "Why is he called the Woodsman? The bodies weren't, uh, chopped up, were they?"

I shook my head. "Hand me that water bottle, will you? Behind my seat? Thanks. Some jackass in the press labeled him the Woodsman and the name stuck. I guess she thought she was being cute, because of the legend, and the boys being found in the woods."

"What's the legend?"

"You don't know the Woodsman and the Bear? The woodsman was a hunter, a lumberjack; a man of the woods. He lived in a remote cabin with a beautiful young wife who didn't mind that her husband was bearded and stinky and probably had squirrel breath. All she wanted was a baby. Well, screw as they might, it just didn't happen. It broke the man's heart to see his wife so sad. Then one day, in town, he saw a sweet, young girl harshly berated by her mother. The woodsman went home and talked it over with his wife and the next day, he went to town and snatched the girl. The wife grew to love the child but the little girl was evil. A few months later, the woodsman returned home to find the child had killed his beautiful young wife in a fit of jealousy. Overcome with rage and grief, the woodsman took the child deep into the forest and strung her up as bait for a bear. The bear appreciated the free meal so much that he struck up a friendship with the woodsman."

Aghast, Sam stared at me. "That's a horrible legend."

I shrugged. "Most fairy tales are. Try reading some of the original European stories. Anyway, the tale goes that if you are very naughty, the woodsman will come and steal you from your home and take you to the woods and feed you to the bear. There are a few old cabins up there, just off the trails, and enough gloom in those forests to give weight to the legend. At least, if you're a kid."

Sam said, "Creepy. I thought our tribal legends were disturbing. So, the real Woodsman—the killer—there were never any leads?"

"We think he was someone local, one of the mine workers, or a day laborer in the orchards. Physically strong, knew the land, and had opportunities to watch the kids and catch them alone, in broad daylight. They just disappeared, Sam. No one saw anything."

He was quiet a moment and then said the very thing that I found myself thinking, day after day. "Thirty years isn't that long ago, Gemma. The Woodsman could not only still be alive, he could be living here in town. Maybe he never left."

I pulled the Jeep into the parking lot of the medical examiner's office, a smaller building annexed to the newer hospital, Saint Thomas's, and turned off the ignition. The old engine grumbled for a moment and then fell silent and I looked at Sam. He was a quick study and would go far as a cop.

"Now you know why I dream about them. Let's go see about a dead clown."

# Chapter Six

Dr. Ravi Hussen was impatient. She greeted us outside the morgue door with a pointed look at her wristwatch and a tight smile.

"My fault, Ravi. The baby was starving and I can't think these days if I don't eat," I said, and rubbed my belly. Her face softened and she jerked a thumb at Sam.

"Who's the kid?"

"Dr. Ravi Hussen, meet Sam Birdshead. He joined the department a few weeks ago," I said.

Sam extended a hand and Ravi shook it, a bemused look on her strong Iranian features.

"He's here to watch," I added, and pushed him toward the men's locker. "Suit up in one of the blue outfits you'll find hanging in the locker marked 'Visitors.'"

Ravi smiled as she led me into the women's room. "Cute."

"Young."

She helped me find an extra large suit to pull over my belly and then changed into her own dressing gown. We added head caps, goggles, masks, gloves, and booties and met Sam back in the corridor. He followed us into the lab.

After the warmth of the August heat outside, the Death Room was freezing. Steel shafts in the ceiling pumped in gusts of icy air, and I shivered as I passed beneath one of the vents. An assistant waited silently by the long, narrow sink that ran the length of one wall, his face as pale and gaunt as the farmer in Grant Wood's *American Gothic*.

At our feet, discreet drains dotted the floor, ready to catch any wayward fluids.

Reed Tolliver's body lay on a metal table in the middle of the lab. Under the fluorescent lights, the white stage makeup on his face glowed a sickly green. The black blood at his neck glistened as though it was, impossibly, still wet. His cheery clown suit, complete with suspenders and squirting flower, added a sense of the macabre, like we'd stumbled through a fun-house door into some kind of sick, twisted carnival act.

Sam swallowed hard. I patted him on the back.

"Please, Sam, if you are going to be sick, use the sink in that corner," Ravi instructed.

She pulled the neon orange wig off Tolliver's head, exposing a generous mess of dark strands, and deposited the wig into a large evidence bag, which she promptly sealed. The crime scene investigators would go over the wig and Tolliver's clothes at length; Ravi's job was to strip him down and expose him at his more base molecular levels.

Leaning close to Tolliver's scalp, Ravi peered at the dark strands and then pulled back a few, exposing pale yellow roots. She nodded to herself.

"He's a towhead. I thought as much when I saw the eyes. You rarely see blue like that on a brunette. His hair has been dyed repeatedly. As a result, it's very damaged, the follicles have almost no elasticity."

Ravi soaked a sponge in a small yellow bucket of water and began wiping Tolliver's face. The makeup coated the sponge with a thick layer of grease, just as it had coated Tolliver, and she had to repeatedly soak and wring the sponge and then begin again.

After ten minutes, Tolliver's face was clean but it was not unstained.

The right side of his face was covered with tattoos. What looked like pagan and Celtic symbols in blue and black danced across his cheek, his eyebrow, half of his forehead, even the corner where his upper and lower lips met. A cascade of inky knots and circles wove here and there, trailing at times up into his hairline. In contrast, the left side of Tolliver's face was stitched with piercings: half a dozen tiny silver and gold studs and hoops crisscrossed his skin like flags on a map.

"Jesus," I breathed. "Are those real?"

Ravi gently tugged a few of the hoops. They pulled away from the skin and then slowly sagged back into place, the elasticity of the living replaced by the rigor mortis of the dead. She examined the tattoos and piercings at length and then stepped away from the body and snapped off her gloves. At the sink, she scrubbed her hands and pulled down her mask to splash water on her face. She dried off with a paper towel and then spoke.

"Many of these were done by an amateur; perhaps even by Tolliver himself. Scarring and recently healed infections indicate they were done quickly and without clean instrumentation. These days, the pros go out of business real quick if they don't use proper hygiene."

"You gotta be kidding me. He did that to himself?" Sam gasped. "Fuck."

I stepped on his toe and whispered "recorded" and pointed at the ceiling-mounted voice recorder.

"Sorry," he mumbled. "But seriously?"

Ravi nodded and slid on a fresh pair of gloves. "That, or a buddy did it for him."

"Some buddy," I muttered.

Ravi carefully cut away the rest of Tolliver's costume and placed the clothes in another of the large evidence bags. Without the oversize outfit, he seemed frail and small, much more a boy than a man. His chest was smooth and the hairs on his arms and legs and pubis the same pale blond as the roots on his head. His body was free of markings; I didn't see so much as a scar on him below the neck.

Evidently, he had decided to limit the self-mutilating to his face, or perhaps he simply hadn't lived long enough to start in on the rest of his natural canvas.

In striking contrast to his clean and naked body, Tolliver's throat gaped open, obscene and violent. The cut extended far enough back that Tolliver's head had been almost completely severed from his body. White bone matter and cartilage gleamed through the blood and muscle.

Beside me, Sam gagged.

I patted him on the shoulder and pointed him in the direction of the sink. He swallowed hard and then shook his head, remaining at the side of the table. Ravi poked and prodded at the wound for a few minutes and then spoke.

"I've never seen a cut like this, Gemma. I actually don't think it's a cut at all."

I stared at her. "I don't understand. If it's not a cut, what is it?"

"A tear. Around noon today, someone literally tore open the throat of this poor kid."

Two hours later, Ravi was finished with her preliminary study of the body. Aside from the injury and the facial tattoos and piercings, there were no more surprises. To be thorough, though, she would still do a complete autopsy and examine the organs and other matter for whatever else might help the investigation. Her assistant, the man with the long pale face and somber air, fingerprinted Tolliver. If he was a street kid, chances were good he'd been caught at some point for shoplifting or busting a car.

If we could get a match on his prints, we might be able to find a next of kin.

"Neosporin baby," Ravi surmised as she tossed her gloves into the bin by the door. Sam looked at her in surprise, and she continued.

"Somebody cared for this boy. They fed him, kept him sheltered, probably discouraged him from playing competitive sports.

They bandaged skinned knees, applied Neosporin to prevent scarring, and got him braces when his teeth came in crooked. He wasn't always a street kid. Somebody out there, somewhere, loved him once."

Ravi walked us back to the locker rooms.

"I'll call with any news. You must be exhausted," she said.

I nodded. It was nearing seven o'clock and I'd been awake since four. Sleep didn't come easy these days.

It had cooled down outside, and Sam and I drove back to the station in silence, each of us lost in our own thoughts. I pulled the Jeep up close to the front door. He took his time collecting his things and under the Jeep's dome light, I decided he looked a little worse for the wear.

I told myself it was for his own good: if he wanted to be a cop, he better get used to seeing the terrible stuff. It wasn't all guts and glory; sometimes, it was just guts.

I'd just started to pull out of the station to make my way home up the canyon, when Sam flagged me down from the front door. I circled back around and rolled down the passenger side window.

"Dr. Hussen's on the phone, she says it's urgent."

That was quick. I parked the Jeep and hurried in.

"Ravi?"

"Gemma, we got the prints back," she said. Her voice was flat and guarded.

I turned around, facing away from the receptionist. "That was fast, Ravi. How?"

She whispered, "We ran them in the state database first, not the national one. I thought we should start with Colorado, on the slim chance he was a local boy. And I knew the results would come back quicker."

She paused and then said, "Gemma, it's Nicky Bellington."

My ears registered her words but my mind took a minute to catch up.

"Fuck me," I said.

Behind me, the receptionist giggled. I ignored her and massaged my suddenly pounding temple.

"No kidding," Ravi whispered back.

# Chapter Seven

The weak light that peeked out from under Chief Angel Chavez's closed door was a soft and muted yellow. He should have been home, helping his wife Lydia get baths ready and homework assignments finished. She worked long days at social services, only to come home to the four little ones and their needs and demands.

Chavez readily agreed that of the two of them, she had the tougher job.

After I told the chief what I needed to tell him, I knew he wouldn't be home before midnight. I offered up a quiet apology to Lydia, and knocking softly on the door, pushed it open. The room was dim, the only light from the small Tiffany-style lamp set at the edge of the oak desk.

Chavez sat, his head in his hands, a ledger and a few files spread out in front of him. In brass letters high on the wall behind him, a Latin phrase: *Familia Supra Omnia*. Those words had been drilled into me since day one: Family above all else. Interpret it how you will; around the station, it referred to the brotherhood of police officers. It meant loyalty, honor, putting the good of the group ahead of yourself. I thought again of Finn's reckless actions on the home invasion case, actions that betrayed that loyalty, that brotherhood, and felt anger course through my mind. I pushed it to the side; now was not the time.

The chief looked up from his desk and while I can only imagine what expression I wore, it was enough for him to stand and cross the room.

"Gemma? What is it?" he asked.

He stood close, as though he thought I might collapse. I suddenly felt tired and took the chair he offered. It was a beautiful antique chair, the woodwork as delicate as lace, but uncomfortable as hell and immediately I wished I had remained standing.

"Close the door, Chief. And then you better sit down, too."

I waited until he'd done both and then took a deep breath. I hated what I was about to bring into the room. The chief of police in a small mountain town can be a thankless job, but Chavez was a good leader and more importantly, a good man. Framed newspaper articles and commendations lined the walls of his office. Few were about Chavez himself, not because he'd never been the subject, but because it was more inspiring for him to be reminded of his team's successes over the years.

I said, "Ravi Hussen ran the prints on Reed Tolliver, the dead clown from the fairgrounds, through the state database. As you know, the database searches for both registered offenders and missing children and adults. She came back with a hit. I asked her to run it again, and her results were the same."

I held up a hand as he started to speak. "I know, I know . . . but I wanted to be sure."

Chavez nodded and sat back. "And?"

I knew whatever happened in the next few hours, days, and weeks would be the direct result of what I was about to tell the chief. And he would never be able to forget this moment, when I opened the floodgates of Hell and let loose the demons.

"Reed Tolliver doesn't exist," I said. "The body is Nick Bellington."

Chavez exhaled noisily. "That's not funny, Gemma. If this is some kind of sick joke—"

I interrupted him. "It's not a joke. Not only did I make Ravi run the prints twice, I also had her pull his dental records. He did a summer camp police internship when he was thirteen, in Denver. They took prints as part of the application process, sort of a 'through the criminal's eyes' kind of thing. It's him, Chief. It's Nicky."

Chavez leaned back in his chair, out of the glow of the lamp. Shadows obscured his face but I could imagine the dozens of thoughts that crossed his mind, just as they had crossed mine an hour ago.

"I'm so sorry. I know this can't be easy."

He leaned forward and raised a hand, whether to brush away the words or acknowledge them, I wasn't sure.

"Please, Gemma. We grieved with Terry and Ellen years ago. And ever since Terry won the election, things have been, as you know, a bit strained," Chavez said. He rubbed his hands over his face and then sat up. "Damn. All right. I want everything. Where are we right now?"

I nodded. The hard words were out. The hard work, on the other hand, was about to begin.

"At this moment, four people know: you, me, Ravi Hussen, and a tech, a young guy named George Aldonado. It has been strongly suggested to George that unless he wants to be charged with interfering in a criminal investigation, he stay quiet for the time being. He's a good kid, he'll play ball."

"What else?"

"Ravi puts the time of death about eleven or noon this morning. The victim bled to death due to his throat being torn open. Ravi's words, not mine. Chief, you should have seen his face when we got that clown makeup off. He's covered in piercings and tattoos. And his hair's been dyed dark, repeatedly. He was unrecognizable as Nicky Bellington, like he was in a disguise, in hiding."

Angel Chavez stood and jammed his hands into the pockets of his pants. He paced the office, a room small enough to get four strides in before he had to turn around. It was like watching a bear swim laps in a Jacuzzi.

"From here on out, we need to be very careful with the words we use. We don't know anything except the fact that Nicky was murdered sometime this morning, and that he'd been working at that circus for what? Two years? I don't want to hear 'hiding' or 'disguise' again, got it?"

I nodded. And then as gently as I could, I corrected him. "Chief, we have to accept something else as fact. Contrary to all accounts, Nicky Bellington wasn't killed in that fall three years ago."

The chief stared at me for a long minute, then groaned and sank back into his chair. "I got another fact for you. I now have to inform the Bellingtons, a couple I've known for over twenty years, that their son has died. Again."

# Chapter Eight

I hated leaving Chavez alone in his office, in a space that seemed too small to contain such fresh grief, but I respected his wish to call the Bellingtons in private. Exhaustion waited patiently behind adrenaline, kindly allowing me to make the winding drive up the canyon safely, only to smack me upside the head as I pulled into our drive. I sat there, in silence, staring at the front of our dark house in a near stupor, until finally Seamus's barks reached me and propelled me up and out of the car.

I went in through the front, turning on a single light in the foyer as I closed and locked the door behind me. Seamus met me and after a final bark, fell silent and took his place at my heel. I kicked off my shoes and socks and walked by the living room, with its hulking leather furniture and upright piano and fireplace partially obscured by plants and a painting that had yet to be hung. Down the dark hall, not bothering with the lights, letting the quiet wash over me.

Coming home has always been a salve to me, a warm bath after a good chill.

Sanctuary.

In the kitchen, I flicked on the big ceiling light and fan and cracked open a window. The house is shaded and high enough up the mountain that it stays cool most of the day, but by evening the air is warm and stuffy. Our nearest neighbors are a quarter mile away and tonight, for the first time in a long while, I wondered what I would do, if I actually needed quick help.

I was confident in my ability to take care of myself. But a baby . . . a mother tethered to her child is both the fiercest fighter and the most vulnerable. Beside the morning sickness, this had been the hardest part of my pregnancy thus far; this feeling of weakness, knowing that very soon, my entire being would revolve around this little stranger. No longer would I answer only for myself. A life would depend on me, and my life would depend on her: her happiness, her joy, her every breath.

Seamus scratched at the pantry, interrupting my thoughts and bringing me back to reality.

"Okay, little one, I'm getting your food," I said. He scarfed down the kibble in three quick bites and then looked surprised when he didn't get seconds. He never gets seconds, yet he remains the epitome of hope. It's quite sad, really.

I poured a glass of skim milk and heated up a late supper of frozen enchiladas and beans. The small cardboard box with its filmy wrapper rotated slowly in the microwave, warming until steam seeped through the tiny holes I'd poked in the plastic. I watched it, one minute, two minutes, three minutes, then took it out at the beep and swore when the boiling cheese dripped onto my thumb. Sweat beaded at my temple and I stripped down to my undershirt, a thin cotton tank top that didn't quite cover my belly.

I couldn't stop thinking about Nicky.

Nicky died three years ago.

Nicky died today.

Nicky was the good-looking teenager I used to see around town every now and then.

Nicky was the pierced and tattooed circus clown.

I ate my microwave dinner slowly. The house grew too still, too dark. Brody wasn't due home from Anchorage until the end of the week and all of a sudden, I missed him like crazy. This was how most of Brody's trips went, at least for me; initial excitement at the chance to have the space to myself for a while slowly faded into a kind of boredom that eventually bloomed into feelings of actually missing him. Even Seamus seemed more mopey than usual. Trust me, you haven't experienced depression until you've lived with a sad basset hound.

After dinner, I stood and stretched and wiped down the counters and put away the milk. I picked up my cell phone and hit the second button on the speed dial. The line rang three times and then a sweet old lady's voice said, "Hello?"

"Hi, Julia, it's Gemma." I leaned back against the counter and looked at the nails on my right hand. They were unpolished and needed a good filing.

"Who is this, please?"

"Julia, it's Gemma. *Gemma*. Your granddaughter . . ." I said. I held my breath and waited. Maybe she was having a good day.

The good days were happening less and less as summer wore on.

"No, I don't need any damn newspapers. Thank you very much for calling," Julia said, and hung up with a resounding whack.

"No, thank you very much," I said into the phone and hung up. It was late; I shouldn't have called, I knew better. I set the phone down then picked it back up and sent a text message to her husband, Bull: "I'll call tomorrow. Sorry, bad day for us both I guess."

I wondered when the bad days would be the new normal, and the good days the exceptions. I wondered if we had until Halloween . . . or Christmas. Maybe pessimism was getting the best of me and we had until next summer. Damn it all. A car accident took my parents in a minute; dementia was taking my grandmother day by day. I still couldn't decide which was worse.

It was the little things at first, lost keys and misplaced utensils. Then it was friends' names, lost, and emotions, misplaced. I was lucky; Bull got her to a doctor who was patient and kind and exhaustive in explaining the horror that is dementia. It might be Alzheimer's, or it might be some other disease. What was known was it would get worse and worse until she died. She would never get better. There was no cure for what ailed her, no magic pill, no miracle exercise.

Poor Bull was bearing the brunt of it. After forty years as a district attorney, the last ten of which he'd spent as a judge, he had looked forward to retirement; long days on the golf course and low-stakes poker games in town. He barely got a taste of that before Julia's symptoms appeared. Now he was nurse, babysitter, and watcher. Bull made sure Julia didn't burn the house down or walk into a street full of traffic. He kept her stylish and attractive, lipstick and pants on before she left the house.

For the time being, Bull managed. But it could be years of this, and I knew Bull's sheer determination and physical strength wouldn't last forever. At some point, we'd need to move Julia into a home, or hire help.

On the counter, my phone buzzed. A reply from Bull: "Need to talk? Julia reading now."

I turned off the kitchen lights and dialed Bull's cell. He answered on the first ring.

"Hi, sweetheart. Julia's been off for most of the day. She's got a *Reader's Digest* now. We just had steaks and potatoes. Do you think I need to watch her cholesterol? I read an article that said too much fat can affect this."

"Jesus, I don't know. I'm sure you could find an article espousing the benefits of fat for dementia. Don't read too much into one recommendation or another. Everything in moderation, right?"

I walked up the stairs as I spoke, moving into the bedroom, crossing the room in the dark. Cool mountain air blew through the windows I'd left open the previous night, bringing with it the smell of pine and night. I turned on a small bedside lamp then crawled onto the top of the bed, got situated, and then leaned back, adjusting a pillow under my ankles to elevate my legs.

Bull sighed into the phone. "Don't take our Lord's name in vain, honey. So what's the story on this homicide up at the fairgrounds? It's some kid?"

I closed my eyes. I was so tired. . . .

"Gemma? *Gemma?* Are you there?"

Eyes open. Jesus.

"Yes, I'm here. Stop listening to the scanners," I said. "I shouldn't be talking to you about this, but I know you're not going to let it go. It was a nineteen-year-old male, a circus employee. The killing was brutal."

"Any leads?"

"Sort of, but I can't speak to them yet. I'll swing by tomorrow; do you need anything?"

"Your grandmother could use a new jar of her face cream, that stuff she gets at the department store, in the yellow jar."

"Clinique?"

"Yes, that's it. But I can order that online, too . . ." Bull trailed off.

I closed my eyes again. "No, it'll be good to take her out, she loves the mall. We'll have fun, a ladies' day out. I can't do it this week, but maybe over the weekend."

"Okay. Gemma, we haven't seen that pretty face in a while. Your grandmother loves to see you, why don't you swing by tomorrow, just for a few minutes? Remind her she's got a great-granddaughter on the way."

"I'll do that. Good night, Bull. Love you."

"Love you, too, honey. God Bless."

Sleep came quickly. When I woke in the middle of the night, the phone was still in my hand, the bedside lamp still burning. The room was cold. I went to the window and shut it, pausing to stare out at the dark night. Somewhere out there was a killer. Did he sleep, satiated from his kill? Or was he a creature of the night, restless and awake and hunting again?

# Chapter Nine

In my second-grade class, our teacher, a lovely woman named Mrs. Hornsby, gave us an assignment to "draw our town." That was it—with pencil or pen, in color or not, draw the town. It's harder than it sounds, especially when you are seven and your perspective tends to skew to grandiose scales or tiny little creatures.

Most of the other kids did sketches of the ski slopes and the Rockies, with wildflowers that looked like poppies, and stick figures of their moms and dads and dogs, each drawing complete with a perfectly square house and a charcoal-colored smoke plume puffing up from a redbrick chimney into a sky filled with, inexplicably, a sun, a moon, a half-dozen stars, and a few puffs of clouds, all at the same time.

I turned in a piece of graph paper with the town divided into four directional segments.

I still think of Cedar Valley that way, broken up into rough quadrants, each with its own subculture.

The south end of town is the working man's land, a busy hub of gas stations and fast-food restaurants, pubs with neon beer signs (half of them missing important vowels), and mechanic garages, and trailer homes spread out on lots teeming with rusted bicycles and washing machine parts and plastic toys. Head to the east, and you'll eventually hit Denver; head to the west, and you'll find yourself in a maze of ski lifts and mountain bike trails and fishing holes and campgrounds.

And to the north, well, to the north is where the beauty and the brains of Cedar Valley reside. It's where the main street becomes Main Street: a quaint row of shops, and Victorian houses, and modern municipal buildings all built to look vintage.

Head north and you hit money.

It was to the northwest part of town that we were headed, Sam Birdshead and the chief and myself. It was just before eight in the morning and we had an appointment with the Bellingtons.

After my lonely and melancholy night, I had been glad to see the chief and Sam. Then I remembered where we were headed, and a cold feeling crept into my belly and remained there, heavy as a rock. Even the Peanut had slowed her kicking and I wondered if she could pick up on my mood, if we shared some kind of sentient connection like that.

I wasn't looking forward to our meeting with the mayor and his wife.

Chavez was driving. He took a left at an unmarked turnoff and we climbed a narrow dirt road. I caught glimpses, through the wall of pine trees that lined the road, of big sprawling estate homes with log sidings and brick chimneys and private driveways. In the mountains, money has always bought seclusion. At the angle we were climbing, I was going to expect nothing less than jaw-dropping views of the valley.

We drove with the windows down. The air was cool, with a hint of early morning moisture and a sweet, pure scent. Temperatures would reach the nineties by early afternoon and the air would be dry then, dry and hot and not so sweet smelling.

We rounded a tight curve and Chavez said, "This is it."

I gasped as the house came into view. Cedar Valley's wealthy tended to favor what I called the Swiss Miss style, big timber chalets built to look as though they sprung from the forest, homes that made use of natural resources and aimed to blend in, not stand out.

But this . . . this was an entirely different sort of animal. The Bellingtons had taste; I just wasn't sure you'd call it good taste.

Solid sheets of glass hung suspended between concrete pillars, meeting one another at sharp right angles and varying heights, so that the house was one big, cold, alien geometrical sculpture. It was, in the words of Brody's twelve-year-old nephew, butt ugly. I couldn't imagine seeing it in the design stage and saying, with all seriousness, yes, let's spend a few million dollars to build *this*.

I glanced at the chief, but he was preoccupied with wedging the Expedition into a narrow spot between a hill of gravel and a shed. Although the house itself seemed completed, it was obvious there was still work being done on the grounds; what looked like the beginnings of a greenhouse sat a few hundred yards beyond the main building.

From the backseat, Sam Birdshead tapped me on the shoulder and pointed up at the house.

"Look," he said.

In the eastern sky, the sun had cleared the tree line and bathed the structure in an amber glow. A dozen rays of early morning light winked back at me, reflected from the enormous mirrorlike windows and glass walls. It was as though we were inside a prism.

"It's beautiful," I whispered, and blinked as a flash of white from within the wonderland caught my eye. From a second-story window, a pale face stared down at us. But the same sunlight that softened the harsh angles of the house blurred the edges of the face and I couldn't make out any features.

After a few seconds, the person withdrew and a curtain fell down against the windowpane.

Satisfied with his parking job, Chavez turned off the engine and we climbed out. My heart rate increased with the exertion at the higher altitude and I took a moment to catch my breath, one palm on the edge of the warm hood of the SUV.

At the front of the house, Sam searched for the doorbell. Smooth walls flanked twin steel doors. There didn't seem to be any button or bell so I shrugged, reached around him, and knocked sharply on the doors.

The chief let out a short cough and when I glanced at him, I was surprised to see he looked nervous. I gave him what I hoped was a reassuring smile.

I was nervous, too.

The door swung open and a tall, middle-aged woman in a simple, dark blue dress beckoned us in. She introduced herself as Hannah Watkins, the Bellingtons' longtime nanny. She looked shell-shocked and I saw firsthand the pain of reliving Nicky's death. Chavez placed a hand on her shoulder and murmured condolences. I was reminded again of the deep friendship the Chavez family shared with the Bellington family, and I told myself to tread carefully.

We followed Mrs. Watkins down a long hallway.

The interior of the house was as cold and sterile as the exterior. The walls and tile floors were shades of gray, the monotony broken only by large pieces of black and white leather furniture and dramatic canvases of modern art. The paintings were abstract images that followed no rhyme or reason, all swirls and waves and crisscross curves that left me with a vague sensation of nausea, as though I'd been on a boat and gotten seasick.

Mrs. Watkins left us in the living room, a plush, sunken space with a view of the valley below. I walked to the floor-to-ceiling window and peered out. The living room must have hung right over the mountainside, because when I looked down, I was standing at the edge of a cliff, looking at the tops of the same trees that minutes before, I had been driving below.

A fresh wave of nausea washed over me and I closed my eyes and rested my forehead against the cool glass.

"Angel, wonderful of you to come out."

I opened my eyes and watched, in the window's reflection, as Terence Bellington strode into the living room and embraced the chief in that half-hugging, half-handshaking way that men of power use with one another.

When I turned around, I saw clearly the deep shadows that darkened the skin under the mayor's eyes. He was comfortable in his body, on the tall side, trim from years of competitive tennis. If you didn't know he was sick, he would seem the picture of health. But the signs were there, if you looked closely. The cancer treatments had left him completely bald. His scalp was free of age marks and freckles and it shone as smooth as an egg, and his eyes were a dark olive green that made me think of wet army fatigues. Up close, he wasn't trim; he was too thin, and his skin hung in places it shouldn't.

The rumor in town was that Bellington saw Cedar Valley as a stepping-stone to the big leagues. He'd won the mayoral election with an unheard of 75 percent majority; with that kind of popularity, he might just be able to skip a term in the governor's seat and go straight to Washington. And after that, the sky was the limit. He certainly didn't have to stop at the Senate; there's always a cabinet post, or an ambassadorship, or the golden egg itself: the White House.

If he lived.

His was a dodgy cancer; many people survived it. Many more did not. The last article I'd read on him, in *People* a month or so back, had quoted his doctors as saying he had a solid 30 to 40 percent chance of kicking this cancer in the teeth. Still, the word "dying" never entered his speeches, never appeared on his Web site.

Mrs. Watkins, the housekeeper, appeared behind Bellington and silently placed a silver tray on a lacquered sideboard and poured tea into four china cups. She whispered something to the mayor. He nodded at her and then she left the room as silently as she'd entered it.

Bellington said, "Ellen will join us in a few minutes, she's upstairs with Annika. They're having a hell of a time with this, as you can imagine."

Chavez nodded solemnly. "Of course. Terry, you remember Detective Gemma Monroe, don't you? And this is Sam Birdshead, the newest member of our department."

I nodded hello at the mayor.

"Gemma, Sam," Bellington said, and handed us each a cup of tea. He sat with his back to the sun, in the room's only armchair, a black leather number that shone like obsidian. The rest of us spread out on the two sofas flanking the narrow coffee table.

"We're so sorry for your loss, sir," I began. "I can't imagine how difficult this must be."

The mayor sipped his tea. "Gemma, you're right, this is extremely tough news. You know, I thought losing my child was the worst thing that would ever happen to me. Now, knowing all these years he was actually alive and allowed us, allowed his *mother*, to think he was dead . . . it turns out I don't even know who my boy was. It goes against everything this family stands for. Cancer is nothing compared to this hell."

Chavez said, "Terry, we're going to get to the bottom of this, I swear. Nicky was a sweet kid. He must have had a damn good reason to do this."

"Easy to say, Angel, harder to believe. He wanted for nothing. Anything he asked for, he got. When I was his age, I worked three jobs just to buy a bike," Bellington said. He crossed his legs, deep in thought. "Why would he do this?"

The mayor set down his tea and rubbed his hands over his face vigorously as though to wash away the thoughts that prickled him. Red streaks bloomed on his cheeks and just as quickly faded away. His hands were small for his stature and I watched him, knowing I might be looking at Nicky's killer.

You always look to the family first. Fair or not, mothers and fathers and spouses are the quickest and most direct connection to any victim. That was something I had told Sam; always start your suspect list small and tight and widen as you go.

Sadly, sometimes you never need to look beyond the family.

The mayor picked up his cup of tea and took another sip and repeated, "Why would he do this?"

"Sir, when we find your son's killer, we might be able to answer that," I said. "Perhaps the two—his disappearance, and now his death—are connected. Murder is usually never as complicated as it first seems."

"Imagine that, Terry. We're now the parents of a murdered child," a woman's husky voice said.

I hadn't heard Ellen Bellington come down the hallway, but there she was, all six feet of her. She moved like a cat, slinking into the room and perching on the arm of the mayor's chair, her severe black pantsuit blending into the leather.

Ellen was stunning, more beautiful at fifty than she had likely been at twenty. A former actress, the years had softened her striking Nordic features and rounded out her angular frame. Hair as pale as corn silk cascaded over her shoulders and down her back like a waterfall, and I couldn't help thinking of that other waterfall, Bride's Veil, that her son had gone over three years ago. Her eyes were the same shade of arctic blue ice as Nicky's.

"I wonder, does it feel any different than being the parents of a child who died in a tragic accident?" she mused. "I suppose only time will answer that particular question."

She patted her husband on the head and then began running her fingers over his hairless scalp as though playing the keys on a baby grand.

"Ellen, please," Bellington began, but she shushed him and dropped her hand from his head to his back. She patted him again like one pats a dog, affectionately and absentmindedly, more because the dog is there than because of any strong desire to do the patting.

Ellen smiled at the chief. "Hello, Angel. Aren't you going to introduce me to your friends?"

"Yes, of course, this is Gemma Monroe. Her grandfather—step-grandfather, sorry Gemma, is Bull Weston, who of course you know. And this is Sam Birdshead, he just joined us from Denver. A recent graduate of the academy."

Ellen said, "Pleased to meet you, Gemma. Bull was the best judge this town ever had. Nothing like that idiot Swanson, he presides over the courtroom like it's a reality show. And Sam. I know that last name. Are you related to Wayne Bird Head, up in Wind River territory? Yes, you must be, I see a resemblance in the skin and the nose. He's your grandfather, isn't he? What was that charming expression I heard? The 'godfather of the Rez?'"

Sam flushed and I felt like punching her. I knew who Wayne Bird Head was and I also knew that family ties or no, Sam was nothing like his grandfather.

Ellen walked across the room and stopped at the window where I'd gotten dizzy. She pressed a palm against the glass. I wondered if hers had been the face I'd seen when we'd pulled up the drive. She remained there, staring out at the valley below, and we watched her until the silence grew uncomfortable.

Chief Chavez cleared his throat. "Ellen, Terry, we don't know a whole lot at this stage, certainly nothing more than we discussed last night on the phone. Nicky's body was found at the old fair-grounds. He was part of a traveling circus doing a clown routine, working there for the last two years. He was hired on in Cincin-nati. From all accounts, he was a good worker. We've got a few of the officers interviewing some of the other circus employees today."

Ellen let out a bark of a laugh. It was hard and short and brusque. "A circus, of all places. What kind of freak did my baby become?"

Chavez sighed. "Not a freak, Ellen. Not our Nicky."

Ellen drew her hand down the window slowly, leaving a long streak on the window. She said, "He was my favorite. I know you're not supposed to say that, but he was, since the day the twins were born. Nicky was the best of us. He was too good for this world, in some ways, I suppose. Do you think me a terrible person? I love my daughter. But I loved my son more."

No one knew what to say to that.

I waited a moment and then spoke directly to the mayor. "Sir, you said your daughter Annika is home? May we speak with her?"

Ellen turned from the window and shook her head, answering for her husband. "She won't come down. She doesn't want to talk with anyone right now. She is devastated."

I gave her what I hoped was a reassuring smile. "May I go upstairs? I won't bother her for too long. Maybe she'll talk for a few minutes, if it's just me?"

A look passed between Terry and Ellen that I couldn't decipher.

"Sure, Gemma, you can certainly try," Bellington said. He shrugged. "Maybe it would be good for Annika to talk with an outsider."

# Chapter Ten

✺⟨⟩⟩✺

Annika's bedroom was on the other side of the house. Mrs. Watkins led me up the stairs and down another long, narrow hallway filled with more of the nausea-inducing paintings. We walked by an open door and at the faint sound of a television turned low I turned my head and looked in the room as we passed. An elderly man sat in a wheelchair, his head bowed, hands clasped in his lap, asleep.

The room was dim but the blue light of the television filled the space with a neon glow. I watched, hypnotized, as a thin line of spit trailed from his chin down to the orange afghan in his lap.

Ahead of me, Mrs. Watkins turned, stepped back, reached around me, and gently pulled the door shut. Her eyes were unreadable and I felt ashamed at peeping into an old man's private slumber.

"Sorry," I mumbled.

"That's Frank Bellington," Mrs. Watkins whispered.

"I know. He was a friend of my grandfather, Bull Weston. I don't think they've seen each other in a while, though."

Mrs. Watkins shrugged and continued down the hall and I quickened my stride to keep pace with her. At the end of the hall, she pointed at a closed door. On the knob was a tag, the kind you see at hotels, that indicates do not disturb. I lifted the pink laminated sign and smiled; it read "perfect angel" on one side and "raging bitch" on the other.

I crossed my fingers it was the angel that was in today, and knocked and pushed the door open.

The room was as warm and inviting as the rest of the Bellington house was cold and sterile. A four-poster bed topped with a plump lavender duvet took up the south wall. On the opposite side of the room, a sprawling wooden desk held computers and stereo equipment and piles of clothes. In the corner, a keyboard and a guitar rested against a tall bookcase crammed with dog-eared paperbacks and thick hardcovers. Tucked in among the books were small ceramic angels, the kind you see in Hallmark stores and *Reader's Digest* ads.

"Annika? I'm Detective Monroe," I said. "You can call me Gemma."

She sat cross-legged on the bed, playing with the ends of long hair that was two shades fairer than her mother's. She glanced up and I looked into eyes that were the same pale blue as her twin brother Nicky's had been, the same blue as her mother's. I saw no trace of her father in her, until she spoke.

Her cadence, her openness, her friendliness—that was pure Terence Bellington. She'd make a wonderful politician and she wasn't yet twenty.

"How do you do?" she asked, and bounded from the bed to me in three steps. She shook my hand politely and then stared at my belly. "Congratulations."

"Thanks. I'm due in three months," I said. "It's sort of crazy, really."

"I bet. I can't imagine," Annika replied. She wore dark jeans and a green T-shirt with the word "Hellkat" stitched across the front in fraying red felt letters. The shirt looked homemade but knowing kids these days, it probably cost eighty bucks at Anthropologie.

She noticed me looking and laughed, a lovely sound completely unlike her mother's harsh bark. "Hellkat is a garage band in New Haven. My boyfriend's the lead singer. Pete. He's got this alter ego on stage, with a costume and everything. Hellkat is like a demented superhero cat. Kind of stupid."

I shrugged. "I don't know, sounds pretty cool. How is Yale? I bet it's a lot different than the schools out here."

I said the words but I didn't believe them. I do that sometimes;

the words tumble out of my mouth as my mind is thinking the opposite. College is college, whether you pay ten thousand or a hundred thousand for the privilege of lectures, narrow twin beds, and crappy dorm food.

She shrugged and laughed again. "The boys are the same. They all just want to fuck you and leave you, blow 'em and snow 'em, as they say. That's why I like Pete, he's different from the rest. He never forced it."

I didn't know if she was trying to shock me with the word she'd used, but somehow, I doubted it. Annika chose the words she used because they were the right words for the situation.

"Is my mom still crying?" she asked. She wandered over to the bed and sat down and patted at the cover.

I joined her. "I don't know. She wasn't just now."

Annika said, "She cried a lot last night. That's how I knew something was wrong. I heard the phone ring and then I heard her scream and then she was crying, and so was my dad, and no one would tell me anything."

She flopped backward on the bed and pressed the heels of her hands to her eyes. "My aunt Hannah was the one who finally told me, you know. Can you believe that? They didn't even tell me themselves."

"Your aunt Hannah?"

Annika nodded. "Our nanny, Mrs. Watkins. I'm sure you met her. She's my father's sister, my aunt Hannah. She practically raised us. Her husband left her when they found out she couldn't have kids. My parents were always super busy so she moved in when we were little."

"I didn't realize that she was a relative. Does she live here, too, then?"

Annika said yes. "Me, Dad, Mom, Aunt, Grandpa. No brother no more."

I lay back on the bed next to her and stared up. Tiny green stars dotted the cottage cheese ceiling in random patterns that vaguely resembled constellations. Growing up, my best friend had the same stickers in her room, the kind that glow in the dark once you turn out the lights.

She and I used to lie like this for hours, legs hanging off the bed, flat on our backs, staring at the ceiling and talking about nothing and everything. We'd light blueberry-scented candles and listen to Tracy Chapman and Chris Isaak and wonder if the boys we liked even knew our names.

"I'm really sorry about Nicky, Annika. I know all of this must come as a huge shock," I said. "Can you think of any reason why he might have done this?"

"You mean disappear? Not get in touch with his family? Let us think he was dead? Or join a circus, work as a clown, and then get himself murdered?"

I sighed. It was an awkward situation; there was no getting around that. "Well, all of that, I suppose."

She sat up and, looking down at me, gathered her long pale hair up and began furiously twisting it into a bun.

"I have no idea. Nicky was the applesauce to my pork chop, the milk in my cereal. He completed me. What we had was fierce and I don't mean in some sick, kinky, *Flowers in the Attic* way. You never met a nicer guy. He made the rest of this fucked-up family better just by sharing our last name. I can't imagine that if he knew how much he hurt us, that he did it on purpose. There's got to be some other explanation."

She bounced off the bed and paced the room with the pent-up fury of a tiger in a cage. "I'm so mad at him I would kill him if he was here right now, Detective."

"Please, call me Gemma. Annika, can you walk me through that day? Three years ago? I've read the reports, of course, but I'd like to hear it from you."

She laughed. "Well, sure, but obviously we missed something, right? I mean, it's not the most accurate account anymore, is it? Considering he lived?"

I nodded. "That's okay. I'd still like to hear it."

She picked up one of the tiny ceramic angels on the bookshelf and held it a moment before setting it back down. In the sunlight that streamed through the window, she looked younger than her nineteen years.

"We were on a trip, an overnight camping trip up to Mount Wrigley. Paul—Mr. Winters—he asked Nicky and I to come along as mentors for his foundation. I think he thought we would be good role models for the other kids. We hiked up Wednesday night and camped Wednesday and Thursday. Friday morning, we packed up and started the hike down. We stopped for lunch at the top of Bride's Veil."

"Whose idea was it to stop at the waterfall?"

She shook her head. "I don't remember. Maybe it was Paul's idea . . . Mr. Winters. Maybe it was Nick's idea? We were hungry and it was a beautiful day."

I nodded again. I remembered; it *had* been a beautiful day.

July 6, a Friday, with temps in the mid-eighties. Paul Winters operated the Forward Foundation; a local youth group whose mission was the empowerment of teens through physical action and decision-making situational activities. Think AmeriCorps meets Outward Bound.

Annika said, "We dropped our bags and set up blankets near the edge of the cliff, but not too close. We weren't dumb. Paul handed out crackers and cheese and cookies and we ate and then kind of stretched out, you know, to enjoy the sun. Like cats."

I knew the spot well. I hadn't been part of the investigation; I'd picked up a stomach bug that week that knocked me on my ass and took ten pounds off my already slim figure, but I'd been up there since, plenty of times. About ten yards off the trail, at the halfway point up to Mount Wrigley, there is an unmarked path that leads to a viewing point for Bride's Veil. The waterfall is eighty feet high and raging by the middle of summer, when the snowmelt is at its peak, and the Arkansas River rages through the Rockies.

There is a small meadow by the viewing point, and this had been where the eleven teenagers and Paul Winters stopped for a bite to eat. The ground is flat, but begins to erode the closer you get to the edge of the cliff. Nicky wasn't the first to fall there; in fact, since the late 1800s, three other people had died, either by suicide or accident, at Bride's Veil.

Annika continued. "At some point, I fell asleep. I'd been up all night, too cold to get much rest, and the lunch and sunshine were so nice that when I closed my eyes, I fell into a deep sleep. Do you know what I mean? The kind of oblivion where you wake and you can't even figure out where you are?"

"Sure."

Annika took a deep breath and stopped pacing and sat back down next to me on the bed. Her skin was unlined and her blue eyes like two crystals, and I felt a moment of sadness at the speed with which time sneaks over us all. My own face, less than a dozen years older, had an ever-increasing map of the worries that had crept my way, and the hours spent in the sunshine, and the laughs I'd had, and the tears.

"I woke up because someone was screaming. Then there was shouting, and more screaming. When I sat up, I saw everyone at the viewing point, looking down. Everyone was there except Nicky. And I knew."

"You knew what?"

"I knew he was gone. Gemma, when we were born, we were holding hands. That's how close we were."

Annika laughed at my look of surprise and I was struck again by the musical tinkle her laugh held, like wind chimes dancing in a breeze. "My mom had a C-section. When the doctors pulled us out, Nicky and I were facing each other, holding hands. They took a photograph of us, it's around here somewhere. I think we were even in some magazine."

She leaned over the bed and started pulling picture albums out. "When we were little, I called Nicky my shadow. He always said he wasn't my shadow but my mirror. When I was about to do some-thing bad, Nicky would appear in front of me and reflect back the naughtiness, even if he wasn't physically there. Does that make sense? He was like my ethics barometer. Weird, huh?"

The bedroom door opened a few inches and we both looked up, startled. Mrs. Watkins—Aunt Hannah—peeked her head in. "The others are finished downstairs, Detective."

"Thanks, I'll be down in a minute," I told her, and stood. Annika rose, too, and to my surprise, gave me a hug. Her body felt thin but strong, like a whippet.

"Thanks for talking to me. It helps," she said. She went to the corner and picked up the guitar.

"They never talk to me about the serious stuff. My parents, I mean. They think I'm weak, fragile. That I can't handle it."

She strummed the chords, her notes deliberate and melodic. "Did you take any languages in college, Gemma?"

I nodded. "French. I haven't spoken a word of it in years."

She continued strumming and I recognized the melody, one I was sure I'd be singing myself very shortly.

*Rock-a-Bye, baby . . .*

"I'm a philosophy major, so I have to take Greek. We're on prefixes right now. Did you know that the Greek prefix *A* means without? As in, lacking?"

*In the treetop . . .*

I said, "That does ring a bell, yes."

*When the wind blows, the cradle will rock . . .*

Annika strummed and hummed, and the rest of the words came to me, words that all of a sudden seemed menacing for a nursery song: Rock-a-bye, baby, in the treetop, when the wind blows, the cradle will rock, when the bough breaks, the cradle will fall, and down will go baby, cradle and all.

*Down will go Nicky . . .*

Annika stopped strumming and laid the guitar down. "My mother was a philosophy major. She's fluent in ancient Greek, Latin . . . all the languages of the dead. I asked my dad the other day which of them named us, Nicky and me. He said it was my mom."

"Nicholas and Annika," I said. A chill crept down my back and I shivered.

I understood but I didn't *understand*.

"Annika: without Nika, without Nick. I am without Nick. It's like my mom knew that someday, he'd be gone, and so she cursed me with this stupid name so I'll always remember. I'll always be without Nick."

# Chapter Eleven

I spent the afternoon at the station, writing up my report and reviewing the initial findings from the interviews conducted on some of the circus workers. The officers' notes indicated many of the employees were reluctant to talk to the police; accordingly, there wasn't much to go on: Reed Tolliver had been pleasant, hardworking. He didn't have enemies. He had a girlfriend, and I made a note to interview her myself, along with Joe Fatone, the general manager.

At four, Finn Nowlin stopped by and dropped a sheet of paper on my desk. "Merry Christmas, Gemma."

"What's this? A list of cities, sweet! Are these locations of active restraining orders against you?"

Finn smirked. "You're hilarious, you know that? It's all the towns that Fellini's Circus has been through in the last two years. You might want to put a call out to our colleagues and see what kind of murders they saw around the same time the circus was in town. Maybe we got a serial killer on our hands."

He knew it was a great idea and he knew that I knew it, too. He also knew it hadn't even crossed my mind.

"Thank you," I managed. "Fatone didn't say anything about any other murders."

"I know, I read the report. There are two things that jump to mind. One, maybe Fatone is your guy. I'd be careful around him. Two, maybe your killer works for the circus and his other victims have all been, uh, townspeople, you know, going to the circus. Maybe killing his coworker is a first."

Finn had some good points. He walked off and I started the tedious task of finding contacts for police departments in those cities. It took two hours and when I was finished, I had a list of more than a hundred phone numbers. I left it, with a cover sheet, on Sam's desk. He could make the calls; cops are notoriously territorial and it would be good for Sam to get some practice at establishing diplomatic relations with our buddies in Kansas, Nebraska, Ohio.

Before I left the station, I made arrangements to meet with Fatone at the fairgrounds the next morning. That would give me an opportunity to review the crime scene, do a walk-around without the presence of the body and all the blood.

I was halfway home when I remembered I said I would stop by and visit my grandmother and Bull. Swearing, I checked my rearview mirror and pulled a 180 in the middle of the canyon.

I headed back into town, back to my childhood home. After my parents died, Julia rented out her property in Denver and moved into the spare bedroom on the first floor. I think she thought she would move back to Denver after I finished high school, but she grew to love Cedar Valley. Then she met Bull, and they married, and he moved in, too.

I always wondered if it was strange for Julia to live in her dead son's house. I never asked her about it, though. After their wedding, she and Bull took over the master bedroom and sold all my parents' furniture, replacing it with shabby-chic country-cute stuff. She let me keep a few things, like my mother's antique jewelry boxes and my father's art supplies. That had been a fight; seven-year-old Gemma screaming at Julia to allow her to keep the half-empty paint tubes and half-finished canvases, fragments of a half-finished life.

It was Bull who finally stepped in, calmly directing Julia to go for a walk. He helped me pack up the paintbrushes and tubes and canvases, and the jewelry boxes, and then drove them to his storage unit on the other side of town. He promised to hold them for me until I had my own place. Bull was a good man, a fair man. It wasn't his fault he fell in love late in life with a woman stuck raising her granddaughter. He accepted me as his own and many times, I've felt closer to Bull than to Julia.

I parked behind his station wagon and stood for a moment next to my car, staring at the house, taking in the open windows, with their white curtains billowing in the gentle breeze, and the neatly trimmed lawn with the pretty flower beds that held dormant irises and blooming roses. A chubby man in shorts and a too-small tank top started up a lawn mower two houses down. He saw me watching him and he raised a can of Coors in my direction. I didn't know if he was toasting me or offering an ode to the lovely summer evening. I raised a hand in greeting and he turned away to his mowing.

The smoky smell of barbecue reached me and I entered the backyard through a side gate, calling out as I did so. My grandmother sat at a white wrought-iron table, a glass of juice before her and a paperback in her lap. A plate heaped with pieces of charred and crispy chicken got my stomach rumbling.

I put a hand on her shoulder and she jumped.

"Ah, Gemma, you scared me. You shouldn't be sneaking up on old people like that," Julia said. "I'm liable to have a heart attack. Give us a kiss."

I leaned down and pecked her on the cheek. Her skin was cool and dry and tanned under a large hat with a straw brim.

"You're not old, Julia. You're just deaf. I called hello as I came through."

She furrowed her brow. "Well, if you say so. Did we have an appointment?"

I shook my head. Movement caught my eye and I turned to see Bull pushing through the back door with a platter of biscuits and coleslaw and corn. Despite the heat, he wore a long-sleeve T-shirt and khaki pants. With his black glasses and white mustache and goatee, trailing the smell of barbecue sauce, he was a dead ringer for Colonel Sanders.

He smiled when he saw me. "Hi, honey. Want to join us for dinner? There's plenty of food," he said. He set the platter down and leaned in to give me a kiss. As he did, he whispered, "She's having a good day. Praise the Lord."

We ate outside, bathed in the dying light of the setting sun, surrounded by the sounds of a summer night in small-town America: the chirp of a cricket, the sporadic lawn mower two houses down, a television turned loud in a neighbor's living room. At the end of the cul-de-sac, I heard school-age boys playing basketball. They weren't very good—there were four shouts for one *thunk* of the ball hitting the basket.

When we were finished, Julia offered to clear the plates and Bull agreed. I could tell he wanted to speak to me alone, and I became worried that something was wrong with Julia, some new symptom. Maybe we would need to look into the home health care sooner than I thought.

Bull waited until she was inside, then he said, "Gemma, I heard a rumor today. You know you don't have to confirm or deny, but if I heard it, you know others will have, too."

"Oh yeah? What kind of rumor?" I asked, toying with my glass of juice.

Bull stared at me over his glasses. "The kind where dead boys come back from the grave."

"Like Jesus Christ?" I said. I respected Bull's devotion to Christianity; I told myself it was good for him to defend it every now and then against a heathen like myself.

Bull rolled his eyes. "No, not like Jesus Christ. Like Nicky Bellington."

I sat up straighter. "What did you hear?"

Bull looked back to the house as Julia came through the back door. She carried a pie in her hands and pride in her eyes.

"Voilà!" She set the pie down and Bull and I stared at it, then at each other. Ice crystals rimmed the edges and the frozen cherries in the middle looked as hard as rocks.

"That looks delicious, Julia. I'm so full though, maybe we could save it for later?" I said.

She shot daggers in my direction. "You are too skinny as it is,

Gemma. You're eating for two these days, damn it. When are you going to start taking care of yourself? I'm going to call your mother and have a word."

Julia picked up the pie and hustled back inside. She slammed the back door so hard the thermometer on the wall next to it shook.

Bull shrugged. "I hope you weren't planning on dessert."

"What did you hear about Nicky?"

"Exactly what I said. He came back. Only he came back as someone else, didn't he? What makes a kid fake his own death?"

I held up a hand. "We don't know that's what happened yet, Bull. Take off your prosecutor hat for a minute, will you?"

Julia came back and sat down at the table. She'd changed into a red nightgown and a pair of slippers I remembered from ten years ago. They were sheepskin, plush, winter slippers. She pulled her knees up and hugged them and looked at Bull and me. Her right hand began to tug at the loose fuzz on her slippers.

"Go on," she said. "Don't mind me."

"What a nightmare. That poor family, first the cancer, now this . . ." Bull said.

I nodded. "They're pretty shaken up. I saw them this morning at their big new house up Foxfield Drive. I saw Frank Bellington, too. I hadn't seen him in years. He's quite old now, in a wheelchair. I remembered he used to come around quite a bit, didn't he?"

Bull leaned back in his chair and crossed his legs. He pursed his lips but didn't say anything.

He looked like a man contemplating a lie.

Julia, though, reached across the table and gripped my arm. Surprised, I turned to her. She stared at me. Her eyes were fierce and the color was high in her cheeks.

"You stay away from that man, Gemma Elizabeth Monroe," she said.

Her grip tightened on my forearm.

"Ow, Julia, you're hurting me," I said. I pulled free and rubbed at the red marks she'd left. She slumped backward in her chair and resumed picking at the fuzz on her slippers.

I stared at Bull. "What the hell? I thought you and Frank were these great friends."

Bull stood and removed his glasses. He folded them carefully and placed them in the breast pocket of his T-shirt. He motioned for me to join him and I did, and I found myself being walked to the side gate.

"Are you escorting me out? What was my grandmother talking about? I do remember Frank coming around, years ago. You two were buddies, you and Louis Moriarty and Jazzy Douglas. You used to play poker every Thursday night. What happened?"

At my car, Bull stopped walking. The lawn mowing man was long gone, as was the sun and the pleasant summer evening. The street was dark and still. Something cramped in my stomach and a sourness rose in my throat. Maybe it was the coleslaw. My arm throbbed where Julia had gripped it.

Bull sighed. "Nothing happened, Gemma. That's how life goes. You are friends with someone until you aren't, and it's usually over some small, silly misunderstanding. I don't even remember what it was. Go home, honey. Get some sleep; you look exhausted. I don't like the thought of you in that empty house, all alone, not a neighbor in sight. When is Brody home?"

"A few more days."

"Are we going to see a wedding before that baby comes?" Bull asked. His tone was gentle. My reaction was prickly; petulant undertones, hated but uncontrollable, crept into my voice. "What, you don't want a bastard great-grandchild?"

Bull gave me a look. "Gemma, stop it. At some point, you need to crap or get off the can. Brody apologized. You're having a child together. Forgiveness heals the giver much more than the receiver. Marriage is a great stabilizer, especially for a child."

"I forgave Brody a long time ago, Bull. Forgive *me* if I'm still not convinced that marriage is the right choice for us. You know what they say, 'Once a cheater, always a cheater.'"

"People change, Gem. They grow and mature. You two were young and in love and things turned serious. Brody got scared. He's a man; at the end of the day everyone knows we're really the weaker sex. We constantly struggle with our biological need to sow our seeds and our desire for a stable home front with one good woman. He loves you too much to hurt you again."

"It's got nothing to do with love. It never has. It has everything to do with Celeste Takashima and all the other beautiful women in the world who turn the heads of men who don't belong to them."

"Well, that's your first problem, Gemma. Brody doesn't belong to you. You go on thinking that way and sure as spit he'll up and betray you again," Bull said.

I didn't have a response to that, so I shrugged and got in the car. Bull closed the door behind me. I rolled down the window and thanked him for dinner then backed out. He stood in the drive, watching me until I reached the street, then he turned and was swallowed by the dark shadows lining the edge of the house.

# Chapter Twelve

I slept little that night. The Peanut was active and every jab and kick felt like a personal attack against any hope of slumber. When I did sleep, my dreams were vivid. Twice I woke, heart pounding, my body covered in a film of sweat that simultaneously chilled and fevered me.

I dreamed I stood at the edge of a great precipice.

Below me, miles below me, a narrow ribbon of indigo water wound its way through a rust-colored canyon. I raised my arms in a swan dive and pushed off the ground, lifting up and over and then I was falling, falling down through the air. What seemed like an eternity passed, and suddenly the river was rushing up to greet me and my face hit the water with a sharp slap.

The green light on the tiny alarm clock next to my bedside read two in the morning. I walked downstairs and got a glass of milk and then splashed cool water from the kitchen sink on my face. After a few stretches, I lay down on the living-room couch. Although the couch wasn't as comfortable as the bed, the room was cooler.

The windows had no curtains and I watched as the pale moonlight made fantastical shapes and shadows on the pine floor: a witch on a broom, then a headless horse, then a silo that shifted and slid into a nameless blob.

I remembered Dr. Pabst's explanation of nightmares as being one of the mind's ways to work through traumatic events. He also said they are a common reaction to stress. My grandmother used to tell me that nightmares were the result of too much sugar and not enough love. When I woke crying from a bad dream, which was a common occurrence in my youth, she would lie with me and shower my forehead with kisses.

Curled up on my side, I called for Seamus. He waddled over from his doggy bed in the kitchen and with a groan, jumped up on the couch. He lay at my feet and passed a squeak of gas and was soon snoring. He was no replacement for my grandmother but he was a comfort nonetheless.

I fell asleep to his snorts and grunts and funny little sighs.

I woke a few hours later from my second dream, one that was as familiar to me as the thin cotton quilt, hand-stitched by my other grandmother, my mother's mother, that lay jumbled in a heap at my feet. I'd been having this same dream for years; it started a few weeks after I found the skull in the woods.

If I was lucky, I went a full month between the dreams.

If I was unlucky, they haunted me three or four times a week.

I stand in a meadow in the middle of a dense forest. The air is cool and silent and still; the pine boughs do not so much as move. I'm in a nightgown, an old-fashioned dress with long sleeves and delicate lace trim, what they used to call a granny gown. The white fabric glows in the moonlight.

I'm a beacon in the dark woods.

The children creep toward me from opposite directions, emerging from the black forest like wraiths. They form points on a compass: Tommy from the north and Andrew from the south. One after the other, they fall to their knees around me, their hands together in supplication, in prayer.

*We are the dead*, they whisper.

*Do not forget us*, they chant.

Tommy is closest and I put my hand on his head in a gesture of comfort, but he is mere ether and my hand passes through his face like a hand through a cobweb.

A noise emerges from the woods, a dragging, clanking, terrible sound. The children rise to their haunches and scuttle backward, their eyes never leaving my face. As they slip back into the darkness at the edge of the trees, a man emerges. He stays out of the moonlight, but I can tell he is a big man, over six feet tall, and strong.

He drags a sleigh. Something lies on the sleigh, something small and shrouded and still.

Strapped to the man's back are tools: A pick-ax. A shovel. A handsaw.

They are a woodsman's tools.


As the old kettle began to babble with the sounds of boiling water, I rubbed the sleep from my eyes and scanned the fridge. The Peanut had taken a liking to cinnamon rolls in the morning and I wasn't going to fight her (although I was a little pissed about all the kicking she'd done during the night). I popped a frozen bun in the microwave and snipped open the corner of the tiny frosting package that had come with it.

Sticky white icing leaked from the plastic wrapper and I licked my fingers and felt the sugar hit my bloodstream.

On the kitchen table, my MacBook beeped. I opened it to see a Skype call waiting so I logged in and Brody's face, slightly hazy and out of focus, greeted me. I waved at him and waited for the connection to improve. His beard looked full and his hair seemed to have grown inches since we'd last Skyped.

"Morning my sweet one, how are my girls?"

I was grateful for the technology that allowed us to not only talk but see each other as well, but I hated how close he looked and how far away he actually was. Anchorage could have been on the moon for all the miles between us.

"We miss you. Four more days, I don't know if we'll make it," I told him. The microwave beeped and my belly growled. "Hang on a sec."

I grabbed the cinnamon roll and a decaf tea and sat down in front of the computer screen. I held up the pastry and mug. "See what you're missing? Momma's on a sugar rush."

He laughed, his smile appearing a millisecond before the sound came through the line. "That looks almost as good as all the salmon I'm eating. It is so beautiful here, Gemma. You'd love it. We'll be back in Denali for a few days, then back to Anchorage at the end of the week and then I'll be home."

This was his third trip to Alaska in six months. He was a contract geologist for the federal government, doing all sorts of technical scientific things I didn't pretend to understand. At the moment, his work involved a top-secret mineral deposit that had been discovered in some ridge or another in Denali National Park. Apparently Brody was one of about five people in the world that could understand its importance.

"I miss you. It's been a rough few days," I said.

Brody's face blurred in and out of focus and I heard something that sounded like "mumble mumble line mumble gee."

"Uh-oh, hon? Are you there?"

I tipped the laptop screen back and forth and he reappeared for a split-second. He was talking over his shoulder to someone behind him, someone I couldn't see, and then he came back to me. I caught a glimpse of a bright pink parka, feminine and fitted, and then Brody's face filled the computer screen. "Honey, I gotta go. Love you both."

"Hey, is that Celeste? Jesus Christ, Brody, is that Celeste Takashima?"

He touched his fingers to his lips and then to the screen. Then he was gone.

And . . . the days just keep getting worse. If that was Celeste Takashima, I was going to kill Brody when he got home.

My mood foul, I finished my breakfast and then I showered and dressed, all the while trying to give Brody the benefit of the doubt. Pink Parka could have been anyone: the bush pilot, the bush pilot's wife, some other world-renowned, highly specialized female scientist that I'd never heard of. Maybe Brody was surrounded with snow bunnies all eager to service the man.

Bull's words came back to me: people change. I pushed down the terrible thoughts trying to claw their way out of my heart and tried to focus on the job at hand.

Seamus followed me around, and I explained to him how frustrating it was to struggle with the buttons on my shirt, a struggle I hadn't had a few days ago. The baby was growing by the minute. I was already in the largest women's size the station stocked. I'd be moving into the men's sizes in another week.

After that I might as well wear a muumuu. God, Finn Nowlin would have a field day if I walked into the station in a muumuu, my handgun on one hip and a radio on the other. If it came to that I was just going to retire and journal my eating habits on a blog. I've heard people can make big bucks doing that, taking pictures of their meals and posting it for the whole world to see.

I headed out of town, my thoughts dancing between two big questions: Who killed Nicky? And what really happened on that beautiful July day three years ago?

It didn't make sense, any of it.

The story of Nicky Bellington for three long years has been one of fate. A tragic slip and a long fall; a matter of timing and improper footwear and recent rains and whatever else you could attribute to the cause of the accident.

But Nicky didn't die. And that changed everything: how we looked at the accident; his family; his life. I thought about Ellen's strange question: is it different, being the parent of a murdered child as opposed to a child who's died in an accident? I thought there was a difference there, but I couldn't see what it was worth, or what it meant. It seemed to me that with murder comes intent, whereas with an accident comes fate.

I realized, as I took a hard right on the steering wheel and headed to the south part of town, there was another question that needed to be answered. Who was the real victim here: Reed? Or Nicky?

# Chapter Thirteen

I arrived at the fairgrounds shortly before ten. The sun was an orange orb in a blue silk sky. There was a sharp quality to the sunlight that only served to highlight the trash and dirt of the Fellini Brothers' Circus of Amazements. I put on my sunglasses and walked to the box office at the front of the fairgrounds, watching where I stepped. The grounds were littered with evidence of visitors. Empty soda cans and cups and crumpled foil wrappers lay scattered among orange rinds and apple cores and paper plates and those cardboard tubes that cotton candy is wound upon.

In the distance, just beyond the red and white stripes of the big top, a man swept trash into a large bag, pausing every few seconds to wipe his brow and adjust his grip on the broom. The air was heavy with the smell of rotting fruit and farm animals. I heard children crying, their voices rising together in panic, and I moved in the direction of their cries until the scent hit me and I realized it was not children, but goats.

Joseph Fatone met me at the closed ticket-taker stand. He was in his early seventies; deep grooves made parallel vertical tracks on his forehead and continued down to bookend his mouth. An unlit cigar hung from his thin pale lips and he patted at the four strands of hair on his head as though making sure they were still there.

"Thanks for meeting me here. It's hard to get away, especially at a time like this. We're all devastated, our family has been broken," he said, his words garbled around the Cuban.

He offered me his hand and I shook it. It was clammy and damp and I resisted the urge to wipe my palm on the seat of my pants. Fatone pointed to an Airstream trailer just beyond the box office and we walked toward it. On the ground, orange raffle tickets lay among the trash like trampled poppies in a field.

"The family?"

Fatone nodded and held the trailer door open for me. "Yes, we're a big family around here. Reed was a son, a brother to us all. He was a real great kid, full of heart and vigor. You don't meet too many kids with vigor these days. Vigor went out of style fifty years ago."

The air inside the trailer was musty and smelled of tobacco and lemon Pledge and burnt coffee grounds. Fatone gestured at the tiny kitchen table with its two mismatched plastic chairs and I carefully lowered myself into the one on the right. There was barely an inch between my belly and the edge of the table and I scooted back in the chair as far as I could.

Fatone sat across from me and picked up a chipped mug.

As he drank, I took a look around the trailer. It seemed to be his office and his home. There was a narrow, unmade bed behind a halfway open door near the back of the Airstream. A stack of dishes filled the tiny kitchen sink. The prints on the walls were hunting and fishing scenes clipped from various men's magazines, mounted in cheap black plastic frames. A sad-looking spider plant hung out of an old coffee can, its tips brown and brittle.

Fatone took another long sip from the mug and his next words wafted toward me on a breeze of booze.

"I still can't believe he's gone. I keep expecting him to turn up at the door with T, hollering that the elephants have gotten loose or that he needs to borrow the car. He was such a jokester, that one. A real wise guy."

He took another sip from the cup and coughed. I smelled tomato juice and put my money on a Bloody Mary.

"T?" I asked.

"Tessa O'Leary. Calls herself T. She and Reed were, uh, well . . . you know. Going together," Fatone said. He touched his head again, found the hairs intact, and returned his hand to his lap.

"Dating?"

In the window behind me, I heard the angry buzz of some small insect beating itself against the pane, too desperate to get out of the trailer to notice the open door a few feet away.

He nodded. "Yup, ever since Omaha. Oh, they were friends before that, everyone is friends, you know. But eventually, they all pair up, even the old ones. Everyone's got a partner."

"Do you have a partner, Mr. Fatone?"

"I had a wife once. It didn't really take, her and I. Now, you might say I'm like an old grandpa," he said. "I have a lady friend every now and then, but nothing serious. Those days are behind me."

I nodded. "Mr. Fatone, how long have you been the manager for Fellini's?"

The old man leaned back and pursed his lips and stared at the ceiling. The short-sleeve shirt he wore was yellow and thin and it strained against his belly. I watched as dark patches of sweat made half-moons in the pits of the shirt.

"Well, I started with them back in the late seventies, when it was just Jack Fellini. Then he got his brother Sam involved, and it became the Fellini Brothers. When Sam was killed in the plane crash in eighty-five, Jack promoted me to general manager. So, yeah, it's been about twenty-five, thirty years. Jesus, the time goes fast, doesn't it?" he said. "Hey, can I get you a soda pop? Or some water?"

"No, thank you. And how's it been, business, I mean? I imagine you've seen a lot of changes over the years."

Fatone nodded. "You know, the circus used to be the greatest thing in town. When that long caravan of trains and trucks would roll in, the energy and excitement was just electric. It was a real family event you know, parents and kids together, having a good time. And then . . . I don't know. Somewhere, I think it was in the late 1980s, everyone sort of lost their innocence. Maybe it was the recession. The circus became this antiquated creature, going from town to town, feeding and then moving on."

I said, "That's a strange way to describe it. You make it sound like some kind of parasite."

He shrugged. "It was bad for a while there, but it's better now. I think folks are ready for joy again in their lives. The kids just adore coming, you know. They love the animals, the cotton candy, the clowns, too. All of it, it's just a blast."

"And Reed Tolliver? Did he like the scene?"

The old man nodded again. He took another sip from the mug and stretched out his legs to the side of the tiny table. I noticed his socks were mismatched and I wondered if he was color-blind. Maybe he just didn't care.

A breeze came in through the open trailer door, ruffling a stack of papers piled high in the corner. I wished Fatone would open the windows, too. The trailer was parked in the shade but the heat was already beginning to rise inside the tiny space.

Fatone said, "Reed was in bad shape in Cincinnati. We had finished our run and were packing up the tents and animals and he showed up at my door. He looked like he hadn't eaten in weeks, real skinny, kind of strung out."

"Drugs?"

Fatone shook his head. "I never saw him touch them. Believe me, I keep my eyes open for that sort of nonsense. Once they start using, they're no good to me. The risk is too high for something to happen, someone to get hurt. You know, Deputy, I'm not a real hard-ass . . . but the one thing everyone around here knows is that I run a clean operation. Yes, ma'am."

He waited for me to acknowledge this statement, so I scribbled a few words in my notebook and gave him a very serious nod. He looked pleased at this.

"What else can you tell me about Reed Tolliver?" I asked.

Fatone said, "I still remember, as bad of shape as he was in, there was this real honesty about him that shone through. Kind of a sweetness."

Tiny beads of sweat popped out on his forehead and he leaned over and cranked open one of the trailer's windows. "I'm sorry, it gets warm in here pretty quick."

"And he asked you for a job?"

He nodded. "Reed said he needed work, and that he'd been in theater. I had him do a few routines on the spot, and he was good, real good. And I'd just lost my best clown, Fred, so what the hell. I don't like to look a gift horse in the mouth, if you know what I mean."

I nodded. "Did you get his story from him?"

"You mean his life story? I don't like to pry, that's not really my business. But I got the sense he was a foster kid, maybe he ran away from a bad situation. You see that a lot these days, really sad shit, pardon my French. Like I said, though, he was a sweet kid. He was the kind of guy who'd chase you down the street to give you the shirt off his back."

That certainly was in line with everything I'd ever heard about Nicky Bellington. It made sense he'd display the same nature as Reed Tolliver.

I consulted my notes. "Is his girlfriend, Tessa—T—is she available? I'd like to speak with her."

Fatone stood. He walked over to a narrow ledge covered in loose file folders and opened one and scanned the contents and then said, "2B. The younger employees are all staying down at the Cottage Inn. She's in 2B. I told her to take a few days off, she's just real tore up about Reed."

The Cottage Inn was a cluster of tiny cabins built along a narrow stretch of the Arkansas River that ran parallel to town. I knew it well. I'd been there just a few months ago, on a domestic call that resulted in a young man shooting his even younger wife in the abdomen. She bled out before the ambulance could get her to the hospital.

It was a beautiful location with bad juju, as Brody would say.

Fatone and I spoke for a few more minutes. He told me Fellini's had more than two hundred regular employees, staying at various campgrounds, hotels, and motels in the area. I consulted my notes again and asked Fatone to put together a list of everyone who hadn't already been interviewed by our officers. Then I called Sam Birdshead and asked him to swing by with a partner and pick up the list and get started on the rest of the employees.

I stood and walked out of the trailer. At the bottom of the steps, I turned around and looked back up at the general manager. "Thank you, Mr. Fatone. I'll be in touch soon."

He leaned down and shook my hand and gave me a sad smile. "Wait, don't say it . . . don't leave town, right?"

I looked up at him. An errant nose hair, gray and tiny, hung from his left nostril, just touching the whiskers that dotted his upper lip.

"It would be better, sir, if you and the others stay in Cedar Valley for the foreseeable future."

Fatone nodded. "We'll lose money, of course, but it'll give everyone a break. We've been hitting the road pretty hard. The towns keep rolling by, week after week. Same story in each of them, until now, that is."

I started to walk away, then thought of something and turned back to him. He stood in the doorway, looking off in the distance at the man I'd seen earlier, still sweeping up the previous day's trash.

"Mr. Fatone, I would also advise you to tell your employees to be careful. Whoever killed Reed did it viciously, without remorse. This person may be targeting certain individuals, or it could be random. We simply don't know yet. So, be careful. And tell your group to be careful, too."

He said, "Absolutely, Deputy. We're all spooked. We'll be on the lookout. That's what families do, you know—we watch out for one another."

# Chapter Fourteen

The midday summer sun beat down on the Arkansas, the sun's rays dancing across the water like thousands of shimmering threads of light. As I drove to the Cottage Inn, I kept an eye on the river. A group of kayakers plucked their way through the rapids and boulders. If I wasn't so big, I'd have been tempted to rent a kayak myself and hit the water for an hour of hard paddling.

There's nothing like a good sweat to loosen old and rusty cogs in the head. At the moment, those cogs were rusted together. I felt like things in the case were progressing slowly, too slowly, and at the same time, too fast for me to hold all the pieces together.

It was a feeling I was used to, one that I knew would eventually pass. Starting an investigation is like dumping a five hundred–piece puzzle out from a cardboard box. All those pieces, random little bits of colors and shapes, and you stare and stare and then you find one that maybe goes with this one, and now you've got two. And then you find a third, and so on. Bit by bit, a picture starts emerging.

I parked and checked in at the Cottage Inn's front office, a tiny room with a desk, a computer and fax machine, and a phone. A teenage girl with bad acne and a noisy wad of Juicy Fruit eyeballed my badge without a word. She waved her hand in the general direction of the river and I took that as consent to enter the property.

A squat wooden post with an inlaid map said that 2B was one of a dozen cabins on the other side, the east side, of the Arkansas. I crossed a narrow footbridge, pausing for a moment to look down into the river, and caught a glimpse of a trout, a real beauty, as she made her way under the bridge. Her ruby red scales flashed at me like a showgirl's feathers and then she was gone, hiding in the rocks at the river's bank.

Rolling up my shirtsleeves and wishing I'd worn shorts, I consulted another wooden post and then continued on to the small cabin and rapped twice on the door and waited.

Inside, I heard shuffling and a low cough and then the door opened and the heavy-sweet smell of pot hit me full force. The face of a plump young woman emerged from behind the smoke. Her eyes were rimmed with a redness that matched her flame-colored hair. She coughed again and then her eyes widened when she saw the badge I held up.

I decided Joseph Fatone was either a liar or an idiot regarding the matter of drugs in the circus. This was clearly not the girl's first time down Mary Jane Lane.

"Uh," she grunted.

"Tessa O'Leary?" I asked. I stepped back to avoid inhaling the smoke and I spoke a little louder than I'd intended.

The girl's eyes grew even wider. With her right hand, she yanked at a loose cuticle on her left hand and then quickly brought the bleeding finger to her lips. She sucked at the blood and her mouth made a wet squelchy sound not unlike that of a boot being pulled from mud.

"Uh," she said again.

Red was seriously stoned.

I gave her a gentle smile. "Don't worry, I'm not here because of the pot. I'm here about Reed Tolliver. Is Tessa here?"

Another young woman emerged from behind the chubby one and gently shouldered her out of the way, until their positions were reversed and Red was in the back and the new girl was in front.

"I'm Tessa," she said. She was petite and compact, with the muscular body of a gymnast. Her hair was cut short, in that pixie style that can look masculine unless the wearer has feminine or delicate features.

Tessa had both; she looked like a fairy.

Thankfully, she didn't seem stoned. Not even high.

"Um, let's talk out here," Tessa said. She was remarkably composed for someone who'd just been caught with a hell of a lot of weed in her house, if the volume of smoke was any indication of the girls' stash.

I stood back as she whispered something to Red and then she joined me on the front porch. As the door closed behind Tessa, I saw Red's face for a moment in the narrow space between the door and the jamb and she no longer looked stoned.

The young woman looked furious.

"Sorry about that. Lisey is really upset about the whole Reed thing. God knows, I am, too, but she's having nightmares and anxiety attacks and stuff. I thought the weed might help," Tessa said. "I have a medical license for it, so it's okay, right? This is Colorado, after all."

"You know what? Let's just pretend I didn't see it, okay? And don't distribute anymore. I'm Officer Monroe."

She nodded, very solemn. "It's for my back. I hurt it on the bars last year and weed is the only thing that seems to relax my muscle spasms and lets me go on with my routine."

"What are the bars?" I asked.

We had, by some unspoken agreement, begun to stroll the Cottage Inn grounds, and we made our way along the river. I was envious of Tessa's T-shirt and shorts; my long black slacks were starting to stick to my legs from the sweat pouring down them.

"The trapeze bars. I'm a trapeze artist; I've been doing it for almost fifteen years and my back is just shot," she said.

My jaw dropped. "Fifteen years? How old are you?"

She laughed. "I'm twenty-two. My parents got me started on

the bars when I was seven. They had me in gymnastics when I was four."

"Wow. That's incredible. Tessa, I think you know I'm here about Reed. I'm so very sorry for your loss, and I'm hoping we can chat for a few minutes," I said. The young woman was composed now but I knew that could change at any moment. Grief is a funny thing; it catches you when you least expect it.

We came across a muddy patch and skirted the edge. I started to slip and Tessa caught my elbow and held me up while I regained my balance. I'd noticed in the last few weeks that the Peanut had really messed with my center of gravity; I hadn't been this prone to slipping and falling since I'd been a baby myself, learning to walk.

"How long have you been with the circus?"

"I was legally emancipated when I was sixteen and I joined up with Fellini's about a year later," she said. She leaped over another mud puddle and I walked around it, careful not to slip again.

"Rough home life?"

Tessa shrugged. "What's rough? Compared to some, I guess; others, not so much. I'm still in touch with them, so I guess that says something. We were very poor; they still live in a trailer park in a tiny town in Idaho.

"How about you?" she continued. "That's a gnarly scar you've got, what happened, bar fight?"

My hand went to my neck, as it does when my scar is mentioned. It begins at the base of my skull and travels around the right side of my neck, down over my collarbone, and onto my chest, in a rough half-circle of knotted, twisted flesh.

"No, it's not from a bar fight. It was a car accident, when I was four," I said. "It was Christmas Day and we were headed home from my grandmother's house, in Denver. We hit black ice on the highway and skidded into the path of an oncoming semi."

"God, how horrible," Tessa said. She shivered. "I've never been in an accident. Do you remember it?"

I nodded. "Bits and pieces. I remember my mother screamed, and my dad, he was driving, he yelled at me to hold on. After the impact, though, it's all sort of hazy."

A lie, one I had told so often it rolled off my tongue as sweet as syrup.

In truth, I remember coming to, upside down, hanging in the car. Blood ran from my neck and face in a steady flow, and I had to wipe it from my eyes to see. The car was silent; my mother and father looked asleep.

But I knew they weren't asleep.

I knew if they were alive, they'd have been frantically calling to me, helping me, urging me to pull myself out of the car.

Tessa noticed my silence.

She said, "Yeah, I don't like to talk much about my family, either. It's hard, you know, unless you've gone through it. And I've gone through some deep shit."

She grew quiet, so I followed her lead. At the academy, we'd had some training in adolescent counseling, and on the job of course, I'd been exposed to a fair share of family crisis situations. But I still felt like I was walking on eggshells when it came to these things. Some kids like to be asked questions and talking seems to help. For others, prying is akin to picking at scabs; painful and apt to reopen old wounds that are desperately trying to heal.

We continued along the river until we came to a sandy beach about half the size of a baseball diamond. Tessa slipped off her flip-flops and went to the water's edge and dipped a toe in. She gasped and then with a deep breath, waded into the river until the water lapped at her thighs.

"It's freezing!" she squealed, and I believed her. The river was high with snowmelt and even the near constant heat we'd had this summer would have done little to warm the water.

I slipped off my shoes and socks and rolled my pants up above my knees. The first touch of the icy water took my breath away but then the cold wrapped itself around my swollen ankles and compressed them and I sighed loudly at how good it felt.

Tessa gave me a weird look.

"You'll see, one day. It's amazing, you spend your whole life getting to know your body and then along comes this alien-like thing and every part you thought you knew changes," I told her.

To my shock, Tessa started weeping.

"I'm sorry," she said as she wiped her eyes and lifted her T-shirt to her nose and blew mightily. "Reed and I talked about having kids one day. I wasn't sure but he said it was something he'd always wanted, to be a dad."

"Did he ever talk about his own dad? Or his mom?" I asked.

I walked with her out of the water and we sat on the sandy beach. We watched as a family of four strolled on the other side of the river, the two toddlers running to the river's edge and then shrieking and running back to their parents.

Tessa closed her eyes. "The first time he mentioned his dad, it was an accident, like, he didn't mean to say anything. When I asked him about it, he clammed up and said something like he had a lifetime of atoning to do and the sins of the father are the sins of the son."

That surprised me. As far as I knew, Terence Bellington was an honest man. I'd never heard the slightest whispers of improper behavior, business, family, or otherwise.

"What did he mean by that?"

She tilted her head to the side, thinking. "You know, I'm not sure. I never got a chance to ask him. We were at some party, after a concert somewhere in Kansas, and we were drunk. He changed the subject real quick. I'd forgotten all about it, until you asked, just now."

"What about his mom? Did Reed ever talk about her?"

Tessa shook her head.

"Never? He never mentioned her?" I asked again.

"No. You know how some kids won't talk about their parents, if something's happened to them? I got the impression she was dead, like maybe she'd died when Reed was real little and he didn't like to talk about it, so I never pushed him," she said.

I nodded. "Tessa, I know this is difficult, but can you think of anyone who'd want to hurt Reed?"

She shook her head emphatically, her eyes filling up again with tears. "No way. Reed was just the *nicest* guy you can imagine. I've never met anyone before who treated absolutely every person they met the same, no matter if it was a freaky performer, or a gasser, or a little kid in the audience."

"Gasser?"

"The guys who fill the balloons with helium. We call 'em gassers because they inhale so much of it their brains are, like, filled with gas. They're pretty much at the bottom of the totem pole, if you know what I mean," she said.

"But not to Reed?"

"No. He talked to everyone and anyone. He was always asking where are you from, who do you know, where's your family, stuff like that. And around here, that's pretty ballsy. Lots of folks don't want their business known, that's why they join up," she said.

Tessa lay back on the sand, pulled her knees to her chest, and rolled first to one side and then the other. I heard a loud pop and winced. She just laughed.

"Oh, that's better. I have to crack my back a few times a day now. It gets so stiff."

I hated to think what her back would be like in another fifteen years.

"I'm not always going to do this, you know," she said. "I've been taking online courses and I'm about three credits short of my business degree. I've done a lot of research, too, into accounting, finance, that sort of thing. I'm aiming for what you might call 'well-rounded.'"

"That's great."

She nodded in agreement. "I want to work for corporate. Fellini's main offices are in Seattle. I talked to a lady there and she said they'd hire me, as soon as I fax them a copy of my diploma."

"Was Reed planning to go with you?" I asked. "To Seattle?"

With his multitude of facial piercings and tattoos, I thought it unlikely Nicky had any plans to go white collar. But hell, Seattle had its fair share of alternative lifestyles. Tessa's face darkened for a moment, but then as quickly as it had come, the shadow passed and she gave me another brilliant smile.

"I don't know. We'd talked, you know, like we'd talked about having kids, but sometimes I didn't know when Reed was serious and when he was messing with me. Like, not to be mean, but sometimes, what he thought was playful kind of hurt my feelings."

I thought of Brody, and the way that those we love the most can rip open our hearts like no one else.

She started crying again. "I can't believe he's gone. Fuck. One minute I forget and then the next, it's like Papa Joe is calling me all over again, telling me something bad had happened to Reed."

"I know this is hard to understand, but it will get easier, Tessa. Not right away, not anytime soon, but it will get better."

She nodded and helped me up off the sandy beach. "Hey, why are you in charge of this case, anyway? I thought detectives investigate murders, not officers or whatever."

"Well, in the bigger cities, that's true. But in some towns, like Cedar Valley, we don't have the manpower to have a separate unit. So, we're all sort of cross-trained on everything from parking tickets to, well, to this," I said. "Burglaries, assaults, rapes . . . you name it, we do it. I'm an officer and a detective."

"Oh. Okay."

We made our way back to the cabin in silence. We shook hands and I handed her one of my business cards.

"Tessa, I asked Joe Fatone to keep the circus in town for a few extra days, all right? I'd like to talk with you again, maybe tomorrow? Would that be okay?"

"Sure. If Papa Joe's not going anywhere, I'm not going anywhere," she said. Something caught her eye at the cabin and when I turned, I saw Red staring at us from the window with the same furious expression she'd worn an hour earlier.

Tessa sighed.

I tilted my head toward the cabin. "She seems mad."

Tessa stared another few seconds at Red and then looked back at me. "Lisey doesn't know what to feel. She was in love."

"With Reed?"

"With me," she replied, and walked toward the cabin. "Give me a call, I'll be around."

# Chapter Fifteen

The station was quiet when I returned. Sam Birdshead sat typing at one of the computer terminals; he had split the workload with another officer and finished interviewing most of the circus employees from the list of names Joe Fatone had prepared for us.

The window shades were drawn against the glare of the southern afternoon sun and the old wooden ceiling fan was on, creaking and groaning and looking as though it might fall at any moment. The fan made a rhythmic whoosh every few seconds that slowed my pulse, syncing it with the scalloped blades. The room was cool and dark and empty, save for Sam and I.

I've often thought being a police officer is akin to being a clergyman, and at that moment the station felt like the hallowed sanctuary of a church.

"Where is everyone?" I asked Sam. I sat down and leaned back and lifted my legs up until my feet were on my desk. With my belly, it was an awkward maneuver and for one horrible moment I thought Sam was actually going to grab my ankles and hoist, but he had the good sense to just watch.

"Armstrong and Moriarty took a call on an accident in Pine. I don't know where Nowlin is," Sam said. "I think the chief is in his office."

I nodded. "Get anything good?"

Sam shook his head. His expression was so hangdog I had to laugh.

"Don't worry about it, that's part of the deal. For every hour you spend on a case, you might get a minute of gold. Just remember that gold makes those fifty-nine other minutes of sweat and tears and blood and bullshit all worth it."

"I guess. It's strange, I get the impression that Fellini's is like its own little society, and everyone belongs to a class, and the classes don't mix," Sam said. "For example, the grunts and the glitter don't ever get together."

"The grunts and the glitter?"

"Yeah, the performers like the clowns and the acrobats, the showmen. They're the glitter, and the grunts are the guys like this Pat Sheldon I talked to, the cooks and the mechanics and the train-ers," Sam said. "The grease in the wheels of the big machine that is the circus."

Hadn't Tessa said something about that? She'd said it was like a totem pole, with the gassers on the bottom.

"Did this Sheldon mention the gassers?" I asked.

Sam nodded with surprise. "How'd you know about them? They're the worst, apparently. The gassers, and the guys who run the kiddy booths; Sheldon called them the peddies."

"The peddies?"

"Yeah, as in peddlers, or pedophiles, depending on if you think they're just selling wares or if they're manning the booths to get up close and personal with the kiddos."

I winced.

"Well, after I called you from Fatone's, I went and saw Reed's girlfriend, Tessa," I said. "We ought to take a look at her roommate, Lisey. Seems there was a bit of a love triangle."

Sam perked up. "Oh yeah?"

I nodded. "Yeah, but not the way you're thinking. Lisey appar-ently has a thing for Tessa."

"You thinking this Lisey killed Reed in some kind of jealous rage?" Sam asked. "That's pretty violent for a crush."

He stood and stretched and handed me an open bag of peanut M&M'S.

"You'd be surprised what can happen when love's involved,"

I said. I knocked back a handful of the chocolates and noticed they were all brown, red, or green candies. "The worst things I've seen were between people who loved each other. Did you pick out all the blue and yellow M&M'S?"

Sam looked at me, aghast. "I would never do that."

"Well, someone did. Did you get anything else?"

Sam shook his head. "Not much. Same stuff we've been hearing, sweet kid, liked everyone, blah blah blah."

I stopped him. "No, not blah blah blah. This is good, and important, and we can't forget it, no matter what else we discover. Consistency tells us a lot, Sam. People are creatures of habit. Everything we know about Nicky thus far tells us he was a good kid, sweet, gentle-natured. Everything we know about Reed thus far also tells us he was a good kid. And what does *that* tell us?"

Sam shook his head and shrugged. "Well, we'd expect that, right? Since it was the same guy?"

"It tells us that even though Nicky went to drastic, extreme measures to change his appearance—the tattoos, the piercings, the hair dye—he didn't, or couldn't, change his personality. On the outside, Nicky became Reed. On the inside, Nicky stayed Nicky."

I stood and walked to the back of the station, where a whiteboard stretched the length of the wall. I erased a few scribbles and a tiny unflattering cartoon of what looked like Chief Chavez and a pack of ponies and rummaged around the markers until I found one that wasn't dried out.

I drew a long horizontal line and then added a tick mark along it.

"Three years ago, in the summer of 2012, Nicholas Bellington left home for a camping trip and he never came back. He was presumed to have died when he what—fell? Tripped? Was pushed? Jumped?—over Bride's Veil. His body was never found."

Sam nodded. He grabbed a marker and some distance from my first mark, added another tick. "Two days ago, Nicholas Bellington, living under the alias Reed Tolliver, turns up in his hometown murdered. This is all we can say for certain, right?"

"Right." I drummed my marker against the wall, thinking. "I think we need to consider the possibility that Reed wasn't the target."

"You mean Nicky was the target. Someone discovered who Reed really was and that's why he was killed; not for something Reed did but for something Nicky did."

Pleased, I nodded at Sam. "You're sixteen. You survive a fall that would have killed anyone else, and then you run. But you don't run to your parents, your school, or your church. Instead, you run as far away as you can and then you change. You change your name, your hair. You destroy your face with tattoos and piercings to the point that if your own mother saw you on the street, she'd walk right by you. Why?"

The room was silent save for the rhythmic whoosh of the ceiling fan. It paced our thoughts like a giant metronome. *Whoosh, whoosh. Whoosh, whoosh.*

"You're scared. You do all that because you are scared to death," a voice whispered into my ear. I jumped and turned around. Finn Nowlin had crept into the room in that silent way of his and he stood, looking at us. Then with a wolfish grin he reached around me and slapped up the window shade on my left. Sunlight streamed into the room and I thought about Finn's words.

I knew there were shades of fear, the same as there are shades of like, and love, and anger, and desire. I was grateful in that moment to have never known the level of fear that Nicky must have felt, to do the things he did.

# Chapter Sixteen

The phone rang for a long time at the Bellingtons'. I was about to hang up when Ellen Bellington answered. She sounded harried, impatient to get off the phone.

"Of course we didn't keep his things. We boxed them up and gave it all away, after the police came and poked their damn fingers through it, touching every little item they could," Ellen replied in response to my question.

"What about his schoolwork, his papers? Did he have a journal, maybe a diary?"

She laughed, that harsh bark so at odds with her beauty. I was starting to believe that laugh was more representative of her true self, the ugly side she kept hidden.

"What do you think? He was sixteen."

"Mrs. Bellington, we need to discover why Nicky disappeared three years ago. If we can figure out what he was doing at the time—"

"Nicky wasn't *doing* anything, Gemma," she interrupted.

I heard a low voice in the background and then a muffled sound, as if she'd covered the phone with her hand.

"I have to go. Frank, my father-in-law, he's not well, I have to go to him," she said. "Check with that basketball coach. Maybe he can tell you more. He was real fond of Nicky, too fond for my liking."

Ellen hung up the phone with a force too strong to be an accident, and I rubbed my ringing ear.

Although school had not yet resumed, Cedar Valley High

School ran summer classes through the end of August. I checked my watch; it was nearing four o'clock. I took a chance and called, and waited while an administrative assistant put me on hold and tracked down the basketball coach.

I paced the office and listened with one ear as Finn regaled Sam with war stories. He was beginning the one about Christmas Eve of '09, and the drunken department store elf, when the hold music stopped and a male voice came on.

"This is Darren Chase."

His voice was low and sounded like he'd spent some serious time down in the bayou; I heard in the ebb and flow of his words days spent on shrimping boats, in swampy wetlands, watching shell-pink and blood-orange sunsets over the Gulf.

I introduced myself and asked if I could see him regarding a student he had coached a few years back.

He said, "Well, sure, of course," then added, "Which student?"

Damn. I forgot the Bellingtons still had not held their press conference.

"Mr. Chase, I'd rather not get into too many details over the phone. Can I buy you a coffee at Rick's?" I said. "I can be there in twenty minutes."

"Make it thirty, and a beer, my treat," he said with a laugh. "Or is it doughnuts that you cops prefer?"

"Very funny, Mr. Chase. I'll see you at four thirty then."

I asked Sam to join me. Chief Chavez hadn't officially made us partners on the case but what the hell, the kid was eager to learn and it never hurt to have a second set of eyes and ears. I didn't want to put the mileage on my car, so I checked at reception and gave Sam a high five when the receptionist tossed me the keys to Olga.

Olga was a piece-of-shit Oldsmobile, a relic from the '80s, but she was the hottest ticket around, on account of her working air conditioner and AM/FM stereo. We clamored into it and cranked the AC and headed over to Rick's Café, a small restaurant that sat in the shadows of the ski lifts, at the base of a black-diamond run called Maverick's Goose.

"I was thinking about what you said the other day, you know, dreaming about those kids, the McKenzie boys," said Sam. He fiddled with the AC vents, opening and closing them like a kid himself. "Do you think we'll ever know who killed them?"

I shrugged. "I hope so, but who knows? You have to understand, back in '85, and then in 2011, when I found the skull, thousands of dollars were poured into the case. Hell, tens of thousands, and not just money, but time, effort, and energy. Finding those bodies opened old, deep wounds in Cedar Valley. There were people in town that would have preferred the bodies never be found. I guess they thought it was just easier to keep thinking maybe the kids had run away."

"But if the Woodsman is still alive . . . well, that would be something, right? If there was some way to find him . . ."

I had to appreciate his enthusiasm.

"Of course. But we went over it, again and again. I haven't given up, but I can't let the past prevent me from giving all to the present. Take Nicky Bellington—we have an opportunity to find his killer and solve *this* case, here and now."

"And what's this Darren Chase got to do with it?" Sam asked.

"He's the basketball coach at the high school. Ellen Bellington said that in the months before Nicky disappeared over Bride's Veil, he was spending all his free time at practice with his coach. She hinted that perhaps there was something inappropriate going on."

"Hinted?"

I nodded. "She didn't come right out and say it, but she has her suspicions."

"And do we? Have our suspicions, I mean? Is this guy on a list?"

I shook my head. "Nope. I checked before we left the station, he's clean. Mr. Chase moved here from the Gulf about five years ago. He's clean as a whistle."

"Hmmm. Something to be aware of, at least. Just because there's no record doesn't mean something hasn't happened," Sam said. He stopped fiddling with the vents and began channel surfing the stereo. "Do you have any names picked out?"

I smiled. The name. Lately, the only thing Brody and I fought about.

"Well, it's a girl. I like Elizabeth, after my mother. But Brody dated a girl named Eliza who was a real bitch, so he hates it. He likes Tara but spelled T-E-R-R-A, like the earth kind of terra, nerdy scientist that he is."

"Different. I like it. But the name Brody's different, too. His parents must have been hippies."

I shook my head. "Nope. They were missionaries in China in the sixties and seventies. His mother came down with a terrible fever while carrying him and she almost died. They were in a re-mote outpost hundreds of miles from any kind of hospital, but the Buddhist villagers saved her life. They'd already settled on the name Matthew but his dad was so grateful to them that he switched it to Bodhi, after the Bodhisattva. But back in the States, when she delivered, the nurse misheard her and wrote Brody on his birth certificate."

"Wow. That's a crazy story," Sam said, shaking his head. He settled on a country-western station and George Strait filled the Olds, singing about an oceanfront property in Arizona.

"After they returned to the States, they had four more children, all girls: Rachel, Mary, Naomi, and Sarah."

Sam laughed. "Biblical names."

"Except for Brody. Can you imagine? I think you guys would like each other; you'll have to come over for dinner once he gets back from Alaska," I said.

Just a few more days and he'd be home; unless, that is, he was planning to shack up with Celeste Fucking Takashima. Maybe she would take him back to Tokyo and they'd eat sushi naked, holding intense conversations deep into the night about geological anoma-lies and surface-level fissures.

Sam was looking at me funny.

"Sorry, I missed that?"

"Your house is up canyon, isn't it? Sort of isolated up there."

"Brody bought it ten years ago. Once we started dating, and

fell in love, I sort of fell in love with it, too. It's just beautiful and peaceful. And the wildlife is amazing; we've seen deer, of course, but also black bear and even a mountain lion once."

"Is it on the grid?"

"Yes and no. We're on a propane system and our own septic, but we've got Internet and cable and electricity," I said with a laugh. "It's not as out there as you might think."

I pulled into the parking lot at Rick's Café. It was empty save for a beat-up Subaru wagon. A tall man leaned against the driver's door, a Red Sox ball cap pulled low over his ears. By his hip, the Subaru's side mirror hung at an angle, held in place with duct tape. I noticed a rear fender was dented, as well.

We met him halfway between our cars and the restaurant. Late-afternoon heat rose from the asphalt. At the edge of the lot, two crows pecked at a dead squirrel. Their loud cackles filled the air and I turned away from the sight of them diving into the squirrel's abdomen, their sharp beaks bobbing back up with bits of flesh.

"Mr. Chase? Thanks for meeting us. This is my partner, Sam Birdshead. I'm Detective Gemma Monroe," I said. I had to crane my neck to look up at him. He was my age, give or take a year or two. His eyes were dark and framed with long lashes, the kind any woman would kill for. When he spoke, I again heard the Gulf in his voice, a low drawl that trod softly over the harder consonants and vowels.

"Darren. And it's no problem," he said. "Look, am I in some kind of trouble?"

"I don't know, are you?" I asked. My intent had not been flirtation, but it sounded that way.

Darren just smiled and shook his head.

Inside Rick's, we took a seat at a table by a window that looked out at the ski slopes, brown and drab and dusty in the summer heat. The ski lift chairs swung gently in the breeze, giant swing sets suspended high up in the air. A handful of mountain bikers crisscrossed their way down the slopes, small clouds of dirt and dust bellowing up from their back tires. We watched as two of the bikers almost collided. At the last second, one angled uphill and the other downhill. Darren and Sam watched them and made small talk while I leaned back and watched Darren. I was curious what he'd have to say about Nicky.

A waitress with hips like a Chevy dropped three menus in front of us. The laminated pages were sticky, as though they hadn't been wiped down after the lunch crowd, and Sam put his down in disgust. He wiped the tips of his fingers on the edge of the tablecloth.

The waitress, whose nametag read "Michelle," came back and placed three glasses of water on the table. The water was iceless, the glasses filled only halfway. Her right hip jostled the table as she shifted her weight. She waited silently, her pen poised above a small notepad in hands that were red and chapped and dotted with age marks.

"Three coffees, please," I said.

She gave me a skeptical look.

"Two regulars and a decaf, then?"

I shook my head. "Three regulars, please. With some cream and sugar on the side."

"Honey, you sure? I don't think you're supposed to have coffee if you're expecting a little one," she said.

She'd taken a step back and placed her reddened hands on her hips. In her black-and-white-striped polo shirt, she looked like a referee, and I expected to hear a whistle pierce the quiet restaurant.

"Hey, Michelle. How 'bout those coffees," Darren said without taking his eyes off the mountain bikers.

The woman's hands dropped from her hips and with a shake of her head she turned back into the kitchen.

The basketball coach took off the Red Sox cap and his hair, dark and thick, fell at an angle down his forehead. He finally turned from the window and looked at me in a way that I hadn't been looked at in a long time.

"So, I think you mentioned a former student, right?" Darren asked. "Is it someone who graduated?"

I swallowed. "Sort of. Nicholas Bellington. Remember him?"

Darren jolted in his seat, and his mouth fell open. "Nicky?"

Sam jumped in. "So you knew him?"

In response, my partner got a withering glare from Darren.

He answered. "Of course I knew him. Not only did I coach him, he was one of the most beloved students at the school. And then, of course, when he died . . . well, let's just say it would be pretty squirrely if I didn't know who Nicky was."

"Would you call him a good player? It sounds like he was at the gym a lot that spring."

Darren's eyes met mine again. He put his hands flat on the table and leaned forward, holding my gaze two seconds longer than what most would consider polite.

"Look, what's this all about?" he asked.

Sam Birdshead started to reply and I kicked his leg under the table.

"Please answer the question, Mr. Chase," I said.

"It's Darren. My dad is Mr. Chase," he replied. "This was three years ago, you know."

I nodded. "I get the feeling you're not the kind of man who forgets things, Darren."

"You'd be right about that. Well, someone's been telling you tall tales. Nicky quit the team right before Christmas. He wasn't that great of a player. I would have tried to get him to stay, but . . ." He trailed off.

"But what?"

"He started missing a lot of practices. We talked and decided it would be best for everyone if he dropped out. I don't think his parents even noticed, they were so busy with that campaign," Darren finished.

"So, where was he if not at practice?" I asked. "What was he up to?"

Darren gave me a smile. "Would you believe he was at the library? He was working on a special project."

"Which was?" I pressed.

He sighed. "Look, I told him I wouldn't tell anyone, okay? I can't break a promise, not one I made to a dead kid."

"The dead don't give a damn about loyalty, Darren. Would it surprise you to know that Nicky's been alive and well these past three years?" I asked.

The coach's reaction was nearly identical to the one he'd had a few minutes earlier. Another jolt, another drop of the jaw.

"It's true. Alive and well, that is, until he had his throat torn open Monday afternoon," Sam added.

Darren's face turned ashen. "I don't believe it."

"Oh, believe it," I said. "The mayor will be holding a press conference today."

Michelle returned with three white mugs of steaming coffee, and a small pitcher of milk and a bowl of sugar. I pushed one of the cups toward Darren. He took a quick sip and then swore as the hot liquid burned his mouth.

Tears welled in his eyes and I wondered if it was the coffee or the news of Nicky that brought them forth.

"We obviously can't give you any more details, but you can see, right, how it might be important to get a picture of Nicky's last few weeks and months? Before he went over that waterfall?" Sam asked.

Darren dipped a napkin in his water and brought the cool cloth to his lip. He shook his head and blinked away the tears so fast I decided they must have been from the burn after all.

"Look, Darren," I said. "I don't want to subpoena you."

"Are you sure? It might be fun," he replied with a smirk. "Look, all I can say is that Nicky was interested, and I mean, very interested, in some local history. He asked me about it once, and I told him to get with Tilly over at the public library."

Sam glared at Darren. "Could you be more vague? What exactly was this local history?"

I glanced at the bikers as I waited for Darren's reply. They seemed to have finished their rides for the day, as they were huddled en masse at the bottom of the slope. A few peeled off their jerseys, revealing lean sweaty torsos and a solitary sports bra.

The restaurant was quiet and when I turned back to the table, I saw Darren staring at me.

"What?"

He laughed. "I was just thinking how ironic it is, you asking what Nicky was researching."

"Ironic?" Sam asked.

"Yeah, it means—"

I lifted a hand. "He knows what it means. Why ironic?"

Darren Chase stood and jammed the baseball cap down on his head. He threw a ten-dollar bill on the table and stretched and as his T-shirt lifted, I caught a glimpse of another lean, tan torso, this one fringed with tiny dark hairs that trailed down into the waistband of his jeans. I swallowed and blamed my raging hormones, and the fact that Brody had been gone for so long, on the thoughts that flitted across my mind.

"Because you were the one who found the bodies, Gemma. Nicky was fascinated with the Woodsman murders. He couldn't get enough of them. From the time you found that skull in what, November? December? Until his death, that kid was obsessed."

I pushed back from the table, shocked. "You're kidding. Why?"

"He wouldn't tell me," Darren said. He shook his head. "Like I said, he came to me one day and asked how someone would go about researching cold cases, old crimes. It wasn't hard to guess which crime he was talking about, so I pointed him in Tilly's direction."

Darren left. Sam and I silently watched him walk away. It seemed I wasn't the only one who couldn't get the McKenzie boys out of my head.

# Chapter Seventeen

By the time I dropped Sam back at the station, I was so tired I didn't think I was going to make it up the canyon. As I watched him walk into the building, his short blond hair turning amber in the setting sun, I was struck by a powerful sense of déjà vu, and for a moment, I waited to see if he would come back, and tell me that Ravi Hussen was on the phone, and the whole damn thing would start over like that Bill Murray classic *Groundhog Day*.

But he didn't come out and I headed home. The last swatches of sunlight were chased across the sky by the deepening twilight. A couple of bats flitted high above me, on their way out for an evening meal. I pulled into our gravel driveway and stared at the house. It was, as it should have been, dark and silent. Immense woods flanked the narrow two-story house on three sides like an open mouth, gaping and black and ready to swallow up the place at any moment.

As I got out of the car, the chilly mountain air hit my bare forearms and I shivered; the intense heat of the day was already a distant memory. I hurried inside and got the lights on and some potatoes and salmon in the oven. I let Seamus out into the yard and left the back door open for him.

We'd spent a grand building the fence; it was nine feet high and reinforced with discreet steel planks hidden behind pine panels. Since its completion a year ago, we hadn't had a single problem with bears in the garbage. And I had stopped worrying that Seamus would become a snack for a mountain lion.

The house was quiet save for the ticking of the timer I used for the fish and potatoes, and the sound of Seamus coming and going through the back door. He'd come in, whine a bit, and then go back out. After his fourth rotation, I pushed myself off the couch and went to the door.

"Seamus?" I called to him. "What is it, boy?"

The backyard was dark and I heard him snuffling in the garden at the side of the house. I flipped the switch for the porch light and waited for the thing to come on but it didn't and I flipped it up and down and then cursed, remembering. The bulb had burned out during a dinner party we'd thrown a month ago.

I thought Brody replaced the light but he must have forgotten.

"Seamus! C'mon boy, come here," I called. The snuffling stopped, and then started up again with another funny little whine. "Seamus! Get in here."

He emerged from the dark with dirt on his nose and a guilty look on his face, and as I pulled the back door shut behind him, I got the sense that something, or someone, was in the yard.

I don't scare easily but the silence was eerie and it made the hairs on the back of my neck stand up. I held my breath and listened and heard none of the usual nighttime sounds of the forests: the screech of crickets, the breeze in the pine boughs or the scratch of rodents.

A deep silence descended over the yard, so deep I could hear my heart thudding in my chest. I stepped back into the kitchen and bolted the back door and drew the curtains on the windows above the sink. I thought of going upstairs and getting my gun but the feeling passed. It was likely a raccoon or bobcat up the street; the prey all seem to play freeze when they sense a predator in the neighborhood.

I ate my dinner on a tray in front of the television and with every news story, grew more and more depressed. Another war in a faraway country, another parent doing something horrible to their child, more bloodshed, more sadness. I switched to a local news station and saw Terence and Ellen Bellington standing at a podium, holding hands, and I upped the volume.

They were in the pressroom at City Hall; I recognized the heavy velvet indigo curtains that hung behind them, embroidered in gold and scarlet thread with the state and town crests. The mayor's chief of staff, a somber old bird whose name I couldn't remember, stood to his left. To his right stood Chief Chavez.

I didn't see Annika. Perhaps she was in the audience.

Mayor Bellington raised a hand for silence and then spoke. "Thank you all for coming, I know the late notice was a surprise. I'm going to read a short statement that my wife and I have prepared. We won't be taking any questions tonight. You can contact my office, or the police department, in the morning for further information."

He cleared his throat and I watched as Ellen gave his hand a squeeze. She wore a navy suit that made her pale hair and skin look ghostly. In contrast, the mayor wore dark slacks and a light blue V-neck sweater, with a pastel tie. Somehow it all worked.

"As many of you know, the body of a young man was found Monday afternoon at the fairgrounds. The victim was a clown, an employee of the Fellini Brothers' Circus. What began as a routine murder investigation took a surprising turn when it was discovered that the young man is none other than our son, Nicholas Patrick Bellington."

The mayor raised his hands again at the chatter that burst forth from the audience, waiting until the room was quiet again before speaking.

"Three years ago, the good citizens of Cedar Valley granted my family privacy and respect as we grieved for our son, Nicky. I ask you now, not as your mayor, but as your neighbor, and I hope your friend, for that same courtesy once again," he said.

The mayor stepped back from the microphone and without another word, walked off the stage with Ellen in tow. The room erupted and Chavez took the podium.

"Chief! Chief Chavez! Do you have any leads?" a squeaky voice rang out above the others. I recognized it as that of our local news anchor, Missy Matherson, a bottle blonde with a little too much ambition and not nearly enough empathy.

"Missy, you heard the mayor. We'll be taking all questions in the morning," Chavez said. He was comfortable at the podium and his genuine manner seemed to settle the room down. For the first time, I realized that he could easily run for office someday and likely win, and I wondered if the same thought had ever crossed his mind.

He said, "Y'all come down to the station about nine, we'll have coffee and doughnuts and I'll tell you everything I can."

The mayor's chief of staff, still on stage, leaned over and whispered something in Chavez's ear. He listened and then nodded.

"The mayor's office will be available for questions, as well, in the afternoon," he added.

"Chief! Is the mayor still planning a rumored run on the Senate office in next year's elections?" Missy Matherson shouted. "What about his cancer, is such traumatic news going to affect his recovery?"

I put down my fork in disgust. The woman was colder than a steak in the freezer.

Chavez had been in the process of stepping away from the podium, but now he came back and leaned into the microphone. If I knew him, he'd have a zinger.

"Folks, it's been a long couple of days. We've got a dead man—a kid, really—and tonight, a good family grieves. I can't speak for the mayor, but I'd guess politics is the furthest thing from his mind at the moment."

I turned the TV off and felt a wave of anxiety wash over me. It was a shitty, shitty world at times and here we were, bringing a baby into it. By the time the Peanut was my age, was there going to be a world worth enjoying? What if something happened to me, or Brody? I knew what it was like to grow up loved, protected, cherished, only to have that security ripped away in a few seconds of screeching tires and screaming engines.

I'd had a few of these panic attacks early in the pregnancy and Brody's response had never wavered. "We're bringing a baby into this world not with fear, but with love. We can't be afraid of life."

I wasn't afraid of life. I was just terrified of how different life might look for my daughter.

I brushed my teeth and used the restroom and put my nightgown on. I climbed into bed; my body was exhausted but my mind refused to rest. Next to the bed, my cell phone buzzed on top of the nightstand. I checked the caller ID; it was my grandmother.

"Julia? Are you all right? It's late," I said.

Silence.

"Julia?"

"We just watched the news. Gemma, listen to me. You've got to be careful now, stay away from him. He's got a sickness. He's a virus," my grandmother whispered. She spoke quickly, her words tumbling over one another.

"Stay away from who, Mayor Bellington? What on earth are you talking about?"

Julia sighed. "Think, you little idiot. What do viruses do? They seep in and infect and spread. Oh no, oh no, your grandfather's done in the can. I've got to go, he can't know I called you. Did you hear me? Stay the hell away from that man."

She hung up and I slowly set the phone down, chilled to my core. She'd never spoken to me that way, and I was rattled. What man did she mean?

I lay back in bed and pulled the covers up as high as they could go before they'd smother me. Slightly over forty-eight hours had passed since we'd discovered Nicky Bellington, aka Reed Tolliver's, body. The people in both boys' lives circled in my thoughts like pieces in a chess game; like vultures in the sky.

There was Joseph Fatone, Fellini's general manager. He seemed harmless enough, but there was something off about him, his answers had come too easy during our conversation. There was more to the man than met the eye. Reed's girlfriend, Tessa, was feisty, driven, and beautiful . . . and complicated. Was it compassionate to live with someone you didn't love—Lisey—who was in love with you? Or was it a cruel power play, an illusion like the ones Tessa created as she flew through the air on the trapeze bars?

At the circus, surrounding Reed, and Joe, and Tessa and Lisey, were the dozens of supporting characters I'd yet to meet: the glitter and the gassers, and the grunts and peddies. They were a motley crew of nomads, making their way from city to city, anonymous, living under the shadows of the big top and the bright lights.

Not for the first time, I thought what a perfect cesspool a traveling circus could be. I'm sure there were good people in there, honest, decent hard workers, but the very nature of the beast dictated that the players were those who liked living on the fringe of society.

And there was Nicholas, sweet, good-natured Nicky. His father was a decent and ambitious man with aspirations for Washington. His mother, Ellen—beautiful and as cold as an arctic queen in a fairy tale. And like any good fairy tale, there was a princess. Only this princess was as smart as her father and as beautiful as her mother and as sweet as her twin brother.

In real life, perfection like that doesn't exist, and when you see it, you know there's something else behind the facade.

Finally, there was Nicky himself. What was he doing three years ago, spending all his free time looking into a thirty-year-old murder mystery? And what, if anything, did that have to do with his death two days ago?

Like actors on a stage, the major players in the case paraded back and forth across my mind, each playing their roles. At my feet, Seamus snored, twitching every few minutes from his doggy dreamland. He shifted and I shifted with him, his body and my legs repositioning themselves until we were both comfortable again.

I must have fallen asleep around midnight, but the Woodsman again haunted my dreams.

I stand in a meadow in the middle of a dense forest. The air is cool and silent and still. I'm in a nightgown, an old-fashioned dress with long sleeves and delicate lace trim at the wrists and hem.

When I raise my arms to look at what I'm wearing, the white fabric glows in the moonlight. The lacework is so fragile it looks as though I've dipped my wrists in cobwebs.

I'm a beacon in the dark woods.

The children creep toward me, emerging from the black forest like wraiths.

They fall to their knees around me, their hands together in supplication as though to pray. We are the dead, they whisper. Do not forget us, they chant. Tommy is closest and I put my hand on his head in a gesture of comfort, but my hand passes through his face and I stumble, losing my balance.

A noise emerges from the woods, a terrible dragging sound, and as the children slip back into the dark edges of the trees, a man emerges. He never steps into the moonlight but I can tell he is large, over six feet tall, and strong. He has the shoulders of a man who spends hours using them, and strapped to his back are the woodsman's tools: pick-ax, shovel, handsaw, hammers.

Behind him is a sleigh, or a wagon, on which a wrapped object lies. The object is not long, maybe four feet, but something deep within me recognizes its general shape and my stomach clenches in a tight fist of fear.

He stops and for the first time in all my dreams, he looks around the meadow as though he senses my presence.

For a moment, I think he doesn't see me. I exhale and step backward but my bare feet hit a twig and in the still of the forest, the noise is a crack of thunder. I freeze and the Woodsman's head slowly turns toward me.

My blood turns to ice in my veins.

My bowels loosen and I tighten my thighs to staunch the flow of urine that I'm about to release. Fear like I've never felt before runs through every nerve, every cell in my body, and I sense a scream building in my throat.

"It's too late," he whispers. "You're already dead."

.    .    .

At six o'clock the angry buzz of the alarm clock jolted me awake. I sat up. The room was cold and quiet; Seamus must have gone downstairs for a sip of water or to commandeer a patch of early morning sunlight on the living-room floor. As I rolled out of bed, my bare leg brushed against a damp spot in the middle of the mattress. Puzzled, I leaned over it and the sharp smell of urine hit me.

I'd wet the bed.

I threw the sheets in the washing machine and left a voice message with Dr. Pabst's office. He was helpful when I saw him before; perhaps he'd have some new insight into my dreams. I reached a secretary who was delighted to tell me that there had been a cancellation and Pabst could see me that morning.

I tried to ignore the shame that crept over my body when I thought about the wet spot in my bed. Fear is a natural human emotion. My bladder was just full; it was the Peanut's fault. Maybe I had a UTI.

I told myself these things but I knew who had caused the bed-wetting.

It was the Woodsman.

I showered and made breakfast and let Seamus out into the backyard. In the morning light, from my perch on the patio, I couldn't see anything out of the ordinary. I thought about crossing the yard and checking the far side of the fence, but my feet were bare and the grass was wet with dew. Seamus did his business and then came right back in, with none of the whining he'd done the night before.

Before I left for the day, I checked my personal e-mail and immediately wished I hadn't. There was only one message, from Brody, laced with expletives and apologies. The team had run into a snag in Denali; some of their core samplings had degraded and were useless. They would need to re-create most of their research, from the beginning. It didn't make sense to return to the mainland, and then go back, so they were staying, possibly as long as another three weeks.

Brody wasn't coming home anytime soon. Celeste Takashima's

perfect face, with her dark almond-shaped eyes and thick black hair, flashed in my mind. Their affair had been brief and intense and was long over. At least that's what Brody had told me. But he'd also told me that part of his contract included a clause by which he had the ability to vet his team, and avoid ever having to work with the woman again.

Some clause.

"Stay cool, Gemma," I whispered to myself. "You don't know that she's up there."

I told myself that but I didn't believe it.

# Chapter Eighteen

Dr. Dean Pabst hid a keen intellect and a wicked sense of humor behind an extra two hundred pounds and a bad toupee. Despite the old saying, the world does judge books by their covers, and as his weight increased over the years, Pabst lost a number of clients, clients who felt that a man who couldn't control his own size certainly couldn't speak to their issues of self-control and life skills.

Pabst was good, though, and I trusted him. He was a keeper of secrets, of dark feelings and tangled thoughts that, in the sanctity of his office, tumbled from my mind and freed up space for the good things. It was strange to admit, but Pabst knew me better than anyone else on this planet.

The doctor settled into the easy chair behind his desk and I took my customary seat in the armchair that faced him. I hadn't been to his office in a few years and I was pleased to see not much had changed. The spider plants in the windowsill looked healthy; the books on the shelves that lined the wall remained dust-free and orderly. The blue carpet was worn and the temperature was pleasant. It was a neutral space conducive to confession and healing.

Pabst began. "He's returned, has he? I was afraid he might. Gemma, I fear the Woodsman will never leave you, not until you put some distance between the children's murders and yourself."

"I know, I know. That's what you said the last time we spoke. But I can't find the distance. I don't know how."

I hated how whiny I sounded. Pabst had worked so hard to get me in the habit of detailed journaling, diary therapy so to speak, and it was no one's fault but mine that I let that practice slip. Life has a funny way of waylaying our best-laid plans; life keeps us busy in ways that seem, at the time, more important than self-care and introspection.

Maybe that was just an excuse, though. Maybe I was too afraid to take such deep, continuous searches into my own psyche.

Pabst stared at me over eyeglasses that were small on his pudgy face. He hadn't worn glasses before; and I realized that Pabst had to be approaching seventy years old. Between his age and his weight, I feared for his health.

He said, "You do know how, Gemma. You've got all the tools, right there, in that toolbox we set up in your mind. You don't give yourself enough credit, my dear. You never have."

I swallowed the sudden lump in my throat. "Dean, I thought we had done it. I really did; he was gone for so long. I don't understand why he's come back, now."

"Gemma, you do know why the Woodsman has returned. You are afraid to say the words out loud, because that will give truth to them. But you must," Pabst said.

I nodded. "It's the baby. This little girl who's not even here yet has changed everything. She's called the Woodsman back, and this time he's brought friends, dead children who seem to think I'm the only damn person who can help them. Why is that, do you think?"

Pabst shrugged. "It's not meant for us to understand the ways of the dead, Gemma. That's not how the world works. You told me once that you've never cried for your parents. And yet you are unable to stop crying, in a sense, for the McKenzie boys. Often, it is easier for us to grieve for those we don't know, than it is to grieve for those we love most."

"My grandmother used to beg me to cry. She said she couldn't stand seeing me so cold; that it wasn't natural. But I never felt cold, Dean. I didn't. I felt there was a dam inside me, and if I cried one tear, the whole thing would burst. That's not cold, that's self-control. That's a good thing."

Pabst nodded. "This is very normal, especially for children. Instead of allowing the grief to heal their pain, they direct their energy toward strengthening that dam, building it up higher and stronger. At some point, though, and that point is different for everyone, the dam becomes too high, and too strong."

"And you think that is what's happened to me?"

"Yes. I think you've displaced the grief you feel for your parents' deaths onto the deaths of the two boys. The ability to compartmentalize your emotions drives your relentlessness, and speaks to your success as a police officer. But it creates the nightmares, too. Gemma, we talked through this a few years back. Will you try the journaling again? I do think it will help tremendously," Pabst said.

He stood up and went to a cooler in the corner of the office. It was stocked with sodas and sparkling water and he handed me a San Pellegrino, knowing my preference. He took a Diet Coke for himself and settled back into his chair.

"The world is full of monsters. It always has been. For every monster, though, there are a hundred heroes. Mankind simply could not survive if the bad guys outnumbered the good guys; you know that, you live that truth every day in your chosen field," Pabst said. "It's natural for you to feel fear and despair now, with the impending birth of your first child. The Woodsman is the embodiment of that fear, a man whose very existence speaks to havoc, a complete void of hope."

I nodded. "So what do I do now? How do I fight this monster of my dreams?"

Pabst smiled. "With science, of course. A bit of rational thinking and some dedicated journaling and you'll be back to tip-top shape in no time. But tell me, Gemma, are you wrapped up in this Bellington mess? I don't like to think of you investigating the young man's death in your condition."

I stood. "What condition would that be, the pregnant condition, or the crazy condition? Thank you for seeing me, Dean. It's been, as always, enlightening. But you know I can't discuss a case."

"And you know I can't let you leave without at least trying to get some juicy tidbit out of you. Do say hello to the Woodsman tonight, Gemma, if he returns. Tell him the good doctor is anxious to see him put down for good."

# Chapter Nineteen

When I pulled into the station's lot, I saw a pack of reporters and cameramen lined up outside the front door like pigs at the trough. They were early; it was barely eight o'clock and the chief had promised them the Q&A at nine.

Using my belly like a small battering ram, I made my way through the throng of people. Officer Armstrong guarded the front door. He opened it wide enough for me to get through, and then quickly closed it with a slam and a roll of his eyes. Six and a half feet of former linebacker came in handy for crowd control.

Chief Chavez passed me in the hallway, a harried look on his face.

"You see this? Sheer madness out there," he said. "We're in HQ."

I unloaded my shoulder bag and joined the others in the narrow squad room at the back of the station. Finn Nowlin and Louis Moriarty and Sam Birdshead sat at the table, notepads and pens ready, a lineup of cops at various stages of their careers. Baby-faced Sam, barely a month into life as an officer; Finn, almost fifteen years into a solid career; and Louis Moriarty, who was already a good five or six years older than the standard retirement age.

Sam and Moriarty nodded at me; Finn just grinned. I took a seat across from Moriarty and wondered again what he was still doing here. He could have been fishing the Arkansas with his buddies, cashing in on a decades-long career with the PD. At the end of the day, I figured he was one of those cops who wouldn't know what to do with his time, if he retired. The job was his life. And he was good at it, still sharp and fit; seventy years old and Moriarty had never once come in less than second in our annual physicals. And this was against guys half his age.

The man gave cause for pause, as they say on the streets.

The chief leaned against the whiteboard. I guessed Lucas Armstrong, what with the door duty, had been excused from this meeting. That was too bad; Luke had a good eye for details that others, including myself, often missed. Plus he was funny as hell and he walked a straight line on the job. I knew Armstrong too was still struggling with the stuff that went down on the home invasion case a few months back. There was an icy quality to his relationship with Finn that hadn't been there before.

Chavez indicated that I should join him at the board.

"You all caught the news last night, right? I had a feeling once this went public, we'd be looking at a whole new tempo," the chief said. "Gemma, can you catch us up with what we know so far?"

I nodded. "Absolutely. Obviously, we have a time of death: sometime around noon on Monday. We've also got a cause of death: blood loss, but we don't have a murder weapon. We don't even know what type of weapon we're looking for; the victim's throat was cut in such a matter, and with such a tool that we can't be sure what was used. Sam and I are knee-deep in interviews with the circus employees, but so far—"

Finn Nowlin coughed and then cleared his throat.

"Something to add, Finn?"

Above his dark eyebrows, a tiny furrow appeared, the smallest imperfection in an otherwise smooth face. "Sorry to interrupt you, Gem, just as you've gotten started, but this is ridiculous. I'm going to need some specifics here. Are you honestly telling me that I'm to be a part of an investigation in which I don't even know what kind of a goddamn weapon I'm looking for?"

He smiled as he watched me realize the implication of his words.

"Chief? What the hell is Finn talking about?" I asked.

Chavez, who'd sat down at the head of the table, leaned

forward with a sigh. His tie was rumpled and his suit was the same he'd worn for last night's press conference but his dark eyes were fierce.

"This case is too big for you, Gemma. The mayor is upset at the lack of progress being made, and we believe you could use the extra help. I'm making Finn your partner on this," Chavez said.

"We?"

"The mayor and I. Don't forget, I report directly to him and city council. His word goes on this."

"All respect, sir, but screw that. Sam and I have got this. We've already interviewed a handful of key witnesses. I've got hours of research in on this damn circus, and I'm working on a new lead for what Nicky was up to, three years ago. There may be some connections here worth investigating."

Sam Birdshead jumped in. "Chief, I think Gemma's right, we are making progress." He looked from me to the chief and back again and then added, "We're a good team. And we're only two days in."

Chavez stood and gave us a grim smile. "I have no doubt you are a fine team. Sam, you'll stay on as backup to Finn and Gemma."

Finn smiled at Chavez. I wanted to wipe that grin off his face more than anything. If things weren't dicey enough between us before, this just pushed us that much closer to a boiling point. This was my case and if things got fucked up because Finn was willing to smudge the line of ethics, then God help me, I was going to tear his head off.

Finn said, "Thanks, Chief. Gemma and I could certainly use the extra help."

Chavez nodded. "That's the kind of cooperative attitude I like to see. Please proceed Gemma."

I took a deep breath and swallowed and counted to ten. "As I was saying, Dr. Hussen can't determine what weapon was used. Nicky Bellington's throat was torn open—not cut, not sliced, but torn. To be honest, the weapon could be anything with a sharp jagged edge. Now, between Sam and I, we've interviewed a number of people. There are two distinct groups at play here: those who knew Reed, and those who knew Nicky. There's not really any overlap."

I paused and noticed Finn had opened one of a dozen file folders that lay scattered on the conference table. He stared at a color photograph of Annika and Ellen Bellington engaged in what appeared to be a very heated game of tennis. The mother and daughter team wore matching tennis whites of tight tank tops, short skirts, and sneakers.

"We'll need to interview these two again," he said with a grin. "Very suspicious looking, especially the daughter . . ."

Chavez put his head in his hands and muttered, "Jesus Christ, Finn . . ." just as I said, "She's nineteen, you dick. Chief, this is exactly the sort of thing—"

Before I could finish my sentence, Finn stood up and began shouting that he wouldn't be called a dick by anyone, and then the chief was shouting at both of us.

I closed my eyes and leaned back and asked forgiveness for what I was about to do.

"Ohhhh," I moaned, and clutched my belly. Then I gripped the back of an empty chair in front of me and gritted my teeth and held my breath until I could feel my face turning red.

"Gemma, what is it?" Chavez was at my side in a flash. He helped me into the chair and yelled for someone to get a glass of water. I waited a few seconds before replying. Peeking through my eyelashes, I saw that Finn had left the room in disgust.

I grinned into my grimace and relaxed my shoulders. "I'm, I'm not sure, Chief. I just . . . the room started spinning and I thought I was going to faint."

Chavez exhaled. "Things got a little heated. I know you and Finn have had your issues in the past, but you two are the best I got. Please, can you put your differences aside? We've got a murdered kid who deserves our best. And right now, that's you two."

I've never walked away from a challenge in my life and implicit in Chavez's plea was definitely a challenge. "Of course. I'm sorry.

I'll try to refrain from calling him a dick, if he can manage not to act like one for ten seconds."

"Good girl. And keep up the good work with Sam. I want him involved, but he needs to understand Finn is lead now," Chavez said.

"You mean I'm lead, and Finn is my partner."

This close up, I could see the shadows under his eyes, and the fine lines that hadn't been there a week ago. He closed his eyes now and nodded. "Yes, of course, that's what I meant."

"Are you okay, Chief?" I asked. I pushed the glass of water that Moriarty had fetched for me toward him. He looked like he could have used a glass of bourbon instead.

Chavez considered my question seriously. "No, I'm not. To be honest, last night was rough. Terry and Ellen think we should know more than we do by now. They want to know what Nicky was up to the last few years. They don't understand this Reed kid he became, and this circus life he embraced. It's a big contrast to the life he gave up and it begs some serious questions. This has made them reexamine how they raised the kids, where they might have gone wrong. You know how important family is to them."

I nodded. "Those are the same questions we're asking, Chief. But it takes time. They've got to understand that."

"I think Terry does, but Ellen . . . she said the family had enough to get through without 'all of this,'" the chief continued quietly, his fingers making air quotes.

I shook my head in disgust. "Well, that's too damn bad if finding her son's murderer is interfering with her husband's political career."

"Oh, she doesn't mean it like that. Honestly, she's more preoccupied with Terry's cancer than with the Senate run. I think in her mind, they grieved for Nicky three years ago. Losing a child . . . well, Gemma, that kind of grief is not the sort of thing you want to go through twice. Ellen is a good woman. You didn't know her before. She's given everything she has to Terry's career. She even invited Terry's sister, Hannah, to move in and watch the kids. She couldn't stand the thought of a stranger, someone outside the family, raising her children. But she can't let herself fall apart again," Chavez said. He stared off into the distance. "Ellen's the glue that holds them all together, you see."

There was something in his voice and eyes that made my blood run cold.

He continued. "She sees herself as a rock for Terry, and more importantly, for Annika."

Chavez rubbed at his face and then looked at his watch and stood. He went to the door. "I've got to let these monkey reporters in and throw them a few bones to gnaw on."

"Chief?"

He looked back at me as he opened the squad door. Sometime between my faking a heat spell and Chavez's impassioned defense of Ellen, the room had emptied. We were alone and I took a deep breath and asked him something that I shouldn't have, but I couldn't let him leave without knowing for sure.

"How long have you been in love with Ellen Bellington?"

I thought he was going to walk out without answering but then his shoulders sagged and, turning his back to me, he answered in a low voice and I wished with all my heart I could take the question back.

"Twenty-seven years, five days, and about fourteen hours," he said, and he left, closing the door gently behind him.

# Chapter Twenty

It was chaos outside the squad room. Our two receptionists desperately tried to herd the pack of cameramen and reporters—about thirty people in all—into our large conference room, where chairs and a podium were waiting.

I wondered why the chief hadn't held the thing at the more spacious City Hall pressroom, and then I realized the cramped quarters would hasten the proceedings. Especially if Chavez closed the door—that particular conference room, facing east, grew hotter than hell in the morning.

Indeed, already the extra bodies had caused the temperature in the station to rise uncomfortably. I decided the day couldn't get any worse and then I saw Tessa O'Leary pushing her way through the crowd, her face red as a tomato.

Sam was behind me and I elbowed him. Together we watched her approach.

"You big fat liar. You liar!" Tessa shouted.

She barreled up to me and spoke in a low voice that was somehow worse than the yell, "You liar. You lied to me."

I backed up a few inches and lifted my hands up, palms out. "Whoa, Tessa. Take it easy. Do you want to talk?"

She took a few deep breaths and then nodded. She noticed the reporters watching her and the color in her face faded from the angry red to a lighter shade of embarrassed pink.

"Let's go somewhere a little quieter. This is Sam, by the way. Sam Birdshead, he's one of my colleagues here in the department."

I led her to one of the interview rooms off the main hallway. Sam followed us. The room was small and windowless, with a low wooden table and two metal chairs. It smelled of sweat and floor polish, like a gym after a high school basketball game.

I took one of the chairs and motioned for Tessa to take the other. Behind her, Sam leaned against the wall and tried to look inconspicuous. I watched her calm down. Her face was free of makeup and her hair was matted in the back in that bedhead style that is somehow both fashionable and sort of gross at the same time. Dried tears left two faint streaks on her cheeks, and her eyes were bright. She looked much younger than her twenty-two years.

I said, "Now, that's better. I couldn't hear myself think out there. What was that you called me? A liar? When did I lie to you, Tessa?"

"I'm sorry I called you that, but I thought I could trust you. I thought you were my friend," she whispered. She started crying again.

Behind her, across from me, I watched Sam grow uncomfortable. He leaned further into the wall as though he wanted to disappear into it, and I got the impression that he, like most men, wasn't good with attractive, crying women his own age.

"Tessa, you can trust me. I'm not your friend, I'm a police officer, and that's better, because it is my duty to watch out for you. My sworn duty," I said. "What did you mean, I lied to you?"

Tessa fidgeted in her seat and picked at one of the designs carved into the wooden table. Over the years, interview subjects and suspects had etched hundreds of sketches and words and doodles using whatever tools they had: pens, pencils, keys, soda can tabs. "Fuck" and "punk" seemed to be the most popular, but swastikas, happy faces, and gang signs were almost as common.

"Tessa? Look at me, please."

She lifted her head and met my eyes. I saw a pain I hadn't expected.

"You should have told me Reed wasn't real. You let me talk about him, like he was . . . maybe you didn't lie, but you omitted the truth and that's worse," she said.

"Yes, I did omit the truth. Sometimes we have to do that in our investigations. And you're wrong, Tessa. Reed was real, he was just as real as you or I or Sam," I said. "And don't ever forget it."

She bit her lip and then nodded. "He lied to me, too. Reed did. Why didn't he tell me he was some rich kid? And his dad was mayor of this fantasyland ski town? You know, this place is so unreal compared to the rest of America. You have no idea how many times Reed and I made fun of places like this. It's so quaint I could throw up."

Tessa took a deep breath and her eyes welled up again and she made a choked-up noise.

Across the room, Sam's eyes met mine. "Hey, you guys want a pop? Or some water?"

"I'd love a Sprite, Sam, thanks, and some tissues, too, please. Tessa?" I asked.

She shook her head. Sam left the room.

"Tessa, you're very upset. Is this all about Reed? Or is something else going on?"

Her gaze fell back to the table and she resumed picking at one of the etchings with her fingernail. Her nails were cherry red and I watched as tiny chips of polish fell into the carving, adding more spots of color to the mosaic.

"Should I have a lawyer present?"

"Well, you certainly could. But you're not here as a suspect, and this is not a formal interrogation. We're just two people, talking."

"I think Lisey may have done something. Something very bad, I mean."

"Your roommate, Red?" I asked.

At that, she smiled. "I call her that sometimes, too."

"Why do you think Lisey did something bad?"

Tessa sighed. "I found a ripped-up photograph under her bed. It was my favorite picture of Reed and me. It was taken a few months ago. I hadn't seen it in ages. I thought I'd lost it, on the road somewhere."

"Why were you looking under her bed?"

"She had the last of my stash, my pot. I know that's where she hides it. My back was killing me. Anyway, it's not just the torn-up picture. There are other things, too."

"Like what?" I asked.

Sam poked his head up at the window in the door and I gave him a tiny headshake. I didn't want anything to interrupt Tessa.

"Lisey's been wearing this T-shirt all summer, this old Ramones shirt that is disgusting but she just keeps washing it and wearing it, washing and wearing. She wore it on Monday and I haven't seen it since."

I considered this. "Well, as you said, she's been washing it. Maybe it's in the hamper."

"I checked. It's not there. It's just . . . gone," Tessa said.

I leaned back and folded my hands on top of my stomach. I understood why some men didn't mind their potbellies; in a strange way, it was a nice little perch for hands and stray potato chips.

"What are you suggesting, Tessa?"

She stared at me. "Isn't it obvious? She's been in love with me for months. She's clearly upset; what kind of person goes around ripping up photographs? Maybe she . . ."

I met Tessa's fierce gaze with one of my own. Destroying a photograph and trashing a T-shirt weren't much in and of themselves. I thought I knew what Tessa's next words were going to be but I had to hear her say them aloud. I had to know how strongly she believed in them.

"Maybe she what?"

Tessa bit her lip again and then said in a rush, "Maybe Lisey killed Reed and threw away the T-shirt because it was covered in blood."

Before I could respond, the interview room door flung open and Finn Nowlin strode in, all swagger and attitude. On his heels was Sam, an apologetic look on his face.

"That's a very strong accusation, young lady," Finn said. He dropped a pad of paper and a pen on the table in front of Tessa.

"I'm going to need you to write down what you just said, word for word."

Tessa stared open-mouthed at him and I swore under my breath. I should have known. The bastard had probably flipped the audio switch just outside the door and heard every word we'd said.

"Go on, now, honey. Write it all down, every single word," Finn said. He squatted at Tessa's side so he was eye to eye with her and placed a hand on her shoulder. "The sooner you do it, the better."

Tessa stared at him another moment and then jammed her hands under her thighs and shook her head. Her face grew flushed.

Finn stood. "Tell her, Gemma."

"Actually, she doesn't have to write a thing. She hasn't been read her rights and this is not a formal interview. But Tessa, if this is what you really believe, you'd be helping Reed out a great deal by giving us a statement."

She stood up so fast her chair shot backward.

"I'm not a rat. I guess I was right the first time. I can't trust you fucking cops. You pigs have no sense of loyalty."

She pushed past Sam and went out the door. Finn made as though to stop her but I grabbed his arm and gripped it tight.

"Let her go. She won't get far."

Finn turned to me and I let go of his arm when I saw the anger on his face.

"You are a real piece, Gemma, you know that? If we go to court, none of what she told you is admissible. She may have just laid Nicky's killer in our lap and we can't do a damn thing about it," he said.

Sam started backing out of the room, and I raised a hand to stop him.

"C'mon, Finn, the finer details of the law have never stopped you before," I said. He turned pale.

"What the hell is that supposed to mean?" he said.

"You know damn well what that means. Anyways, we certainly wouldn't be very good cops if we had to rely on the offhand comments of a twenty-two-year-old girl to catch a killer. Sam, you got my Sprite?"

Sam grinned and tossed it to me and then yelled, "Don't open it" as I popped the top and soda sprayed all over Finn's three-hundred-dollar suit.

# Chapter Twenty-one

I caught a small break. The one place I needed to visit next was the one place I could theoretically hope to find some peace and quiet: Cedar Valley Public Library. Before I left the station, I grabbed a few of the files on Nicky's accident three years ago. That's what we had called it then: an accident.

I had eyeballed the case notes on the investigation yesterday; Finn had been lead, Louis Moriarty, second, and their distinct signatures filled the bottom of each page—standard operating procedure on any documentation. I looked at the table of contents, the first page in the first folder, but saw no mention of the library.

But then, the investigation had been conducted from the start under the assumption that Nicky had gone over the waterfall and died, his body washed down the Arkansas River straight on into the Gulf of Mexico.

There was never a reason to suspect anything else.

I made my way across town to the redbrick building that housed the library. Although it was still early in the day, thunderclouds, dark as charcoal, filled the horizon like ghostly specters, coming in low and fast over the Rockies. Judging from the speed they were moving, and the strange green-blue tint of the sky behind them, there would be rain by noon.

With the windows down, the moisture in the air hit my lungs like a welcome tonic. The humidity was a nice change from the heat we had experienced all week but as I breathed in the cool air,

I couldn't help but feel a sense of dread. Summer storms have a way of bringing more than rain and wind to town.

Before I'd left the station, I'd heard whispers that the Bellingtons planned to hold a memorial service on Saturday for Nicky at Wellshire Presbyterian. At least this time around they'd have a body to bury.

I parked and hurried across the lot, battling wind that blew against my cheeks, teasing up my hair and then releasing the dark strands just as quickly. Inside the library, a kid in baggy Adidas gear answered my questions with a nod. He pointed a finger down a short hallway and at the end of it, at a reference desk cluttered with paperback novels, tape dispensers, assorted stamps and ink pads, I found Tilly Jane Krinkle.

Surprised, I recognized her at once. I had just never known her name. Like most people in town, I simply called her the Bird Lady.

Orange hair stood in tufts on her scalp, as though a child had commandeered her head as an art table and left a mess of paint and cotton balls. She wore a pair of rhinestone cat-eye glasses, and a blue denim jumper over a cotton blouse, upon which was printed dozens of tiny red and green hearts. The jumper stopped at her calves, exposing thin pale legs that ended in red high top sneakers. On her shoulder a stuffed bird sat, a silent sentinel whose eye, at least the one that I could see, was cloudy as a cataract. The parrot's feet were glued to a thin branch, which in turn was fastened to Tilly's jumper with an intricate silver clasp and chain set.

The woman wore no socks and smelled of lilacs and talcum powder and glue. She looked up at me, took in my badge, and asked how she could help.

"Ms. Krinkle, my name is Gemma Monroe. I'm with the police department."

"Well, of course you are," she answered. Her voice was husky, a smoker's voice. "Petey told me you were coming. Call me Tilly."

"Petey?"

"My parrot," she said, and pointed at the stuffed bird that stood on her right shoulder. "She is very wise."

"I see. Um, hello, Petey," I said, and half waved at the bird.

The woman gave me a black look. "Don't expect a hello back, missy. Petey can be very shy. You're here about Nicky Bellington, aren't you?"

I hadn't told anyone I was coming, not even Finn or Sam.

"How did you know that?"

Tilly said, "I watch the news, girly. I saw the press conference. It was only a matter of time."

She stood, tsked-tsked, and motioned for me to follow her across the main reading room. The red sneakers squeaked against the linoleum and she walked on her tiptoes as though that would quiet the sound, but it just made her look as though she were about to sneak up on someone. I giggled and an elderly man in a suit at a study table frowned at me over the top of his half-moon glasses.

I shrugged back and mouthed an apology.

"I knew sooner or later someone would come about Nicky. I thought it would be sooner, but here you are," Tilly whispered. "I've been waiting three god dang years."

"Did the police talk to you after the accident?" I whispered back. "After Nicky fell at Bride's Veil?"

She shook her head. "Nope, not a one of them. I waited but no one ever came."

Damn Finn.

But then, would I have done any different? No matter what you think from watching *CSI* or *Law & Order*, we don't tend to go looking for mysteries when there are simpler answers there for the taking. And the simple answer back then was, Nicky died in a tragic accident.

Tilly led me to a locked door at the back of the library. She inserted a stubby silver key into the handle and jiggled it back and forth, cursing up a storm when it wouldn't catch. She took a deep breath, whispered something to Petey the bird, and then tried the key again. This time, the tumbler flipped back with a gentle click. The door popped open, and I followed the older woman down a wide flight of stairs that ended in a shadowy, cavernous room.

"The town archives," she whispered to me.

Tilly instructed me to wait at the base of the stairs and then she walked into the dimness, keeping one hand on the wall, disappearing from my sight. She muttered more choice words and then one by one, rows of ceiling-mounted fluorescent lights buzzed on high above me.

The rest of the space remained dark and it was impossible to get a good sense of the room's layout.

A tall bookshelf at my left held row after row of thick volumes. I pulled one out at random, sneezing as a layer of dust drifted off the scarlet leather cover. The title on the front read "Congressional Reports, Denver County, 1899–1901."

"Hokay," said a low voice behind me. I jumped and sneezed again, my heart pounding.

Tilly grinned at me, exposing all twelve of her remaining teeth.

"Jumpy, are we? Well, come on. I don't have all day. Wouldn't you know, I wait three dang years and you come on the day I have got a doctor appointment; it's the cancer in the breasts. Hereditary. My mother had it. Her mother had it. Our whole dang family has it."

I murmured some sympathies and followed her down one labyrinthine aisle after another, pausing as she switched on another row of lights. When she did, the lights behind us flickered off. Once, I stopped and turned and saw an emergency exit sign mounted high up, back in the direction of the stairs. The green glow seemed far away.

Then Tilly was telling me to come on, and I hurried to catch up with her.

She stopped abruptly in front of a study carrel. It was a cubicle-size space; the desk piled high with books, binders, folders, boxes of loose-leaf papers, and a magnifying glass, a tablet of paper, and a pencil.

"What is all this?"

Tilly shook her head at me and said to Petey in a low stage whisper "amateur."

She pointed at the cubicle and said, "That, my dear, is the town's complete archival materials on the McKenzie boys slash Woodsman murders."

I swallowed. Research had not been my forte in school. "And this is what Nicky was doing when he came here? Reading all this stuff?"

"Yessiree," she said. The sequins on her eyeglasses caught the reflection of the ceiling lights and a thousand tiny bulbs sparkled back at me. "That boy spent about four months down here."

"And when was this? Exactly, I mean?"

"Oh, springtime, early summer of 2012. The last time he came by was two days before he went on that camping trip, in July. You know I'm up there a few times myself every summer? There's a beautiful camping spot, just near that lookout point. Only place I can ever find some dang peace and quiet. Anyway, he told me I could pack all this up, that he had what he needed and thank you very much but he was all done," Tilly said.

She stroked the stuffed parrot as she spoke, and I could have sworn I saw its emerald-green wings shudder at her touch.

"Why didn't you?" I asked. "Pack it up, I mean?"

"Because he died, dummy. And I thought someone would come asking and I sure wasn't about to put it all away and then go find it again, was I? Do you know how long it took me the first time, to gather all of this for Nicky? A week," she said.

I looked at the overflowing cubicle and then at her. "Are you telling me this has been here for three years? Untouched? Doesn't anyone else use this room? Or this material?"

She shook her head sadly. "You're the first. Oh, I dust it all every week. But no one is interested in the past. If they were smart, they would be, for the past tells us all we need to know, if we listen. But no one takes the god dang time to listen."

"Why didn't you call the police and tell them to come check this stuff out?"

Tilly scoffed. "I did. I left a message at the station and no one ever got back to me. Time passed, and then it seemed silly to keep pestering you all. I figured if someone was interested, they would have come."

I considered that, and Tilly's age. If she was a native of the area, her answer to my next question might help frame things a bit.

"Did you know them? The McKenzie boys?"

Tilly nodded slowly, her eyes growing wider. She continued caressing the dead bird on her shoulder but her touch slowed, her finger making one long rhythmic stroke from crown to tail, and then beginning again.

"I was forty when they disappeared. Oh, but it was hot that summer. Hotter than a clap infection, so hot you could walk outside and feel like you could lie down and just die. I knew Tommy's father, peripherally of course. We used the same dentist and we must have been on the same schedule, because every six months like clockwork we'd find ourselves waiting together in the little reception area at the dentist. Dr. Whitman. He's long dead, by the way. Brain tumor."

Tilly continued. "I remember the parents, John and Karen McKenzie, and Mark and Sarah McKenzie, they were everywhere that summer. Putting up posters, hosting folks who'd come in from out of town to help search . . . the newspapers interviewed them every week it seemed."

She paused and for a moment I thought she was finished. Then she smiled sadly again and said, "And I couldn't see that it made a damn difference. It was like those boys went up in smoke. They were here and then they were gone."

She stopped stroking the parrot, her eyes locked on something very faraway, lost in the summer of 1985, the hottest summer on record in Cedar Valley, a summer where the sky was bright and children disappeared.

I asked her the same question I asked Darren Chase. "Did Nicky ever say why he was so interested in the boys?"

Tilly shook her head. "Nope. I'm a librarian. You're the cop. It's none of my damn business why people are here. I just show them how to access information and do good research. Nicky was polite and he treated the materials with respect. He was a good boy. This town loses more good boys than it keeps."

# Chapter Twenty-two

I left Tilly with the promise that either I, or a charming young man by the name of Sam Birdshead, would return soon and go through the materials in the cubicle. I added a second promise; when we were finished, truly finished, Tilly could pack it all up and place the whole dang caboodle back where it belonged.

The clouds could contain themselves no longer; it was pouring when I emerged from the library. I dashed as fast as I could to the car and climbed in. The rain beat down on the roof of my car like a drummer on a drum set, pounding out a steady tempo, drop-by-drop, beat-by-beat.

I called Sam. As it rang through, I held the phone between my ear and my shoulder as I undid my belt buckle. Something I'd eaten that morning wasn't agreeing with me, and my stomach was making noises like a diesel truck at a stop sign.

Sam picked up on the fourth ring.

"How's it going over there?" I asked.

"Not bad. The reporters are about done. The chief was awesome, he gave 'em exactly what they needed to know and not a drop more."

"Good. I've been at the library. There's a ton of stuff we need to go through here, Sam. You know the Bird Lady? It turns out she is the librarian that Darren Chase, the basketball coach, referred Nicky to three years ago. She's kept Nicky's work *exactly* as it was when he went over Bride's Veil."

"No kidding? You find anything?"

"Sam, there's so much stuff there, I didn't know where to begin. But I'm going to come back tomorrow. Darren Chase was right; all of it is about the disappearance of the McKenzie boys, the Woodsman murders. Nicky could have been writing a dissertation on this stuff, for all the original material that's there. I've got a little project for you: comb through the original files on Nicky's accident, would you? I've got the basic report here with me, but I know there's another report or two at the station. We need the inventory of what was found in Nicky's room when the police first visited the Bellingtons."

"Would they have done a search of his room? Wasn't his fall tied up as an accident pretty quickly?" Sam asked.

I said, "Ellen Bellington said something strange yesterday when I spoke to her on the phone. She said she'd boxed up his things *after* the police inventoried his room. Finn Nowlin and Louis Moriarty are no fools. They may have missed some things—this library angle, for instance—but I'm starting to get the impression they were maybe a little more thorough than you'd expect on a routine accident report."

Undoing the buckle had helped; I lowered the seat behind me and lay back, taking the pressure off the small of my spine. My stomach gave another rumble and I shifted to the side.

"Are you thinking there was something going on?"

I shook my head and then remembered Sam couldn't see me.

"Not exactly. To be honest, I'm not sure what to think. I found the bodies in November of 2011. By early spring of 2012, at a point when we were scratching our balls and admitting defeat, Nicky was obsessed with the case, to the point that he was spending all his free time poring over newspapers from 1985. But by July, he tells the librarian he's done, that he's found what he needed."

"What did he find?"

"I have no idea. But two days later, he's gone over the waterfall and the world thinks he's dead," I said.

I heard a thump outside and looked out the car window but the rain came down in sheets and all I saw was the blurry red hatchback of a Saab that was parked next to me.

Sam was silent a moment. "So if we find what he found, maybe we find what happened in those two days to make him fake his own death."

"Fake his own death . . . or take advantage of an accident," I said. "Nicky was a smart kid. There are easier ways to fake a death than to jump over an eighty-foot waterfall. In fact, doing that just about guarantees a real death."

"What kind of other ways?"

"Oh, car explosion . . . house fire . . . there are ways. You pay a guy at the morgue enough money and you can buy a body that fits your description. Burn it bad enough, bam. You've convinced the world you're dead."

Sam laughed uneasily. "It sounds like this is something you've given a lot of thought to, Gemma."

"Not really. Let's just say I'd put money on Nicky being incredibly lucky to survive a fall, and then maybe deciding to take advantage of it."

Sam said, "So, this other report on the original investigation, would it be in the records room?"

He murmured something else and then I heard the dull clink of metal on metal, followed by a low fizzing noise.

"Should be."

"Okay, I'll get on it," Sam said. I heard a grin in his voice.

"What?"

"I just opened a Coke and I couldn't help reliving that moment a few hours ago when you sprayed Finn with the Sprite," he said.

"That was terrible." I laughed. "Just terrible. Speaking of the devil, is he there?"

"Yeah, hang on . . ."

I waited and then Finn's voice came on the line, still angry.

"Gemma? What the hell? I thought you were changing your shirt, not going out. I've been waiting here all morning. You got to keep me updated, remember? That's what partners do," he said with an emphasis on "partners."

I groaned and popped the seat back into an upright position.

"That's why I'm calling you right now," I said. "I'm going to call on the Bellington family. Come with me. I could use the extra eyes and ears."

"Uh-huh. You going now?"

"Yep, just leaving the library. Meet me there?"

He sighed a heavy sigh. "All right. But tell me, what are you doing at the library?"

I filled him in on my conversation the day before with Ellen, and subsequent chats with Darren Chase and Tilly. "I want to know if the family was aware that Nicky was looking into the Woodsman murders. And when I ask them about it, I want to see their reactions, face-to-face."

"I don't understand why they never mentioned the library," Finn said. "I specifically asked them if they had noticed anything odd in his behavior; you know, in case it was a suicide."

I shrugged. "I don't think they knew, Finn. Remember, Ellen Bellington pointed me to Darren Chase. She told me Nicky was with him all the time, at practice with the basketball team."

I thought again of the strange tone in her voice, the implication that there had been something more to Darren and Nicky's relationship than strictly coaching, and I wondered if that was Nicky's doing. Maybe he was planting seeds, throwing misdirection. Purposefully keeping his mother away from what he was really doing.

Finn said, "I'll meet you there."

I hung up and stared out into the rain for a moment, the way the water came down, washing the dirt and mud away from my car, erasing where I'd been. There was a spot, though, on my front windshield, a stubborn bug splat that had been there too long to be washed away.

I started the car and thought the case was like that, too. Time had come through and washed away plenty, but like the bug, a few stains were left behind. I wondered if they would be enough to solve two mysteries: Nicky's death and the Woodsman murders.

For the first time in years, I allowed myself to seriously consider the possibility that justice might finally be given to the McKenzie boys. With that came the darker realization that I had spent the last four years, ever since I found the skull, living in the shadow of the Woodsman.

He haunted my dreams and drove me in a relentless and likely self-righteous pursuit of putting the bad guys away.

Who was I if I wasn't chasing the Woodsman?

I realized something else, too, as I pulled out of the parking lot and fell in line behind an empty school bus. Putting away the Woodsman meant freeing up emotional energy that sooner or later, I'd need to direct toward figuring out my own head and heart. Bull said I needed to crap or get off the can, and I knew he was right.

Brody wouldn't wait forever. He wanted a wife, not just a live-in lover and partner. And I wanted my daughter to have stability, to drown in the kind of stable, loving home life that I only got to sip from as a tiny child.

# Chapter Twenty-three

Finn waited in the Bellingtons' driveway. He must have left the station right after our call, whereas I had to make a pit stop at the Conoco station, and then a second at the McDonald's on the north end of town. Whatever I'd eaten wasn't finished ravaging my insides. Both stops were uncomfortable enough to make me consider calling the visit off.

But the image of Finn questioning the Bellingtons alone, his baby blues batting at Ellen and Annika, gave me enough motivation to grit my teeth and carry on.

Finn sat in the driver side of his Porsche, a hot ride that was impractical in Cedar Valley. He drove it four months a year, and a Suburban the other eight, and every time I saw the sports car I cringed. He had a way of working that car into a lot of conversations.

I parked as close as I could to the house and together we dashed through the rain to the front steps.

"You really ought to think about getting a stick, Gemma. The Porsche handles so great on these mountain roads," he said. He gave the car a fond look and I wondered if he was as attentive to his girlfriends, he might have better luck with his relationships.

I ignored him and knocked on the door.

After a long minute, Annika opened the door. She wore an oversize men's navy sweat suit and tan sheepskin slipper boots. Her long pale hair was piled on top of her head in a messy bun and she looked like she had just woken up.

"Hi, honey, is your mommy or daddy home?" Finn asked.

Annika stared at him a moment and then looked at me. "Gemma?"

"Annika, hi. We have a few questions we'd like to ask your parents, and you, too, if you all are free."

She nodded and let us in. "They're in the living room with Grandpa. They thought he might enjoy watching the rain. Sentimental fools, they think he can still enjoy stuff like that."

We followed her down the same long hall that just a few days before, Mrs. Watkins had led Chief Chavez, Sam Birdshead, and me. The pouring rain and general gloom outside only served to emphasize the cold atmosphere inside and I shivered. Finn noticed and for a moment I thought he was going to offer me his jacket, but he only rolled his eyes and gave me a look.

"Mom? Dad? The cops are here," Annika announced. The living room was silent and her words fell like thunder.

Terence Bellington jumped. He sat next to his father on the couch. The older man's wheelchair was folded in, leaning against the coffee table. Across from them, Ellen sat with her legs tucked up under her, a coffeepot in one hand and a mug in the other. She didn't look up, but kept her attention on the hot liquid she was pouring.

Finished, she set the mug down and said, "A call would have been appreciated."

I nodded. "I agree, but there wasn't time. I apologize for disturbing you, Mayor, Mrs. Bellington. Something has come up. We'll only take a few minutes of your time. This is my partner, Finn Nowlin. You may remember him, he headed the investigation on Nicky's accident, three years ago."

Finn buttoned his suit jacket and stepped forward and put his hand out to Terence Bellington. After a moment, the mayor stood and shook it.

"Of course, of course. Have you found Nicky's killer?" he asked. Like his daughter, he wore a navy sweat suit and slippers.

"No, unfortunately."

I glanced at Frank Bellington. The elderly man seemed unaware of our existence, let alone his own. He stared in Ellen's direction but I don't think he really saw her. Annika was probably right; her grandfather was beyond enjoying much of anything these days.

The Frank Bellington I remembered from my childhood was a boisterous man with a naughty sense of humor and a never-ending supply of hard butterscotch candies. He was attractive and compelling; a businessman who built up an empire selling real estate and properties in what was to become a booming ski town. I wondered again at what had happened between him and Bull, why their weekly poker nights had stopped, why one day Frank was family and the next he was persona non grata.

My grandmother Julia's words came back to me. Was Frank the man she warned me to stay away from?

"Is there somewhere else you'd prefer we talk?" I asked.

The mayor shook his head. "No, please, take a seat. Coffee? Annika, hon, bring us some more cups, would you? My father is having a good morning. He adores the rain."

I looked at Frank Bellington again. The mayor saw my skepticism.

"Well, he used to adore the rain," he corrected. "He's got his good days and his bad days and lord knows, we try to make the good days count for something. Gemma, I know you understand what I'm talking about; I was so sorry to hear about your grandmother's diagnosis. Finn, are your parents still with us?"

Finn nodded. "Yes, sir. They live down in Florida. Fit as a fiddle, both of them. They just won a bridge tournament. My dad, he's great. He can't keep his hands off my mom, and they're going on seventy. It gives a man hope."

"Well, consider yourself blessed. It's terrible, just terrible watching a parent decline like this," Terry said.

Annika returned with two more cups and Ellen poured for us. Unlike her husband and daughter, she was dressed to the nines. A soft gray cardigan hung on her narrow shoulders, over a white silk blouse. Her black trousers were cut wide, palazzo style, and her beaded flats looked expensive. She noticed me looking.

"I had a meeting this morning with one of the charities I'm involved with," she said. "And this evening I'm meeting with Reverend Wyland. I'm sure you've heard; we have a funeral Saturday. I expect you will both be there?"

Finn and I nodded.

Ellen continued. "We've had an awful time with the Reverend. We are, of course, using the same plot for Nicky but the man is insisting we pay a surcharge for the *re-laying* of our son. I don't know how he did things in whatever dark cave he crawled out of back home in Africa, but I simply won't tolerate that here. It's not about the money, but it's the principle of the thing, you see. We have already paid for one funeral for our son."

I swallowed and set my coffee down and turned to the mayor. I didn't want to be in this house one minute longer than I had to.

"Sir, we've made an interesting discovery. I'm not sure how much relevance it has to Nicky's disappearance three years ago, or his murder this week, but we've got to look at everything that comes up," I began.

As I spoke, Ellen leaned forward and spooned something white into Frank's half-open mouth. The substance, pale and jiggly, sat there for a moment and then Ellen pushed it in further with the silver spoon. Frank obediently closed his mouth and swallowed and I thought that age is not a progression at all, but a return. We emerge helpless and dependent and the end, for many, is marked by the same helplessness and dependency of infancy.

Terry stared at me. "Well, what is it?"

"It appears that in the months leading up to the accident at Bride's Veil, Nicky was spending most of his free time at the local library, researching the murders of the McKenzie boys. By all accounts, he was there every day after school, and not at basketball practice, as you may have thought."

The mayor's mouth fell open. From her end of the couch,

Annika sprang up like a jack-in-the-box. She knocked her cup of coffee to the floor and swore. Ellen continued to calmly spoon more of the gooey white curd into Franklin's mouth. Hannah Watkins chose that moment to join the party. She came in quietly, somehow aware that she'd just missed a bombshell.

Annika spoke first. "That's crazy, I would have known if he had been looking into that old mystery. We didn't keep secrets from each other."

If that was true, either Annika was lying and she already knew what I had just revealed, or Nicky had decided to keep something to himself. I watched as the same realization struck her and she slowly sank to the floor, a confused look on her face. She began to pick up the broken shards of her coffee cup.

Bellington looked as confused as his daughter. He said, "He never mentioned anything about the Woodsman murders. How do you know about this? Murders, death, mystery, that sort of thing didn't interest Nicky at all. He was into sports, and if I remember right, that year he was obsessed with perfecting his basketball game. He was determined to make captain his senior year."

"He may have told you he was practicing, but he was at the library most afternoons after school," Finn said. "In fact, he quit the team right before Christmas."

Mrs. Watkins was silent through the exchange. She shooed Annika away from the mess on the floor and pulled a towel from her pocket. She dabbed at the stain gently, careful not to rub the coffee into the carpet.

"Thanks, Aunt Hannah," Annika said. She watched as her childhood nanny picked up the shattered pieces of china. It was clear Mrs. Watkins knew her way around broken things; she carefully stacked the shards into a tidy pile on the table and then scooped them all into the towel with the edge of her hand.

Finn finished off his coffee, reached across the table, picked up the pot, and poured himself another cup. He added a dollop of milk and dropped in a sugar cube that splashed into the hot liquid with a wet plop.

He took a slurp and smacked his lips. "This is great coffee, ma'am. Is that Starbucks house blend? It sure tastes like it."

Ellen ignored him and scooped the last of the white gunk—I'd decided it was tapioca—into her father-in-law's mouth. She said, "I knew he was at the library."

Surprise hit me. If she'd known, why point me to the basketball coach, Darren Chase? Had Ellen thought she was sending me on a wild goose chase? Before I could ask, though, the mayor spoke up.

"You did? You never said anything," Terry protested.

"Darling, you were up to your ears at the office. You had just decided to leave the private sector and make the move to politics. You were courting every person who might have a connection to someone, anyone, who would help get you elected," Ellen said calmly. "You were kissing every ass that you could get your lips on, except mine, to be frank. You were utterly and completely distracted."

Ellen wiped the silver spoon on a white napkin and then leaned forward and, with the same napkin, gently wiped at the corners of Frank's mouth. The elderly man continued to stare at her; his hands idle in his lap, his shoulders hunched forward.

"So, what? He told you but not me?" Annika asked. A hurt look replaced the confusion on her face and tears welled up in her bright eyes. She glared at her mother. "He never said a word about any of this."

Ellen sighed. I could feel the exasperation in her breath.

"He didn't tell me. I went at the school one afternoon in, oh, I don't know, late April or May. I thought I'd surprise him at practice and take him to an early dinner at Enrique's. But the coach said Nicky had quit the team, to concentrate on his studies. I was shocked, of course, but you know Nicky wasn't that great of a player. I think it helped the team to lose the dead weight," she said.

Annika gasped and a deep bloom rose in her mother's cheeks as she realized her poor choice of words. Ellen bit her lip, and then went on. "Well, anyway. Everyone knows Nicky was no athlete."

She folded the white napkin she'd used on Franklin into a neat, tidy square, tucked the silver spoon into the napkin and set it down on the table, and then poured herself a fresh cup of coffee and took a sip. She noticed Mrs. Watkins was still on her hands and knees, dabbing at the carpet.

Ellen said, "Hannah, dear, don't worry about the stain. I'll have the cleaners work on it tomorrow. You've done enough. I think your father's probably ready for a nap soon."

Mrs. Watkins rose from her knees and picked up the towel, with the broken shards, and left the room with a nod. I watched her leave and wondered not for the first time what she thought of her sister-in-law.

As though reading my mind, Ellen said, "We're so lucky to have Terry's sister with us. Quiet as a mouse, she spends her days watching over my family. Such a shame she couldn't have children of her own; she adores kids. Everyone thinks I'm the strong one in the family, but I'll let you in on a little secret—that woman is a rock."

Annika said, "Mom, don't try to change the subject. Why was this a big secret with Nicky? *Everyone* in Cedar Valley was obsessed after you found the bodies, Gemma. They all thought they were going to solve the 'mystery of the century.' Why didn't Nicky just tell us the truth?"

"I don't know," I said. "Regardless, two days before he died he told the librarian at Cedar Valley Public Library that he was finished with his research. I think he may have found something, something big, and in between telling her that, and going over Bride's Veil, something happened to scare him. Scare him bad enough to go on the run."

"That's ridiculous," the mayor began, but Ellen interrupted him.

"Is it ridiculous? Nicholas was a puppy dog, trusting everyone, eager to please. He could never have made it in politics."

She turned to me and continued. "If you're right, and so far I haven't heard anything to think you might be wrong, perhaps Nicky revealed this big find to the wrong person."

I nodded. "That's exactly what I think."

"Nick was a smart kid. If he'd figured out who the Woodsman was, he wouldn't have gone up to the guy," Terence Bellington said. "That's just stupid and my son wasn't stupid. He would have gone to the police . . . or me."

He stood and paced the living room, one hand rubbing the back of his neck so vigorously it turned scarlet. After a moment, he stopped pacing and jammed his hands into the kangaroo pocket at the front of his sweatshirt and stared at us.

Finn spoke first. "Maybe he wanted to blackmail the guy."

Ellen laughed and to my amusement, I saw Finn jump at her harsh bark. "Are you completely retarded? Do you have any idea what our worth is? Nick's allowance was more than you make in a week. Money doesn't matter to this family. We just happen to have a hell of a lot of it."

Finn turned bright red and my amusement grew. He'd finally met a woman who first, wasn't charmed by him, and second, wasn't afraid to chew him up and spit him back out in pieces. I felt like letting Finn sit there and stew in it, but that wouldn't accomplish much.

I thought Finn might have a point, too. Maybe Nicky wasn't as smart and sweet and wonderful as everyone seemed to think he was.

I stood up and tapped Finn on the shoulder.

"Sir, Mrs. Bellington, we've taken enough of your time. We'll be in touch if anything else comes up. Thank you for the coffee," I said. "Annika, nice to see you again."

The mayor and his wife nodded at me. Annika stood and wiped her eyes. "I'll walk you guys to the door."

She led us back down the long hallway.

"Do you think it's true?" she whispered to me at the front door. "Would Nicky keep something like that from me?"

She looked so sad, and small, in her oversize sweats, that I felt my own eyes welling up.

"I don't know, Annika. But I do know that you guys loved each other very much, and that's what matters, doesn't it? The love endures," I said. I gave her a little pat on the shoulder and then followed Finn out the door.

"The love endures?" he snickered. "You're a bad Hallmark card."

"Yeah? And you're a real piece of work. . . . I wonder if you might be on to something, with the blackmail. Nicky seems a little too good to be true."

Finn paused at his car. He licked his finger and rubbed at a spot of mud on the rear left light. "Say he did figure out who the Woodsman was. Would he really go to this guy and threaten him? Nicky may not have been perfect but I haven't heard anything to lead me to think he was foolish. The blackmail angle is intriguing but it's probably a dead end."

Everywhere I turned in this case was a dead end, it seemed.

# Chapter Twenty-four

I decided to call it a day. The rain continued to fall, and in the wet, dim light, the streets were a foggy sea of red and yellow taillights and bobbing black shapes I could only assume were umbrellas. I wanted a warm bath and a mug of hot tea and my own oversize sweats, the pair that was so worn there were holes in the armpits and the elastic in the waist barely kept them up.

I drove slowly up the canyon, my windshield wipers rocketing back and forth. The wipers needed replacing and their worn rubber strips put cloudy streaks on the windowpane that left me craning my neck to and fro to peer around them.

When I pulled into the gravel drive, I saw a brown car parked by the side of the house, under our big pine tree. In the rain, I couldn't see much beyond the color of the sedan, certainly not the plates or the occupants.

I sat in my car a moment, letting the engine idle, remembering Seamus's strange behavior the night before, and the feeling that someone had been in the yard.

Finally I turned off the ignition, grabbed my things, and opened a newspaper over my head. I hurried to the front door and then turned and stared at the sedan, waiting. It looked like there were two people in the car, but I couldn't be certain. Beyond the porch, the rain left the world as blurred as a wet watercolor.

After a minute, I decided to go inside, but then the driver side door opened and Tessa O'Leary tumbled out and ran to me. Her hair was soaked in a matter of seconds and she shook her head like a puppy under the front eave.

"Tessa? What are you doing here?" I asked. And how do you know where I live? I thought.

"I wanted to apologize for my behavior earlier. I'm really, really sorry I acted like that at the police station," she said. She wore jeans and a thin T-shirt and she shivered. I sighed, knowing better but still saying, "Well, come in, you'll catch your death out here."

Inside, I put down my things and found an old sweatshirt of Brody's. Tessa put it on and thanked me and then immediately made her way over to the fireplace mantel and picked up one of the framed photographs there.

"Is this your husband?" she asked. "Wow. Bet you have to fight all the ladies off."

My mood darkening, I muttered, "You have no idea, kid."

It was an old black-and-white shot of Brody on his mountain bike. In the picture, he is wearing a jersey and shorts and an Afro wig; it was some costume charity race he had done years ago. I joined her at the fireplace and gently took the photograph out of her hands and put it back in its spot, next to a framed picture of my parents and another one of my grandmother and me, taken at my high school graduation. I look incredibly young in that photograph. As I've aged, I find myself looking more and more like my mother.

I catch my reflection and wonder what she would have looked like at fifty, sixty, seventy years old. She'll always be thirty-five in my mind, frozen in time, young, beautiful, vibrant.

She was full of life, until she wasn't.

I rubbed my lower back and grimaced at the knot I found. "Tessa, it's been a long day. I'm beat. I appreciate the apology, but it wasn't necessary. I should apologize to you, my partner wasn't trying to trick you or get you to rat out anyone."

She looked at me with concern. "Do you want me to rub your back? I can get those knots out, if you want. I've studied massage therapy."

I said, "No, thank you. I need to lie down and get some rest. Can we talk tomorrow?"

I put a hand on her shoulder and gently steered her toward the front door. She stopped halfway there.

"Is that your dog? He's so cute! Here, puppy, puppy," Tessa squealed.

Seamus ambled over and she knelt and ruffled the fur around his ears. He flopped to the ground and exposed his belly with a big grin, in doggy heaven.

I sighed and counted to ten and then tried again.

"Tessa?"

"Sorry, he's just so cute. Yeah, yeah, tomorrow's fine. We've got a performance, why don't you come by and watch?" she said. She peeled out of the sweatshirt and handed it back to me.

I was surprised. "Fatone is having you perform?"

She laughed at my response. "Don't you know, Gemma? The show must go on. We're losing buckets of money if we sit here in town, not doing our thing."

Tessa closed the front door gently behind her and I leaned against it, the wood cool against my forehead. She was a strange one, mature one moment, angry the next, then childlike, then solicitous.

I fed Seamus and let him out and then locked the back door and drew a warm bath upstairs. I lay in the hot water, a rolled hand towel for a headrest, and stared up at the darkness in the ceiling. A few years back, Brody installed a skylight above the bathtub. The rain struck the glass window with fat splatters and the sky beyond was dark and moonless.

A distant boom of thunder thudded somewhere, a few miles off, and through the skylight I watched as the night filled with a white glow that danced away as quickly as it had flashed by.

Another clap of thunder, this one much closer, was followed by a loud thud downstairs.

I sat up in the bath. "Seamus?"

There was no answer. Although he could be a real pain in the

ass, that dog was trained to the teeth. If I was in the house, anywhere, and called him, he came.

"Seamus?" I called a little louder. "C'mon, boy."

Another loud thud and I propelled myself out of the bath and
into the white terrycloth robe that I'd tossed on the counter. At the
same time, the lights in the house flickered once, and then twice,
then went out completely.

I froze and listened to sounds that crept in, replacing the space
where once there had been light. The rain was loud, much louder,
as though the plunks and plinks and splats now came in through
an open window.

Maybe through an open door.

I had lived in this house on the edge of the forest long enough
to know most of her more intimate noises. Her winter noises, when
her eaves and shingles crackled with frost and ice; her summer
noises, when the wooden planks in the floor expanded and con-
tracted with the heat. And her settling noises, the occasional creaks
and squeaks as the foundation shifted imperceptibly.

I crossed the hall to our bedroom, moving quickly but silently,
adrenaline kicking my heartbeat up to double time. Under the
bed among a flurry of dust bunnies lived a long, flat box. Kneeling,
awkward with my big belly, I opened the box and slid out the
12-gauge combat shotgun. The thought struck me that soon with
a baby in the house we'd need to get a proper gun safe. Here I was
worried about gun safety, with a possible intruder downstairs, and
a hysterical laugh caught in my throat. I cursed Brody for leaving
me alone while he went gallivanting around Alaska with Celeste
Fucking Takashima.

Working in the dark, by feel, I groped in the nightstand drawer
until my fingers felt the long, narrow metal shaft of a penlight. The
light was weak but I was running on instinct and experience, as-
sembling the rifle and sliding the rounds in the dim light as smoothly
as I might assemble a sandwich.

Sixty seconds after I'd heard the second thud, I was at the head
of the stairs locked and loaded. I kept my finger off the trigger and

held the shotgun out in front of me, aimed at the ground but ready to lift at the first target that crossed my way.

I took a deep breath and peeked around the wall and looked down. A deep blackness filled the stairwell. I might have been at the bottom of the ocean for all I could see. Hesitant to use the penlight but knowing I couldn't safely risk a descent without a quick look, I flicked the light on and off and saw in the second or two of illumination the front door gaping open at the bottom of the stairs.

I flashed the light again and watched as a gust of wind, ice cold and mean, tore in and gripped the door with tendril-like fingers. Caught unawares, the door traveled along the wind's retreat, slamming back against the wall with another heavy thud.

Had I locked the front door after Tessa left? I thought through my actions of the night and could only remember for certain locking the back door.

"Seamus?" I called out once more and then began walking down the stairs, keeping the gun in front of me like a shield. With each step I felt a tremor make its way down my arm and into my hand. At the bottom, my bare feet took a final step and touched down on wet fabric; the area rug, soaked through from the rain.

I swore and started to close the door then paused and called one last time for Seamus.

He came bounding toward me from the side of the house, his coat soaked, his feet muddy, a ghost-dog in the dim moonlight.

"You dingbat."

I pulled him in, shut the door and, in the dark, felt for the old towel from the hall closet and rubbed him off. As I dried off the last of his short legs, the house lights flickered and came on.

With Seamus at my heels, and the shotgun in my arms, I made my way through the first floor, room by room, checking windows and closets, taking my time.

There was nothing.

There was no one.

I felt silly, but the front door was heavy and even unlocked,

I didn't think it could blow open without assistance. I double-checked the back door and found it secure.

Upstairs, I repeated my search, room by room. I almost skipped the bathroom, as I'd been in there when the noises had started, but as I passed the half-open door, I noticed something strange.

The bathroom was dark.

I was almost positive I'd left the light on when I had bolted from my bath. I wouldn't have taken the extra seconds to turn it off. And the power had gone off after I had put on my robe, hadn't it?

I couldn't remember.

Weariness fell on me like a cloak and suddenly I was too exhausted to care much.

I had a gun. I was trained. I was tired.

I set the tip of the shotgun against the door and slowly pushed it, swinging it inward, opening it all the way. The air was heavy with the smell of the citrus bath oil. The light from the hall spilled into the small room, revealing the toilet, the sink, the tub with the shower curtain hooked to one wall. In the shadows, they were all soft shapes, safe and domestic.

Familiar.

I leaned in and flipped the light on and stared at the sticky red substance that came off the switch and on to my finger. It was moist but not wet, waxy but not malleable, and as I brought my fingers to my nose, the smell I experienced was similar to that of melted crayons.

I lifted my eyes and saw the message on the bathroom mirror. Written in a tidy print, its author must have been as unhurried in his writing as I had been in my searching of the house:

> The next message I leave will be written in your
> blood. Leave the past in the past if you want to
> have a future Bitch.

A gold tube of lipstick, the cap removed and the scarlet wax smashed down, rolled to and fro in the sink, a relic from my dating years. It was one of a dozen I kept in an old shoe box in the bathroom cabinet. I watched the tube come to a stop and saw it was Kiss My Face #47, an old favorite, with a sexy color and a name that used to make me laugh: Killing Me Softly Rose.

I sank down to the floor, my legs finally giving out.

# Chapter Twenty-five

I couldn't figure out when the message had been written.

I would have heard the intruder on the stairs, or Seamus would have. That dog still barked at the mailman, and poor Mr. Ellis had done our route for years.

I took a picture of the note with my digital camera, and careful not to touch the edges of the smooth tube, sealed up the lipstick in a plastic baggie. When I held the bag up to the light, I saw faint ridges on the tube from a fingerprint almost touching the small label at the bottom.

I did another round of the house and checked every closet, under the guest bed, and in the garage, pulling out the bikes, camping gear, and stacks of junk that piled up month by month, year by year. There was nothing out of the ordinary. The only disturbing thing I found was a mouse taking the big sleep in an old ski boot.

At midnight, I grabbed a pile of blankets and made up a bed on the living-room couch. I set the gun on the floor, and put my cell phone under the pillow. My sleep was deep, free of dreams, and when I woke, I found myself in a twisted, sweaty heap of blankets and loose cushions.

The rain had stopped sometime around dawn. I stumbled into the kitchen and tripped over Seamus's water bowl, as I did most mornings, and swore. Later, on the back patio, I sipped from a pot of hot tea and scarfed down a plate of bacon and eggs and toast.

The sun was shining and already the dozen or so puddles of

muddy water that dotted the yard like miniature ponds were beginning to dry up. Two matronly robins, their breasts plump and rosy hued, picked at fat worms that had drowned in the storm. Their sharp beaks picked up the thick pink tubes and neatly sucked them down like housewives at an oyster bar.

In the light of day, the sun warming the air and my skin, it was hard to believe the previous night's events. Other than the lipstick and the photos I'd taken of the message, there was no sign of my visitor. I took a look in the front yard, but the tire treads I saw were my own and those from Tessa's car.

After a shower and quick check of my e-mail, I locked up and carefully backed out of the driveway. The mud was thick, and the west-facing front of the house was deep in shadows, not yet graced by the sun's heat.

Driving down the canyon, I saw evidence of the storm's destruction everywhere. The creek ran fast and high, racing over tree limbs and submerged boulders that two days ago had stood dry. Ahead of me, a silver Honda minivan slowed to a crawl and then carefully maneuvered around a pine tree that lay across the road like a felled giant.

Perched delicately on one of the pine's limbs, a single crow, its feathers black as ink, bobbed his head up and down into the tree's nooks and crannies. A pickup truck from the local utility company was parked just beyond the tree, and as I drove by, the driver gave me a halfhearted wave.

I passed the turnoff to Scarecrow Road, a winding stretch of dirt and cement that culminated, four curvy miles away, in an abandoned mine shaft. The signpost's sketch of a once-friendly scarecrow had faded over the years. Vandals had gouged out his cheery eyes and widened his mouth into more of a leer than a grin.

Someone had taken a red Sharpie to the figure, drawing devil horns on the scarecrow's head, and a protruding tongue from his mouth, lascivious, its tip forked like a snake's. The scarecrow's crotch was filled with crude, obscene sketches that only vaguely resembled anything like standard male equipment.

I drove past the turnoff, making a note to talk to the county about a replacement sign.

I drove, and I remembered.

In March, before the forest fires came, before school let out for spring break, but after the last big snowfall, and after the junior prom had come and gone, a group of six teenagers, two boys, four girls, sat in a basement, bored out of their minds. Inspiration struck and they piled into Greta Tobias's father's minivan—a van identical to the silver Honda I'd been caught behind just a few minutes before—and headed to Scarecrow Road.

Their final destination was the old mine shaft four miles beyond the turnoff.

As teenagers are apt to do, they drove distracted, half of them texting, the other half hollering at one another to change the radio station. But Greta was a good driver, and she tuned out her friends and concentrated on the icy road. The two fatal errors the group made on their way out of town could hardly be blamed on these distractions.

The first error was stopping at Shane Montgomery's house. While Mr. and Mrs. Montgomery sat in the den watching an old movie on the Turner Classic Movie network, their son—star football player, straight-A student—grabbed a bottle of tequila and a bottle of vodka from the liquor cabinet above the refrigerator.

The second error was poor arithmetic, plain and simple. The van's gas gauge was broken; it had been for weeks. Greta's father was a busy man, and he traveled a lot for business. He simply hadn't had time to get the damn thing fixed. So, he had shown Greta how to do the math—fill it up, drive it down. If you knew how many gallons the tank held, you could estimate how far you could go at any given time.

Only that night, Greta's math was off.

Of course, when we arrived at the scene, we didn't know about any of these fatal errors. We only got the details the following day when the five surviving teens told us the gruesome tale, piece by piece.

They had arrived at the mine shaft just fine. They drank by the light of the van's headlights, passing the vodka and tequila bottles around and around, over and over. Lisa Chang-Hughes dared Shane to strip naked and run through the woods. He did, and then he dared Lisa to climb down into the mine shaft.

It was supposed to be a short trip, a few feet down and then back up again. But her heeled boot caught a rotted rung, and her hands, numbed by the cold and the tequila, were slow to react.

She fell fifteen feet.

Frantic, her friends called her name, but there was no answer. They waved the beams of their flashlights into the pit and saw her legs, and then one hand.

The rest of her body lay in darkness.

In a panic, they tried to dial 911 but not one of their cell phones picked up a signal. They were too far into the woods, out of range of all the satellite towers. They decided to split up, and a couple of them would drive into town and get help.

It was a good plan but it went to shit when the van's ignition caught and then died. The gas tank was empty.

In darkness and cold, the two boys ran the four miles back to the main road, and then another three into town. But it was past midnight, and store after store was closed, some with dim interior lights cruelly illuminating phones that were just out of reach. It was another twenty minutes before the boys got to the all-night Mc-Donald's, where they persuaded the manager to make the call.

And it was almost two in the morning by the time we arrived on the scene.

To this day, I can close my eyes and feel the heartbreak that flooded their faces—the boys who'd run seven miles for help, and the girls who sat by the mine shaft, long after their flashlights had died, in the cold, in the dark—when we told them in quiet, gentle voices that Lisa was dead. She had died instantly, breaking her neck when she hit the hard frozen ground of the old shaft.

Hours later, exhausted, I managed to make it to my yearly physical and drug screen, an appointment I had already pushed back twice. The doctor called me at home that night with the news that while my urine test had been negative for narcotics, it had been positive for hCG, a very specific hormone with a very specific purpose.

There is no way for me to drive by Scarecrow Road without remembering that day. A day that opened with the cold, unyielding, unforgiving truth that death comes for us all. A night that closed with the bright, shining truth that with each day comes new life.


I picked Finn Nowlin up at the station and continued downtown, past the coffee joint and the bookstore and the new flower place I'd yet to visit. A young man in cutoff jean shorts and an electric green T-shirt stood just outside the shop door, arranging pink rosebuds in silver buckets that lined the window ledge. He stopped two elderly women as they strolled by, their arms linked, their backs hunched, their hair pulled up in low, matching buns, and handed them each a rose with a dramatic bow. The curves of their backs kept their faces turned to the ground, but I liked to imagine the blush that flooded each cheek was the same shade of pink as the rosebuds they clenched in their gnarled, arthritic hands.

For once, Finn was quiet.

He sipped his coffee and stared out the window, his eyes shaded by dark aviator-style sunglasses. I'd told Finn I wanted to stop at the circus on our way to the library and chat with Tessa.

I didn't tell him about the message on my mirror. Not for the first time, I cursed Chavez for sticking me with Finn. I wondered if Sam Birdshead was making any progress on the old police files that detailed Nicky's fall at Bride's Veil.

We pulled up to the circus grounds a little before ten o'clock and searched vainly for a parking spot in the main lot. Finn finally told me to get out, that he'd park the car up the road. As he pulled away, he muttered in a low voice something about women drivers.

I waited for him at the front gates and watched as ticket after ticket was purchased. It was a warm day, getting hotter and more crowded by the minute. Closing the circus for a few days only seemed to whet the town's appetite; that, or it was morbid curiosity to see the fairgrounds where a murder occurred just a few days before.

Finn joined me and we flashed our badges to the ticket taker and bypassed a line that snaked around the corner of the tent and continued into the parking lot. I knew what our first stop would be and I paused at one of the game booths to get directions. A hand-painted wooden sign read "Toss the Coin in the Bottle—You Pick Your Price."

For a moment, I was confused, and then I realized "price" was meant to read "prize."

Behind the counter, a young man in battered jeans and a black leather biker vest and dirty T-shirt leaned against a metal stool that must have once been a shiny red but was now a peeling dull rust the color of a dried scab.

I asked the man where we could find the trapeze artists.

"Ah, lady, you don't want to watch no trapie show. You want to play the bottles, I can tell these things. Get your boyfriend here to ante up and give us a dollar. You'll get ten throws with a dollar," he said.

The man peeled himself off the rusty stool and ambled toward me. His face was marked by an unfortunate eruption of acne, and as he rubbed at his chin, a blister broke open. He drew his hand away and looked down at it with all the introspection of a man watching the traffic roll by, then he slowly wiped it on the back of his jeans and stared at me with eyes that were tiny, bird-like and bloodshot.

Finn pulled his badge. Neither of us was in uniform, and the young man did a double take at the brass. He rubbed his chin again and said, "So this isn't your woman, huh?" and Finn shook his head.

If he'd shaken it any harder, he'd have gotten whiplash.

The young man grinned at me and I winced at the tobacco-stained Chiclet-like teeth that crowded his mouth. "Well, now, I'm going to be getting off in a few hours, how's about you and I grab a beer tonight?"

"Listen, that's tempting but as you can see," I said, and turning sideways, pointed at my belly with both thumbs, "I'm already taken. Now, my partner has identified us as police officers. If you don't tell me, with the next words out of your mouth, where I can find the trapeze artists, the only coins you'll be collecting will be the quarters you'll need to use the pay phone. At the jail."

The man sighed. "Ah, I was just having a little bit of sport with you. No harm intended, right? My daddy was a policeman. They're all up in that tent, up that way . . . that big blue one, see? They'll be rehearsing right about now."

We cut across the grounds toward a blue-and-white-striped tent, dodging strollers and shrieking kids with sticky fingers and tall clowns with bunches of balloons floating like tethered clouds above their wigged and hatted heads.

Next to a hot dog stand, one of the clowns jumped in front of me and I reared back as he stuck his face into mine.

"Wanna buy a balloon?" he whispered. Black paint as thick as axle grease covered his entire face and a large floppy hat was pulled down low over his ears. I said no and moved to go around the clown but he leaned to the side, blocking me.

"Wanna buy a balloon?"

I shook my head and went to the other side and the clown mimed my movement, blocking me again. Ahead, I saw the back of Finn's head moving farther away as he continued toward the tent. All around me, kids swarmed; their heads brushing against my hips and thighs, their cries and shrieks of laughter piercing my ears like the call of a thousand tiny birds.

They closed in on me, surrounding me, filling the air with their small bodies. So many small bodies! I couldn't catch my breath.

The clown lowered his bunch of balloons over both of us, blocking my last point of reference, the sky.

I panicked.

My heart hammered and I couldn't draw enough air into my lungs. I wheezed and the clown seemed to loom closer and then farther away, up and then down and then up and I saw the ground rushing up to meet me and then an arm gripped my elbow.

"Gemma, c'mon. You can get a hot dog later," Finn hissed in my ear, and pulled me toward the blue tent. I drew in a big breath of air and yanked free of his grip.

I turned around in a circle, scanning the crowd, but the clown, and his balloons, was gone.

I was really starting to dislike clowns.

# Chapter Twenty-six

The blue-and-white-striped tent was deceptive; small from the outside, it was enormous on the inside, easily the size of a large theater space. I suddenly understood why they were called big tops. Bleacher-style seats ringed the inside edge of the tent, and in the middle, a large dirt space had been circled off. Above the dirt, a green net stretched between four pillars, and above the net, five trapeze bars swayed gently in the air at varying heights.

I watched as four people began climbing two sets of ladders at either end of the tent. They wore Zorro-like masks and black costumes that obscured their faces and bodies. Their feet were bare and they climbed quickly, confidently, like monkeys. A sense of déjà vu came over me, and I remembered something that I had forgotten, from a long time ago. I would have been about three, and my father was home for the weekend, a rare occurrence. He was a pilot for Southwest Airlines and he flew the Denver–Las Vegas route, Thursdays to Sundays.

He must have been sick, or maybe it was a holiday, I don't remember. But he was home, and I was thrilled when he packed me in the station wagon and took me to the summer fair. It was here, on these same fairgrounds, and we saw acrobats perform in a similar tent. I remember how small my hand seemed in his, and how his long mustache would tickle my ear when he kissed my cheek.

The memory made me sad; my father would have enjoyed being a grandpa.

"Gem, check it out," Finn said. He pointed up to the top of each ladder, where a long plank, similar to a diving platform, was set with handrails made of thick twine, and rope strung waist-high. The ladders were at least fifty feet in the air and I gulped. Heights have never been my thing.

"Scary, isn't it?" a voice said behind us.

I turned around and shook Joe Fatone's hand. I introduced him to Finn.

"Wonderful to be back in business. We carnies go real crazy, sitting around like a bunch of goobers," Fatone said.

Finn asked, "Has anyone ever fallen?"

Fatone shook his head. "Not on my watch. Couple of close calls, of course, but no real fatalities."

Except in the clown department, I almost said, but instead asked, "Is Tessa around?"

"Oh, she's around. She'll be down in a few minutes," Fatone said with a laugh, and jerked a thumb at the ladders. I looked closely and noticed one of the masked figures had a petite build and cropped pixie-like hair.

"You gotta see this," Fatone said. We followed him to the benches and took a seat. High above us, the group paired off so that two figures were on each of the platforms. They stretched their arms and legs and backs, leaning into and against the wooden planks and the rope rails and each other.

Fatone whispered, "That's Tessa there, the little one . . . and Doug Gray, the one on her right. That's Twosie McDonald on the other platform, with Onesie, her sister."

"Twosie and Onesie?"

"Yeah. Onesie, because she's only got the one eye. Twosie . . . well, hell, I'm not sure why they call her Twosie, maybe since she's got the two eyes," Fatone said. He belched, a low burp that wafted toward me and smelled of peanuts and beer. "Pardon."

I asked, "She has one eye and she can still do the trapeze?"

The sisters mirrored Tessa and Doug's actions on the opposite platform. Then they pretended to sword fight, pushing one another to the edge of the plank, feigning fear, and then pushing back toward the ladder, their arms the swords.

Fatone nodded and let out another burp. "Excuse me, damn heartburn is going to kill me. The trapeze is never about sight, Deputy. It's about touch, and timing, and illusion. The best trapeze artists in the world can do their routines blindfolded. Damn it, I can't explain it, but it's like they've got a sixth sense."

We watched, spellbound, as Tessa skipped to the end of her plank and then without so much as a pause swan-dived into the air and grabbed the trapeze bar closest to her. She swung up and hooked her legs over the middle bar and then swung down and looped over the third. As she hung, upside down, one of the sisters on the opposite platform did a swan dive of her own and landed on the middle trapeze bar. Then, the remaining two jumped in and soon all four were swinging up and over one another, sometimes holding on to one another, sometimes holding on to the bar, sometimes appearing to float in midair before grabbing a leg or an arm.

"They make it look so easy," I breathed.

Fatone nodded. "It takes years of practice to get that good. Up there, it's like a secret world."

I felt his eyes on me.

"Speaking of secrets, seems like Reed had some of his own, didn't he?" Fatone asked. He pulled a cigar out of his shirt pocket and stuck it in his mouth, but didn't light it. "Or should I call him Nicky?"

"Don't most of your people have secrets?" Finn asked. He watched the trapeze artists, as mesmerized as I'd been. "I mean, isn't that why they run off and join the circus?"

Fatone smirked around his cigar. "Everyone has secrets. I'm just saying Reed seems to have had more than his fair share."

Fatone pointed up as the acrobats did a particularly spectacular maneuver that involved Tessa standing on one of the trapeze bars, very still for twenty or thirty seconds, and then she swooped down toward the other three acrobats and they bounced up, like startled birds.

"You know, every single one of these moves has a name," Fatone said.

"Really?"

He nodded. "That one they just did? That's called Scaring the Crow."

I laughed uneasily, thinking about Scarecrow Road.

"Uh-huh," he continued. "She stands still, you see, almost frozen, and then tumbles down like a falling scarecrow and the artists are the crows, surprised into flight. It's the moment the decoy—the scarecrow—comes to life."

"Like the other circus acts, sort of an illusion?" I asked.

"Magic, illusion, call it whatever you want. You see something, and you think you know what's going on and all of a sudden the universe shifts and reveals it to be something completely different," Fatone said. "And that, my friends, is the story of life, isn't it? You think you know."

He stuck the unlit cigar back in his shirt pocket and gazed up at the artists as they hooted and hollered and fell, one by one, into the big green net.

They bounced up and down a few times, laughing, then rolled to the edges of the net and jumped down to the floor. All but Tessa headed to a table in the corner, where a watercooler and paper cups waited. Instead, she looked at us and then walked over, removing her eye mask.

"Hiya! Like the show?" she asked. She leaned back, stretching with her hands on her hips, and I saw Finn give her the once-over. He seemed to have gotten over his anger at her departure from the sheriff's station yesterday.

The black costume was a basic long-sleeved, long-panted leotard that hugged every curve and muscle on her compact frame. Finn was practically drooling.

I said, "That was amazing, Tessa. Really magical."

She smiled and looked at Fatone. "Papa Joe?"

"You did good, kid, real good," he said.

She high-fived Fatone and then turned to Finn. "Hey, it's

Mr. Nowlin, right? Sorry for how I acted yesterday. I was really upset."

"These things happen. No big deal," Finn said with a slight shrug. He smiled at Tessa. "And call me Finn, everyone does."

Fatone stood and excused himself. I waited until he was out of hearing distance and then turned to Tessa.

"Tessa, last night . . . did you come back? To my house, I mean?"

I watched her carefully but her expression didn't waver. "Huh? What do you mean, come back? I left, don't you remember?"

Finn was watching me with narrow eyes but he stayed quiet. I'd have to catch him up on Tessa's visit later.

I nodded. "Yes, but later, you didn't . . . never mind."

"No, what is it?" she said.

She looked at me with genuine concern and I began to think I'd been mistaken in suspecting her. Why would Tessa have left that message scrawled on my bathroom mirror? She had no ties to Cedar Valley, no connection with Nicky Bellington other than knowing him, and dating him, as Reed Tolliver, not Nicky.

"Nothing. I found a hat and thought maybe it was yours," I improvised. "But I just remembered, you weren't wearing a hat, so forget it. Hey, when's the real show?"

She gave me a squinty-eyed look, and then answered. "Twenty minutes. You guys should stay and watch, it's going to be great. We've worked out this whole new routine to this really cool Spanish-funk music, to go with the Zorro outfits. And, for the show, we're using swords!"

Finn looked impressed. "Real swords? Up there?"

Tessa nodded and clapped her hands together and bounced on the balls of her feet. "Uh-huh. Very, very cool."

"Sure, we'll stay. But then I want to talk to you again, after, okay?"

She nodded and then bounced away toward the other trapeze artists. The male acrobat, Doug Gray, grabbed her by the waist and, lifting her in the air, spun her around until her squeals were so loud we could hear them from across the tent.

"I don't like that guy."

"You don't even know him. Or her," I said, and turned Finn by the shoulder until he faced me. "I'm serious. She was Reed's girl-friend. Her roommate, a redhead named Lisey, is in love with her. You heard Tessa at the station yesterday—she practically accused Lisey of murder. Last night, she was in my house offering back rubs. It's all a bit messy."

"Yeah, yeah . . . wait, what? She has a lesbian girlfriend? That's kind of hot. . . ."

I rolled my eyes and dragged him out of the tent. "If we're going to watch the show, I'm going to need that hot dog."

We ordered and ate at a picnic table under an awning, next to a teenage couple with their hands in each other's back pockets, and a harried-looking mother with five children. Blond hair stuck out of her ponytail like pieces of straw, and she'd lined up the buttons on her pink shirt wrong, so that the shirt hung slightly crooked on her small frame.

Three of the kids, towheaded boys with light eyes and fair skin, were definitely hers, but the other two must have been friends of the family. The mother was nicer to those two.

My hot dog was delicious and I chased it down with a freshly squeezed lemonade. A breeze blew over us and in the shade, my hunger satiated, I could almost imagine a decent conversation with Finn.

"So, Finn, three years ago. The Nicky Bellington case: round one. You were lead, right? With Moriarty?" I asked.

He leaned back, pleased to be asked. "We got the call around one in the afternoon. One of the kids had run down the trail until he was in cell phone range, and he'd called his parents. They'd called us. We hit the trail hard and got to the overlook around four. It was a mess. Kids crying, Paul Winters in shock. He'd just started up that youth group, the Forward Foundation, remember? It seemed like it was going to be the hottest thing in town. Annika was there, too, of course. She looked different back then, kind of chubby. Not so pretty."

"Were the Bellingtons there? The mayor, or Ellen?"

"No, while we were hiking in, Chavez drove over to tell them in person. The first time we spoke to them on record was a few days later."

"When you searched his room, right? What made you do that? Wasn't it clearly an accident?"

Next to us, the teenagers had left, and the mother was packing up the five kids. Another breeze blew in, stronger than the first, and suddenly napkins and plates were flying all around us. The kids laughed and jumped about for paper goods and the mother sat down and sighed.

I gave her a smile and she rolled her eyes and then smiled back and shrugged.

Finn continued. "It was Moriarty's idea. We were pretty sure by then the whole thing was just a tragic accident, but he wanted to be certain, if he was going to sign off on the report, that there wasn't a suicide note. Plus, you know, he was pals with Frank Bellington, Nicky's grandfather. I think he felt a responsibility to cross every *T* and dot every *I*. So, we did the whole enchilada. We inventoried every damn thing in the kid's room while his mom's standing in the doorway, sobbing hysterically."

"When we were at the house yesterday, it seemed like you all hadn't met."

"C'mon, Gemma. Like they're going to remember the cops who searched their dead kid's room three years ago?" Finn said.

He leaned forward and ate the last bite of his hot dog. His suit was spotless, as usual, while I'd managed to sprinkle my sundress with tiny drops of mustard. A couple of crumbs from the bun rested on my tummy and I brushed them away. They fell to the ground silently, joining dozens of other crumbs and bits.

The blond woman finally got the kids corralled and marched them off to a trash can, their small hands full of wayward napkins and paper plates. They stuffed the trash into the can and then ran off toward one of the game booths, and I remembered the term for the guys that ran them: peddies.

As in peddlers. Or pedophiles. I shivered.

"It was strange, though," Finn said. He traced a circle on the picnic table with his finger.

"What?"

"How insistent Moriarty was that we search the kid's room. I understood his concerns. But there was nothing, absolutely nothing that pointed toward a suicide. I tell you, if we'd have found a note, I'd have immediately suspected it was planted and that the whole thing was murder," Finn said. "Everything about that day screamed accident."

"Huh. Sure doesn't anymore, does it?" I stood and tossed my trash and picked up a napkin the kids had missed, a smear of dried ketchup staining the center of it like a bloody thumbprint. "We should get back, the show's going to start any minute."

# Chapter Twenty-seven

The tent was packed and we found seats toward the back, up high in the stands. Colorful flamenco music competed with the chatter of the crowd, and all around us, families shared popcorn and cotton candy and peanuts. I watched as more than one person cracked a peanut and then tossed the fibrous shell onto the ground.

In the front row, slightly to my left, I saw a familiar head of red hair: Lisey, Tessa's roommate. She sat next to another young woman, a blonde in a white tank top. The two were speaking to each other and although I was too far away to make out any words, the conversation appeared heated. Lisey's posture was rigid, and her hand repeatedly rose as though to dismiss her companion. Finally, with a look of disgust, Blondie stood and stormed out of the tent.

Lisey watched her go and then shook her head and turned her attention to the ring in the middle of the tent, where a tall man in a black tuxedo stood. His height was exaggerated even more by a top hat and cane that he bandied about before him.

I nudged Finn and pointed to the back of Lisey's head and said her name. He lifted an eyebrow.

"The lesbian?" he whispered, and I rolled my eyes and nodded.

The music died and the ringmaster said, "Ladies and gentlemen, boys and girls, may I be the first to welcome you to the most impressive, the most incredible, the most amazing death-defying show on Earth."

He had to be almost seven feet tall, all arms and legs, like an enormous alien insect. He bandied about his cane and the crowd cheered in response.

"What you are about to see might shock you . . . it may surprise you . . . but it *will* stun you," he roared and the crowd roared back.

The man next to me had just tossed a handful of popcorn in his mouth and when he shouted his approval at the ringmaster, he sprayed the back of the head of the woman in front of him with a fine mist of butter-tinged spittle.

I winced and scooted closer to Finn.

"Put your hands together for the greatest group of acrobats on Earth, the Fellini Brothers' Amazing Trapeze Troupe!" he said. With another flourish of his cane and a tip of his hat, the man bowed to the audience and stepped out of the spotlight. The music came back on with a vengeance, louder and more pulsing than before.

From the four corners of the tent, the acrobats emerged like boxers at a match, each sprinting to the center and doing a jig to pump up the crowd. They wore the black leotards we'd seen during practice, but true to Tessa's word, they each carried a long saber with a wicked-looking tip. Red sashes held the swords to their waists, and as before, each acrobat wore a black Zorro-like mask.

The crowd went wild with cheers and applause and the performers strutted before the audience like court jesters, high-fiving the children in the first row. After a few minutes, the four met back in the middle and huddled, then broke apart in pairs and climbed the long ladders at either end of the tent.

There was something different from what we'd watched in rehearsals but I couldn't put my finger on it.

Once on the platforms, the four drew their swords and began their daring dances on the narrow planks. To the right, Tessa and Doug teased and taunted each other. Tessa danced backward, Doug's sword at her belly, and then she lunged forward, pushing him back toward the ladder, away from the plank's edge.

The audience gasped as he feigned a slip and fell to one knee, then cheered as he regained balance and resumed his attack on Tessa.

On the opposite plank, the sisters, Onesie and Twosie, fended off imaginary assailants. They stood back to back and slashed their swords at the air, moving to and fro along the platform as one unit. The silver weapons flashed in the spotlights like strobes and I closed my eyes, feeling the beginnings of a migraine. Between the late night, my lack of sleep, the heat of the day, and now the pulsing lights and music, plus my hormonal swings, I knew I didn't stand a chance against the vise slowly tightening around my forehead.

As the music switched from the flamenco guitar to a steady, throbbing Latin dance beat, the acrobats laid down their swords and shook hands and hugged. As in rehearsals, Tessa was first off the plank. This time, though, she did a stunning dismount that involved a backward flip that left the audience gasping. She grabbed the first bar and the audience sighed with relief and the show went into full swing. The other three acrobats joined Tessa and soon they were jumping and twisting and diving with, literally, the greatest of ease.

In front of me, a child whispered to his father, "What if they fall?" and the father whispered back, "They won't, honey, they're professionals," and I realized what was different from the rehearsal we'd watched earlier.

The green safety net had been removed.

If someone did fall, it would be a forty-foot drop straight to the ground. I gulped and felt the hot dog I'd eaten turn inside me on a wave of nausea.

"What's a pofresshunal?" the child whispered, and the father answered, "It means they are so good at their job, they won't fall."

With the realization the net was gone, watching the acrobats was suddenly a nerve-racking event. I held my breath through the next ten minutes, until finally they swung themselves, one by one, back to the platforms. They paused, panting, on the planks as the audience gave them a standing ovation.

As Finn and I stood and clapped, I looked down to the left. Lisey was gone. Scanning the room, I saw a flash of red at one of the side exits. "C'mon," I said, and grabbed Finn.

"Don't you want to talk to Tessa again?" he asked, and followed me as we made our way through the stands. Every second person had to turn sideways or stand back up to let us by.

"Yes, but she can wait," I said. "I want to talk to Lisey first."

I wondered if Lisey was the second person in Tessa's car last night. If so, maybe she had come back to my house on her own, later, and left the message. But really, what would have been the point? I was finding it harder and harder to believe that anyone from Reed's life had been involved in his murder, especially given the wording of leaving the past alone.

Everywhere I turned seemed to point right back to the past . . . to the McKenzie boys, and the Woodsman.

To this town.

Outside, I threw up an arm against the glare of the bright sunshine. I'd left my sunglasses in the car, and as I squinted and waited for my eyes to adjust, the throbbing in my head increased. I slowly turned, scanning the throngs of people that milled on the midway between the various booths and tents and food stands and Porta-Potties and rides.

All I could see for miles was kid after kid, clown after clown.

"Where did she go? Do you see her?"

"I don't know, I don't . . . wait, there? Is that her?" Finn asked. He pointed to a small open space about fifty yards away.

Lisey stood, her back to us, one hand raised to her hair, the other on her hip. She wore a tight yellow T-shirt, too small for her voluptuous frame, and men's carpenter-style jeans that hung loose from her hips and sagged at the rear.

We pushed through the crowd. When we were a few feet behind her, I grabbed Finn's arm and held him back.

Lisey was speaking but there was no one else there, and I realized she was on the phone.

"I told you, I'm through," she said. There were tears and anger in her voice. "No, no more. You promised. I don't care how much, it's not worth it."

Finn looked at me with raised eyebrows, as Lisey screamed, "No, screw you! I'm done. Don't call me again!"

She threw the phone in an arc toward the woods that surrounded the fairgrounds. After a moment, she sighed and then stomped off and started searching the ground.

Finn and I walked to her.

"Lisey?" I said softly.

She jumped and turned and stared at me without any sign of recognition. Her face was tear-stained and I saw that when she wasn't scowling, or stoned out of her mind, she was actually quite beautiful. Her skin was the color of fresh cream, her eyes an amber brown. Her cheekbones were wide and with her ample body, she could have been a model for Titian or Rembrandt.

"Yeah?"

"Do you remember me? I'm Detective Gemma Monroe, I visited with Tessa at your cabin a few days ago?" I asked.

Lisey shook her head. "It's not my cabin anymore. I moved out yesterday."

She started to turn away, then stopped, twin roses blooming in her cheeks. "Oh, I remember. I was, uh, incapacitated when you stopped by."

I nodded. "That's right. Are you feeling better? I understand you were upset about Reed's death."

Finn bent down and picked up a pink sparkly object. "This your phone?"

"Thanks," Lisey said. "I . . . dropped it a few minutes ago."

We stood there awkwardly for a moment. I took a deep breath and said, "I don't mean to be nosy, but why did you move out of the cabin? I thought you and Tessa were friends?"

"Tessa doesn't have friends. She uses people like toilet paper and then flushes them out of her life," Lisey replied, dropping down to the ground. She sat cross-legged and jabbed at the keypad on her phone. "Shit, I think it's broken."

"Let me take a look," Finn said. He bent and plucked it from her hands.

Lisey started to protest but he shushed her. I watched as she eyeballed him, top to bottom, and then she closed her mouth with a pretty little pout. Finn's blue polo shirt matched his eyes and his slacks were clean and pressed, and I tried to see him as she did, but it was no good. I knew him too well.

I squatted down beside Lisey and within a few seconds, my knees and quads were screaming, so I lowered myself all the way down to my butt. The ground was grassy and comfortable and I sighed, the weight off my feet. It was going to be a hell of a struggle getting up but for the time being, I was content.

"Lisey, I don't follow," I began. "I was under the impression that you and Tessa were . . . close."

She smirked. "Is that what she said? The first thing you should know about Tessa is that she is supremely talented. The second is that she's a pathological liar. You do the math."

I asked, "So if Tessa told me that you were in love with her, that was a lie?"

Lisey fell backward to the grass with a hysterical laugh. She lay there, chuckling, and when she sat back up, her eyes were again filled with tears. A lock of auburn hair fell across her face, and she pushed it away.

"That's hilarious. I had my first boyfriend when I was eleven. I'm about as far from that as . . . as . . . ." She faltered off as she tried to think of a suitable comparison. "As Jennifer Lopez!"

Finn handed the pink phone back to her. "I think I fixed it for you."

"Yeah?" she said, and pushed a few buttons. "Hey, thanks! It's working."

Finn gave her a wink and sat down next to us. "So, Lisey, no girl-on-girl action? Why would Tessa tell us you had a thing for her?"

"Like I said, she's a liar. And she's really good at it; it's second nature to her. Sometimes she lies even when there is nothing to lie about. Like, I'll ask her if we need milk and she'll say yes and I'll check and there's a full carton. Stupid shit like that."

I asked, "Did Reed know about the lying?"

Lisey snorted. "Of course he did, the idiot. But he was such a nice guy, and he was in love with her, like straight up Romeo and Juliet love. He worshipped her. He thought she would change."

"Tessa told us she found a torn-up photograph of herself and Reed under your bed. Did you do that?"

Lisey looked startled. "What? Why would I do that? I liked Reed; he was a good guy. He was kind of freaky, with the piercings and tats, but hey, he was a gentleman. Tessa didn't deserve him, that's for sure. And if I did tear up some photo, why would I keep it under my bed for Crazy Pants to find?"

She had a point. If Lisey was telling the truth, then I couldn't believe a word Tessa had said. But if Tessa was telling the truth, then Lisey was a jealous woman with a good reason to hurt Reed. Maybe even kill him.

The one thing I believed was that they both couldn't be telling the truth.

But that didn't mean they both weren't lying.

Finn leaned back on his arms and stretched his long legs out in front of him, so his left shoe was touching Lisey's right foot. He gave her a little kick and she looked at him.

"What do you do, anyway, Lisey? I mean, here," he said. "At the circus."

She smiled, displaying a mouth full of crooked teeth that somehow made her look even more beautiful. "I'm a costume designer. I make all the costumes, for the performers, the clowns, even the animals, like the elephants' headpieces and the vests for the monkeys."

"All of them?"

She nodded. "I have a couple of assistants, day laborers we pick up in the cities, but I design the outfits and do most of the sewing and beadwork. The pay is shit but I love the work. And it's sort of fun, you know? Getting to see the world, one crappy town at a time."

"Where are you from originally?" Finn asked. He'd withdrawn his foot and crossed his legs but his eyes hadn't left Lisey's face.

"Salem, Massachusetts. I got my degree there, in fashion design, and then had what you might call a falling-out with my dad. I left Salem and stayed with some friends in Chicago for a few months, working for a shop out there. The owners knew Papa Joe—Mr. Fatone—and well, one thing sort of led to another," she said. She plucked at a few pieces of grass and began threading them together in her hands. "Tessa was the first friend I made."

"So you're what, twenty-three? And this is what you want to do for the rest of your life?" Finn asked. "What about a family? Career?"

"I'm twenty-five. And yes, this is what I want. These guys, the performers, the workers, they are my family. My dad wants me to come home and work for him at his construction company, but I hate that stuff," Lisey said. "Accounting, taxes. Death by office work."

She looked down at the phone in her lap and then up at me.

"I was just talking to him. He said he would pay me fifty thousand a year to run the front office, plus health benefits. But a desk job would just kill me. I tried it last summer, when the circus was having some financial trouble and there was talk of layoffs. I cried every night. Talk about soul-numbing."

High above us, a jet engine roared. We watched the plane pass over us, heading southeast, no doubt to the big Air Force base in Colorado Springs. The jet left a trail in the sky like someone had brushed a streak of white paint across a cornflower-blue canvas.

I took another gamble. "We couldn't help overhearing you, Lisey. So that was your dad? You sounded pretty angry."

"Oh, that's just how we talk to each other. I mean, I love him and I know he loves me."

I thought of asking her about the Ramones T-shirt, the one Tessa said had vanished, but decided against pressing my luck. I also decided it was unlikely Lisey had been the other person in Tessa's car last night.

We'd gotten a lot out of her. I just wasn't sure what it all meant yet.

She stood and brushed at her backside. "I got to get back, see if there's any repairs I need to do before tonight's show."

I awkwardly rolled to one side and half pushed, half lunged my way to a standing position. In another few weeks, I was going to need assistance getting up. The thought of asking Finn to pull me was horrifying and I hoped to God we'd solved this case by then.

"We'll be in touch, Lisey," I said.

Finn pulled out a business card so fast I almost got whiplash watching him, and he presented it to Lisey as though it were a flower.

"Don't hesitate to call. If you need anything, that's my cell number on the bottom."

He shook her hand and I noticed her give him another one of those top-to-bottom glances. She walked away, Finn watching her all the while.

"Earth to Finn. I got four words for you: twenty-five and murder suspect."

He laughed. "Oh, c'mon, you don't really think she killed Reed. If you did, you'd have brought her in for questioning. In fact, I think you kind of like her."

He was right. I did sort of like her. She was plucky and independent.

We headed back to my car. The fairgrounds were calmer; the late afternoon heat seemed to have sucked the energy out of every living thing. Even the pine trees in the woods at the edge of the circus looked tired, their boughs sagging low to the ground. A few teenagers roamed through the booths, halfheartedly playing the games, but most of the families with children had left for the day.

Thinking about Finn's words, I shook my head and wagged a finger at him, feeling an awful lot like Chief Chavez. And sounding an awful lot like Chief Chavez, with my next words.

"First truth of being a cop: be a cop. It doesn't matter who we like or dislike. Instinct is everything, but fact is king."

"What'd you do, memorize Chavez's little black book? Jesus, Gemma. If you were any farther up the chief's ass, you could start charging as a proctologist," Finn said. "Be a cop . . . fact is king . . . Jesus."

I stopped. "Is that really what you think? That I'm some kind of kiss-ass?"

Finn kept walking, and after a moment I hurried to catch up with him. "Well? Is it?"

"Let's say the chief seems to favor you quite a bit, Gemma. Like he's grooming you," he said with a shrug. "Just be careful. You can make a lot of enemies on the way to the top. Some of the others don't exactly appreciate getting passed over for plum cases like this one."

I grabbed Finn's shoulder and spun him around. "Are you kidding me? Chavez didn't give me this case. I was in the fucking room when the call came in. It's that simple. It always has been. You get the call, you get the case. Who's got the problem with me? Moriarty? Armstrong?"

He sighed and thought a moment. "Look, I'm only telling you this because we're partners, now, right? All for one, and one for all? I know you've been holding that home invasion case against me, but the truth is, I got nothing against you, except when you don't shut up and listen when you should. No one was going to answer for that little girl who got killed, and the DA and I did what we needed to do to make sure those assholes didn't hurt another kid. Am I proud of what we did? No. Would I do it again? You bet! You can quote Chavez's little rule book all you want, Gemma, but when push comes to shove, it's our job to put the bad guys away, no matter what it takes."

"Even when that means crossing the line yourself?"

Finn nodded. "It's always been about the lesser of two evils, Gemma. Always."

I understood his rationale. I just wasn't sure I could ever live it.

"Who's pissed at me?"

"Yesterday I heard Moriarty bitching to someone on the phone that maybe Chavez put you on the Bellington case as the department's fall guy," Finn said. He shrugged. "That was all I heard."

I was stunned. First, that Moriarty would say that. I've never had a problem with Moriarty. And second, that there was even the slightest possibility that the chief would do that to me . . . give me a case, thinking that I'd fail him.

Fail the department. Be the fall guy—for the family, the press, and the town. The guy the shit rains down on when the case goes unsolved.

"Who the hell was on the other end of the line?"

"It doesn't matter. When Moriarty saw me, he got off the phone real quick."

As if I didn't have enough to deal with already. Well, Moriarty could just sit tight and watch me solve this case. And just maybe solve the Woodsman murders, too, with a little help from Nicky Bellington.

We got into my car and I tried to shrug off Finn's words. I relived our conversation with Lisey.

"Do you think Lisey was telling the truth? About that being her dad on the phone?" I asked.

Finn didn't answer, and I looked at him as I started the ignition. He lifted his right index finger to his lips and dialed a number on his cell with his left hand.

"Ah, yes, sir, this is Mr. Smith with the U.S. Census department. We've had a bit of a sticky situation with our records, and I'm just calling folks in town, confirming current residents," Finn said with a perfect Boston accent. He listened for a moment and then held the phone away from his ear.

"All right then, sorry to trouble you, sir. You have a great day."

Finn clicked off the phone and smirked at me. "Well, she's a good little liar, I'll give her that much."

"How on Earth—" I began and the image of Finn holding Lisey's phone flashed across my mind. "You sneaky son of a bitch."

"The sneakiest," he said, and leaned back against the headrest and closed his eyes. "Dude was pissed. Said he didn't have to talk to no fucking census department because he didn't fucking live there and was only a fucking renter because the fucking government couldn't get him a fucking job and fuck you, motherfucker, for ruining my beautiful fucking day."

"Wow, that's some real pretty language. Get a name?"

Finn shook his head, his eyes still closed. "Nah. But we can trace the number when we get back. I don't think the dude's going anywhere."

# Chapter Twenty-eight

While Finn's charms may have worked on Lisey, they had no effect on Tilly Jane Krinkle. I introduced the two of them and she paid about as much attention to him as a cat would to a saucer of sour milk. The librarian led us down into the basement archives, and as she stroked the stuffed parrot and cooed to it, I saw Finn's mouth open.

I quickly elbowed him and shook my head. The last thing we needed was to piss off Tilly.

She said, "All right, kiddos, the space is all yours. Now, there are a couple of rules and yes, I know you are police officers but I don't give a god dang rat's butt, you follow the same guidelines as everyone else. And I ain't asking, I'm telling."

Tilly waited until we nodded our heads and then continued.

"There will be absolutely, positively, no marking, drawing, or otherwise writing on these materials. There's a copy machine around the corner. If you remove something from a box, place it back in the same god dang spot. Don't shelve or return anything yourselves; you'll put it in wrong and then we'll never see it again."

Tilly cocked her head and closed her eyes and then jerked to the side with a violent spasm. Finn and I jumped at the sudden movement.

"Petey says go deep or go home," she said. "She says you'll know what that means."

With that, she left us in the basement.

As before, the space was dark save for our small corner. In the stillness, I smelled Finn's cologne, and old paper, and a musty odor, like the air inside a summer cabin that's been closed up all winter.

Finn pulled a second chair over from another study carrel. He removed his wallet and cell phone and keys and placed them to the side and then sat down and took a stack of newspaper clippings from the top of the messy pile.

"What did she mean by that? Who's Petey?"

"Petey is the parrot," I said. "And I have no idea."

I joined Finn and reached for one of the heavy, gray three-ring binders on the table. When I opened it, a dead black spider, its desiccated corpse as light as air, fell into my lap. I brushed the bug away and it struck me that the last person who had touched this stuff was Nicky.

Had he really found something here, in these old articles and photos and scraps of a forgotten time, something the rest of us had missed?

The binder was stuffed with newspaper clippings from the spring and summer of 1985. A few of them covered the sad story of Rose Noonan, the young woman whose strangled body was found tangled in the reeds on the banks of the river in August. Her murder, like the Woodsman murders, remained unsolved. The police always figured her killer was a drifter, a highwayman. Rose had lived in town only a few months, and judging from these clippings, her death, while shocking to Cedar Valley, didn't light a candle to the disappearance earlier in the summer of the two local boys.

I held up a black-and-white Xerox copy of Rose Noonan's driver's license. She was pretty, with dark curly hair and laughing eyes. She wore a necklace with a dangling charm, and earrings that kissed her jawbone. "Remember her?"

Finn nodded. "The forgotten one."

I looked at him. After a moment, he spoke again. "You know what I mean. She's the forgotten one. When you think of 1985 and Cedar Valley, you think of the McKenzie boys. But there were three victims that summer. Four if you count the mayor's death. I always figured the stress from everything that happened brought on his heart attack."

"You think it was the same guy?"

Finn laughed at my expression. "Now hang on, that's not what I meant. Different M.O. She was assaulted and strangled and thrown in the river like a piece of trash, a month after the boys disappeared. The kids weren't touched that way. They were kept somewhere, killed, and then buried, properly, in the woods. I just meant that no one ever talks about her. You know they couldn't even determine a date of death for her? Her body had been in the water too long."

He was right; no one did talk about the woman.

"Do you think it would have made a difference three years ago, if you and Moriarty had gone through all this stuff?"

Finn shrugged. "I don't know. Bottom line is that Nicky was gone. I suppose it would have been interesting to know about, but really, the only reason we're down here now is because Nicky was murdered. Back then 'all this' would have been just a quirky footnote to Nicky's life and tragic accidental death."

I nodded and again thought he was probably right. Finn stood and leaned over the table and went through a few more of the piles.

"Why do you think he came back?" I asked.

"Who, Nicky?"

"No, Frank Sinatra. Yeah, Nicky. Sounds like they've got people drop in and out of the circus all the time. He had to have known what the next stop was—Cedar Valley. Why would he return? He could have checked out for a week or two and joined back up with the circus in Idaho," I said. "What's different now?"

Finn sat down and hugged a stack of files and folders against his chest. He played along. "You abandon your family—your parents, your sister, your grandfather, your friends—and run away for three years. You change your appearance. You're running, or hiding, from someone. What is the one thing that could bring you back?"

I ran through the last few years, looking for some change, some difference, something new. The *People* magazine article on the Bellingtons from a month or so back came to mind. It was a two-page spread on the Bellingtons that touched on the tragic loss of their only son; Ellen's former career as an actress; and Terry's struggle with cancer. "His dad. Nicky came back because of his dad."

"The cancer?" Finn asked. He thought about it. "I think you might be right. If I thought my dad was dying, that would be enough to bring me home."

I nodded. "Something to think about. It's been splashed all over the news, maybe Nicky saw it in an article somewhere."

Finn was into the files and folders now. "It seems like there's a good mix here of reporting from '85 and from 2011."

He handed me a photocopy, this one the front page of the *Valley Voice* dated two days after I found the skull. There was a photograph of Chief Angel Chavez and me. Under the image was a headline that read "Missing No More—McKenzie Boys Found in Local Woods."

I scanned the first paragraph.

*In a stunning discovery early this week, the remains of Tommy and Andrew McKenzie were found in shallow graves in the woods a few miles off Highway 50 by backcountry skiers Gemma Monroe and Brody Sutherland. Monroe, an officer with the Cedar Valley Police Department, declined to comment for this article, but Chief Chavez issued a statement, calling the discovery "an opportunity for closure for the families, and for the town." The disappearance of the two children in 1985 will be reopened as a murder investigation. In town, a new title has already been bestowed upon the case: The Woodsman Murders.*

I stopped reading. The byline was Missy Matherson; at the time, she had been a bit reporter for the *Voice* and had not yet climbed the ranks to television anchor. Even then, she'd irritated the hell out of me and had been the main reason I'd declined to comment.

That, and what would I have said?

That already I felt finding the bodies had altered the course of my life?

That when I closed my eyes, I saw Andrew's skull grin at me, his eye sockets wan and empty, his teeth even and white?

The dreams hadn't yet started but they were sure as hell on their way.

Finn muttered, "Shit, these shouldn't be here."

He held up a stack of manila file folders, each stuffed with loose-leaf sheets of paper. He angled the cover of the folder on top and I saw the distinct blue-and-green stamp of the police department emblem.

"You're kidding me," I said. "Ours?"

He nodded. They were classified reports. How long they'd been down here, tucked among these public records, was anyone's guess.

"What are the dates?"

Flipping the first few folders opened, Finn scanned the contents. "From 1985. They're from the original missing persons investigation."

"Well, at least it won't be our butts that will be in the hot seat," I said.

If case files from 2011 had been down here, free for any person off the street to find, there would have been hell. But most of the cops from '85 were retired, dead, or had moved away.

"Uh-oh," Finn said quietly.

He stopped reading the folder in his hands and put it on the bottom of the stack.

"What?"

He shook his head. "It's nothing. I just remembered, I had an appointment this afternoon."

"You're many things, Finn, but a good liar you aren't," I said. "Give me the damn thing."

"I really don't want to," he said, but he handed it to me anyway.

A sticker affixed inside the folder read *September 18, 1985.*

*Interview 245-A, Officers Dannon and Cleegmont. Subject Daniel David Moriarty. 4:15pm. Moriarty residence, 1763 Lantern Lane, Cedar Valley.*

"Our Moriarty?"

Finn nodded reluctantly. "Danny was his son. He died a few years ago in a bar fight; he was stabbed to death. From what I've heard, the kid was always sort of a bad seed. In 1985, Danny would have been what? Sixteen? C'mon Gemma, the cops back then interviewed every male between the ages of thirteen and sixty-five. It doesn't mean a thing."

"That's bull, Finn, and you know it. Moriarty's a cop, a cop who happened to be a lead on the investigation into Nicky's accident. And now come to find out his son was a suspect in the very murders Nicky was obsessed with? I don't believe in coincidences."

"*Subject*, Gemma. Not suspect," he said, and leaned back with a sigh. "Well, go on, read it. Let's see what it says. I know you're not going to let this go until you do."

They were only a few sheets of paper in the folder. On the first page, a tiny notation referenced a recording, and I assumed the transcript was word for word. With a deep breath, I began to read.

> **Moriarty, Daniel:** Do I need a lawyer?
>
> **Dannon, Officer:** You have the right to an attorney if we take you downtown. Right now, this is just a friendly conversation, son. Your dad does this sort of thing all the time with folks.
>
> **Moriarty, Louis:** He's right, Danny. Just answer the officers' questions.
>
> **Cleegmont, Officer:** Please, son, have a seat. As Officer Dannon said, this is just a nice friendly little conversation. We're visiting everyone in town. Heck, we talked to your neighbors just a few minutes ago.
>
> **Moriarty, L:** That's right. And I talked to a bunch of your friends, and their parents, last week.

**Moriarty, D:** Okay, Pop, I get it. What do you guys want to know?

**Dannon:** Okay, Danny. Says here you're a junior at the high school? Is that right? On the football team?

**Moriarty, D:** Yes, sir, a junior. No, sir, baseball's my game, sir.

**Dannon:** Baseball? Now that's a real American sport, isn't it? You pitch?

**Moriarty, D:** Yes, sir.

**Cleegmont:** You know, I played a little ball in my day. I can see by your arms you've probably got a real nice throw, son.

**Moriarty, D:** I do okay.

**Dannon:** You lift?

**Moriarty, D:** Coach has us do weights in the afternoons in the gymnasium, sir.

**Cleegmont:** Would you call yourself a strong young man, then?

**Moriarty, D:** I suppose so. Strong enough.

**Dannon:** Now, I heard from one of the families down the road that you and Tommy had a beef awhile back. Can you tell us about that?

**Moriarty, Elsa:** Oh, that old nonsense? That boy was bothering Danny, following him around. He got in the way all the time. He wanted to be just like Danny.

**Dannon:** Now, what do you mean, he got in the way?

**Moriarty, Elsa:** Well, he—

**Moriarty, D:** Ma, let me handle this. It was nothing. We just had a scuffle last spring. It wasn't a big deal.

**Cleegmont:** Was this before or after you stole lunch money from Andrew McKenzie on the bus?

**Moriarty, D:** Someone has been lying to you guys. Andrew's poor as dirt. I never stole anything from that kid.

**Dannon:** You think this is funny? He's eleven. His birthday was two days before he disappeared. And I have more than one person who can testify you were giving him a hard time a few months back.

**Moriarty, L:** Okay, fellows, I think you made your point. Danny's a good boy and he sure didn't have anything to do with the missing boys. I think this interview is about done.

**Dannon:** Lou, you know better than anyone that we've got to talk to everyone. We got two kids missing, and according to our records, your son has, at various points within the last year, had "issues" with each of them. We also know your son's got a file an inch thick at the school. Now, we can go about this the easy way or the hard way. What's it going to be?

"Is that it?" Finn asked.

I nodded. "The page ends there. Seems like there should be more to the report, but . . ."

"Wow. I mean, wow. Moriarty. What do you want to do?"

What I wanted to do was to sink my teeth into a big steaming slice of cheese pizza with olives and mushrooms, and forget I'd ever opened the folder.

I shrugged. "Let's keep this between us for now. Like you said, they would have interviewed everyone. There weren't that many kids in town; they were all bound to know one another, at least peripherally. But, it does make me wonder. A father's loyalty to his son is something to consider, especially if the kid had a reputation. The cops would have been all over that."

Finn said, "What are you saying, Gemma? That Danny Moriarty was the Woodsman? And his dad covered up the crime? No way. No, I know the guy too well. Lou Moriarty didn't cover up the murder of two boys and then spend the next thirty years in the same damn town, all the while knowing the bodies were rotting a few miles away."

He stood and pulled at his hair, something I had never seen

him do before. He paced the aisle to our right, stopping at the edge of the dark void and then coming back. "And then what? Sixteen-year-old Nicky discovers this and Moriarty kills him, too? That is complete and utter bullshit."

I thought a moment, recalling Finn's words. "You said it yourself. Moriarty was insistent on searching Nicky's room. What if Nicky *had* approached him, and threatened to expose him, or his son? Maybe Moriarty was looking for something Nicky had, some piece of evidence or proof?"

"Like what?"

"I don't know. *Something.* When you searched the room, did you have a pack with you, something to collect evidence?"

Finn nodded. "Yes, but I carried it. Moriarty couldn't have taken anything without me seeing. I remember that day, we met at the Bellingtons'—their old place— and we looked like the freaking Bobbsey twins, both of us in khakis and maroon polo shirts. Moriarty didn't have anything else with him, no briefcase, no bag, no nothing."

"But if it was something small . . . something he could have slipped in his pocket?"

Finn stopped pacing and stared at me and then started pacing again. "What the hell. Sure, I suppose."

I thought about Louis Moriarty. In 1985, he would have been in his mid-forties, smack dab in the middle of a distinguished career with the Cedar Valley Police Department. From the police transcript, it sounded as though he was still married at that point, living with a teenage son with a history of getting into trouble with the other kids.

Lou was big and strong; I had to imagine his son Danny had been as well. How much easier for a kid, known from the neighborhood, to get close to the two young boys than it would have been for a stranger? Maybe there was something there.

I thought about something else, too. Lou was one of the men that used to play poker with my step-grandfather, Bull Weston, and Frank Bellington and a couple of other guys from town. Thirty years ago, they were all accomplished, middle-age men, running the town in various ways: lawyers, cops, businessmen, and politicians.

And then, about twenty years ago, there was a falling out. The group disbanded, the men went their separate ways. What could have been at the root of something like that?

The lights above us buzzed off for a second and came back on and then flickered again and then went completely out. I stood and waved my arms, hoping to trigger a sensor but nothing happened. The space was dark, so dark that when I lifted a hand in front of my eyes, I couldn't see it. I couldn't even make out the green glow of the emergency exit sign.

Maybe the entire building had experienced a power outage.

"Gemma?"

"I'm here, by the desk. Just stay where you are, I'll see if I can find a switch," I said. I groped blindly with my arms outstretched in front of me low, to protect my belly. I felt the edge of the table and ran my hands up the sides of the study carrel and then up and on to the wall.

Left or right?

Tilly had mentioned a copy machine around the corner and I headed that way, keeping a hand on the wall like a tether.

"Gemma? I'm going to come back to the desk," Finn called. He sounded far away, much farther than if he had indeed stayed where he was when the lights went out.

Maybe it was a trick of the dark, causing our voices to ricochet and bounce around in space. My hand ran along the smooth flat surface of the wall until it hit an edge. I reached around and decided it was a corner and rounded it, careful to keep my other hand stretched out to fend off any tables or chairs.

I hit the copy machine with my foot and stopped and felt along the wall, but there was no button or switch . . . just more of the same smoothness that seemed to stretch on into infinity. With no idea what lay before me, and getting farther and farther from my partner, I was hesitant to keep going.

"Finn?"

I listened and heard nothing but the ticking from my Timex, and a low shifting noise as though the building itself was settling in for the day.

"Finn? Are you there?"

The darkness had a weight all its own, and the silence around me grew. It pressed against me and I took a deep breath and slowly exhaled, willing my nerves to settle.

A few feet away, a soft scuffling noise, like a sneaker catching on carpet, caused my heart to hiccup.

"Hello?" I called softly. "Tilly? Finn?"

Another scuffle and I backed up against the wall next to the copy machine. For the second time in one week, the feeling of being watched by someone unseen slipped over me and settled in my bowels like a shard of ice.

I held my breath and listened and almost screamed when I heard the low, steady inhalation and exhalation of someone else breathing. My heart felt like it was going to crawl up out of my throat and my hand went automatically to my belt, where I found . . . nothing.

I was in the summer dress I'd worn to the circus. My Glock was locked in the gun safe in the trunk of my car.

"Who's there?" I called. "I can hear you breathing, damn it."

A low laugh, followed by, "Yes, I'm here."

The voice was too low to tell the age or sex of the speaker but there was a familiar quality to it, one that I couldn't quite put my finger on. The words were enough to make me slide down the wall and land on my rear end. I wrapped my arms around my knees and shrank into myself and closed my eyes and tried not to breathe.

I heard another soft scuffle, this time closer.

The stranger was approaching me, one slow step at a time. He, or she, was just on the other side of the copy machine now.

"Gemma," the voice whispered in a singsong voice. "Where are you?"

A low electrical hum began and the copy machine gave a shake and lit up with red and green buttons. In a far corner of the cavernous space, lights began flickering on. Then running footsteps and a door slamming and as the lights came on in my corner, dazzling and blinding, I stood and jogged down the corridor in the direction of the noise.

"Gemma?" Finn called.

"Down here!" I said. "Hurry."

I reached the end of the corridor and saw a door to my right and one to my left.

Damn.

Which door, which door . . . I ran to the door on the right and pushed against it and then looked down and saw a rusty padlock gripped by an equally rusty chain.

Finn met me on my way to the door on the left. "What is it?"

"There's someone else down here," I panted. I hadn't run this much in months.

Next to me, Finn bent down and removed a small snub-nosed revolver from an ankle strap.

"Nice," I said as I pushed open the door.

"Like my American Express and condoms, I don't leave home without it," he replied.

Above us, a dark staircase loomed and I hurried up it as fast as I could, Finn behind me. We reached the top and I pushed open another door and we emerged into bright afternoon sun at the back of the library in an old parking lot.

It was empty, save for the tangled weeds and trash that lay in the cracks and holes of the cement. A tall chain-link fence lined the perimeter of the parking lot and I sighed as I saw a dozen different holes cut into the wire.

We spun around but there was no one in sight. From the looks of it, no one had been there for months.

# Chapter Twenty-nine

"So it wasn't you?" I asked Finn. We were back in the basement, picking through the materials to decide what to take home and what to leave for another day.

"How could it be? I was clear on the other side, trying to find a light switch."

"But you didn't answer when I called."

He sighed and looked at me. Rubbing at the five o'clock shadow on his chin, he replied slowly, "Because, as I just said, I was on the other side of the room. I didn't hear you."

I put a few folders in my shoulder bag and looked around.

"Anyway, are you certain someone else was down here? You know, it was pitch-black. Our minds can play, ah, tricks on us sometimes," Finn said. He held the folder with the Danny Moriarty transcript and I watched him flip through it, alarm bells going off in my head.

I looked back at the desk. A mountain of stuff, piles of it, and in the first few minutes of searching, we found a decades-old confidential police report pointing a big fat finger at one of our colleagues.

Scratch that, *we* hadn't found anything.

Finn had found the folder.

Finn.

How many times had I watched as the two of them, Finn and Lou, left work together, headed to one of the taverns on the south side, their heads together, their laughter comfortable, familiar? Too many times to count.

I tried to keep my voice casual. "Finn, how well do you know Moriarty?"

He shrugged and tucked the folder into his briefcase. "Well enough, I guess. We've shared a few beers, you know, the usual. I mean really, Gemma . . . how well do any of us know one another?"

We drove back to the station in silence, each lost in our own thoughts. I dropped him off and wondered, again, how it was that I ended up driving everyone around so much. You'd think some-one would give the pregnant lady a break here.

My stomach growled and the next thing I knew I was parking in front of Chevy's Pizzeria and Arcade. I squeezed through a group of teenagers and entered a world of pinball machines and arcade games, comforting lights and sounds and laughter. The smell of mozzarella and garlic and roasted tomatoes hit me hard and I made my way to the back of the restaurant and found an empty booth near the restrooms.

I sank into the leather seat. And then I looked up and saw Darren Chase emerging from the men's room, his ball cap angled low over his eyes, but not low enough to miss seeing me.

"Hi," he said.

"Hi."

He slid into the booth before I could stop him. "Are you here alone?"

I nodded. Out of habit, I'd taken my cell phone out of my purse and laid it on the table. I started playing with it, turning it over in my hands. "You?"

He leaned back and took off his ball cap and ran a hand through his dark hair and nodded. "Yup."

A waiter stopped by and set two menus down, then gave Dar-ren an exaggerated gasp. The young man's laminated name tag read "Fitch," and he had decorated it with more glitter and sparkle than I'd seen since my high school homecoming dance.

Fitch eyed Darren the same way I eyed the pepperoni pie the waiter carried against his hip.

"You can't still be hungry, sir. You had the Double Triple Threat," Fitch said.

Darren laughed. "No, I'm full. I'm just keeping the lady company."

Fitch drew a hand across his brow. "Phew. I was about to get the boys on the phone and tell them we had a tiger loose at Chevy's."

The waiter gave out a tiny roar and winked at Darren and then turned to me. "Uh-oh, what's this? Eating for two, are we? What can I bring you, babe?"

"Oh, I'm not staying. I'd like a large cheese with mushrooms and black olives to go? I . . . I just needed to sit down," I said. Fitch looked at my belly and nodded, then eyeballed Darren again and spun around and left.

When had I decided to make it a to-go order?

When Darren Chase had sat down. All six feet three inches, two hundred lean pounds of him.

"I'll wait with you till your order comes," Darren said. He smiled and I couldn't help smiling back.

"So . . ."

Why couldn't I stop playing with my phone? My hands were spinning it around on the table like it was a roulette wheel. And was I sweating? Jesus. This was worse than a middle school dance.

"So . . . hey, thanks for the tip about the library. Tilly is, uh, great. She's very helpful," I said. I looked around the arcade in hopes of spotting someone, anyone, I knew, but all I saw was a sea of Abercrombie hoodies, low-rise jeans, and trucker hats, inexplicably on the heads of teenage girls.

I wasn't yet thirty and trends were passing me by like messengers on bicycles, fast and furious.

Darren said, "Gemma."

I looked at him and he leaned forward and placed a hand over mine, stilling the spinning phone. "I'm not going to bite. I can leave if you want me to."

I jerked my hand back and put it in my lap.

And then felt like an asshole.

I said, "No, that's okay. I'm . . . it's been . . . there was someone in my house last night."

Tears rolled down my cheeks and I bit my lip. "Damn it, I'm fine. It's just shaken me up a bit."

Darren grabbed a handful of napkins from the silver dispenser at the end of the table and handed them to me. I dabbed at my face. Fitch dropped off a pitcher of water and two glasses and I waited for him to leave before speaking.

I was beyond embarrassed and surprised that I had lost it like that.

"I'm sorry, I'm normally a little more composed. It's been a rough week."

Darren nodded. "There's no need to apologize. Is there anything I can do?"

"Not really," I said. "Unless you can catch Nick Bellington's killer, solve a thirty-year-old murder mystery, and deliver a baby in, oh, about three months. Preferably vaginally, so she doesn't miss out on the whole birth canal experience. Apparently that's very important, and if I have to have a C-section, she could end up going to state school, dropping out halfway through, and doing nails at the Nail Express on Highway Nine."

"My mom does nails, on South Street. You might have seen her shop—Speedy Salon?"

Oh, shit. I felt my cheeks grow hot.

He grinned. "You should see your face. I'm kidding. Although I went to state school and I ended up fine."

I blew out my breath. "Jokes are going over my head these days, Darren. I never cared about stuff like this before, but now I have crazy aspirations for the Peanut, like she's going to go to Harvard and then medical school and then be the first female astronaut on Mars. I guess it's true, kids will break your heart before they're even born."

"The Peanut?"

I nodded. "That's what we . . . um, Brody and I, that's what we call her."

"And Brody is?"

Baby daddy didn't sound exactly right. "He's my partner . . . my boyfriend?"

Darren started to say something but Fitch arrived with a cardboard box, steam escaping from the side, and a bill. I looked at the box and knew I'd never make it home without tearing into it.

"Would it be all right if I actually ate some of it here?"

I signed the bill and left an extra large tip and when Fitch saw it, he gave an exaggerated sigh and said, "Well, I guess that would be okay. Thanks, doll!"

I opened the box and inhaled the heady air. Darren watched with amusement as I ate two pieces slowly, in silence.

"So, you and Brody, not married?" he asked. He reached over and took a slice of my pizza and folding it in half, took a bite. He took a second bite, and with the third, the slice was gone.

"No, we haven't done that deed yet. We're . . . well, to be honest, I'm still working out some issues. And don't ever touch a pregnant woman's pizza, if you value your life."

He ignored me and reached for a second slice. "I thought all you young fillies ever dreamed of was the big white dress and the fancy affair."

"That's a pretty broad stereotype, don't you think?"

He shrugged. "So, what's the hold up? He's got cold feet? Thinks he can do better?"

"You don't know anything about me or my relationship. Brody very much wants to get married. I'm the one with cold feet. Haven't you ever been spooked before? Jesus, where does it all go?"

I happened to know that Chevy's Double Triple Threat was a stuffed double-crusted, two-layer pie the size of a tractor tire. I couldn't believe he'd eaten a whole one and was now starting in on a second slice of my pizza.

He looked at me and blinked. "Where does all what go?"

"The food you eat."

"Fast metabolism, I guess," he said with a shrug, and finished off the slice. A glob of tomato sauce stuck to the corner of his mouth and without thinking, I leaned forward and wiped it off with my finger.

Without breaking eye contact, he took my hand and for a moment, I thought he was going to lick the sauce right off my finger.

Instead, he wiped it with a napkin and then released my hand and I pulled back.

What the hell was going on? I'd been with Brody almost five years. We were expecting a child together. I wasn't the sort of woman who even entertained the thoughts that were now flying across my mind like rolls of thunder and lightning, booming and sparking every which way.

I blamed it all on Celeste Takashima. I wasn't about to cheat on Brody but if I did, he could hardly point a finger. He set the standard long before I ever lay eyes on Darren Chase.

I said, "I should get going. I need to rest before . . . tomorrow."

"Nicky's funeral? I'm planning on going as well," Darren said. He stood and watched me gather my purse and the pizza and then push myself up out of the booth. "I'll see you there, I guess."

"Uh-huh," I said. "Sure."

Then we stood there, in a Technicolor sea of hoodies and low-rise jeans, staring at each other, until finally I broke eye contact and turned and walked out of Chevy's Pizzeria and Arcade.

And found all four tires on my car slashed.

# Chapter Thirty

We drove up the canyon in silence. It was too late to get a tow, so I left my car at Chevy's and reluctantly, but with little choice, accepted Darren's offer of a ride. The inside of his Subaru was as beat as the outside, with a missing dashboard panel, broken cup holder, and seat covers that were heavy with fraying, fringy threads.

I ran my hand under my thigh and over a small tear in the cloth, poking my finger against the seat's squishy interior foam cushion.

"You ever think about fixing this up?"

I was in a dark mood. The slashes on my tires were deep and I knew I would have to replace all four. Not only had someone been in my house, and scared me in the dark of the library, now they were messing with my ride. I knew it would be an expensive repair.

Darren glanced at me. "She runs fine, Gemma. I know she's not much to look at, but the engine's strong. I can't really afford a new car right now. Sometimes it's more important what's on the inside than the outside."

How this guy kept making me feel like a jerk, I didn't know.

"I'm sorry. Thanks again for the ride, I appreciate it."

He turned on the radio and found an oldies station. The up-beat music of the Temptations filled the car, and I found myself humming along.

"Do you need a lift to the funeral tomorrow?"

I shook my head. "No, thank you. I'll call Mac Neal—do you know him? He's got an auto shop on Fifth?"

Darren nodded slowly. "I think I do, that little gray building? Set back from the road?"

"That's the one. He's great," I said. "Oh, up here on the right."

Darren pulled the car into the driveway. In front of us, the house was dark and quiet. He put the car in park but left the engine running.

"I think I should go in with you."

He must have seen the look on my face because he rolled his eyes. "Gemma, your tires were slashed. Someone's been on your property, in your house. Your boyfriend is in Alaska. I don't think you should go in there alone. This has nothing to do with me wanting to get you in bed."

My cheeks flushed. He wanted to get me in bed?

"I do have this," I said, and opened my handbag and flashed him my gun. Before we left the parking lot at Chevy's, I had grabbed it from the trunk of my car.

Darren looked doubtful. "I don't know. I'd feel terrible if something happened to you while I sat out here like an idiot."

"How about I go in, and look around real quick, and I'll come back and wave at you if everything looks okay?"

I gathered up my things and was out of the car before he could protest. The thought of Darren in my house, this late at night, was somehow more terrifying than the thought of a killer inside waiting. Besides, I was a cop. I was more prepared to take on an intruder than a high school basketball coach ever was.

I strode to the front porch, deliberately not looking back at the Subaru, and fished my keys out of my bag. The cool, heavy weight of them in my hand brought a sense of normalcy to the situation, and I stuck the silver house key, with its purple fob, into the lock and pushed the door open.

As I'd expected, the house was quiet.

I felt, and sensed more than anything, that there was no one, except for Seamus. He looked at me with heavy eyes from his spot by the kitchen door. He stood and passed gas and then waddled over to the back door and sat and waited. I went room to room and turned on a few lights but kept most off; I didn't like the sense that Darren was out there, watching me walk through my house.

Finally, I went to the front door and waved. He honked twice and backed out of the driveway. I closed the door and slid the wooden chair we keep in the foyer across the tile and angled the back of it up and under the doorknob. It wasn't much but it would make a racket if anyone tried to get in.

I let Seamus out, watched him do his business, and called him back. I did the same chair trick with the back door, and the door to the garage. The sliding glass doors on the side of the house had Charlie bars that we rarely used, but I engaged them, dropping the bars from their vertical position to horizontal.

Then I went upstairs and pulled off my dress and fell into bed without bothering to brush my teeth. The next thing I knew, the heat of the morning sun was warming my cheek. I cracked an eye open and groaned when I saw the alarm clock.

It was ten in the morning.

Saturday. Nicky's funeral, his second funeral in three years.

My mouth was dry and tasted of garlic and tomato. I pushed myself up and staggered into the shower and let the hot water shake me from the grogginess that seemed to permeate my brain.

Out of the shower, naked and dripping wet, I stood in front of my closet and cursed. The day would be hot but the church would be cool. Wool was out, as were my printed summer dresses, my dark slacks, and my uniform. Jeans were inappropriate, as was my black cocktail dress, my navy long-sleeved pants suit, and every other damn thing.

I finally settled on a knee-length black skirt, a cream-colored silk blouse, and a printed yellow scarf. I looked like a banker but the clothes fit around my belly and breasts and I wouldn't be too hot or too cool.

Mac Neal picked me up in his Goblin. The Goblin was a Ford F-150, with a lacquer cherry finish as sleek as freshly painted nails, and cattle horns on the front, and a Right to Life sticker on the back. He helped me up into the cab of the truck and we drove to

Wellshire Presbyterian, humming along with Garth Brooks and Kenny Chesney.

Mac dropped me in front, where Sam Birdshead and Finn Nowlin and Chief Chavez were gathered, all solemn in dark suits and sunglasses.

"Thanks, Mac, I owe you a million," I said, and gave him my keys.

He nodded, his long salt-and-pepper beard shaking with the motion, his thick mustache obscuring his mouth. "I'll leave the car at the police station, all right, kiddo? Keys under the back tire well?"

"Great. Leave me the bill—like I said, I owe you big time."

He drove off, leaving a small puff of black smoke in his wake like a calling card.

"Nice ride, Gemma. Brody know you're tooling around with that old fart?" Finn asked.

I ignored him and instead greeted Sam and Chief Chavez. We headed inside, one by one, into a church that was already full. Most of the crowd seemed to be Cedar Valley's elite, the families who owned the ski resorts and the city council members. I recognized a few other politicians, like Senator Morrow, and Congresswoman Peters.

A couple of children played in the aisle, dodging out of their mother's grasping hands, ignoring her whispered threats to get back to their seats.

"Don't you think that's weird, bringing kids to a funeral?" Finn said in my ear.

I shrugged. How the hell did I know what was weird these days? I'd spent the last few hours fantasizing about a basketball coach with a Louisiana accent who wanted to get me in bed, in spite of my belly and my not-so-single status.

"I think it's smart. They've got to get used to all of life's curve-balls, the good and the bad," Sam Birdshead said. He edged into one of the pews and Finn and I scooted in next to him.

"On the reservation, death is celebrated the same as weddings and births," Sam continued. "I saw my first dead body when I was four years old. There isn't anything to fear. The mother's wise to bring them here."

I realized I didn't know much about Sam's upbringing. "Did you grow up on the reservation?"

Sam said, "Nah, not after my parents divorced. Mom took me back to Denver with her, to live with her parents, my grandparents. But every summer, she let me go spend a few months with my dad in Wyoming. Those were the best times of my life, those summers. By then my grandfather was out of prison. He's nothing like what you've heard."

He started to say more but the big organ, high above us in an alcove, started up and the opening notes of *Amazing Grace* floated down upon us like snowflakes.

A man in black stood at the pulpit and looked out at us, and he must have seen what I can only imagine was a sea of faces, somber suits and dresses, and a few bold hats. In front of the man, on a low stand, lay a coffin. Its deep mahogany finish shone in the white light that streamed through the high windows of the church. A single bucket of white roses with baby's breath graced the ground before it, an offering that spoke of innocence and purity and sweetness.

I hadn't seen the Bellingtons; I could only assume they were seated somewhere up front, in the first pew. Across the aisle, I caught sight of Joe Fatone, and behind him, Tessa O'Leary. She gave me a little wave and I waved back. And a few rows behind her, I saw Lisey. She sat with the same blond girl I'd seen at Tessa's trapeze show, and the two looked friendly.

In fact, from this angle, it appeared Lisey and Blondie were holding hands.

The man at the altar cleared his throat and began to speak. He was black, and I assumed he must be the Reverend Wyland that Ellen had spoken of. His voice was low and it filled the church like hot fudge poured over ice cream, melting into every nook and cranny of the place. He opened the service with Psalm 23 and I thought once again that if a more reassuring ten sentences existed, I'd never heard them.

He spoke for only a few minutes. What is there to say, really, about someone who was buried three years ago? There was no mention of Nicky's secret life as Reed Tolliver, or of the circus. It was as though the last three years hadn't existed, and I wondered if that was a conscious choice on the part of the Bellingtons, or a suggestion from Reverend Wyland.

Fifteen minutes after we'd sat down, John Lennon's "Imagine" started up and we all stood, followed the coffin as it was carried out on the shoulders of six men, and filed out of the church and made our way to the gravesite.

The cemetery was a sprawling mass of rolling hills and low-hanging trees, offering plenty of shady places to sit and contemplate life in the land of the dead. I found a deserted bench and sat, resting as I watched the mourners make their way to the grave. The Bellingtons hadn't procured a second site after all; they'd simply dug up Nicky's original grave and removed the empty coffin, to make room for the full one.

I inhaled deeply. The smell of grass recently cut hung in the air, heavy as a blanket, and in the distance, in some unseen part of the cemetery, a lawn mower roared to life. Above me, the sky was clear save for one cloud, elongated like a stretched-out athletic sock, gray on the bottom, white on the top. On the ground, by my shoe, a small snail slid across the dirt, leaving a trail of slime in its wake. Its shell was the size of a quarter and I watched as its tiny antennae quivered in the air. The snail was a specimen millions of years in the making, its sole protection a thin casing no thicker than my fingernail.

A miracle, in and of itself, and I watched it make its way slowly toward the shade of the bench, each millimeter a triumph of perseverance.

"Want some company?" a voice chirped behind me. I turned around and nodded at the young woman.

"Sure."

Tessa sat next to me, rearranging her long crimson skirt so it hung straight. She wore a short-sleeved cardigan open over a black top, and a thick gold chain that hung down and came to rest just past her breasts.

Out of the corner of my eye, I studied her. I saw no traces of the angry woman who'd been at the police station, or of the hyper-friendly woman who'd visited me at home, or even of the active acrobat I'd watched yesterday.

Instead, she seemed small and sad and lonely. She played with the pendant on the chain, a gold coin that flashed in the sunlight as she twisted it with her right hand.

I was starting to think maybe she had multiple personalities, and then I remembered being in my early twenties, and the angst, and the awful feeling of not knowing your place in the world, and I decided she was probably absolutely normal.

She'd also just attended her boyfriend's funeral. There was no acknowledgment of Tessa from the reverend or the Bellingtons, and I wondered if they even knew Nicky had spent the last few months of his life with a pretty and talented young woman who loved him.

"That's lovely, your necklace," I offered.

She lifted it and looked at it, then let it drop back to her chest.

"I suppose. My parents gave it to me on my sixteenth birthday. They gave it to me, and I gave them court documents to sign to emancipate me."

"Was it really that bad?"

She shrugged. "What's bad? We had food to eat, and clothes on our back, and no one hit me. They put every spare nickel they could into my gym training, and then my bar training. I was their princess. But I knew I was only going to go so far on their dime, in little old Keylock, Idaho.

"Once they signed off on the papers, I couldn't get out of that trailer fast enough. Without their financial support, I was free to get all sorts of training fees waived, and scholarships, too. And then Papa Joe came along, and well, you know the rest," she continued.

"Now I do everything I can to make sure I'll never live in poverty again. Hence, all the classes I'm taking, the finance and accounting stuff. I feel like if I can understand how money works, how it really works in the real world, I'll be that much more ahead of the game."

I nodded and looked back at the gravesite.

I saw Terence and Ellen Bellington take up places next to the raised coffin. They stood on either side of Annika; all three dressed in black. In front of them, Frank Bellington sat in his wheelchair. Across from the Bellingtons, Darren Chase took a place next to Paul Winters, the founder of the Forward Foundation, the group that had been camping together when Nicky had gone over Bride's Veil.

The men hugged, and then Darren patted Paul on the back.

I hadn't realized they were friends.

Whenever I saw Paul Winters I thought of that actor, the one that played George Costanza on *Seinfeld,* whose real name I could never recall. Paul was short, rotund, and wore wire-rimmed glasses. He was balding on the top of his head—round as a cue ball and rapidly getting sunburnt—but wore the rest of his dark hair in a tidy ponytail that reached his collar.

I watched as Paul leaned toward Darren and spoke into his ear. Darren murmured something in response and then clapped Paul on the back again. The older man had eschewed a suit; instead, he wore dark slacks and a gray short-sleeved dress shirt with a red bolo tie. When he lifted his hand to push his slipping glasses back up the bridge of his nose, his massive watch caught the sunlight and reflected it like a solar panel. The thing was the size of a cell phone and I'd have bet serious money it was fully loaded with every accoutrement you could hope to get into a watch.

I didn't know much about Paul.

He made a bucket of cash in the dot-com boom and was lucky enough to pull out before Silicon Valley went bust. He tooled around South America for a few years, starting up but never completing schools for orphans, and somehow found his way to Cedar Valley.

He'd been here less than a year before opening the Forward Foundation.

Tessa interrupted my thoughts. "Gemma, what do you hope for, most of all, in the whole world?"

She'd resumed playing with her pendant, and her fingers slid the pendant up and down the gold chain, back and forth. I started to answer and then stopped, really considering her question.

What did I hope for, most of all, in the whole world?

"Well, I think hope is a funny thing. It's not quite want, is it? And it's not quite desire, either. I guess what I wish for, really, is probably the same as most people. I want my life to count for something good."

Tessa watched the crowd at the gravesite. "I get terrible insomnia sometimes. I lie in bed and all these thoughts spin around in my head, so fast, and I can't sleep. I lie there and think and think and think. I just want to be somewhere I can stop thinking. Stop worrying about my routine, my future, having to move back to Keylock, living with my parents in their two-bedroom trailer, failing."

How do you tell a twenty-two-year-old that the worries only get worse?

You don't, unless you are the cruelest kind of person.

"Tessa, you seem to have a good head on your shoulders. I think you'll do fine," I said. "But, there's something I want to ask you, and I have a feeling you're not going to like it. But I'd like the truth, here, right now, just the two of us, woman to woman, okay?"

She looked up at me.

"I heard that Lisey moved out of the cabin. What's going on with you two? I hear one thing from you, and something else from her," I said.

I paused and then added, "To be honest, I'm not quite sure who to believe."

Tessa's face flushed and she stood up. "What did she say about me? Did she tell you I was a liar? That I'm psycho? She is such a bitch."

I stood, too, and sighed, and stretched to the side. I couldn't find a comfortable position anymore. Sitting, standing, walking, laying down, it all hurt these days.

"I'm just asking what happened. Did you two have a fight? When girls fight, especially girls as close as you two, sometimes nasty things get said."

A winch started up at the gravesite and I glanced over as the coffin was slowly lowered into the ground. The crowd began to disperse, but the Bellingtons, and Darren and Paul, and a few others remained.

"We did have a fight, a really bad one. There's this girl, Stacey, that Lisey . . . likes. Not like she loved me, but she just likes her and I don't know why, I think she's messed up and fake and gross. And I told Lisey that, and Lisey started screaming at me, that I was psychotic and couldn't be trusted and—" She trailed off and her face went red again.

"That's her, over there. Look, see that blond whore? That's Stacey."

I looked in the direction Tessa was pointing and saw Lisey with Blondie. Their backs were to us, and we watched in silence as they each threw a rose onto Nicky's coffin. They held hands as they followed the rest of the crowd back to the church, and then Lisey threw her free hand, her left one, up and over her head and tossed a middle finger in our general direction.

"Whore," Tessa uttered under her breath. "I'm out of here."

She took a step and I closed my eyes at the small crunch that followed her heel coming down. She stomped off and I considered how easily death falls on those who are too small, in size or character, to offer resistance.

I'm not an overly sentimental person, but I knelt and covered the crushed shell and sticky remains of the tiny snail with a single, perfect leaf before I made my way to the gravesite.

Roses filled the space around the mahogany coffin, whites and pinks and yellows and a few lilacs. Spring colors in the middle of summer. They had changed the headstone to reflect Nicky's actual day of death, last Monday. Like the other headstones in the family plot, it was creamy marble run through with rivulets of black and gray. The plot next to his was his grandmother's, Terence's mother. Her headstone read Rachel Louisa Wozniak Bellington, beloved mother and wife, followed by the dates of her birth and death, and a single flower. I did the math; she was sixty-five when she died.

I touched Nicky's headstone and whispered a vow. No one was there to hear my words, except for the grass, and the wind, and the sun, and that was fitting, somehow. Bull used to say that ethics are determined by what you do when no one is watching, and I thought that was about right.

I repeated my vow and left the cemetery, tired of all the death around me.

# Chapter Thirty-one

We agreed to gather at O'Toole's, a pub on Fifth Street just a few doors down from Mac Neal's auto shop. Sam Birdshead drove us over in his smoke-gray-colored Audi.

I sat in the front seat and caressed the soft leather under me. "This is a nice ride, Sam."

He grinned. "It was a graduation present from my grandfather. My sisters call me the Little Prince; I seem to get the brunt of his generosity. Youngest child, only boy, you know how it goes."

I didn't, but nodded anyway.

In the backseat, the chief yanked off his tie. "Christ, I'm glad that's over. It was not as bad as the first time, but God-awful in its own way. Listen, Gemma, how's it going with Finn? You guys working out together okay?"

"Sure. When he's not hitting on young women or making fun of the Bird Lady. Or calling me fat."

"Bird Lady?" Sam said. "Who's the Bird Lady?"

He took the next corner a tad fast and I gripped the door handle but the Audi's tires took it like a demon. In the backseat, Chavez cursed and strapped on his seat belt.

I said, "You know the Bird Lady, that woman who stalks around town, with the orange hair and the dead parrot on her shoulder. That's Tilly, the librarian."

Chavez said, "Matilda Jane Krinkle."

"You know her?"

"Of course I know her, I'm the goddamn chief of police. Sam, slow it down a bit."

"Yes, sir," Sam said as he downshifted, and the Audi purred in response. Ahead of us, Finn's Porsche pulled into a spot by the front door. Behind us, Ravi Hussen's Honda kept a conservative distance. We had run into her at the reception and invited her to join us at the tavern. Actually, I'd invited her while Finn and Sam had stared and drooled. Only Ravi could get away with short sapphire-blue silk at a funeral.

O'Toole's was mostly empty. The bar was cool and dark and felt apropos after the solemnity of Nicky's service. A couple of old men sat at the bar, the cool condensation on their beer long since wiped away by the warmth of their hands. They gave Ravi the once-over, completely ignored me, and then returned their focus to each other, and their Coors, and the bowl of peanuts that sat between them.

Their conversation, like their hair, was sparse and thin; they seemed to grunt more than carry on actual sentences.

We took a table in the back, near the dartboard. Sam grabbed our orders and headed to the bar. I sat down next to Ravi, across from Chavez and Finn, whose cell phone buzzed against the grain of the table. He glanced at it.

"Moriarty's on his way."

I pulled off my scarf and draped it on the chair then undid the top button on my blouse and fanned myself with an old copy of the local newspaper that I'd grabbed on the way in. I was still warm from the ride over.

"Why's Moriarty coming?"

Finn gave me a look. "Because he's one of us, and this is our place. No one wants to be alone today."

I pushed back. "Was he at the funeral? I didn't see him."

"Gemma, just because you don't see something, doesn't mean it didn't happen. He was there, he snuck in late and left early," Finn said. "You're not this all-seeing, all-powerful being."

"I know I'm not. I never claimed to be," I said.

I turned to Ravi. "Do I act like that? Like I know everything?"

She looked from Finn to me and then back again to Finn and exhaled noisily. "Honey, this is one cat fight I'm sitting out. Honestly, you two should screw or call it a day."

I think both of us turned pale at that. Finn may have gagged a bit.

Sam returned with a waitress, drinks, and promises of potato skins, nachos, and hot wings. The waitress set bottles of beer in front of Finn and Chavez, and a martini before Ravi, and a cranberry juice seltzer next to my hand.

A glass of merlot remained on her tray, and this she set down in front of Sam Birdshead. He looked at it and with a deep breath, picked it up and took a sip. We watched as he swallowed with a wince and then gently set the glass back down.

"Didn't take you for a wine guy, Sam," Finn said with a snicker.

Poor Sam. It was so obvious you almost felt sorry for the guy, trying to impress an older woman by requesting what he thought would be a more mature drink.

He blushed and tried not to look at Ravi. "I . . . I like wine."

I caught Ravi's eye and gave a head tilt toward Sam. She smiled gently.

"I like wine, too, Sam. You know they say that beer drinkers are fun, but wine drinkers last longer?"

The grins faded from Finn and Chavez's faces.

"I've never heard that," the chief scowled.

"Oh yes, it's very true. Wine drinkers are proven to have a longer lifespan than beer drinkers. All those antioxidants, you know," Ravi said, and sipped her martini. "What did you think I meant?"

At the front of the pub, the door opened and Moriarty came through. He looked at me and I thought I saw him grimace, but the room was dim. By the time he reached our table, he was all smiles and handshakes.

The waitress brought our food, and a beer for Moriarty, and we talked shop.

"Anything new with the reports, Ravi?" Chavez asked between a potato skin and a sip of pale ale.

"Unfortunately, no. The tests all came back negative. We don't have fibers, hairs, prints, anything," she said.

Moriarty signaled the waitress and asked for another round for everyone. "So we got jack shit."

It was going to be one of those nights, then. My mouth was open and the words out before I could help myself. "I wouldn't say we have nothing. In fact, I think someone's worried that we're getting too close."

Chavez asked, "What are you talking about?"

He double-dipped a celery stick into the small pot of ranch dressing and Finn muttered something under his breath.

"Well," I began, "well, my tires were slashed last night. At Chevy's."

"And?" Moriarty said.

"And I don't think it was the football star feeling up his girlfriend in the car next to mine."

Chavez held up a hand. "Whoa. Whoa. Just hold on a damn second. Your tires got slashed and you're only just now telling me?"

"Did you want me to tell you before, at the funeral? I'm telling you now, aren't I?"

Chavez said, "Anything else going on that I should be aware of?"

If I didn't tell him now about the message on my mirror, he'd probably find out anyway, and then be pissed I hadn't told him. I gave them an abbreviated version of Thursday night's events and ended with "So, I'll forward you the pictures, and we can start a file, but honestly, I don't think there's much else we can do. Maybe it's all a prank, someone playing a sick joke at the expense of a murder case."

Chavez slammed his hand down on the table and we all jumped. Sam was sipping from his wine and he jumped so hard he spilled the rest of it all over the front of his shirt.

Chavez said, "Goddamn it, Gemma. Why am I always the last to find out about these things? We should have had a squad car parked at your house for the last day. We could have dusted for prints."

I found a lone chip with cheese and no beans and scooped it from the platter. I ate it and waited for Chavez to calm down.

"Chief, the last thing we need is a cop sitting in my driveway twiddling his thumbs. We can't spare that kind of manpower," I said. "Besides, I hardly think the Woodsman is going around slashing tires and sneaking around houses. I'd have heard him. And I didn't hear anything. So, like I said, I think it's just some local kid fooling around. The tires and the message on my mirror probably aren't even related."

With his beer bottle halfway to his mouth, Louis Moriarty froze. "What the hell does the Woodsman have to do with the murder of Nicky Bellington?"

Shit. I hadn't meant to bring up the Woodsman yet. The rest of the crew didn't know about that angle. I glanced at Finn but he refused to meet my eyes.

So I was on my own, then. Some partner.

"Well, you might as well all know. At the time he went over Bride's Veil, Nicky had just wrapped up three or four months of intense—and I mean intense—research on the Woodsman murders. Intense as in consumed."

Silence.

Moriarty, Chavez, and Ravi stared at me.

Sam shook his head slowly and continued to wipe at his shirt.

Finn stared at the plate of slowly congealing nachos.

Finally Moriarty muttered, "Is this another part of your, uh, obsession with that case, Gemma? Because this is getting kind of old."

"This has nothing to do with me. Nicky was down in these archives at the library almost every day, digging through wads of old newspaper articles and reports. He spends more than three months down there and then all of a sudden, announces to the librarian that he's done. And a few days later, the world thinks he's dead." I stared at Moriarty. "You were there. Finn told me you had your suspicions. You thought suicide, didn't you? Why? In a perfectly normal kid with no prior history of depression, why would you think suicide?"

Chavez, Ravi, and Sam looked from me to Moriarty and back again like they were watching a Ping-Pong game. Finn stood and mumbled "men's room" and made his way to the back of the bar and ducked through a dark curtain that hung at an angle.

Moriarty pursed his lips and nodded slowly. "Yup, he was perfectly normal. Normal kids do stupid shit all the time, screwing around things they shouldn't, daring one another, showing off for the ladies. One false step, a loose rock, and bam, it's over, just like that. Except Nick wasn't *that* guy. No one remembers him messing around like that. He wasn't a risk taker. One minute they're eating Cheetos, the next he's gone over a waterfall. There wasn't anything *normal* about *that*."

Finn returned from the men's room and took his seat. A single hot wing remained on the platter in the middle of the table and he picked it up and sucked the meat from the bone with a smack.

I thought back on the reports I'd read three years ago, the transcripts of the kids, the other campers and the statements they'd given the police. But my memory was hazy. Sam had the reports in his possession, but I didn't want to alert Moriarty to that.

"Did anyone actually see him go over?"

Moriarty glanced at Finn then shook his head. "Not a single person."

"And everyone's first thought is that he'd fallen off the cliff?" I asked. "Did anyone search the woods? What if he'd waited for the perfect moment and simply snuck away?"

The chief interrupted me. "Gemma, you're forgetting two things. We found his Windbreaker the next day, five miles downstream. He'd worn it tied around his waist all weekend. One of the searchers spotted it, tangled on the banks of the river. And we found footprints in the dirt, right at the edge of the cliff. Size eight Adidas. Nicky's shoes."

Anybody could toss a Windbreaker in a river.

And anybody could leave prints.

Maybe Nicky had survived his big fall over Bride's Veil by not falling at all.

Moriarty said, "You ever stop to think this is all one big, fat coincidence? You're so busy chasing after your damn old demons you've already made up your mind on this. Leave the past alone, Gemma. There's nothing there worth kicking up."

He tilted the tip of his beer bottle in my direction and continued. "Did Finn tell you how many Stephen King books we found in Nicky's room? And the posters, Christ, with what's his face, that Manson rocker. I think the Woodsman murders were just one more dark, spooky thing that kid was into. I bet you a hundred dollars, none of this old shit has anything to do with the fact that a week ago his throat was torn open."

Moriarty polished off his beer and set the bottle on the table hard enough to rattle the empty platters of food. He stood and clapped Sam on the back of the neck and squeezed. "How 'bout a game of darts, son? I got ten bucks that says I beat you in best of three."

I leaned back and chewed the inside of my lip while I tried to make sense of the tangled webs this case was bringing to light. The others chatted and drank and let me alone with my thoughts.

Louis Moriarty had just told me to leave the past alone.

The same words my visitor had left on my bathroom mirror in a scarlet shade of lipstick that had taken ten minutes to scrub clean.

Louis Moriarty's son Danny was at one time considered a suspect in the McKenzie murders.

Louis Moriarty had been close to Frank Bellington and Bull Weston.

What it all meant, I wasn't sure.

Frank Bellington was a man taking a long, slow slide into the big sleep. Bull Weston had lied to me the other night, I was sure of it, about not remembering what made their friendship die all those years ago. Louis Moriarty was a fellow cop—a brother of my extended family.

At the moment, I didn't trust a single one of them.

Moriarty bested Sam in three rounds and then left without a good-bye. Finn announced he was walking Ravi to her car and she followed him with a roll of her eyes and a peck on my cheek. Sam looked at a loss but perked up when a trio of curvy grad students took a table near ours. A brunette with turquoise eyes caught his attention and within five minutes, he was in a game of pool with the beauty and her friends.

Chavez muttered something. He was on his fourth beer and I hoped Sam was still planning on driving both of us home. Or at least back to the station so I could pick up my car.

"What did you say?"

He groaned. "I shouldn't have said that, what I said before."

"Said what?"

"You know what. About Ellen," the chief said.

He rolled the half-full bottle back and forth in his hands. They were big hands, rough with calluses formed years ago working the land on his parents' farm in eastern Colorado.

"I'm not really in love with her. It was a long time ago."

"What happened?" I wasn't sure I wanted to know but when life hands you answers, you take them, no matter how uncomfortable the telling.

"Terry happened."

Chavez took a long sip and then belched into his fist. "We were best friends, you know, at Harvard. Roommates freshman year, co-captains of the tennis team, study buddies. And then one day this stunningly beautiful creature walked across the cafeteria and that was it, man. Ellen freaking Nystrom."

"And?"

"What do you mean 'and'? And nothing. She chose Terry. After, of course, she gave me a night to remember her by. You know I was a virgin? Twenty years old and I was a virgin. Christ," he said. The chief lifted his beer then set it back down. "Christ."

"Chief—" I began. I didn't need to hear any more.

He waved a hand in my direction. "What the hell, bygones are bygones, right? We got over it. I met Lydia the next year. And when I got recruited for this job, I honest to God never made the connection between the small dust hole Terry spoke of and the booming ski town I came to in the late nineties."

"Does Lydia know? About Ellen?"

Angel Chavez gave a deep laugh, the kind that starts in your belly and comes out somewhere at the crown of your skull. "Gemma, you don't get to be married for twenty years and not know every damn thing about your spouse. 'Course she knows. She also knows that I'd never trade what we have for even a minute for life with that Nordic devil. That woman has more angles than a geometry book. Not all bad, of course, but angles and sides you never want to see."

"What do you mean?" I asked, but Chavez was done. He shook his head and watched Sam move a few inches closer to the grad student with the turquoise eyes.

"That kid's got his whole life in front of him, doesn't he? Do you remember being that young? 'Course you do, what am I saying," he said. "Christ. What a week."

I stifled a yawn and waved at the waitress and signaled for the check.

"It was surreal when I got here, though. I'd heard so many stories from Terry, about how screwed up his family was, especially his dad, Frank," Chavez said. "His mom was a bit of a head case, too. She was born in Poland, just after the shit hit the fan. Her parents were Jews, wealthy, and they managed to get the family across the border and into Switzerland. Two years later they arrived in New York."

That explained the Polish surname I'd seen on her gravestone—Wozniak.

The chief continued. "Anyway, Terry's mom was real quiet, sneaking around the house like a mouse, always popping up right behind you when you least expected it. Like Terry's sister, Hannah, that old bag of a housekeeper. Jeez, but she was a beautiful lady, looked like Elizabeth Taylor. But to hear Terry tell it, Frank

Bellington was a real son of a bitch. Quite the racist; n word this, n word that. But I never saw it. I don't know. Maybe that sort of thing fades with age."

I couldn't agree. The worst racists I'd ever met were older folks who had years to deepen their hatred for the Jews, the blacks, the Asians, the gays. The bigotry never faded; the bigots just got better at hiding it as the rest of society evolved around them.

I tried to reconcile Chavez's words with the jokester who used to pull my pigtails and sneak me butterscotch candies, with the old man I'd seen slurping pudding from a spoon, his gaze on some distant horizon that would never get any closer.

We untangled Sam from the grad student as they were bumping iPhones. It used to be you exchanged a business card, maybe a phone number. Now you had to do cell number, e-mail, Facebook, Twitter handle, blog address, and any other number of social networking tools. How anyone found the energy to hook up after all that, I didn't know.

At Sam's car, we did an awkward shuffle of courtesy and practicality that ended with Chavez in the front seat, Sam driving, and myself in the back. Our drive took us past the edge of the forest and I watched through the window as the trees streaked by like ghosts, their gangly branches like outstretched arms linked to one another for all time.

Sam dropped me at the station, where I found my car, as promised, the tires gleaming with the shine of rubber that's barely been around the block. As the Audi pulled away, the passenger-side window rolled down and the chief stuck his head out.

"You were wrong about something tonight, kid," Chavez said. He raised a hand to his forehead and rubbed at the skin between his eyes. I saw creases there I hadn't noticed a week ago.

"Yeah, what's that?"

"When you said you didn't think the Woodsman was running around slashing tires, and breaking into your house. You're already presuming there's a connection between Nicky and the Woodsman. Don't confuse one with the other. There's absolutely nothing linking them. All you've got is one young man's obsession with a sad bit of local history."

The Audi pulled away with a squeal.

I stood in the dark lot; the moon had grown shy and hid somewhere up in that great black sky. The stars were few and far between, sprinkled like garnish against the darkness. Somewhere in the distance a coyote howled, its cry as plaintive as a newborn's, and still I stood, thinking about Chavez's words.

# Chapter Thirty-two

I woke Sunday with an energy I hadn't felt in weeks. My sleep had been deep and quiet. In the pantry, I spied an old box of Bisquick and I found enough eggs, butter, and oil in the fridge to make a stack of pancakes.

I took the pancakes and a pot of tea and a warm saucer of syrup to the dining-room table and inhaled the first few in a matter of minutes. The Peanut gave a little kick; she liked the sweet, chewy starch. Between bites, I pulled my laptop close and fired it up and waited for my browser to pop open, but when I opened the mailbox icon, there were no new messages.

To be truthful, that wasn't completely unusual—when Brody was in the field, we sometimes went a few weeks without talking. But I wanted to fill him in on the case, and give him a heads-up that our joint checking account was about to be a few hundred dollars lighter, thanks to my new tires.

I also wanted to ask him point-blank, without any warning, if Pink Parka was Celeste Takashima. If it was . . . well, as they say in space, Houston, we have a problem.

Seamus nudged my ankle and I looked down into his deep brown eyes. He panted and a thin line of drool fell from his mouth and landed on my toe.

"Gross, buddy," I muttered. I knew what he wanted and it was disgusting, but I did it often enough that he had come to expect it, so I placed my plate on the floor and watched as his long tongue swept across the surface, slurping the last dregs of syrup and the

tiny crumbs that I'd missed. Content, he left the plate and waddled across the room and scratched at the floor, then turned around
twice and with a low burp, settled back into his spot.

Replacing the computer with the stack of files I'd brought home
with me, I opened the top folder, with its thin tab marked 1985.
As I read through the pages, thin and faded with age, I found myself once again asking why.

Why *these* two boys.

Thomas and Andrew McKenzie. Cousins, thirteen and eleven.

They were average students, well liked by their teachers and
classmates. Tommy's father, John, owned a chain of discount mattress stores across the state, and his wife, Karen, was a stay-at-home
mom. Andrew's father, Mark, was a line cook at a fast-food chain
and his wife, Sarah, did day care out of their basement. Her business was spotty, though, and most years she barely made enough
to cover her license fees.

All four parents had been thoroughly investigated. Nine times
out of ten crimes against children are perpetrated by close relatives
such as parents, siblings, or an aunt or uncle. Although you'd never
know it listening to the media, abductions, molestations, and murder at the hands of strangers are the very rare exception, not the
norm.

The McKenzie families represented about as close to the average slice of life as you could hope to get in small-town America,
circa 1985. John and Karen McKenzie were upper-middle class,
not extravagantly wealthy but comfortable, especially for Cedar
Valley. Mark and Sarah hovered somewhere much closer to the
poverty line, but they made do.

Mark and John both smoked. Karen drank, mostly in secret,
but sometimes at a ladies' lunch in town in full sight of anyone who
cared. Mark had three prior arrests. Sarah, the day care provider,
had at one time been the star of an amateur porn video. All paid
their taxes, owned their homes, and had two automobiles registered to each household. They spent Easter and Christmas together, and the rest of the time mostly ignored each other's families.

The boys, though, Tommy and Andrew, had gone up through elementary school together, and shared the same middle school. They were buddies, as close as John and Mark had once been.

Each of the parents was carefully and thoroughly exonerated in the disappearance of their children. They spent most of fall and winter of 1985 in meeting rooms across town, spaces that reeked of despair and curiosity, frequented by psychologists and detectives and reporters.

I pushed the papers away and stood and stretched. There was nothing here that hadn't been looked at hundreds of times, by the best eyes the state was able to hire. I didn't know what I hoped to find. I thought that if a sixteen-year-old kid could find an answer in these old papers, I could, too.

In the kitchen, I made a fresh pot of tea and watered the tiny pots of herbs we kept on the narrow ledge of the windowsill that lined the sink. Movement in the backyard caught my eye and as I lifted my head, I saw a fat rabbit hopping around in the grass. He must have crawled under the fence; there were a few spots where the wooden posts didn't quite meet the ground. He snuffled along, his back quivering, his button nose twitching.

Above him, perched on a low-hanging tree branch, a crow watched too, his head cocked, his eye bright. I watched him watch the rabbit for a few minutes and then returned to the files.

I thought about the parents again.

I leaned back and stared at the files before me. I blinked at an irritant in my eye and for a second, my contact lens shifted, leaving the world before me a blur. Then I blinked again, and the table and files came back into clarity, and the thought crossed my mind how different things look when, even for the smallest of seconds, you shift your focus.

The parents. What if they *were* the link?

What if the children had been chosen not because of who they were, but because of who their parents were?

Somewhere in the other room, my cell phone buzzed against whatever hard surface I'd left it on last. I ignored it and doodled on the back of a file folder, drawing the same circle over and over, letting my mind wander. The phone was silent, then buzzed once more and was still. A voice mail I could check in a few minutes. Some thing, some thought, danced at the edge of my brain like a tiny gnat, big enough to draw my attention but too small for me to see it clearly.

It would have made so much sense . . . except.

Except in 1985 and again in 2011 every single one of them was cleared as a suspect. And if they weren't suspects, what on earth would they have in common to cause someone to kill their children? Tommy had two younger sisters, Anna and Jennifer. You'd hope that if the parents had done something to earn the wrath of the Woodsman, whoever he was, they'd have copped to it and sought protection for their other kids.

But the parents had been as mystified as the police.

I skimmed through the first set of interview transcripts. The parents were interviewed multiple times, over the course of a year, until finally the police closed the file on the missing four in late summer of 1986. I paused at the transcript of Sarah McKenzie, Andrew's mom.

I remembered reading these transcripts in 2011, when we reopened the missing persons investigation as a murder case.

I didn't think I could stomach it again, especially now, the part of the transcript that describes Sarah screaming at God for taking her son. She'd lain on the floor of the interrogation room, facedown, and beat the concrete until her knuckles left brushstrokes of blood against the gray cement. It took three officers to get her out of the room and into the arms of a physician, who promptly sedated her.

The transcript indicated the interview had to be postponed until the following day.

Everything I've read says nothing can prepare you for parenthood, but nothing I've read yet prepares you for the scale of worry that begins the moment you discover you have life inside you. I felt the panic creeping in then, the quickening of my breath and heartbeat, the prickling of sweat on my skin. I forced myself to sit still and breathe deeply, and think rationally.

What happened to these children was not going to happen to the Peanut.

Brody and I talked, not seriously at first, then very seriously, when I hit the two-month mark in the pregnancy. The Peanut had been an accident; I'd gotten pregnant in between filling my birth control prescription. Kids—as in our kids—were always something on the horizon: when we had more money, more time, more trust, more stability.

It had taken me a long time to make peace with him after his affair with Celeste Takashima. Things were finally getting back to normal.

The bedroom was warm that night.

I had woken sweating and sobbing from a nightmare, a terrible dream in which the Earth was a series of scorched cities, burnt-out remnants of what had once been great societies. Men walked the land in despair: naked, hungry, crying, hateful.

I'd shaken Brody awake and told him I wanted an abortion, that I couldn't handle bringing a child up in a world that showed as much whimsy in its cruelty as it did in its beauty. He asked me to wait one week, and if after that week I still wanted to terminate the pregnancy, he would support me.

Of course, by the end of the week I'd come to peace with keeping the baby. What else is a child, but hope? Hope for the future, hope for one's own salvation, hope for a tomorrow that shines as bright and warm as the best yesterday you can remember.

Hope can be a rare thing. I think when you find hope you must embrace it. You must hold it close and you never, ever give up on it.

But I'm not naive and in my line of work, especially, I've seen how easily hope can be stolen. Hope can vanish as quickly and as quietly as it appears.

In the other room, my cell buzzed again, drawing me out of

the melancholy that had crept over me like a fog. I checked the caller ID then answered.

Finn was agitated. "Jesus, woman, you on the can, or what?"

"Yeah, you want to hear all about it? What's going on?"

His voice was high, strung-out. "I think you're right."

"Coming from you, that's a first. Right about what?"

"I got a dead crow nailed to my front door, Gemma, with a ticket stuffed in its mouth," Finn said. He coughed into the phone. "A goddamn ticket, one of those you grab from the dispenser at the deli, you know the kind? The kind that means your number's up, baby. . . . Did you get any special deliveries?"

I thought of the bird eyeing the rabbit in my backyard.

"I don't think so, let me check."

I pressed the phone to my chest, muffling Finn in the middle of whatever he was muttering. From the middle of the hall that runs through the center of the house, it is possible to see the front and back doors simultaneously. I looked at both, but all I saw was the white light of the sun streaming through the edges of the doors.

"Finn? Hang on, I'm going to open the front door," I whispered.

"Why are you whispering?" he asked with another cough.

"I don't know," I said, and returned the phone to my breast. I grabbed a walking stick from the umbrella stand in the corner, and then opened the door.

I peeked out. "No, there's nothing here."

"Well . . . that's good. Maybe this prick is more intimidated by me," Finn said.

I didn't bother to remind him that I'd already had my own message, *inside* my house, and my tires slashed.

"Anyway," he continued, "anyway, it's disgusting. The thing looks like it's been dead a few days. The eyeballs, Jesus, the eyeballs look like SpaghettiOs. All mushed up."

"You said it was nailed to the door? When? Did you hear anything?"

Finn coughed. "It wasn't there last night, that's for damn sure.

I came home from O'Toole's, worked out for a while, then went to bed. I didn't hear a thing."

Finn lived in the middle of town, on a busy main street in an old Victorian that had been converted into two units. The other Victorians on the block were filled with young couples and families, and there was a corner store with late hours across the street.

"Ask around, maybe someone saw something," I said, then paused. A dead crow with a deli ticket nailed to a cop's door sounded like something out of a bad Mafia movie. Come to think of it, so did leaving a message written in lipstick on a woman's mirror.

"Finn, this all strikes me as a bit over the top. Theatrical almost. And it doesn't make sense. We're to believe a hardcore killer—a guy okay with tearing open Nicky's throat—resorts to silly threatening messages?"

He sneezed into the phone. "I don't know, I just know it's creepy as hell. What am I supposed to do with this thing? Fingerprint it?"

I sighed. "Keep the ticket, bag the bird. Bring both to the station tomorrow."

"Where the hell am I going to put a dead bird?"

"I don't know, Finn. Put it in a box or something. Jesus. You sound like a twelve-year-old girl. Don't you have an empty shoe box? Double-bag it and put it on your porch. Maybe the raccoons will ignore it."

He muttered a few words I chose to ignore, then he was back on the line. "What are you doing anyway? Eating bonbons? Watching *Sex and the City*?"

I rolled my eyes. "I think we need to take a closer look at the parents."

"The Bellingtons? The mayor's a little busy with chemo treatments and collecting votes. He's hardly out trolling the streets and nailing dead birds on his officers' doors."

"No, the McKenzie boys; their parents. Finn, what if . . . what if the kids were killed because of their parents?"

It sounded so crazy when I said it out loud. This was old history.

Finn was silent.

"Hello?"

"Yeah, I'm thinking. They were all cleared, weren't they?"

I paced the house, stepping over Seamus, who watched me like I was an idiot. Any walking other than outside was sort of pointless in his mind.

"Yes, they were cleared. And on the surface, they don't have any one thing in common, not all of them together. But what if there's something else? What if, I don't know, there's some event, something in their past, that ties them and the Woodsman together?"

Another cough. "Like what?"

"I don't know. What's with all the hacking, don't tell me you're getting sick."

"Nah, it's the damn cat. Fucking allergies," Finn said.

I stopped pacing. "I thought you said it was a bird?"

He replied after the briefest of pauses. "It is a bird. The cat is Kelly's."

And then I heard another voice in the background, screechy and squeaky like a tire taking a bad turn, and I laughed.

"Don't tell me Kelly Clameater is back to Kelly Maneater?" I asked. I couldn't help myself.

"Don't be crude," Finn said. "You know her name's Clambaker."

Finn must have walked into another room; I couldn't hear the squawk anymore. Kelly had what you might call a five-alarm set of pipes, the sort of voice that stopped people in their tracks and made them pray to the Lord to just make it stop.

"I thought after she went, um, after she decided she was more into girls, you guys were finished?"

"She's had a change of mind," Finn replied, and I could hear the smirk in his voice.

"Uh-huh. She brings her cat?"

"Sometimes."

"Uh-huh."

A double beep saved me from any more details. I checked the caller.

"Finn, it's Sam. Let me call you back," I said, and changed lines. "What's going on, Sam?"

"I'm not calling too early, am I?"

His voice was muffled by a low whirring noise that suddenly picked up in intensity.

"No, not all—but Sam, what is that? A blender? Can you turn it off? I can barely hear you."

The noise stopped. "Sorry, yeah. It's a juicer; I just bought it. I had one of those coupons for Bed Bath and Beyond. So listen, I was going over the inventory from Nick's room, you know, the one Moriarty and Finn did? Three years ago?"

"Uh-huh," I said, back at the dining-room table. I glanced over at the thick stack of files I had yet to go through.

"Everything seems pretty typical, normal, you know, for a kid," he said. "But under his bed, they found a piece of paper and a gold necklace, both items tucked up into the mattress, sort of hidden. The necklace has a pendant, maybe a daisy. I'll read you what was on the piece of paper. You got a pen?"

I grabbed my notebook and ripped out a clean spiral-edged sheet. "Go."

Sam cleared his throat, then said, "I can only see death and more death, till we are black and swollen with death."

"Is it Nicky's writing?"

"No, I don't think so," Sam said. He chugged something and swallowed thickly. "Creepy, though, isn't it?"

I nodded. "So they found a necklace and a note under the bed. Anything else?"

"I'm still looking. Oh, and Gemma, I got a message at the station. Some lady called looking for the chief and that new temp, what's her name, Angie, she passed the message on to me. The lady's name is Kirshbaum, with a K. She said she's got important information, for the chief's ears only. Ring any bells?"

I flipped through a mental Rolodex and paused at the K's, then kept flipping through. "No, I don't think so. . . ."

"You sound unsure," Sam said.

I snapped my fingers. "You know those late-night lawyer com-mercials, where they get you off a murder charge for two hundred bucks? I swear, that's the guy's name. Kirshbaum. Carson, or Kyle. Something like that."

"Hang on," Sam said. "I'll Google it."

I waited and gnawed at a dry cuticle.

"Canyon Kirshbaum?"

"That's it. Canyon Kirshbaum. Is there a photo? He's kind of a big guy."

Sam grunted. "No photo, just a crappy Web site. What kind of a name is Canyon? So, what? Maybe it's his wife that called?"

I shrugged. "I don't know. Might not even be the same Kirsh-baum. I'll give them a call tomorrow. I'm sure it can wait a day. She's probably some local busybody playing Agatha Christie."

"You mean Miss Marple. Agatha Christie was the author," Sam said.

He grunted again and then in the background I heard a door-bell ring. "Just a sec, Gemma."

There were voices and then Sam was on the phone again. "Hey, can we talk later? A couple of the guys are here, we're going fishing."

"Sure. Have fun. Oh, and Sam—"

"Yeah?"

I was about to tell him to be careful, considering Finn's dead bird.

"Nothing. Catch a beaut, ok?"

"Yes, ma'am," he said, and clicked off.


Hours later, I would recall that moment, how the click was like a period at the end of a sentence.

I would recall how I almost called him back and told him fish-ing could wait, that we should call Kirshbaum right now and make something out of our Sunday.

That's what cops do, after all. They chase the leads while the leads are white-hot.

But I didn't. Not that day.

Instead, I picked through the weekend paper and read about war and famine in Africa and a super-strain of malaria resistant to all drugs and George Clooney's latest blockbuster.

I wondered, later—much later—if I had called Sam, if he would have stayed, and gone with me to Kirshbaum's house.

I think he might have.

# Chapter Thirty-three

I met Chief Chavez in the hospital waiting room. He came straight from his daughter's soccer tournament, and under the fluorescent lights, he was pale, his legs surprisingly skinny in black and white gym shorts. Dark stains under his armpits made half-moons on his gray T-shirt, and when he removed his Nike visor, patches of hair stood up in a half-dozen cowlicks.

Chavez said, "His parents are on their way in. The dad was in Cheyenne, his mom in Denver. I got hold of the older sister, too, she's swinging down to the Springs to pick up the younger one."

"Where is he?"

Chavez leaned against the wall and closed his eyes. "He's in surgery. Gemma, it's not good. He lost a lot of blood, and . . ."

He sagged down to rest on his heels, and put his head in his hands.

"And what?"

Chavez shook his head and bit his lip. "They might not be able to save his leg. If he makes it through surgery, they'll likely amputate as soon as he's stable."

Fuck.

"I can't believe no one saw anything. For Chrissakes, Lou Moriarty and three other cops were less than a hundred yards away," I said. "We got to get on this, Chief. Witnesses, tire treads, there's a security camera at the 7-11 on the corner of Blair and Third—maybe it caught a car on the way up the road?"

Chavez nodded slowly. "I called in a favor, Avondale's sending a team over to the site. They'll work the case, Gemma. We should be here, for Sam, in case . . ."

In case.

In case he lived.

In case he died.

I slid down the wall and sat next to Chavez as he told me the story. The guys had driven up to Wally's Pond, a quiet fishing hole twenty minutes outside of town stocked to the reeds with trout. There were two trucks; the beds were loaded with coolers of sandwiches and beer and bait. Sam followed them on his road bike and then took it past the fishing hole, up the road for another few miles. His plan was to ride down and join them, getting in both a workout and some relaxation on the river.

It was a good day for fishing.

A couple of hours later, seven trout were resting on ice chips, gutted and filleted, their innards thrown to the birds, birds that had waited and watched as the fishermen tied their flies and threw their casts.

And somewhere, somebody else had waited and watched.

When they were finished fishing, the guys loaded up their gear and headed back into town, Sam coasting behind the second truck. At some point, the driver noticed Sam was no longer in his rearview mirror. He turned around and backtracked and came upon a red Ferrari pulled over on the side of the road, the driver frantically yelling into his cell phone.

It was a hit-and-run.

The impact knocked Sam off the road and down the ravine. One of the officers scrambled down and got a tourniquet on Sam's bleeding leg. That action probably saved his life. His bike was in pieces. Sam was unconscious and broken and scratched all to hell.

Ferrari Man wasn't much help; he'd noticed a white sedan with muddy plates, possibly a passenger in the backseat. Possibly it was just shadows. He thought it might be a Honda or a Toyota.

It didn't make sense, any of it. Sam was a twenty-two-year-old kid with a few weeks on the job and a girl with turquoise eyes waiting for him. He was supposed to be a cop, a good cop, not a desk jockey with one working leg and a psychological scar a mile wide.

Maybe he would turn out okay, we told ourselves, Chavez and Moriarty and I and a half-dozen other cops. We sat in the sad, cold hospital waiting room. We waited for Sam's family to arrive; we waited for an update from the surgeon; we waited to see if one of our own would pull through.

# Chapter Thirty-four

Sam Birdshead lost his leg at midnight, about the same time that Frank Bellington died in his sleep. News of both events came by text message early the next morning. Chavez let me know about Sam; Bull sent me word about Frank.

I called Bull right away, before I got out of bed.

"I'm so sorry. I know you were close to Frank."

Bull sighed into the phone. I heard a cuckoo clock chime in the background and knew he must be in his study. "We certainly were, once upon a time. It's hard to grieve when I know he's with our Lord Jesus now, but I would've liked to speak with him one last time."

"What would you have said?"

Bull was silent.

I watched through the open bedroom window as the rising sun overpowered the gray morning light with vibrant shades of pink and orange. It was going to be a beautiful day. Seamus jumped on the bed and nuzzled into my hip. He curled himself into a tight ball and I scratched behind his ears, glad for the companionship.

"Bull?"

"I would have asked him if he had made peace with our Savior. Frank was a complicated man, Gemma. He had demons, secret demons, more than anyone really knew."

I sat up in bed, the cover falling from my shoulders. "Bull, what happened, all those years ago? Why did your friendship with him end? Why did Julia tell me to stay away from him?"

Bull inhaled sharply. "When did she say that?"

"She called me a few days ago, after the news conference the mayor and his wife gave, about Nicky's murder. Julia told me to 'stay away from that man,' and I have to assume she meant the mayor or his father. Why would she say that?"

Bull coughed and I heard another noise in the background, the familiar set of beeps and commands of a computer starting up. He was definitely in his study, a room he kept a few degrees colder than the rest of the house. It was his private space, his retreat, a room lined with his volumes of state-revised statutes and other legal tomes.

"Why don't you come by the house; there's a few things we should talk about. Your grandmother made a quiche, it's delicious," Bull said. "By the way, Brody e-mailed me. Gemma, I don't like the idea of you all alone in that house, being so isolated. You want to stay with us for a few days? I can make up your old room."

"Brody e-mailed you, huh? He can't seem to find the time to get in touch with me," I said. "Did he tell you Celeste Takashima is with them, in Denali?"

"No! What? Brody wouldn't . . ."

"Don't 'Brody wouldn't' me, Bull. You know damn well he would. You men all think with your little brains. I'm fine staying here, but I'll come down and see you guys. I'll be there in an hour."

I showered and dressed quickly. Before leaving the house, I called Chief Chavez. He had gone home to catch a few hours of sleep and a change of clothes and then returned to the hospital. Chavez said Sam was resting comfortably after his surgery. Sam's prognosis was good; he faced months of physical therapy but he was alive and he would heal.

I drove to Bull and Julia's house. The streets were quiet as I made my way through town. I saw empty parking lots and just-waking stores. A lonely bus passed me on its way headed somewhere south, a single passenger silhouetted by the interior dome lights. It was a woman, young, with long pale hair and a dark scarf wrapped around her neck. She looked cold and lonely and I hoped she was making her way somewhere warm and happy.

I wondered, not for the first time, if that's what I should do. Head south, to a warmer clime, maybe a little border town on the beach. Raise my daughter in a place that I don't associate with so much death. It would be a place where winter never fell, where the sun shone and the beer was cold and the ocean came to our toes and then receded and then returned in a never-ending pattern. We could learn to surf and she would spend summers with her father, in exotic locales around the world.

As I pulled into the driveway of my old childhood house, though, the dream of leaving floated away as quickly as it had come. They say you can never go home again, and I'm too afraid that might be true, to ever really leave.

This is home, for better or worse, in good times and in bad, till death do us part.

Bull met me at the front door with a plate of quiche and a cup of hot cocoa. He wore a bathrobe, a navy blue-and-black plaid wrap that clashed with his green pajamas. The robe was last year's Christmas present from Brody. I remember Bull modeled it for us, right after he unwrapped it, and then we all took turns wearing it, pretending the hallway was a runway.

"I haven't had hot cocoa in years."

"You always used to drink cocoa when you were a girl, Gem. When I first met you, you were six years old and cute as a button, until you heard the word no. Then Lord help us but you were a little terror. I learned very quickly never to say no to you when it came to cocoa," Bull said. His expression grew sad. "I guess you couldn't stay my little girl forever, could you?"

I shook my head. "Cedar Valley never was never-never land. Where's Julia?"

"Mrs. Delmonico took her to the mall. Julia was getting antsy about her face creams. I would have taken her, but I think your grandmother's tired of this old mug."

I forgot I had promised to take Julia shopping. "So, she'll be gone a few hours?"

Bull nodded. He watched me behind his dark-rimmed glasses, his eyes unreadable. The lines and shadows in his face were obvious, though. He was tired.

We show the world what we want it to see, don't we? I saw a man slowly changing from old to elderly; a man who had lived most of his adult life defending, protecting, and upholding the laws of the land. A man who was learning law and order don't translate so well to chaos of the mind. Julia's memory and emotions would come and go until she'd seem a stranger.

Bull would walk alongside her on her journey, but I could see, in his weariness, the terrible toll it would take on him.

"I'll have to catch her another day. I take it we should meet in your chambers?"

His "chambers" was the nickname we'd given to the small study just off the front living room. I'd always loved touring his real chambers at the courthouse and after he retired, it felt appropriate to rename the study.

It was where we'd had all our serious talks, after all. I learned about the birds and the bees in that study. It was where I received an hour-long lecture on the dangers of drunk driving after I came home late one night from a high school party, blasted out of my mind on cheap wine and marijuana. It was where we'd talked, after Julia's diagnosis, about next steps and future plans.

We took our usual seats in the study; Bull behind the desk, me on the leather couch. I set the hot cocoa down on the coffee table. The thought of drinking the thick, sweet chocolate made my stomach turn.

I took a bite of the quiche. "This is pretty good."

"Your grandmother always was a good cook. It's a funny thing, moving from a state of bachelorhood to a state of matrimony. It hasn't always been easy, Gemma, but I wouldn't trade my family for anything. That's the most important thing in this world, besides friends and faith," Bull said.

He loosened the belt on his bathrobe. "Don't ever retire, honey. I've gained fifteen pounds and an ache in my ass since I left the bench."

I set the quiche down and clasped my hands in my lap. "Family, friends, and faith, huh. Sounds good in theory. What happens when it all goes sour in real life?"

Bull sighed. "What do you remember, Gemma?"

"What do I remember when?"

"Come on, we're both talking about the same thing here. What do you remember of Frank Bellington, of Louis Moriarty, Jazzy Douglas . . . the other guys?"

I closed my eyes and thought. "I remember Frank was a wise guy with a penchant for candies. Louis was bigger than life, I remember he always had his piece on him, in a shoulder harness. Julia hated that he brought it around the house. Jazzy was the first black man I remember seeing in my life. The others are sort of blurry."

I opened my eyes. Bull was nodding.

He said, "Frank always did like the sweeter things in life. Candy, money. Women. Louis was just trying to make it as a single dad, his wife split when the boy graduated high school."

"Danny Moriarty."

Bull was surprised. "How did you know that?"

I shook my head. "You first, Bull. The truth."

"I've never lied to you, Gemma."

"Yes, you have. I don't care about that. I want to know what broke up your little group. Was it something to do with the Woodsman? Did one of you kill the McKenzie boys and the others knew, or guessed?"

Bull's face paled. He leaned forward and gripped the edges of the desk. I saw the color go out of his fingers. I tensed, ready to run, but then Bull sat back and covered his face with his hands. To my surprise, he started weeping.

"It was horrible. It was maybe ten years after the McKenzie boys disappeared. You were probably eight or nine years old. I don't know. We were downstairs, in the basement, knee-deep in a poker game, all of us drunker than a bunch of sailors on leave. Your grandmother kept sticking her head down and telling us to shut up. Frank got up at some point, needed to use the facilities. After ten or fifteen minutes, one of us sobered up enough to realize he'd been gone a long time. I came upstairs. Frank was gone. Your grandmother was sobbing in the kitchen."

Bull paused to take a tissue from the box on his desk and blow his nose.

"What happened?" I didn't remember any of this.

Bull wadded up the tissue and threw it in the small, metal trash can next to his desk. "I asked Julia the same thing. She refused to answer, just kept crying. Then I asked where Frank was. I was dim-witted, drunk and stupid. I didn't put two and two together."

"He attacked her?"

Bull nodded. "Thank God he was too drunk to do much more than paw at her. He left bruises on her jawbone, her arms. She was able to push him off with a slap and a few sharp words and Frank sobered up enough with the slap to realize what he was doing. He fled, distraught, embarrassed."

"Jesus."

Bull pointed a finger at me. "Gemma, I mean it. Don't take His name in vain in this house. But yes, your reaction is appropriate, given the circumstances. Of course, I was beyond furious. I wanted to chase Frank down, give him a beating he wouldn't forget. Julia was distraught but even then, her kindness shone through. She begged me to let it go, said Frank was too drunk to realize what he had tried to do. She wouldn't let me go after him."

"So that was it? Did Frank ever apologize?"

Bull shook his head and took a sip of his hot cocoa. "Julia made me swear that I would forget it happened. Of course, I couldn't, so things just took their natural course. A deep coldness seeped in between Frank and me and as a result, the poker group fell to the wayside. I'm not very good at keeping secrets, though, and I ended up telling Lou. He was aghast and embarrassed and the whole damn thing was just a big mess. Friendships ruined over a night of cheap whiskey."

"Do you think Frank could have assaulted other women? This probably wasn't his first time, Bull. You should have gone to the police."

"And told them what? It would have been Frank's word against Julia's. Most of the people in this town were in his pocket, from real estate developers to the mob, and half the folks in between. He was the most powerful man in the valley. She was just a home-maker. And Julia was mortified at the thought of a scandal. She just wanted to forget the whole thing. Frank didn't really do any-thing . . ."

"Bullshit! He tried to rape her. If you hadn't been in the basement . . . if she hadn't managed to stop him . . ."

Bull sighed. "I'm not proud, Gemma. But you've got to under-stand, this man was one of our closest friends. There was alcohol involved. It was a shock and we tried to do the best we could with what we had."

"You didn't answer my question. Do you think there were other women?"

Bull sat back and steepled his fingers. "I don't know. I think . . ."

"Yes?"

"I think so. Over the years, I've watched Frank. He hid it well, most of the time, but I think a deep violent streak ran through that man," Bull said, nodding. "I'm almost positive there were others."

"Rose Noonan?"

Bull sat up. "Rose? No, oh no. Gemma, Frank may have been violent, but he wasn't a killer."

"Before that night, I bet you thought he wasn't a rapist, either," I said, biting my lip. "Bull, you worked a lot of cases, first as an attorney, then a judge. You and I both have seen the damage that comes when the beast in man's true nature emerges. Killers, rap-ists: they've got mothers, partners, brothers and sisters. Friends. And every single one of them is always shocked when they find out their son, their husband, is not the person they thought."

Bull was shaking his head but there was a light in his eyes that hadn't been there before. He leaned forward. "Something has bothered me about that woman's murder, Gemma, for years. I read the autopsy report on Rose Noonan. Her body wasn't, uh, fresh when it was dragged out of the river."

I'd never read her autopsy report but I remembered Finn had said something along the same lines, something about difficulty determining her date of death. "What are you saying?"

"I'm saying, maybe the boys weren't the first victims that summer. Maybe Rose Noonan died first."

I chewed on the inside of my lip, thinking. "So Rose first, then the boys. I don't know that it does make a difference."

Bull shook his head, frustrated. "Of course it makes a difference, Gem, if it was the *same killer*. He kills her first, then the boys. But he purposefully stages it so her *body* is found second. Why do that? She was new to town, lived alone in a studio apartment south of the tracks. She had no friends, knew only a few people. No one reported her missing. She could have been dead a month or two before her body was placed in the river. Maybe her body was dumped, sometime after the boys went missing, to throw us all off. Looked at that way, it changes things, doesn't it? You're the detective; doesn't it change things?"

"I don't know. She was raped and strangled. The boys were killed by blows to the head. She was dumped. The boys were buried. Either it makes a difference, or it doesn't. If the Woodsman killed both Rose Noonan and the McKenzie boys, what's the connection? What's the motive? Crimes of passion are usually single events. Rarely do we see someone progress to a serial killer based on one heat-of-the-moment killing," I said, thinking out loud. "Did you know Louis Moriarty's son was interviewed for the McKenzie murders?"

Bull took another sip of his hot cocoa and nodded. "Everyone was, Gemma. Me included."

"Louis has been giving me grief about digging around in the past," I said. "Jesus, that would be something, if Lou's son was the Woodsman and Frank killed Rose Noonan. And they all went right on living here in town, innocent as could be."

Bull stood. He tightened his bathrobe belt and went to the window, his hands deep in his bathrobe pockets. An expression crossed his face that I remembered well from watching him on the bench. It was the expression of a man at odds, wrestling with his base instinct to trust and love his neighbor, and his seasoned experience that no man is above sin.

I waited.

"Gemma, I wish I had more answers for you, but I don't. Lou struggled with Danny for years. He was a headstrong young man, and he gave Lou and Ella a real tough time. I think Lou himself always wondered if Danny could have killed those boys. It was a relief when Danny graduated high school and left Cedar Valley. He was sort of the town bully, but we didn't call it that in those days. He was just the tough kid everyone shied away from," Bull said. He scratched at the back of his head and then checked his fingernails. "As for Frank, well, you're right, of course. I never thought he was a killer. I never should have thought I knew him well enough to say one way or the other."

Bull paused, then continued. "But just because a man is weak in the bedroom doesn't make him a killer, Gemma. You know that better than anyone."

My face flushed and I stood up and grabbed my purse.

"Thanks for the breakfast, Bull. Say hi to Julia when she gets home. And thanks for talking to the police, finally. I hope it's a weight off your self-righteous chest."

Bull stared at me, sad. "I'm sorry, honey, that came out all wrong. Brody is nothing like Frank Bellington. He adores you. He regrets what he did."

I nodded. "Sure. I'll see myself out."

# Chapter Thirty-five

Frank Bellington's funeral was a few days later. Like most funerals, the telling of the dead brought equal parts tears and laughter. Sorrow for the loss, joy for the life. I decided the measure of a life well lived must be how easily the tears and the laughter ebb and flow from each other. How the sweetness of a single memory is strong enough to push away, even for a second, the tragedy of it all. Terry Bellington and his sister, Hannah Watkins, both gave eulogies that were full of references to Frank's quick wit, his love for his wife—their mother—and his fondness for the town.

I left the church halfway through the service and waited for my partner. He had taken a phone call from Avondale PD.

It was Thursday.

The skies were hazy, the breeze gentle. Across the street, in a neighborhood park, a man in an orange and purple Lakers jersey chased a little girl with tiny pigtails. She squealed as he caught her and then the two posed for an older woman holding a camera.

Nearby, a man in a wide-brimmed hat shuffled along with a German shepherd, their steps in unison. They had gray in their faces and weariness in their steps and it was hard to tell who was walking whom.

Finn met me outside. In the reflection of his mirrored sunglasses, I saw a weary-looking woman, heavy in the belly, her dark hair loose around her face.

"Anything?"

He shook his head. "Avondale's a joke. They got very little, barely even a skid mark on the road. One good piece of news, they did retrieve a few shards of broken glass from a front headlight. No way to tell if it's our guy, but the preliminary reports put it at a Toyota, late model. Whoever hit Sam did it nice and slow and hard. They interviewed Ferrari Man again, nothing else he can tell us. I called the hospital, too. Sam's still in a coma."

"So we're looking for a late-model white Toyota. Great, only about a million of those in Colorado. It doesn't make any sense, Finn. This guy's a schizo, a real nutjob. He starts with homicide, downgrades to silly threats and tire slashing and a dead bird, and then bounces back up to attempted murder? I don't get it."

I followed him to the parking lot. At my car, we stopped and Finn cleared his throat. I looked at him over the roof.

"What?"

Finn said, "Are we even sure it's the same guy? I mean Sam barely had a finger in the Nicky Bellington case. He wasn't a player."

He pulled a toothpick from his breast pocket and stuck it in the corner of his mouth and shrugged. "What if the one has nothing to do with the other?"

"You're joking. Get in the car."

We slid in and I continued. "You're telling me you honestly think the two are unrelated? That in the midst of investigating a murder one of our partners randomly happens to be the victim of a hit-and-run?"

I started the car and checked my mirrors. The lot was clear; I figured there were another ten or fifteen minutes left to the service. Unlike the reverend at Nicky's funeral, this minister was a real character. He worked the altar like it was a stage.

Finn talked around the toothpick, rolling it cheek to cheek and back again.

"I'm just saying, we've got nothing that ties the one to the other. We need to be careful."

I peeled out of the lot, my brand-new tires taking the turn like a bastard. "Careful? I will tell you who needs to be careful. Our guy. I think he's scared. I think we can't see it yet, but somehow, we're closing in on him."

Finn listened as I told him what Sam had discovered, the necklace and poem found in Nicky's bedroom.

"Yeah, yeah, I remember that. It was some kind of flower pendant, I think. But that doesn't mean anything. He probably found the necklace at school. Maybe the poem was part of a love letter. You'd be shocked if you knew half of what kids are into these days, Gemma."

"It wasn't a damn love letter, Finn. Sam finds it and a few hours later, he's nearly dead."

I slammed on the brakes so hard the car spun to the side. Finn's hand hit the dashboard with a thump. Behind me, a Volkswagen honked, long and loud. I released the brake and slid forward until I was parallel with the curb. "Son of a bitch. How did he know?"

"Don't ever do that again. I know it must be real rare for you to get an epiphany but shit, my elbow feels like it's in my shoulder," Finn said. He massaged his arm and started rolling his neck in a slow, loose circle. "How did who know what?"

I stared out the window and talked to myself. "Three possibilities. Sam's phone is tapped. My phone is tapped. Sam told someone."

"Four. Sam was being watched," Finn said, picking up on my train of thought.

Shaking my head, I said, "No, that doesn't make sense. You said it yourself; Sam wasn't a player in the investigation. Why watch him?"

I restarted the car and drove slowly. "If you're our guy, you watch me. Or you—but not Sam."

I ran through the sequence of events in my head. Sam finds the evidence sheet describing the piece of paper and the necklace. He calls me. Our call is interrupted—the guys are here, we're going fishing. Sam is pumped. Maybe he talks, maybe it's to Louis Moriarty. Sam asks Moriarty if he remembers finding the paper and the thin gold necklace tucked up high under Nicky's bed. Maybe Moriarty does remember.

"Louis Moriarty was in the first truck, we know that for sure, right?"

Finn stopped rolling his neck and groaned. "Give it a rest, will you? It's not Moriarty. And this isn't the grassy knoll. He didn't have a damn partner run Sam off the road."

I parked outside of the narrow Victorian and checked the address. I turned to Finn.

"Okay, so maybe it's not Moriarty. But you've got to admit, every damn thing seems to lead back to him," I said.

I watched Finn gnaw on the toothpick. "I think you've got it backward. It all comes back to Nicky. He found something three years ago that made him run away. Then he came back. And someone, despite Nicky's best intentions, recognized him and killed him. And now we're on the same path Nicky was on, looking in the basement records, reopening old wounds. Only now, it's us in the frying pan, getting picked off. One by one."

Something about old wounds struck a chord in me. "It doesn't all come back to Nicky. It all comes back to the McKenzie boys and the Woodsman. Without them, you've got Nicky alive and well, home for the summer from Yale or Harvard."

"So what now?"

"We talk to the Kirshbaums."

# Chapter Thirty-six

Canyon Kirshbaum was a large man in his late thirties. We sat in his backyard, sipping iced tea poured from a crystal pitcher, with slivers of lemon rind and honey. The bench Kirshbaum sat on was low, and his massive thighs puddled around him like ice cream melting on a hot day. He wore a charcoal suit and an ivory dress shirt with the first few buttons open, and dark shoes that shined from a recent polish.

Kirshbaum was a gracious host. "How's the Lipton? More honey? We purchase it at the farmer's market on Tenth and Spruce. There's a lovely young woman, a Haitian, who does a wildflower blend infused with Palisade peaches. It is simply divine."

"That sounds wonderful, this tea is just fine as is," I said. "This is a lovely garden."

Kirshbaum glanced around the expansive yard as though seeing it for the first time. The space was narrow and long, with enough shade to be pleasant and enough sun to grow spectacular plants.

"My wife's got the green thumb. I don't get out here often enough to enjoy it," Kirshbaum said. He mopped at his brow with a pale lavender handkerchief. "I couldn't tell you the names of half these things. I have a law degree with honors from Chicago, but I can't tell a rose from a lily."

I pointed to a particularly stunning flower with scarlet petals that looked like velvet and had a heady, sweet perfume. "That's a rose."

Kirshbaum smiled. His lips were thin and his teeth large and he said, "Yes, I suppose I was exaggerating. Perhaps I should have said I can't tell the difference between an amaryllis and an orchid."

I shrugged. "A flower is a flower is a flower. . . . Anyway, we don't want to take up any more of your time than we have to. Thanks again for meeting us; we could have come to your office."

Kirshbaum waved a dismissive hand. "My office is a disaster. We're remodeling and there's junk everywhere. My wife will be glad someone's using the yard. She's out of town at the moment and my mother lives with us, so this is good. I can keep an eye on her and give the day nurse a few hours off."

Finn swallowed the last of his iced tea and sucked on the lemon rind for a minute before spitting it back into the glass. "I don't know how much my partner told you, sir, but it seems like it's really your mother that we need to talk to."

Kirshbaum stared at Finn. "I have to tell you, my mother does have her moments. But to be honest, she's been in and out of it for months. I'm surprised she was able to place a call to the police station."

Kirshbaum poured Finn another glass of the tea and topped mine off.

"Well, your mother was quite insistent that she speak with someone, and we're obligated to follow up on any leads. As you probably know, we're investigating a homicide—"

"Ah, the Bellington boy, correct?"

"Yes, Nicholas Bellington. Did you or your mother know him? Or the Bellington family?"

Kirshbaum leaned back and steepled his fingers and thought a few minutes. "Well, of course, his father Terry is the mayor so we're familiar with the name. But personally, no, I don't think so."

He mopped his brow again and then stuck the lavender handkerchief in his breast pocket. Then he leaned over and snapped the red velvety rose off at the stem with his fingernails. The chlorophyll from the plant left thin green stains under his thumbnail.

Kirshbaum slid the flower across the table to me. "A rose for a rose. Let me see if my mother is awake. I'll be right back."

He pushed himself off the bench and ambled through the back door and into the house, out of sight. I stood and leaned back, my hands on my hips, and caught a glimpse of another rose bush, brimming with flowers of the most unusual shade of pale purple. The bush bloomed along the back wall of the garden, a good fifteen feet away.

"Have you ever seen roses that color, Finn?" I asked, and he shook his head, distracted by the ring of his cell phone. I picked my way along the flagstone path until I stood before the bush, admiring the flowers.

As I turned to leave, I stubbed my toe on the base of an alabaster birdbath, nearly hidden from sight by an aggressive vine that wrapped itself around the marble like a vise.

The basin held a few inches of stagnant olive-green water, thick with slimy, moldy leaves. A pair of mosquitos buzzed just above the surface, their tiny bodies throbbing like microscopic drones. I backed away and when I did, I saw a plaque at the base of the column of the birdbath. The vines were pushed back and I saw the plaque bore an inscription, and a raised relief of children dancing, holding hands in a circle.

Two boys.

I slowly walked back to Finn, and Canyon Kirshbaum, who'd returned. They were deep in conversation when I interrupted.

"Sir, did you grow up here?" I asked. "In Cedar Valley?"

He nodded. "Born and bred. Aside from school in Chicago, I've been here ever since."

"And your mom, she was an artist?"

He nodded again. "In her younger years, she was quite wonderful. She painted, drew, even dabbled in sculpture. How did you know that?"

I jerked a thumb toward the birdbath. "Her name is on that piece, right below the dedication to the McKenzie boys."

"Well, I'll be. That's right," Kirshbaum said with a snap of his fingers, his face brightening. "I'd forgotten all about that old birdbath. They had it up at City Hall for years and years, right in the front, by that fountain, and then it cracked, at the base, so my mother brought it back here."

Finn stood and peered back at the birdbath. He looked at me, his eyes wide, and then he asked Kirshbaum, "Did you know them? The kids?"

The heavy man moved his head in a half shake, half nod. "Sure, I was a few years behind them in school. I was quite young."

"Your mother, she knew them?"

"Of course. Everyone knew them," he said. "Cedar Valley is a small town. It was even smaller thirty years ago."

I thought of what I'd told Moriarty in the bar after Nicky's funeral, about not believing in coincidences. The cop in me places a deep-seeded trust in facts, figures, and cold, hard evidence. But I've always thought that there are currents running through our world and our lives, threads if you will, that touch and connect all things. Events, years after they've happened, leave faint fingerprints that linger and change the surface of places over time.

I've known that the Woodsman left his mark on Cedar Valley thirty years ago. Chills ran down my spine as I realized, truly, completely, for the first time, just how deep that mark might run.

Kirshbaum said, "My mother's ready for you, if you still want to speak with her."

Oh, boy, did I ever.

He motioned us to follow him. The house was dim; window shades were drawn against the heat and the air was cool and smelled of floral potpourri and something else, like sawdust or a woodshop.

Kirshbaum led us to a narrow stairway. He said, "Come on, she's upstairs."

I pushed Finn in front of me with my elbow and we headed up the stairs after Kirshbaum, his enormous behind swaying before us like the rear of an elephant. At the top, the attorney took a sharp right. We passed a room with a door half-open and I heard a low cackle.

I paused by the door and while I didn't sense anything was

amiss, we were in a strange house with a strange man. "Is there someone else here, Mr. Kirshbaum?"

He stopped at the end of the hallway and came back to us and pushed the door open the rest of the way. Inside the room was a daybed, covered in a pale blue and white quilt, and a sewing table, and a wooden cage the size of a person. Inside the cage, perched on a thick branch, a black bird with an orange beak and legs stared at us. The bottom of the cage was lined with wood chips and over-ripe pieces of fruit.

The bird cackled again and then said, "Honey, I'm home," in a woman's voice with a harsh New York accent.

"Jesus, that's creepy," Finn said.

Kirshbaum laughed. "That's Margaret, my wife's Mynah bird. They are incredible mimics. Margaret likes to imitate my wife."

"That exercise bike won't pedal itself," Margaret said, and laughed. Kirshbaum's face darkened and he reached around me and pulled the door shut.

"My mother's waiting," Kirshbaum said, and led us down to the last doorway at the end of the hallway. He called into the dark-ened room and a quiet, firm voice answered back.

Kirshbaum whispered to us, "We keep the lights low, my mother has sensitivity issues with her eyes. The dimness seems to help."

We followed him into the bedroom, a small space with framed lace handkerchiefs on the walls and faded oriental rugs on the floor. An older woman, somewhere in her early seventies, lay in the bed, propped up against a stack of ivory silk-covered pillows. Her gray hair hugged her head in tight curls, framing an attractive face. She was petite, and the handmade quilts and afghan blankets pulled up to her chin almost swallowed her.

I introduced myself, and Finn, and sat on the edge of the bed. Finn stood in the corner, his hands in his pants pockets, his ex-pression saying he'd rather be anywhere than here, in this woman's bedroom, where she'd likely stay until she died.

I touched the threads on the top blanket.

"This is an echo quilt, isn't it?"

Her voice was worn but steady. "Yes, it is. Are you a quilter?"

I shook my head. "My mother had a real passion for quilts. She couldn't afford to buy many, so she took pictures of them instead. I have a whole scrapbook with photographs. I always loved the names: album, clamshell, crazy, memory, in-the-ditch, echo."

"It's a lost art, quilting. I had to ask Canyon to take away my television; I couldn't stand all the horrible shows on TV now, where women attack one another. There used to be a real sisterhood. Women would come together and share their stories and their troubles and together, create something from nothing—like this quilt," she said.

I thought of Tessa and Lisey and the cruel things they had said about, and to, one another. "There are a lot of things that are different nowadays, aren't there?"

Mrs. Kirshbaum eyed me out of the corner of her eye and nodded slowly. "Canyon, make yourself useful, dear. Make us another pitcher of that iced tea, would you?"

Kirshbaum stood at the foot of the bed and excused himself. Finn's cell buzzed again, and after checking the caller ID, he too left the room.

"Ma'am, you've lived here a long time, haven't you?" I asked.

She sighed. "Yes, a long time. It won't be much longer, though, I think. My time is coming and there's nothing anyone can do to stop it. Not that I'd want to stop it, mind you. I'm ready. I'm tired."

There was a confessional tone to her words and her voice and I thought of the birdbath in the backyard, and the effort it would have taken her to call the police station.

Something weighed on this woman's mind, something dark and heavy.

I said, "In all the years you've lived here, how much evil have you been a witness to? I'm talking about real evil. Like two kids disappearing thirty years ago. Like a young man being killed last week. Like a cop—a friend of mine—getting hit by a car and losing his leg."

Her face paled but her voice never wavered. "Do you believe in God, Detective?"

I nodded. "Yes, I believe there is a higher purpose, a higher power."

"I do, too. I knew there would be a day when I would be asked to answer for my sins," she said. She leaned back and closed her eyes. "I'll tell you a story, dear. I'm not proud of it, but I think it's getting on late for this old bird. Sunset is a-coming and dirty deeds best be aired before night comes."

Her eyes opened. "That's something my grandfather used to say. He was a fearful, superstitious old codger."

She grasped at the quilt with gnarled pale fingers that looked like claws. "Would you like to hear a story, Detective? It's a story about a secret that's been kept for thirty years."

# Chapter Thirty-seven

It took an hour for Mrs. Kirshbaum to tell her story, and by the end I was an emotional wasteland. She paused early on, listening to the heavy steps of Canyon as he made his way up the stairs and down the hall and into her room. He set the tray down and gave us each a glass of iced tea. Then he sat in the corner, watching his mother, and at some point he joined in the story, adding details that only he would have known. In a way it was that much worse, hearing the two of them tell their sad tale, a nice enough mother and an accomplished son so intrinsically linked to Cedar Valley's most notorious mystery.

The tale itself was straightforward enough.

But Sylvia Kirshbaum wasn't just telling me a story; she was reliving the past, one excruciating memory at a time. And in my mind, I could see her: prim and proper, with her hair done up, and her dress hemmed to hit just about midpoint on her knees, and her pumps, sensible one-inch heels. This was 1985, after all.


Canyon was inconsolable that afternoon.

It was early July, one of those perfect, warm days that occur a handful of times between late spring and early fall, when the air is hot and the sky is blue and the world seems bursting with life and color.

Canyon was a delicate child, not yet showing the body type he inherited from his late grandmother, she of the narrow shoulders and the wide buttocks. Seven years old, skinny as a twig, with a nose that ran constantly from allergies and wet eyes that were red-rimmed and sensitive to bright lights.

"But why?" he asked and it sounded like "bud way."

Sylvia Kirshbaum wiped her son's nose again—the rate this child went through hankies!—and gripped his fingers around the cup of tea. His were pale, thin fingers that were longer than they should have been for his age and size, like a piano player's fingers or a surgeon's.

"Because, my dear heart, you'll catch your death. Now, you must rest here while Mama goes to work, and when I get back, we'll make a surprise for Daddy. How does that sound?" she asked.

If she was late again, Mr. McGuckin would call her into his office and make her sit there on the black leather sofa and he would stare at her over those horn-rimmed eyeglasses and scold her. Scold her, a grown woman, for punching in her time card one minute past her expected return from lunch.

There were no words. Canyon simply wailed as she checked her handbag, fished out her heavy brass key ring with the funny owl tchotchke, and locked the door behind her.

For one hour, he was safe and sound, inside the house.

Every minute of that hour represented an opportunity for something, anything, to occur to prevent him from going outside and setting into motion the terrible events of that summer.

But the clock went tick and tock and Canyon occupied himself, with no idea that Fate waited patiently just outside.

The familiar squeal of the postman's truck brought Canyon to the door and gingerly down the front steps. He snatched the new issue of *Boy's Life* from the tin box, leaving the Sears catalog and two slender envelopes behind. Back inside, in the kitchen, he poured a big glass of milk from the bottle in the icebox, and then checked the pantry again, in case his mother had managed to hide a box of cookies. But she hadn't, so he contented himself with the glass of milk and a slice of cold pie. It was cherry, though, and slimy as snot, and he dumped half of it into the sink.

He whispered *shitpie* as he watched it slide down into the drain and then giggled and said it again.

*Shitpie!*

In the living room, Canyon lay on the floor on his stomach, his body carefully angled to catch a single ray of sunlight. He read the magazine, wiping his nose every few minutes on the back of his hand. He sneezed and pretended not to see the wet spots that appeared on the page in front of him. Instead he focused on the newest clue in the Mars Attacks! Mystery. With his tongue between the gap in his front teeth, he carefully penciled in the code and added it to the notebook he kept in his back pocket.

Movement outside the living-room window caught his eye. He peeked out and saw something very interesting. The Kirshbaums lived at the end of a cul-de-sac, just beyond which was a big meadow filled with pines and aspens and a trail that led down the creek and deep into the wooded open space. Making their way down the trail were two blond, older boys. Canyon recognized them from the middle school that adjoined his elementary school.

It was 2:15 p.m.

Moving fast, he pulled off his pajamas and left them in a heap on his bedroom floor, and yanked on a pair of cotton shorts and a dirty old shirt his mother kept trying to toss. By the time he got outside, the boys were almost to the end of the trail. By the time he caught up to them, he was out of breath and snot caked his upper lip. The boys turned as they heard him approach.

"Hey, guys, whatcha doing?" Canyon asked.

It took a minute for them to understand what he had said, and he blushed at the congestion and stutter that turned his words into indecipherable mush.

"He's showing me a secret," the younger of the two boys said, pointing to the older, taller boy.

"A secret, huh?" Canyon said. "Can I come?"

They looked skeptical. "I don't know. You're just a baby. A sick baby."

"Please? I'm not a baby."

One of them asked, "How old are you?"

"Nine," Canyon lied. The older boy scoffed. "Okay, eight but almost nine. I'm just small for my age. Jeez."

The two boys went off to the side of the trail and conferred in whispers. After what seemed an eternity, the older one beckoned to Canyon with his finger.

"You can come but you got to keep your mouth shut, okay? This is my secret lair and I don't want a bunch of babies finding out about it."

They went off the trail and walked along the creek for a ways until they came to a little hill. Just beyond the crest of the hill was a bramble of bushes, thick with berries and thorns. Canyon had never ventured this far in the woods and the bramble looked menacing and dangerous, like something out of the fairy-tale books his mother read to him.

The younger boy noticed Canyon's pause. "C'mon, he's not going to wait for us."

In fact, ahead of them, the older boy had disappeared. Laughing, the younger one hurried to catch up to him. Canyon wiped his nose on his shirt. The bush swallowed up the older kids, and the sound of laughter sounded far away.

And then all of a sudden it was quiet, and Canyon stood in the sunlight, alone.

He wiped his nose again and took a deep breath and pushed into the thicket. The leaves and branches weren't too thorny, after all, and he caught sight of the boys squatting in a small meadow, passing something between them. It was small, about the size of a cigarette, but it smelled different, sweeter.

"What's that?" Canyon asked.

The blond boys looked at each other knowingly.

The younger one said, "Weed. Want some?"

Canyon shook his head.

"Come on, *Canyon*. Live a little," the older boy said. He put the funny-looking cigarette to his mouth and inhaled, holding the smoke in as long as he could and then exhaling it in one big breath. He started coughing and hacking, his face turning beet red. The younger boy laughed but Canyon didn't dare. He'd seen that big kid wallop too many boys at school.

Over the sound of the coughing and the songs of the birds in the meadow, Canyon heard the low rumble of a diesel truck.

"You guys, shh. Someone's coming."

The older boy quickly ground out the cigarette under the heel of his boot. "Oh, shit. We're royally fucked if we get caught with this. I stole it from my mom's jewelry box."

"What do we do?" the younger boy said. He was in a panic. His dad was twice as mean as the older boy's dad.

"Quick, up there," the older boy said, and pointed up a small hill. "We can hide."

The boys took off running toward the hill. Canyon quickly fell behind, his breathing labored, his nose more stuffed up than ever. He felt too hot and he wondered if he had a fever. Stupid idiots. He should have known better than to follow a couple of losers like them into the woods.

He reached them finally, and found them lying flat on their bellies, on the backside of the small hill.

"Wha—" he started to say, and then the older boy was grabbing him and pulling him down on the hill and wrapping a hand across his mouth that smelled of tuna fish salad and motor oil. Canyon struggled against the big kid and then stopped when he saw what they were looking at, down at the creek below them.

Canyon's eyes grew wide as saucers. He watched, afraid to look away, afraid that if he did, the man would move and maybe make his way across the creek and up the hill to them.

The man wore a dark shirt, and blue jeans, and a ball cap pulled low against the sun. The woman wore a red dress, fitted at the waist and collar, like the one Canyon's mother wore to dinner with his father sometimes. A pickup truck was parked in the shade, under a tree. Someone sat in the passenger seat, hidden in the shadows, a cowboy hat pulled low.

The woman lay on the sandy bank of the creek, and the man

tugged at her arm, pulling her toward the water, but she was stuck, caught on something. He cursed, loudly, and gave a mighty heave, and the woman's head flopped back so that her eyes stared up at the children.

But they were beyond seeing a thing, those eyes, and Canyon felt a slow trickle make its way through his jockey shorts and down his legs. The older boy felt the wetness and pulled away from Canyon and then realized he still had his hand over the boy's mouth, so he pulled that away, too.

The man got the woman's body to the edge of the water. He whispered something and paused, brushing his hands on the seat of his pants.

And then Canyon sneezed, a great honking noise that filled the air like a flock of geese.

The man's head jerked up, so fast the kids never had a chance. The man looked across the creek and up over a small hill and saw two boys staring at him, their eyes filled with horror. The top of a third head, Canyon's, was bowed, the aftereffect of his sneeze, and by the time Canyon got his eyes back up, the man was knee-deep in the river, crossing over to them.

"Run," the older boy shouted. He and the younger boy took off toward the trail while Canyon panicked. He rolled down the hill and landed in a thicket, under thorny brambles and deep foliage. He heard the sound of a car door slam and he froze. He knew the passenger in the truck was joining the chase.

The hunt.

Canyon tucked his head down and curled into a tight ball and closed his eyes. He stayed there for hours it seemed, until finally he heard doors open and slam again, and the diesel truck's throaty engine start up and peel out of the woods on the old lumber road that led back into town.


Canyon Kirshbaum paused, took a deep breath, and wiped at the tears that streaked his cheeks.

His mother tsked-tsked from her spot in the bed. "When I came home from work, I found him in his bedroom, his clothes soaked in dirt and urine. He was in shock. I got enough out of him to piece together what had happened, and then I put him in a hot bath and we never spoke of it again."

I stared at her in disbelief. "You never went to the police, even after news of the missing boys hit the next day?"

The old woman shook her head. "Canyon never told me who he was with. He just said it was some kids from school, some older kids. I didn't know it was those boys. Besides, those cops would never have believed a word I said. And I couldn't risk it, for Canyon's sake. I just couldn't."

Finn swore. He stood in the doorway of the bedroom, a look of disgust on his face. "And you, Canyon, you never saw the man again?"

Canyon shook his head and shrugged. "I don't know. Maybe. Maybe not."

"What the hell does that mean?"

Misery filled the big man's eyes, prompting a fresh round of tears. "That's the damnable shame of it all. We never saw his face, none of us. He saw the cousins', but we never saw his goddamn face. That hat blocked everything. If only he'd known he was safe. I don't know if he even knew I was there. Otherwise, they'd have kept hunting."

I couldn't believe it. The woman in the red dress had to be Rose Noonan, whose body had been found downstream a month after the boys disappeared. The Woodsman had killed the McKenzie boys, thinking they could identify him as her killer.

And Canyon had lived, simply because the man hadn't seen his face. Unbelievable. The universe was filled with enough mystery that sooner or later, you stopped questioning it and started seeing the perfect, the goddamn perfect, sense of it all.

Beneath me, the bedsprings shook and then settled. Mrs. Kirshbaum was pale but dry-eyed. She stared at me. "I suppose you think I'm contemptible, don't you? You'll see, once you have that baby. You'll see."

"See what?" Canyon demanded. "All I know is that you had an opportunity to help those kids, and you didn't. You let me—no, you *made* me—forget what I'd seen. Like it never even happened. All those years, all those nightmares I had growing up . . . You kept telling me none of it was real, that I'd just imagined all of it. My God. To think that a part of me knew, that a part of me *remembered* all this time what happened to those poor little boys."

Canyon pulled a tissue from the box in the windowsill and blew his nose. He continued. "When you started talking about that afternoon, it felt like I was drowning and your words were an arm, reaching down to me, pulling me up and out of a big, black fog. I remember. I remember everything. And I'll remember until the day I die, long after you're gone. You were wrong not to go to the police, and you were wrong to let me think those years of nightmares were the result of a naughty, overactive imagination."

"You'll see. A mother's love doesn't know right or wrong. A mother's love just . . . is," Mrs. Kirshbaum whispered, and closed her eyes. "What should I have done? Gone to the police and told them my son *thinks* he saw a dead woman about to be disposed of? That he and some kids were doing drugs—drugs!—in the woods? They'd never have believed me. And if it was true—*if* it was true—well, then Canyon would have been in danger."

Understanding bloomed. "You had a record, didn't you? That's why you were afraid the cops wouldn't believe you."

Her eyes still closed, the old woman lifted a hand to her sagging breast and rubbed at it. Her hand traveled to her throat and she began to scratch at something on her skin.

"I never stole a dime from anyone. I cleaned that woman's house for ten years and she blames me when her silver goes missing. Not the Mexican gardener or the black plumber. Me, the Jew whore. She turned everyone in town against me. It was only by the grace of God that Mr. McGuckin was so desperate for help that he gave me a job. But he watched me like a hawk, you bet he did."

Canyon sighed. "Mother—"

"Canyon, I know you want to see the good in everyone but the world doesn't work that way. The cops were the worst. Sworn officers, give me a break. They put their hands on me. I was driving home, late, after work, and they pulled me over, two cars with lights and sirens and badges that entitled them to act like animals. There were four men. They made me stand against the car and then they took turns, patting me down, patting me up, patting me every which way they wanted. And then one of them, a big man who by the light of day tipped his hat to me at the grocery store and called me ma'am, he squeezed my breast and said 'Jew whores don't feel any different than regular whores, do they, boys?' and then he laughed. He laughed, Canyon, and I knew I would die before I put trust in a system that broken."

Canyon stood and crossed the room and bending over, took his mother's hand from her chest and replaced it in her lap. He kissed her on the forehead and whispered, "Mommy, hush now."

Mrs. Kirshbaum stared up at her son with eyes full of horror and grief and pain.

"I couldn't go to them, Canyon, I couldn't. Not after that."

# Chapter Thirty-eight

We left Mrs. Kirshbaum and Canyon in the bedroom and let ourselves out. I felt dirty, like I'd watched something obscene. And in a way, I had. What kind of a woman—what kind of a mother—would hide a thing like that? For thirty years?

Finn took the car keys from my hand. "I'll drive."

We got in the car but then sat there, too numb to leave. I rubbed my belly and leaned my head back against the headrest.

Finn said, "There's no way Nicky Bellington knew all of this, right? I mean, how could he? Mrs. Kirshbaum just called us. Nick's been dead almost two weeks."

He leaned his head back, too, and then turned and stared at me. "Right?"

"I don't know. I don't know anything anymore, Finn."

I took a deep breath and blew it out. My head was pounding. I opened the glove compartment, hoping for a bag of trail mix, a chocolate bar, anything. I found a dusty old bag of peanuts and I tore into it.

"I give up, this whole thing; the kids, Nicky, the circus, all of it. I don't care anymore. I just want Brody back from Alaska, and to deliver this baby, and to forget this whole miserable thing ever happened."

I chewed a few more of the peanuts and sucked the salty grease from my fingertips.

Finn glanced over at me. "You don't mean that. You're just upset."

I threw the empty wrapper at my feet and nodded. "Damn right I'm upset. I'm furious. We should arrest that woman for conspiracy, for aiding and fucking abetting. If she had gone to the police that day with Canyon's story, maybe she could have saved those boys."

"You heard her, she was scared. Would you have gone to the cops, if they'd done that to you?"

I was silent. Finn started the car and pulled away from the curb.

Finn continued. "Gemma, I need you to be here, okay? Wherever you are right now, come back. We need to get to the station and get all this written up. We need to figure out how this plays into Nicky's murder. We've got a motive for the McKenzie murders—the Woodsman thought they could identify him. And we know the Woodsman had a partner. Jesus, it changes everything. We've got to talk to Chief Chavez."

My cell buzzed against my hip and I checked the caller ID. "Speak of the devil—"

I answered and listened to the chief for a few minutes without speaking. He finished, and I said, "We'll be there in ten," and hung up.

I leaned to the left and looked at the dashboard. Finn was doing thirty-six in a thirty zone.

"What?"

"Annika Bellington's missing."

"Ah, hell," he said. He hit the lights and sirens and accelerated the car until we were streaking through the town in a haze of blue and red lights and shrill, ear-piercing sirens.

A dead son. A missing daughter. I didn't know what Terry and Ellen Bellington's breaking point was but I had a feeling we were approaching it.

# Chapter Thirty-nine

Angel Chavez fumed. "What the hell is going on?"

We stared at him. The suit he'd worn to Frank Bellington's funeral was rumpled. A coffee spill roughly the shape of Italy stained his white dress shirt. His eyes were bloodshot, his cheeks unshaven.

The chief asked again, "What the hell is going on?"

The small conference room was hot; there were too many of us in it. Finn, myself, Moriarty, Armstrong, Chief Chavez, two secretaries, and Mayor Bellington's chief of staff, that somber old bird whose name I could never remember. Her navy dress was impeccable, her pearls—*Pearl Gold.*

That was it. That was her name. No wonder it never stuck.

She was the first to respond to the chief. "Angel, if I may?"

He nodded and took a seat and pinched the bridge of his nose.

Pearl Gold removed her eyeglasses and folded them in her right hand. As she spoke, she tapped the pair against the palm of her left hand, one tap for each sentence. Her skin was an origami artist's practice paper; thin, delicate, full of lines and creases.

"Mayor and Mrs. Bellington believe something has happened to their daughter, Annika. They are terribly worried. She's not responding to the countless messages they've left on her cell phone."

I asked the obvious question. "When was the last time they spoke with her?"

Pearl Gold shrugged. "The last time anyone remembers seeing her was at the funeral this morning. Her car is at the house, and her clothes and personal effects seem untouched. She's simply . . . gone."

"A few hours? And we're already worried?" Louis Moriarty asked.

Pearl nodded. "Unfortunately, we are in this case. Annika wouldn't have missed out on her grandfather's service this afternoon."

Moriarty said, "Let's think about this. The girl is what, eighteen? Nineteen? She's young, cute. She probably found herself a boyfriend and she's holed up somewhere with him."

"That doesn't sound like Annika. And she's got a boyfriend— he's a band guy in New Haven," I said, remembering the first conversation I'd had with her. "Paul, or Pete. He goes to Yale, too."

Pearl Gold cleared her throat and attempted a smile. "Erm, yes, it's not *exactly* like Annika to up and run away. But she has done this before; she and Nicky, when they were quite young, maybe twelve or thirteen years old. They left a note that said they were running away from home. The mayor and his wife didn't worry, though, you see, because the children had taken sleeping bags, tents, a loaf of bread, and two jars of peanut butter. They knew when the children got tired of peanut butter sandwiches they'd come home."

Chief Chavez stood and paced the tiny room. "I'm guessing the Bellingtons have checked, and there's no peanut butter missing this time?"

Pearl Gold nodded. "Correct. The only thing missing is Annika."

"Her brother was murdered less than two weeks ago, I think we need to take this seriously, Chief," Finn said. He didn't bring up the Kirshbaums; we'd agreed to stay quiet on that until we knew more. There were still too many unanswered questions. We didn't know who the Woodsman was. We didn't know who his partner was.

Partners. That word was dancing across my mind a lot. Brody and I were partners—what kind of trust was there? Moriarty and

Finn, Finn and I. Partners could be friends, too, like Bull Weston and Frank Bellington and Louis Moriarty.

Did the Woodsman have friends? Was he a regular old guy, someone who'd been a monster once and who had found a way to still those demons?

The chief stopped pacing and sat down. "I agree; we need to take this seriously. The clock starts now. She's an adult, so we've got a forty-eight-hour window before this goes official. Pearl, you let the Bellingtons know we're going to do all we can. Finn, Gemma, keep working on the Nicky case. Lou, take Armstrong and give Avondale a hand. We got shit on Sam's hit-and-run, which means we've still got a would-be cop killer out there."

# Chapter Forty

If you're talking an eon, hell, if you're talking a century, two days is nothing, a single grain in a gallon jug of sand.

If you're talking a missing young woman, just out of childhood really, forty eight hours is an agony. A minute feels like an hour, an hour a day. Time passes and you look at the clock and you realize it's only noon, and not five or six or seven o'clock, as you'd hoped.

I was worried. The Annika I knew was sensible and sensitive. I couldn't fathom her up and leaving without a word to her parents; not after what they had just been through as a family. There was some piece of this puzzle that was missing, something that didn't add up, and it scared me. I felt like we were puppets being strung along by forces I could not identify, allowing us to see just enough of the final picture and then pulling us away.

Finn and I waited until we couldn't wait any longer, and then we tried to push Annika to the back of our minds and refocused our attention on her brother; on Nicky. But to do that, we needed to recover the original case files, the files I'd asked Sam to look into.

We parked across the street and stared at Sam's apartment building. Sam had woken from his coma but had no memory of the crash. He was just starting to understand what he'd lost—his leg, possibly his livelihood.

Finn said, "This is weird."

I nodded. "Tell me about it. Did you ever come here with Sam?"

"No. We met up a few times after work but always out at a bar. Do you think our guy was here?"

I shrugged. "Maybe, maybe not. Guess we'll see."

We locked the car and entered the building, a three-story World War II construct. The lobby was uncomfortably warm and heavy with the smell of stale disinfectant and burning incense. One wall contained twelve tin mailboxes, each with a locking door and a neatly printed label. On the opposite wall, hanging askew next to a faded watercolor of a pack of wild horses, a pockmarked bulletin board held business cards and a few brightly colored fliers.

The manager, a Vietnamese man with sad eyes and poor English, met us in the lobby. We followed him to the second floor and down a narrow hallway until he stopped in front of a door crossed with yellow crime scene tape.

Reaching under the tape, the manager slipped a key into the lock and then stepped back. The door opened with a sigh, releasing cool air out into the warm hallway.

"We got it from here, bud. Thanks," Finn said. He gave the man's back a hearty thwack. "We'll let ourselves out."

The manager nodded and moved away, his slipper-clad feet sliding across the parquet floor as quietly as feathers falling to earth. Finn pulled a switchblade from his back pocket and sliced the yellow tape, then held it to the side and motioned for me to enter. I squeezed by and found the light switch.

The apartment was nothing special. It was neither large nor small, with a living area, two bedrooms, a bathroom, and a kitchen. I started there, as it was closest to the front door, while Finn took a bedroom that seemed to double as an office.

Cabinets stained in a color last popular forty years ago held canned goods, plates and bowls, a few boxes of rice and cereal. But the appliances had been updated in the last few years, and the steel refrigerator hummed along, keeping milk, eggs, cheese, and deli meats cold for someone who wasn't coming home anytime soon. On the counter sat a juicer, its glass pitcher reflecting the cherry red of a toaster on its left and the deep black of a Mr. Coffee machine on its right. I left the kitchen and went to the other bedroom.

I glanced over a double bed, dresser, and nightstand. Sam's closet was organized and neat; clothes on hangers all hung to face the same way, and his dress shirts and uniforms were pressed and crisply ironed. On the dresser, a shallow bowl held a watch, a half-empty box of matches, a few dimes and a nickel, and a pair of cuff links. These I fished out of the bowl and felt the heaviness of solid silver. They were engraved with Chinese or Japanese symbols, and I wondered what they said.

On the bedside stand, a couple of paperbacks—an old Michael Crichton and a newer Stephen King—were stacked under a half-empty bottle of water. The nightstand had a drawer and I hesitated a moment, not wanting to invade Sam's privacy, but Sam was beyond caring and I couldn't leave the apartment without a thorough search.

The drawer stuck halfway open, caught on its tracks. I gave a mighty tug and a bottle of lubricant rolled forward and hit a box of condoms. The condoms were unopened; the lube expired by a few months. I thought of the pretty turquoise-eyed woman Sam had met at the bar, and a weight like a rock hit my chest. I sat on the edge of the bed and willed the tears that fell from my eyes to stop. Sadness comes in strange packages sometimes; today it was in the form of a box of condoms. I ached for what was taken from Sam, and from Nicky, too. And then I thought about Brody, and wondered if it was a sin to mistrust so much of our relationship.

I wiped my eyes and then reached my hand into the drawer and stretched to the back, grasping empty air with my fingers until I was sure I had covered the whole space.

"Got anything good?"

Finn stood in the doorway, a look of amusement on his face. He watched me untangle myself from the drawer and I looked away as I answered, not wanting him to see my tears.

"No, you?"

Finn shook his head. "Not yet. In the office, the paperwork is mostly bills and correspondence with his dad and his grandfather. There are lots of letters to and from the reservation. Luckily, the original Nicky case files all seem to be here. If our guy came by, he either couldn't get in or he wasn't looking for the files."

I nodded. The apartment had felt undisturbed.

"Avondale PD didn't come through, did they?"

"No, the chief asked them to lock-and-leave it until we'd done a sweep."

I left the bedroom and went to the living room. There, I paused a moment and then turned in a circle.

Sam was everywhere.

They say you can tell what's essential to a person by what he surrounds himself with, in the sacred spaces of his own home. If that's true—and I think it is—Sam's culture and ancestry were of utmost importance. The place was filled with tribal textiles and artwork.

Black-and-white photographs, portraits mostly, covered the wall above a maroon leather sofa, framed in different metals and woods. I knelt on the couch and looked up at them. All of them seemed to have been taken on some reservation; the same run-down government-issue buildings and dusty, dirt roads appeared in the background of most of them.

I pushed off the couch and bumped into the coffee table. On it, a wooden tray held a half-dozen candles, some melted down into mere puddles of wax; a handful of incense sticks; and a bundle of what looked like horse hair, wrapped into a short switch. In the center of it all was a chipped ceramic ashtray filled with bits of burnt paper, tissue-thin.

A breeze blew in then and lifted the crisp black pieces a few centimeters and then floated them gently back down. As the air caressed my bare shoulders a rash of goose bumps broke out across my flesh. The breeze retreated and I heard a whisper at my ear, one word said so faintly I might have imagined it.

*Go.*

Finn came out of the bedroom that doubled as an office, his arms heavy with files and folders. "This is everything, every damn note and file Moriarty and I wrote three years ago."

"Sam was thorough. He would have been a good cop."

Finn said, "Hey. He is a good cop."

"Yeah. Let's get out of here, we're wasting time."

"Do you want to look through this stuff, make sure we're not missing anything?"

I shook my head, more chilled by the second. "This doesn't feel right, being here. Close that window, would you, and let's go."

Finn tilted his head to the right and peered around me. "The window's closed."

I turned around; he was right. I walked to the glass and looked at the clasp. There was no need for a lock; thick putty-like paint held the latch shut. The view out of Sam's living room was uninspired: a parking lot with an army green Volkswagen bus parked at an angle, taking up three spots. A few slots down, a hot pink Vespa sat in the shadows of a Harley. Dumpsters, two for trash, one for recyclables, completed the tableau.

I jogged to the bedrooms and checked the sliding glass doors in each. Locked as well, each leading out to a narrow balcony.

"Gemma?"

I spun around. "Did you open these?"

Finn shook his head, watched me. I went back to the living room and reached up, waving my hand under the ceiling vents. Nothing.

"Gemma?"

I was fatigued and emotionally spooked. My stomach growled. "Forget it, I'll buy you lunch at Frisco's."

We ate a silent lunch at the restaurant, our hands and mouths busy with the steaming platters of enchiladas and fajitas until finally, we were sated. Finn waited until our server had refilled our iced teas and whisked away our plates before he pulled an interoffice manila folder out of his briefcase.

"What's that?"

Finn opened the flap and withdrew a black-and-white photograph, eight and a half by eleven inches. He took a look and then slipped it across the Formica table to me.

The photograph was of two objects: a necklace, and a notecard-sized piece of paper, with a single line written on it in block print.

"I can only see death and more death, till we are black and swollen with death."

Finn took a long swallow of his iced tea. "Yup. The actual necklace and notecard are in the evidence room, at the department's offsite storage center. We can go look at the real thing, but if we don't, at least you've seen what the necklace looks like and the note. No idea if they're relevant but they were sure hidden up high under Nicky's bed."

I stared at the photograph and then swore. "Finn, I've seen this necklace somewhere."

Finn tore open a pink packet of sugar substitute and poured it into his tea. He stirred it with the straw. He looked at me and said, "Yup."

"Tell me."

He sighed. "The other day, at the library? You showed me her driver's license. The forgotten one."

"Rose Noonan. Of course! The pendant is a rose, isn't it?"

The photograph of the necklace was blurred, but once you knew what you were looking at, you could see the petals and the budding leaves on the stem of the flower growing up the gold chain like it was a vine.

Finn said, "The question is, what was Nicky doing with a dead woman's necklace and a D. H. Lawrence quote on rotting corpses?"

He saw my look and continued. "I got curious after we found it, I looked it up on the Internet."

"You continue to surprise me, Finn, you really do."

He shrugged, finished his tea. I sat back in the booth, the faded teal leather squeaking as I moved.

I closed my eyes, watching the scene unfold, like a silent film produced for an audience of one. It's late in the day, but in the dark, cool basement, it might as well be midnight on the moon. Time moves slowly here, and Nicky has found an entire afternoon can pass by in the blink of an eye. Since that lady cop found the kids— the bodies—he's been here most days reading these old, dusty case files from the '80s.

If asked, he would be unable to explain his fascination.

He prays to God that he is never asked.

He thinks it has to do with the fact that life, for him, has always run so smoothly. Good looks, enough talent and smarts to get by, money to waste; yes, he was handed not just the silver spoon at birth but the damn golden ladle to boot. He's never known cold, never known tragedy, never known loss, except for the death of his grandmother, of course, and well, she'd been so sick, it was really a blessing, wasn't it?

But these kids, the McKenzie boys. The Woodsman. They represented another side to life that Nicky had no knowledge of but was desperate to understand. The dark, grim, *real* side, what the rest of the world experienced on a daily basis.

So he loses himself down here, asking the same question the cops did in 1985, and again in 2011: why these two? What made them special to him, to the Woodsman?

Because they *were* special to him, they had to have been. For if it was just random, what did that mean? What kind of a universe— what kind of God—allows that?

Then one day, he stumbles on a newspaper article about another special one, a woman, Rose Noonan. He looks at the picture they've included in the article, an old black-and-white photo that is obviously a reprint of a driver's license.

He stares at the picture, and then he sees *it*.

Nick's heart seizes for a second, two seconds, three seconds, and then it lets out a mighty beat and the blood and the heat and the oxygen race through his body and he gasps.

He has to hide this article, but where? That old librarian upstairs checks the workspace every night after he leaves, he knows she does. She'll know something's missing. He thinks and thinks and then realizes, *duh*, that if he puts it back in the same place no one would ever be the wiser.

And no one is.

I opened my eyes and slapped the table with the palm of my hand. "He recognized the necklace. Finn, he recognized the necklace. He must have."

Finn nodded and drained his iced tea. "It feels right. He recognizes the necklace, and puts two and two together and instead of four, he gets Rosie Noonan's killer. But how does he know it's the same prick that killed the kids, too?"

I thought on that. "Maybe he doesn't know for sure. Maybe he thinks it would be a hell of a coincidence if it weren't the same guy. Think about it, Finn. How many unsolved murders do we have in Cedar Valley? Three. Every death, every other death in the whole damn town, we can account for."

Our server, a cheery man in a sombrero, returned with the bill and I fished a twenty out of my wallet and laid it on the black tray, weighing it down with the pen he had provided in case of payment by credit card. Finn added a five for tip and we left.

At the front door, though, I stopped and then backtracked to a wall I'd noticed when we first came in.

Portraits, dozens of them, lined the wall. Taken over decades, they depicted different threads of the same family. The same dark eyes and heavy brows filled many of the faces and I thought about what gets passed down, parent to child, year after year, generation after generation, the visible lines of paternity and fidelity, and the invisible strains of legacy.

With one hand on my belly and the other at my mouth, worrying at a cuticle, I returned to Finn. He had continued on outside and waited by a bench, a toothpick in his mouth, hands in his pockets, briefcase at his feet.

I pulled him by the elbow toward the car. "We've got to find out how Nicky got that necklace. It's the key to everything."

# Chapter Forty-one

The station was quiet, and in spite of all that had happened, life in Cedar Valley went on as usual, chugging along as reliably as a locomotive on an engineer's schedule. I had an inch-high stack of paperwork to deal with, routine court notices on prior cases, a few summons that I would need to appear for, as a witness for the prosecution, an unpaid annual permit license fee that I could write off for tax purposes, and a dozen other things that had taken a backseat to the Nicky Bellington case.

Thoughts of Annika continued to bloom in my mind and I felt myself interrupted again and again with worry.

I spent a few hours working the pile, then called it a day at seven.

At home, more mail and correspondence had built itself into a tower that threatened to topple over if I breathed on it wrong. I spent an hour paying bills, filing paperwork, and tossing a backlog of catalogs and circulars into the blue recycling bin we kept out back. Seamus ate and then I ate, a bowl of shredded wheat with blueberries and walnuts tossed in for good measure.

I hoped for a word or two from Brody but my electronic in-box was empty. Thinking about Brody made me think about Celeste Takashima. I hated someone that I'd never even met. I hated that she knew me—she knew the man I loved and made love to, the eyes and mouth I woke up to, the genes that I carried in my belly.

Stop it, I told myself.

I crawled into bed and instead of the Woodsman, I dreamed

of a wide snowfield in Alaska, white and pure and empty as far as the eye could see. It should have been peaceful but it filled me with panic, all that space and nothing to fill the horizon. A frozen wasteland, a barren land void of humanity or life.

At six, my cell rang. The shrill ring beat my alarm clock by fifteen minutes.

It was the chief. "How soon can you get to the Bellingtons'?"

I was already pulling off my pajamas. "I can be there in thirty. Annika?"

"Terry found a ransom note rolled up in his morning copy of the *Denver Post*," Chavez replied. "Half a mil."

I whistled. "Cash?"

"What else? See you in twenty-five," he said, and hung up.

I skipped a shower and instead threw on clothes and brushed my teeth and ran a hairbrush through my hair and pulled it up high into a ponytail. The roads were clear and I made it to the Bellingtons' in just under a half hour.

Their driveway was full. I recognized the chief's car, and Finn's Porsche. The others, a black Range Rover with government stickers, and a mud-colored Jeep, and a red Ford Focus, I'd never seen before.

This time we met in the library, a dark-paneled room that was crowded. In addition to myself, Finn, and Chief Chavez, there was Pearl Gold, Terry and Ellen Bellington, and a lawyer who introduced himself as Dick Tremble. There was also a man in a black suit whose name I didn't catch. He stood against the wall, his hands in his pockets, his eyes half-open.

A fed.

We were in the midst of ten different conversations when the lawyer, Dick Tremble, began waving his arms and clearing his throat. When that didn't work, he called out "excuse me" and then said it again, louder.

"Excuse me, can we get a little order in here?" he asked.

We looked over at him, a tall, thin whippet of a man with a fringe of hair above his ears and below his nose. His mustache covered his upper lip and drooped down, like Yosemite Sam in that old cartoon. But his accent was pure Boston and his suit Savile Row all the way.

Once he had our attention, though, he seemed to lose focus. He stared first at the mayor, then at the chief, and finally at the federal agent, who stared back with a smirk, his hands still in his pockets, his eyes taking in everything.

Chief Chavez took control. "Let's see the note, Terry."

Mayor Bellington held up a clear ziplock bag, inside of which was a typed note. He read, "We have your daughter. If you want to keep her in one piece, do as we ask. We'll expect five hundred thousand dollars to be deposited into this account. You have forty-eight hours."

The ten-digit number for a bank account in Europe was scrawled in pen below the typed message.

Pearl Gold let out a whistle, her rouged lips continuing to pucker long after the sound had ended. "Half a million dollars. Sir, if this got out, this could set a bad precedent—"

The mayor interrupted her with a tone like a slap. "My daughter, Pearl. I'd give everything."

He walked across the room to a sideboard and poured brandy out of a crystal decanter and into a low tumbler. He held the glass up to the light and swirled the liquid, admiring the deep amber glow. Then he tossed it back in one long swallow.

Ellen Bellington sighed and pinched the bridge of her nose. She leaned against the long desk that anchored the center of the library, its surface bare, its lines sleek. "Dear, it's not even eight o'clock in the morning. I really don't see how drinking can—"

The sound of shattered glass cut Ellen off in her tracks, and she sighed again. Pearl Gold patted her on the shoulder, then walked over to the far wall and knelt and picked up large shards of the tumbler.

The mayor casually picked up a second tumbler and poured another inch of brandy. "Leave it, Pearl. Dear wife, I wish you'd stop treating me like a fucking child. And I wish, that for once in your goddamn life, your frigid soul could show a little warmth. Our daughter's life is in the hands of greedy, bad, evil men."

Ellen hissed back at him. "Screw you, you slimy worm. Just because I don't go to pieces like a ninny doesn't mean I'm not heartbroken. That girl *is* my heart. The only way I could even comprehend accepting, let alone understanding, Nicky's death was because of her. And now she's gone, too. And you, horrible man that you are, are all I have left."

Chief Chavez raised his hands, "Ellen, please—"

But she turned on him, too, and raised a hand in his direction, holding it high like a witch casting a spell with her words. "And you, you are worthless. Why don't you go back to what your people are good at, namely washing my car and picking produce in the field."

The chief's face paled and his hands fell to his sides.

The lawyer, Dick Tremble, cleared his throat and stepped forward, his mustache moving up and down with each word. "All right, we're all under a hell of a lot of stress here. None of this is going to help get Annika back. And that's our goal right now, isn't it?"

He waited until we all nodded. "Terence, Ellen, what's the bottom line here?"

Mayor Bellington set the tumbler down and, coming to some decision, nodded. "Dick, I'd like you to prepare the money. Angel, you and your team have done a hell of a job but this is out of your league. On my attorney's advice I've reported Annika's kidnapping to the FBI."

At this, the still unnamed fed removed his hands from his suit pockets and stepped forward. He stared at Chief Chavez. When he spoke, it was like ice cracking in March, thin and cold and unforgiving.

"Take an hour and get your files together."

Angel Chavez shook his head slowly. "I can't do that, partner. We are this close"—he held up two fingers and squeezed them together—"to solving the murder of Annika's brother. This kidnapping is, I'm sure, related."

The man with the voice like ice brushed an invisible speck of dirt from his arm and then one at a time straightened out his shirt cuffs. "Oh, you can keep your dead, my friend. We just want the live one. Ransom, possible state line crossing, this is big-boy stuff."

Had I missed something?

"What do you mean, state lines?"

The federal agent swung his head in my direction, his shoulders and torso and legs remaining still. His eyes made their way down my body, resting a moment on my swollen belly, then swung back up and stopped somewhere between my neck and my eyes. Then he grinned, and I decided he could keep his smile to himself. I preferred the blank look of contempt.

"We have reason to believe the kidnapper, or kidnappers, have taken Miss Bellington out of Colorado. I can't say more without compromising the case."

"You've seen the same ransom note we have. Is there something else?"

But the fed was silent, and at my side, Finn gave me a nudge.

There was more talk, of the European account—probably Swiss—and next steps, but I was only half listening. I thought the chief was right, the kidnapping and Nicky's murder were related. But it was unclear *how.* The obvious thought was some kind of a vendetta against the Bellington family, but that didn't add up when we factored in the Woodsman and the McKenzie boys. Maybe Annika's kidnapping wasn't related at all, but simply the action of someone taking advantage of Terry Bellington's fragile state in light of his son's recent murder and his father's death.

The fed and Dick Tremble and Pearl Gold huddled at the desk, strategizing. Chief Chavez and Finn sat on one of the couches, speaking in low tones. Ignoring Ellen and the mayor, who hadn't spoken directly to each other since their ugly outburst, I went in search of Mrs. Watkins, the nanny, Terry's sister.

I found her in the kitchen, putting together a tray of breakfast items that would in all likelihood go uneaten. Her eyes were swollen and her nose bright red. Not for the first time, I wondered at

what she saw and heard inside the Bellington manor. I wouldn't
have traded places with her for all the gold in the world.

Her hands were busying with a thin-bladed knife and a cedar
plank heavy with smoked salmon.

"I know most of you have already eaten, but I really don't know
how else to help," she said without looking up.

"I'm sure the chief and my partner won't pass up an offer of
breakfast, Mrs. Watkins."

Mrs. Watkins set down her knife. "Call me Hannah, please. If
Annika were here, I'd be making pancakes, her favorite. Lord
knows where the pancakes go; she's as thin as a reed. She'll eat a
dozen of 'em in one sitting, covered with syrup and butter, with
bacon extra crispy on the side. Ever since she was a little girl, she's
loved her sweets and her salty."

Her smile dropped and she sniffled. "I shouldn't tell you this,
Detective."

"What's that?"

"Annika told me I'm more of a mother to her than Ellen Bellington has ever been," Mrs. Watkins said, her voice low and proud.
She was tall and for the first time, I saw the resemblance between
her and Terry and Frank. It was faint, the way it is sometimes between male and female relatives, but it was there nonetheless.

"Nicky and Annika were the best part of my life. All I've ever
done is try to keep watch over those kids, protect them from all
the crap that life can throw at you. Well, I've sure done a piss-poor
job, haven't I? One kid dead, one kid kidnapped," Mrs. Watkins
said. "And now Dad's gone, too."

"I'm so sorry, Hannah. From what I can tell, you've taken care
of the entire family."

With a nod, she thanked me and began spreading cream cheese
on toasted bagels. "I always have. My father made it clear, family
is the only thing you've got at the end of the day. Friends come and
go; lovers will leave you in the morning. But family? Family sticks
together."

Her eyes filled with tears and she paused to wipe at them with a paper towel. "Sometimes I feel like this family is cursed. So much death . . ."

It was the most I'd ever heard the woman say at one time. It was as though her father's death and Annika's disappearance had loosened some dam in her. I took a gamble.

"Mrs. Bellington thought you might know where Annika kept an address book? I hate to search her whole room, as I know the FBI will do so later today."

Ellen Bellington hadn't said anything of the sort but I thought it worth a try.

Hannah Watkins shook her head. "No, you know kids these days. Everything's on their phones."

She gave me a sly look and slid something out of the pocket of her white apron. I couldn't tell what it was, other than the object was small and dark.

"I should probably have given this to that FBI agent," the housekeeper said. "But he isn't a very nice man."

She slid the shiny, black object across the counter to me and then began arranging the bagels on a tray. She said, "I guess I'll just have to tell them I don't remember the last time I saw it. Truth be told, I'm not sure what good it will do you. She's got another phone, a newer model, that she uses now. This one probably doesn't have much information on it."

It was better than nothing.

I whispered a thank-you and left the kitchen, tucking the phone into my purse as I went. In the library, I found Finn still on the couch, awkwardly seated next to Terry Bellington, looking at a photo album that Terry balanced on his lap. Chief Chavez and the fed were looking at something on the desk. Dick Tremble and Ellen Bellington were nowhere to be seen.

I gave Finn a jerk of my head, a "let's go," and he half shrugged in response, an "I'm trapped" kind of message.

I was anxious to take a look at Annika's phone and start calling her friends, maybe even her boyfriend, but I needed Finn's stronger tech skills to bypass her password. I sighed and sat in one of the wing chairs and crossed my ankles to keep my feet from bouncing.

*C'mon, c'mon.*

The Peanut did a few flips in my belly and my thoughts drifted away to Brody and Alaska and a parka as pink as Pepto-Bismol.

I half listened as Terry slowly turned the pages, pausing to point to something and murmur a name or a date. I heard him mention Nicky's name, and Annika's. At the big desk in the middle of the room, the fed and Pearl Gold continued examining some documents. They were soon joined by the lawyer and Dick Tremble. The lawyer got on the phone and spoke in low tones with the head of some bank.

Someone lit a fire in the fireplace and the room was warm and twice I felt myself drifting off, thinking a nap would be lovely. At some point, I looked up and over at the duo on the couch, just as Terry was turning another page.

I watched as the color fell from Finn's face.

His eyes first narrowed and then grew as wide and as bright as suns. Slowly he raised them until he was looking right at me, and his mouth fell gently open.

Then Terry was elbowing him, and turning the page, and the color rose back into Finn's face and then some, until his cheeks were as flushed as roses.

# Chapter Forty-two

Outside, Finn was cagey. "Meet me in town."

"What happened back there? What did you see?"

We stood between his car and mine, the midmorning sun laying a blanket of warmth to the world around us. We were the first ones out of the house and it stood over us like a silent glass sentinel, keeping its secrets to itself.

Finn shook his head vigorously. "Not here. Um, the bookstore on Twelfth Ave? There's a coffee shop."

"Not the station?"

"No, somewhere more private. The bookstore," he said again. He slid into the Porsche and gunned the engine and pulled out of the driveway without another word.

The chief and Pearl Gold came out the front door with the FBI agent behind them. He paused and stared in my direction, his eyes obscured by mirrored sunglasses. Then he tipped an imaginary hat at me and pointed a hand in the Range Rover's direction. Its doors unlocked with a sharp click and the engine started before he was completely in the car.

Nice what federal money could buy.

I headed back into town and found a parking spot a few blocks down from the bookstore. Inside, a few customers strolled the aisles. The coffee shop at the rear of the store was nearly empty. Finn sat at a small table beneath a stained glass window, his head in his hands. A latte sat before him, its foam peaks untouched.

Finn jumped as I approached. I sat down and said, "Spill."

He looked near tears. "That fucking family, Gemma. I mean, how screwed up can one family be? Is it something in their DNA? Or do they all go crazy because of one another?"

I felt like slapping him but sat on my hands instead. When he was ready, he would talk. Finn pulled the latte toward him, spilling a few drops onto the table. His hands were trembling.

"Hey," I said, reaching across and taking the cup from him. "Hey, breathe, buddy. That's it, in and out."

I breathed with him, keeping my eyes locked on him, until he broke contact. He blushed and the old Finn came back with a vengeance and for the first time in my life, I was glad to see it. "Jesus, Gemma, I'm fine. This isn't my first rodeo. It's the fucking *grandmother*, you know?"

No, I didn't know.

He continued. "In that book, the photo album, you saw it? It's right there, plain as the nose on my face. Frank's wife, Terry's mother. Nicky's grandmother. She's wearing the goddamn necklace."

"You saw a photograph of Rachel Bellington wearing Rose Noonan's necklace?"

Finn didn't respond, just stared glumly across the table. Now I did tap him, gently on his cheek with the back of my hand. "Earth to Finn, come in."

"Yeah, yeah, I saw a woman wearing the necklace. The same woman Terry Bellington had just pointed out to me as his dear old dead mother."

I sat back. It all made sense. Perfect sense. Frank's attempted assault on Julia; his mean, racist streak that he kept so well-hidden.

Finn said, "Frank Bellington was the Woodsman. He killed Rose Noonan, and then killed the McKenzie boys to keep them from identifying him. And then—he's so goddamn smart, I can't believe it—then he holds on to Rose's body for a month and *then* dumps it. No one can connect the disappearance of two little boys with the murder of a young woman."

I couldn't even nod in agreement. We should have known, as soon as we realized Nicky recognized the necklace.

Finn was saying something, something I'd missed. The roar in my ears was loud, like a train driving through my head. Implications were bouncing off each other.

"What?"

"Do you think there's more? Others? He was never caught, so maybe there was no incentive for him to stop killing. God, I hope there's not more."

I hadn't even considered it. "If there are, they weren't from Cedar Valley. We can look for patterns, check the national databases . . ."

My words trailed off. Here we were, talking about other possible victims, and we hadn't even made the first steps toward any kind of legal proceedings. We could never charge Frank, of course, but we could sure as hell make sure this town knew who had been terrorizing our dreams all these years. We would need to gather evidence, go through his things. There would be counseling needed for the rest of the family . . . the rest of the family.

"Finn, stop a sec. Sure, okay, we've got Frank as the Woodsman. But he was housebound, so there's no way he killed Nicky. And he certainly didn't kidnap Annika and stash her somewhere, holding her for a half mil in ransom. Think of everything else; Sam's accident, the creepy messages left for you and me."

When Finn picked up the latte this time, his hands were steady. He sipped from it.

"You're right, it's not possible."

He set the cup down and gripped his hair in his hands. "Just when we get something concrete, everything else falls apart. One step forward and ten steps back."

I thought about our visit to the Kirshbaums. "Don't forget, if Canyon's story is true, then the Woodsman had a partner. Maybe he's the one doing all of this."

"But who was his partner? And don't say Louis Moriarty, Gemma."

"Why not? Finn, it makes the most sense that Frank's partner would be one of his close friends. Hell, it might have been my step-grandfather, Bull Weston. Or Jazzy Douglas . . . or any number of guys he hung around with."

"You don't really believe Bull had anything to do with this, do you?"

I shrugged. "Well, no, but I'm just saying—we can't rule anyone out."

I recounted Bull's story of Frank's attack on Julia to Finn. He was surprised and then said that Rose's killing certainly seemed to fit a pattern in Frank's life.

Finn finished his coffee and started shredding a paper napkin in his hands, pulling it apart, strip by white paper strip. "What I don't understand is how that old son of a bitch lived here for the last thirty years, normal as you please, all the while a murderer. He raised a family, saw his son become mayor, no problem, just your average old guy, playing with the grandkids."

"Doesn't that happen a lot, though? I mean, BTK . . . probably the Zodiac Killer . . . hell even Ted Bundy's neighbors thought he was just your normal average dude," I said. "And sooner or later, they all get caught. A feeling here, an inkling there . . . sooner or later, someone connects the dots."

Finn nodded. "Nicky did that. He made the connection. But why not tell someone? He had the proof; he had it all right there. The necklace links Franklin to Rose Noonan's death. And Kirshbaum's story links Rose Noonan's death to the McKenzie boys."

I shook my head slowly. "But Nicky didn't know about Canyon Kirshbaum, remember? All Nicky suspected was that his grandfather killed Rose Noonan."

"Maybe he did tell someone. Just the wrong someone."

I felt like tearing my own hair out. Everything fit and nothing fit.

Finn exhaled. "Bear with me. In 1985 Frank Bellington rapes and kills Rose Noonan, maybe she wouldn't let him do her; maybe it's a fit of passion, whatever. He, with a partner, takes her body to the river to dump it. He's probably hoping she'll float all the way down to Mexico. Unfortunately for old Frank, though, just as he's about to dump Rose, he notices some kids watching him. Well, shit. His plan is screwed. He and this unknown partner go after them instead. And then he's still stuck with a dead woman. So, he holds on to her body for a while. He's smart; he doesn't want the killings connected. Then for thirty years he lives in the same town, in plain sight the whole time. He would have watched the town go crazy with grief, searching for the kids. All that time goes by, and then boom, you—completely by accident—find the bodies. It's big news; so big that Frank's grandson gets interested. Nicky starts digging around and he finds a photo. He recognizes a necklace that his grandmother wore and puts two and two together. Then *he* dies, in an accidental fall. Only, he doesn't really die, he disappears for three years. Then he returns to Cedar Valley and within a day or two, he is killed, for real this time. And now his sister's been kidnapped."

I nodded. "Yes, I think that about sums it up. What we're still missing is what happened in between Nicky's discovery, and Nicky's first fake death. *Who did he tell?*"

"And what the hell did they say to scare Nicky enough to make him go on the run?" Finn asked. He finished his latte and wiped his mouth with the back of his hand. He continued. "Jesus, Gemma, I thought I was going to lose it in there. When I saw that picture . . . I was sitting right next to Terry, you know? His dad's the goddamn Woodsman and I'm sitting right next to him."

But I barely heard Finn.

Something else, something Annika had said to me, was flitting around the edges of my mind, creating some very unpleasant thoughts.

"Finn," I said slowly, "Finn, I know who Nicky talked to. I know who he told."

He stared at me, this man that most of the time I loathed but who I was also growing to respect quite deeply. Someone I didn't know that well, but with whom I would have trusted my life.

Partners are like family. They can challenge you, irritate the heck out of you, but ultimately, if you're lucky, they'll always have your back.

If you're not lucky . . .

I pushed away from the table and fished the phone Mrs. Watkins had given me out of my purse.

"We have to find Annika. She's the key to everything."

# Chapter Forty-three

Four hours later, I'd called most of the contacts in Annika's phone. A different picture of her was forming in my mind than the one I'd carried with me over the last few weeks. Most of the people who answered my calls were reluctant to talk much, once I told them why I was calling.

The picture I got was of a young woman; smart, beautiful, gifted with every grace possible since birth, but cold in spirit and mean as a snake.

Cruel but controlled.

One of the girls I spoke to had been a fellow student in Annika's English lit class the previous spring. She used words like master manipulator and sociopath, and I felt the knots in my stomach twist harder and harder.

"She even had our professor under her thumb. I don't know what she said to him, but he was so cowed by her that she got an A after missing half the semester. The days she was there, she'd sort of saunter in and bully people," the young woman told me. "I always thought that one day she might just come in and start shooting."

I was at my desk, the phone to one ear, taking notes with my free hand. "What do you think made her tick? Why did she act that way?"

Silence on the other end and then the young woman sighed. "Honestly? I think she was bored."

. . .

Chief Chavez checked in before he left for the night. There'd been no word from the kidnappers. I caught him and Finn up on the latest with Annika.

"Do you know what you're saying? This is totally nuts," the chief said.

I knew it was nuts. The whole case was nuts.

I said, "I've talked to dozens of people. They all say the same thing—and these are people she kept as contacts in her phone! No one crosses Annika Bellington, certainly not back East. Maybe she's different here, at home, but there? Half these people are scared to death of her."

Finn added, "She manipulates them to get what she wants and then lords their weaknesses over them. Classic bully behavior, Chief. Narcissism to the extreme."

Chavez sighed as he loosened his tie, and then removed it completely. He took a seat at the edge of my desk, his hiked-up pant legs exposing a pair of mismatched socks. He held the tie in his hands, his fingers running back and forth along its silk edges.

We still hadn't told him our suspicions that Frank Bellington was the Woodsman. I didn't know why we were waiting, Finn and I, except that when we did break the story, we wanted to tell the *whole* story.

And without knowing who kidnapped Annika, or why, the story was incomplete.

"Okay, okay, I get it, Annika's not the nicest person around. Look at her mother, the girl probably never had a chance," the chief said. "What's your plan?"

Finn and I looked at each other and then answered in unison, "Work the case, Chief."

It was soon too late to continue calls to the East Coast due to the time difference. I decided to make one last call, to a Peter Dillen, whose phone number was saved in Annika's phone contacts list under the nickname "Honey Bunches."

I figured he had to be the notorious garage band boyfriend

Pete, so I left a message and asked him to call me back as soon as possible.

We reconvened at nine o'clock the next morning. As I walked into the station, Finn met me with a cup of tea in one hand and a piece of paper in the other hand.

"For me?"

Finn handed me the tea and the paper. I took a few sips and read the scribbled message: call Joe Fatone at the circus A.S.A.P.

"We're leaving town, Deputy," Fatone said when I got hold of him ten minutes later.

I leaned back against the counter and cradled the phone against my shoulder, peeling an orange. I'd found it in the staff lounge next to a snack-size package of crackers I planned to eat next.

"On whose authority?"

"Chief Chavez's," Fatone continued. "He cleared us this morning. He said you all got what you needed from the crime scene and that he'd get in touch if you needed anything else."

I sighed. Yes, we had what we needed evidence-wise, but the thought of the circus packing up and leaving left me glum. There were unanswered questions there. I'd never know the real truth between Lisey and Tessa, if all their drama really was about a complicated love triangle.

"Well, c'mon by, then, if you've got time," Fatone said. I heard ice clink in a glass and he swallowed, the sound loud and clear through the phone. "I've got something for you."

# Chapter Forty-four

If a circus coming to town is the greatest thing on Earth, a circus leaving must surely be one of the saddest. The workers and performers looked happy to be moving on to their next destination, but there was a sense of finality to the scene, a sense of ending, that made me melancholy.

"Where will you go next?"

Fatone and I walked the perimeter, him stopping every few yards to check on rigging or instruct a worker to change how they were doing something. Decaying food and bits of trash were ground into the dirt below our feet, the remnants of one great, big party.

"We have a contract in Santa Fe, so we'll make our way down there and stay a few weeks, then head west to Arizona," Fatone said. "We stayed here too long as it is."

"I'm sorry. That couldn't be helped," I said. "What about Tessa? And Lisey?"

He shrugged. "What about them? They're like sisters, fighting like cats and dogs one minute, hugging and crying the next. One big family, that's what we are. They'll be fine. They always are."

I wasn't sure if he meant the girls specifically or the entire lot of them.

"I've got big plans for Tessa," Fatone said. He bent to pick up something sharp and rusty and tossed it into the woods, overhand like a baseball pitcher.

"I want to put her in a one-person act and make her the star. She's ready."

"Can you do a trapeze act with just one person?"

Fatone squinted into the distance, looking east toward Kansas. "Do you think those pioneers would have crossed all those thousands of miles if they knew what monstrous mountains awaited them?"

I shrugged. Above us the sun grew higher still, rising up on the waves of the very heat it pulsed down.

"Hell, who knows, but we're going to try. It might revolutionize circus acts for time immortal," he said.

"You said you had something for me?"

Fatone nodded and took my elbow, tugging me toward his trailer. "A box of Reed's—Nicky's—things. I just found it so your cop friends must have missed it. It was sitting under the bed in his cabin."

Nicky hid a lot of things under his bed, I thought.

The inside of the trailer was as warm and airless as I remembered. In the window, a fly buzzed against the closed pane, a few fallen comrades like desiccated raisins in the sill beneath it.

Behind me, Fatone gently closed the door. "It's there, that shoe box, on the table."

I sat and he leaned across me, pushing open the window. The fly sailed out on the first breeze, and I removed the lid from the box, staring at the objects that lay inside.

"Did you look inside?" I asked Fatone.

I knew he had, he must have, but he shook his head and shrugged.

"It didn't feel right. I knew it was his, being under the bed and all, and I didn't want to handle it more than I needed to," he said, taking a seat across from me. "It's a dirty business, all around."

It was an interesting choice of words, considering what the box contained.

There were half a dozen Polaroid shots of Nicky and Tessa in various stages of undress, limbs and clothes draped strategically over their bodies. The pictures didn't contain anything you wouldn't see in a bathing suit, but there was a sense of intimacy to them that made me feel as though I was violating something sacred.

Under the photographs was a stack of vintage postcards, from what looked like the 1950s and 1960s, each with a cute saying or cheesy line. They were all addressed to Reed—Nicky—and signed Tessa. None had been mailed, though, and I imagined she collected them, and then left them for him, maybe on his pillow, or in a book.

A surprise, from a girlfriend to her boyfriend, and I wondered who had taken the photographs. The angle seemed impossible for a tripod.

"Do you think I should have given the box to Tessa?" Fatone asked. He pulled a cigar from his front pocket and wet the tip of it with his tongue, but didn't light it.

I didn't know what to do with the box. I felt a great sense of fatigue creep over me and I wanted to put my head down and close my eyes and sleep for a hundred years.

"Why don't I hold on to it for a while," I said. "If it turns out we don't need it, I'll forward it on to Tessa in the mail."

Fatone nodded. He stared out the window, noticed the dead flies in the sill, and brushed them out with the edge of a magazine. Against my hip, my cell buzzed. I didn't recognize the number, but it had a Connecticut area code so I answered. When I heard who it was, I excused myself from Fatone's trailer and stood just beyond it, under the shade of a large pine.

"Pete? Thanks for holding. My name is Gemma Monroe, I'm a detective in Cedar Valley, Colorado."

# Chapter Forty-five

Annika's boyfriend had been sick, was still sick, and so our conversation was punctuated with coughs and great, heehawing squawks as he repeatedly blew his nose.

"Like I said, I haven't talked to her in weeks. She's batshit crazy, man. I couldn't take it anymore," Pete said.

He sneezed and swore. "I hope to God she's not coming back in the fall."

"Can you tell me anything else? I get that your breakup was bad, but some details would be really helpful."

Pete spent the next ten minutes describing the living hell Annika put him through for the majority of their relationship. I asked him the same question I'd asked the others—why?

Through the phone I heard a sigh and then he spoke again. "I don't know why, man. She's rich, privileged. You know, bored."

Pete's voice was a mere croak by that point and I decided to let him get off the phone, but he had one more thing to say.

"Hey, ask that bitch if she's got my hand," he said. He coughed, a wet hacking sound that was thick with phlegm.

I wasn't sure I'd heard him right. "Your hand?"

"Yeah, my hand. My claw. I haven't seen it since the night we broke up. The thing's custom-made, cost me eight hundred bucks."

I was confused. "What does this claw look like, Pete?"

"Check out the clip of our show at the Oriental in July, in Concord. That was the last time I had it on stage. Hellkat's just not the same without it."

"Do you have a video you can send me?"

Pete sighed and coughed again. "YouTube it, lady."

He hung up and I stood a minute, under the tree, searching online, but the browser on my phone seemed to load at a snail's pace. I went back to Fatone's trailer. He answered on the second knock, and I could see that I'd woken him from a nap.

"Just lay down for a minute. This heat—" he began.

I interrupted him. "Do you have Internet?"

He shook his head. "Sorry, no."

"That's okay but I've got to go, Mr. Fatone. I'll be in touch," I said, and left with the box of photographs and postcards and headed into town. At the local Starbucks, I pulled into the parking lot and sat, my engine running, the air-conditioning pouring over my body like a salve. I fished my laptop from the trunk of my car and checked the browser—the signal was at full strength, the wireless from the coffee shop powerful.

On the video-sharing Web site YouTube, I typed in the words Hellkat, July, and Concord and ten links popped up.

I clicked on the first linked video.

It was grainy, likely shot on a cell phone, but then the person recording zoomed in to the stage and the band crystallized into focus. Pete was center stage, screaming into a microphone. The drummer was going nuts behind him, and a couple of bass players flanked him, their long hair waving in the breeze supplied by two giant fans on either side of the stage.

And then Pete raised his right hand and waved it in the air.

I saw the claw and my heart stopped as another large piece of the puzzle fell into place. I watched one more minute and then threw the laptop on the passenger seat and raced out of the parking lot.

I had to get to Ravi Hussen.

The medical examiner was at the morgue, finishing up on an elderly man. The attendant whispered "heart attack" to me as I paced the hall, anxiously waiting for Ravi to wash her hands and slip off her sterile robes. The minutes dragged by like hours.

"Gemma, what is it? You look ready to burst," she said.

I pulled her into an empty side room and popped open my laptop. I'd bookmarked the site and it was up and running in under a minute.

She watched the clip and then hit the back button and watched it again, her forehead furrowed.

"Hmmm," she said.

"Well? Don't you think?"

I played it again and paused at the moment where Pete's arm was first lifted. The claw glittered in the stage lights, each two-inch nail picking up the flashes of strobes and cameras. It was wicked looking, a cruel parody of a cat's paw. It was an instrument of torture.

It was an instrument of death.

Ravi exhaled and sat back and stared at me. "Yes, it could be. Without seeing it in person, and matching the claws to the wounds on Nicky's throat, I'm not willing to go on record as saying it's a match."

"How about off record?"

She nodded. "Off record . . . yes. The length of the nails, the edges, it could definitely be our murder weapon. Now tell me who the hell that is, and where that thing might be."

"I can't. Not yet. I need to check on a few things first," I said, and grabbed my laptop and purse.

"Gemma—" Ravi started to say but I'd left the room before she could finish her sentence.

I needed to find Chief Chavez, and fast. The kidnappers' deadline for the money transfer was coming up and once that half million dollars left the Bellingtons' account, all bets were off.

# Chapter Forty-six

Five o'clock in the afternoon, and the police station was empty. The lone receptionist—a temp—sat at the silent switchboard, her neon green nails flicking the pages of a newspaper with a crisp efficiency.

Outside, an evening shower had crept in, and rain fell gently against the windowpanes.

I was out of breath and I couldn't get my pulse to slow down. "Where is everyone?"

The temp looked up at me and smiled. "I'm not sure, honey. Chief Chavez left a message that he was going to be gone the rest of the day. I think he was attending some political dinner tonight. A couple of guys took a call on an accident out east. Everyone else is out on patrol. You know."

Yeah, I knew all right.

I was halfway down the hall when the temp called me back. "Oh, I do have a message for you, from Finn. He said he got a tip that he's checking out, but he'll be back real soon and you shouldn't wait for him. He signed it 'dear,' now isn't that sweet?"

She flipped the note around so I could see the word scribbled at the bottom but I barely noticed it.

"Did he say what the tip was? Or where he was going?"

The temp shook her head and resumed her newspaper perusal, each flip of the pages sharp-sounding in the silent station.

Shit.

I paced at my desk for half an hour, calling, and then leaving messages, for Chief Chavez and Finn. I tried the Bellingtons, but no one answered. Not even a machine picked up, and I cursed again. I called the mayor's office and some man with a snooty voice explained that Mayor and Mrs. Bellington were attending a fund-raiser dinner and would be unavailable for the rest of the evening.

Nothing kept this family away from the voters, it seemed.

I left another round of messages. "Call me, it's urgent, very important. Call me."

Where the hell was everyone? At six-thirty I couldn't wait any longer. I stopped at the front desk on my way out.

"You tell the next damn cop that walks in that door—I don't care who it is—to call me, all right? I don't care what time it is. Call me."

The temp nodded, her eyes solemn at the seriousness in my face, and in my voice. I pointed a finger at her, probably closer to her face than she would have liked.

"You tell them to call me," I said again on my way out the door.

# Chapter Forty-seven

The Bellington house was dark and still, a giant glass spaceship asleep for the night. I stood and watched as the rain hit the black windows and gray concrete and thought about the stains in life that can't be washed away.

To anyone watching me from the house, I would have looked menacing—a hooded figure, cloaked in a black raincoat, hovering about the edge of the forest like a masked killer.

I had parked in a turnoff a quarter of a mile down the road and walked the rest of the way. There was a chance that Mrs. Watkins—Aunt Hannah—might be home. I had the element of surprise on my side and I wanted to keep it that way.

A single light burned above the front door. I knocked heavily, three times, and waited.

Nothing. Maybe I got lucky and Mrs. Watkins was out for the evening, too.

Doubt crept over me and I shivered in the cool, wet air.

I must be insane, to be here.

I walked around the perimeter of the house on a narrow footpath, setting off a motion-sensor light. The sudden brightness made me jump. The rain came down in a light mist that dampened instead of drenching. I adjusted the hood on my rain jacket and passed by a small, fenced-in garden, guarded by a bright blue wheelbarrow, a bag of sod, and an orange hose looped on a hose coil. A pair of gardening gloves lay in the soil, abandoned by their owner.

The strong smell of mint hit me and I had an inexplicable craving for sweet tea. The Peanut gave a single kick and then stilled and I felt another shiver pass through me.

What was I doing here?

You know what you're doing here, I whispered to myself. You're searching for goddamn evidence. If my theory was right, once her parents completed the money transfer according to the directions in the kidnappers' note, Annika would bail. She'd leave Cedar Valley half a million dollars richer. I hoped I was wrong, that Annika didn't kill her own brother and fake her own kidnapping.

That she hadn't tried to kill Sam Birdshead.

That her grandfather's violent, murderous streak hadn't skipped a generation and blossomed in the charming young woman whose involvement in the case I'd been blind to, since the day I interviewed her in her room.

I kicked at a rock in the middle of the footpath and set it soaring off into the dark air. It landed somewhere with a dull thud and I wished I could kick something more meaningful. I'd been distracted by the Woodsman murders, and by the thought of Brody canoodling with Celeste Takashima in the arctic tundra.

Annika had been there all along, in plain sight.

I'd missed taking the close, hard look that I should have at Nicky's family; at his sister, his twin sister, the one person closest to him in the whole world. Annika was a narcissist and a bully and a killer.

And somewhere in that house was the evidence.

I reached the end of the path and saw a four-car garage connected to the house by a covered-walkway. Breaking and entering, searching a property without warrant or probable cause . . . Finn's words came to me like a permission slip from God himself: the ends justify the means.

I told myself to remember the cliff, the overhang just beyond the house. It would be easy to lose my footing in the dark, easy and fatal. At the garage, I paused by the first door and felt around the front of it, down low, toward the ground. There—a handle.

I twisted and turned it to the side and then heaved and I was rewarded with a squeak that sounded like a gunshot. Pausing, I looked back at the house again. The great glass spaceship was still dark.

The rain began to beat down harder.

I wished Finn was at my side, but he wasn't, so instead I tried to channel his arrogant Devil-may-care attitude and lifted the door high enough to duck and squeeze under, and I did, emerging into blackness deeper than the night I'd left outside.

On the wall, I found a switch. I flicked it up and down but the power was out. The garage seemed to grow even darker, as though I were in some kind of black hole that was swallowing all and every source of light. My breath seemed to come faster. I forced myself to close my eyes, embrace the quiet rather than fear the dark, and *think*.

What had I grabbed from the car? My cell phone, my gun . . . and a tiny flashlight, no more than a penlight really. I pulled it out from the pocket of my rain jacket and turned it on.

The light bounced around in a narrow, thin beam that made the rest of the darkness seem immense. There was enough light, though, to make out three cars and a fourth spot, empty.

If Terry or Ellen drove to the fund-raiser, that meant one car was Annika's, one car probably belonged to Mrs. Watkins, and one car was either the mayor's or Ellen's.

The rain came in through the half-lifted garage door, splashing my lower legs and soaking my tennis shoes. I moved to the front of the cars. There was a space of just a few feet between the cars and the back wall of the garage. Along the back wall were hung bicycles and sporting equipment, hockey sticks and skis and a goalie net, folded up and draped awkwardly like a massive, long-forgotten spider web.

Slowly, I walked down the line of vehicles.

The first one was a black Lexus SUV with a personalized pink breast cancer awareness license plate that read "Elle-1." Ellen's car. The exterior was spotless and I shone the light through the driver's side window. Clean, tan leather seats. A stainless steel coffee tumbler sat in the cup holder. I tested the door; locked.

The second car was a navy blue Honda Accord, maybe two or three years old, with a sheepskin cover over the steering wheel and a Yale license plate holder around out-of-state plates. I figured it must be Annika's car. It had been recently washed and waxed and it gleamed in the beam of the flashlight. I peeked in the window, and two things gave me pause.

The first was a day planner about the size of a hardcover novel, printed with photographs of different breeds of cats. The second was a receipt from Same Day Clean Way Laundry. The name on the receipt was Hannah Watkins and it had yesterday's date stamped at the top.

The Annika I knew would drop dead if she was spotted carrying that day planner, which begged the question, was Mrs. Watkins borrowing Annika's car? And if so, why?

Maybe Mrs. Watkins's car was in the shop. I shrugged and passed by the empty spot. An old fluid spill stained the concrete floor, and I moved on to the third and last car in the garage.

It was about the size of Annika's Honda Accord, some kind of four-door sedan. I couldn't tell the make or model or color for the vehicle was completely hidden by a light gray car cover.

I took hold of one corner of the cover and slowly pulled, tugging the cloth until it puddled at my feet in a large heap.

I stared at the car and my heart stopped.

An old white Toyota Camry with a busted right headlight winked at me.

*Deep breaths, Gemma, deep breaths.*

I pulled out my iPhone and took a picture, using the phone's flash. I stared at the photograph on my screen and saw something glinting in the broken headlight.

I looked back at the car and didn't see anything. Another look at the picture—yes, there was definitely something in the headlight.

I crouched down and shone my flashlight in there.

"What the hell is that?"

I stuck my hand into the light's cavity, mindful of the broken glass, and pulled out a piece of silver rubbery-like material. I held it up and shone the flashlight on it.

And then I realized what it was and I wanted to scream.

It was Lycra, from a pair of biking shorts.

Jesus.

This was the car that hit Sam.

A noise behind me, by the half-open garage door, then the bright white beam of a powerful flashlight hit my eyes and I threw an arm up to block the blinding light.

"Gemma? What are you doing here?"

"Mrs. Watkins, is that you? Turn that light away, please," I said.

The beam moved off my face to the floor. In the gloom, I saw the tall, older woman standing by the front of Ellen's black SUV.

"Uh, hi. I know this looks bad but I can explain. I knocked on your door a few minutes ago and didn't get an answer, so I came around back, thinking someone might be home. I thought I heard a cat, crying, coming from the garage," I stammered.

I felt the ridiculousness of the lie in the silent space between us.

I felt Mrs. Watkins's eyes on me, but I couldn't see her features.

She was quiet a moment then said, "Well, come inside the house. You'll catch your death out here."

"Oh, no, really, I should just be going home."

"Then why knock on the door?" Mrs. Watkins replied. She turned and ducked out of the garage. I sighed and followed her, caught in my own web of deceit.

We moved in silence through the covered walkway, from the garage and into the house. I pulled the hood back from my head and removed my rain jacket, careful to bundle it up so that it didn't drip all over the polished marble floors.

In darkness, Mrs. Watkins led me to the kitchen.

There she had set up a trio of thick white pillar candles, and she set a kettle of water to boil on the stove by the light of the flickering flames. She directed me to take a seat on one of the two stools that stood next to an island in the middle of the kitchen.

"We lost power an hour ago. If you're looking for Terry or Ellen, you're out of luck. They're in town, attending a fund-raiser. The show must go on, I suppose. Dad's barely in the ground; Annika's missing; and they just buried their only son for the second time," Mrs. Watkins said. "I'll never understand it."

She went to a cupboard and opened it and stood, looking at contents I could not see. "Herbal tea? I have chamomile, lemon, or mint. Or I can get you black, decaf or regular."

The candles cast strange shadows in the large kitchen and I began to feel drowsy in the dim, warm room, out of the cold rain. I struggled to concentrate on Mrs. Watkins's words.

"I don't know, some people cope with grief by staying busy, I suppose. If you've got sugar or milk, the decaf black tea would be just fine, thank you."

Mrs. Watkins looked back at me over her shoulder. "The Bellingtons are not 'copers,' Gemma. That implies making do with situations. We tackle our problems head-on."

She pulled two mugs from another cupboard and began opening the tea bags. She whistled as she worked, a funny little smile on her face.

"Speaking of head-on, is that your Toyota in the garage? You've got a busted headlight."

Mrs. Watkins looked up at me. "Why do you think I've been using Annika's car? She took mine out at some point in the last few weeks, God knows why, and returned it in worse condition than she found it. She hit a parking pole, apparently. Until I get it fixed, she said I could use her Honda. I wouldn't want to get a ticket for the headlight."

"Ah, I see. Hannah, forgive my bluntness, but you seem rather in a good mood. Have there been any further updates about Annika? Any more word from her kidnappers?" I asked.

On the stove, the kettle began to whistle. Mrs. Watkins turned away without answering me and went and removed the kettle from the burner. When she turned back, she'd stopped smiling.

"No, no word from the kidnappers. Let's just say I have a feeling Annika is going to be okay. She and I are alike that way. We're survivors. We do what has to be done," Mrs. Watkins answered.

She poured the boiling water carefully and then dropped a tea bag into each mug. Something behind me caught her eye and she looked up and then away, quickly, but it was too late. I'd noticed her movement and in the space before I heard anything, I sensed a presence behind me, in the darkness.

"Gemma," a voice called.

Slowly, I turned around.

# Chapter Forty-eight

Annika laughed, that musical laugh of hers that sounded like wind chimes. "You look like you've seen a ghost!"

She was just a few feet from me, in jeans and a hoodie sweatshirt. Her feet were bare and her toenails painted a scarlet red.

It's odd what we notice.

"Annika, go back upstairs," Mrs. Watkins said. "Finish packing."

Annika paced the edge of the room, shaking her head. She moved in and out of the candlelight, there one minute, gone the next. Maybe she was a kind of a ghost, after all. Maybe I'd been living in a horror story all these long days and nights.

"Gemma's here. I need to know why."

I said the first thing that came to mind. "I talked to Pete this morning. He wants his claw back."

Annika stopped pacing on the other side of the island and gave another laugh. "He's such a child. You wouldn't believe the things I let him do, and now he wants his little prop back?"

"He sounds like a nice guy, you should give him another chance. Although I don't think he'd take you back."

"*I* broke up with him," she shouted, and resumed pacing.

Mrs. Watkins sipped her tea, watching the two of us. "What claw, Annie? What is Gemma talking about?"

Annika stopped pacing and stared at me with pleading eyes. I looked at the older woman, confused.

"Wait, what?" I asked.

Annika said, "Gemma, don't . . . Pete doesn't have anything to do with this. I just want my money; money that I would have got-ten anyway, so I can leave. This family, this town . . . I need to get away!"

"And you will, my love, you will," Mrs. Watkins said.

She moved toward Annika, her arms outstretched, pleading. "But you must hurry. You need to be packed and gone before your parents get home. That's the only way this plan works."

Understanding bloomed in my head.

"You don't know, do you?" I asked Mrs. Watkins.

Behind her, Annika was frantically shaking her head and mak-ing shushing motions. Unbelievable.

The older woman stared at me. She glanced back at Annika, then at me again.

"Know what?"

"Annika killed Nicky. And she tried to kill my partner, Sam Birdshead, with your car."

The mug fell from Mrs. Watkins's hands and shattered on the kitchen tile with a sound as sharp as a shotgun's blast. She stag-gered forward, her hand on her heart.

"You're lying," she gasped. She reached the edge of the island and gripped it as though holding on for dear life. "Tell me she's lying, Annika."

Annika was silent, chewing on a fingernail.

"Annika!" Mrs. Watkins shouted. "Answer me this minute."

Annika sighed and said, "You know I can't lie to you, Aunt Han-nah. I never could." She kneeled down and began picking up the shards of the broken mug. She worked quickly and carelessly and when she stood up, bright spots of blood bloomed on her finger-tips.

Mrs. Watkins stared at her in shock. "I don't . . . I don't under-stand. You killed your brother? And ran that police officer off the road? Why?"

"Sit down, Aunt Hannah, before you stroke out. You thought we didn't know about your heart pills, but we do. You don't have to hide them, you know," Annika said.

She stood there, bleeding, until her aunt obeyed and took a seat on the other stool, next to me. Only then did Annika move to the trash can, dump the broken mug, and yank a bunch of paper towels off the paper towel holder. She held them to her bleeding hands.

"I don't understand," Mrs. Watkins said. She trembled and I took a good look at her face. Her skin was pale, with sweat beginning to bead at her temple. I thought back to my first aid classes and remembered sudden news—good or bad—could cause shock in a person. The adrenaline rush could be fatal to someone with heart problems.

Annika looked at me.

I shrugged in response and said, "I don't understand either, Annika. Why don't you explain things for us?"

She blew a strand of loose hair from her forehead and bit her lip. She was quiet, thinking, and then came to some decision.

"Nicky had a hard time keeping secrets. The rest of us are pretty good at it. He held it in for a day or two, and then he burst on that camping trip, up at Bride's Veil. He told me everything that night. How he was messing around with some old articles at the school library, and came across a story about that dead woman, Rose Noonan. He didn't pay much attention, until he saw the photograph. She was wearing the same necklace our Granny always wore! Nicky couldn't believe it. Granny used to call it her 'good luck' charm, and said wearing a flower at her throat was like carrying springtime in her heart. So, Nicky decided to play detective. He went to 'investigate' the cold case at the public library. He decided Grandpa must have killed the lady, and then given the necklace to Granny," Annika said. "He got sick while he was telling me about it. He puked in an empty plastic bag in our tent."

What were the chances, I thought to myself? A thousand to one? A million to one? That one day, a killer's grandson would see an old photograph and both solve a murder mystery and start a terrible chain of events?

Annika peeked under the paper towels on her hands and nodded, satisfied with what she saw. She said, "I stopped the bleeding.

Just a little pressure, like they taught us in Girl Scouts. I was a great scout, Gemma. The uniforms just got too ugly for me to keep going."

"Do they also teach you about shock? I'm worried about your aunt."

At my side, Mrs. Watkins groaned. She leaned forward and put her head in her hands.

Annika ignored my question. She continued with her story. Once started, she wouldn't or couldn't stop. "Our father was running for office. Our family is one of the most respected in the state. I'd never get into Yale if people knew my grandfather was a killer. Jesus, we'd be like the Manson family."

"But Nicky wasn't worried about those things, was he?"

Annika nodded. "You're right. Nicky wanted to tell Mom and Dad. He wanted to go to the police. He mentioned you by name; he remembered you from some Career Day fair. Nicky said we owed it to the woman, Rose Noonan."

"God, dear God, what have I done," Mrs. Watkins murmured. "Oh, please. Please, make this stop."

Annika said, "Aunt Hannah, don't worry. Things are going to be fine, once I get my money. You were so right; I do deserve a fresh start somewhere amazing. I have my whole life ahead of me, I shouldn't have to live it under anyone's thumb. I'm a fucking Bellington, for God's sake."

Mrs. Watkins started weeping into her hands, her shoulders shaking with each sob.

Time seemed to slow down then in the warm, dim kitchen. I needed to know what happened to Nicky, I had to have the whole story. At the same time, I tried to watch Mrs. Watkins out of the corner of my eye. I was worried about her; if she was going into shock, we needed to call for help here in the next few minutes. I shifted in my seat and felt the reassuring weight of both my gun and my cell phone in my rain jacket.

Annika went on. "I told Nicky I'd kill him if he told anyone. I said I'd rip his heart out before he'd ruin our family. He asked me how I could say such a thing, and I said it was easy, that he and I were the same, and while I'd miss him, I'd go on living his life and mine, and it would be just as if he'd never been born at all."

"How did Nicky survive the fall over Bride's Veil?"

"I asked him the same thing before I slit his throat," Annika said. "He'd been playing around the spot a few weeks before our camping trip, and he discovered a deep pool, one without boulders or rocks, just to the left of the waterfall. He decided that night, after we spoke, he would just leave and have nothing more to do with our family. He would forget what he knew, what I had said to him. He could start over; start fresh somewhere. The coward could run away as if all this had never happened. When he saw his chance the next day, he never hesitated. Nicky jumped, knowing if he positioned himself right, he would land in the pool, the one without rocks. And that's just what he did."

She stepped forward, into the candlelight, and I saw a strange gleam in her eyes. The little narcissist was proud of her brother.

Keep talking, Annika, keep talking.

"And then three years passed, and what? You recognized him at the circus?"

Annika laughed. "Yes, three years passed. I finished high school, went to college, and started my own life. I came home for the summer and was anxious to get back to Yale. And then I got an e-mail from my dear dead brother, asking to meet behind a tent on the grounds of a circus that would be arriving in a week."

She went to the trash can and tossed the bloodied paper towels in and then poured herself a glass of water from the kitchen sink. She took a long drag and then wiped at her mouth with the back of her hand. "God, it feels good to tell all this to someone, you know?"

Annika took another long sip of water and then placed the glass inside the dishwasher. Beside me, Mrs. Watkins was still and silent, her weeping stopped. She watched Annika. I tried to watch them both.

"So I met him. He told me how he survived the fall and he

begged me to reconsider telling the authorities about Grandpa. He spent three years running from the truth and he couldn't do it anymore. Nicky read somewhere that Dad was sick and he got it into his head that all these lies and cover-ups were at the root of Dad's cancer. He was convinced that if he could somehow right the wrong of Rose Noonan's killing, Dad would be cured. Nicky said he was going to see Dad whether I agreed or not. It was an easy decision. I couldn't agree, so I killed him."

"Just like that, you killed your own brother?"

Annika nodded. "In a way, I wasn't killing him but saving him. I knew he'd never live with himself if he ruined this family. Family is everything, isn't it, Aunt Hannah? That's what you've always told me. It's all about the collective good, not what I or you or Nicky or even Mom or Dad want. We must always ask ourselves, 'What is best for the family?'"

Mrs. Watkins stared at her niece in horror. "Yes, yes I have told you that. But I didn't mean . . . you can't have thought I would condone murder . . . My, god, your poor brother . . ."

"How did you get away? There was a lot of blood, Annika," I asked.

Annika smiled. She said, "In his e-mail, Nicky had explained he'd been working as a clown. So, I took a clown suit with me. It was one of those big jumpsuit style costumes. I pulled the whole thing up and over my bloody clothes and voilà! It covered everything."

In front of me, one of the candles went out and I moved to relight it with the lighter that lay in the middle of the island. Mrs. Watkins touched a hand to my thigh. I looked at her. Keeping her eyes on Annika, she gave the slightest shake of her head.

Don't light the candle.

"What about Sam? Why try to kill him?"

"Sam was a diversion. You and your asshole partner, Finn, you guys spooked me when you came to the house. If you knew Nicky was looking into the Woodsman murders, it was only a matter of time before you started connecting the dots."

"You didn't know, did you?" I asked.

Annika looked confused. "Know what?"

"Sam was closer than you thought. He had the files of the evidence collected in Nicky's room. He had a photograph of the necklace, and part of a poem. Finn saw a picture of your grandmother, wearing the necklace, at your house, while we were busting our chops trying to solve *your* kidnapping."

Annika said, "Now that is irony. I had no idea. I just figured Sam was the easiest to get to, seeing as he's not even a real police officer yet. But you sure are, aren't you Gemma? So now, maybe you can answer something for me. Did my Grandpa kill those boys, the McKenzies?"

I nodded then shook my head.

"Well? Which is it, yes or no?"

"I think he did, but I can't be sure. There was a third boy there, the day the McKenzies disappeared. He saw the whole thing. Your grandfather was about to dump Rose's body. He had a partner with him, someone waiting in the car. When Frank saw the boys, he and the partner went after them. They were afraid of witnesses. So, I don't know who killed the boys—it was either your grandfather, his partner, or both," I replied.

Outside, a bolt of lightning lit up the sky, followed by a low roll of thunder. For a moment, the entire kitchen was illuminated. I saw Annika, pacing like a caged tiger. She held something in her hand, some small, silver thing that I couldn't make out.

"Jesus Christ," Annika said. "Who was his partner?"

# Chapter Forty-nine

At my side, Hannah Watkins let out a thin, keening moan. She had been through so much. I eased the cell phone out of my rain jacket pocket and held it close, under the edge of the island, ready for my first opportunity. Somehow, I needed to call for an ambulance for Mrs. Watkins and backup assistance to arrest Annika, without her realizing I was making any calls. I had a feeling she wouldn't go easy.

"Well? Who was his partner?" Annika asked again.

"I don't know," I said. "Somebody incredibly close to him, a friend, someone willing to enter into the darkest of acts to protect Frank."

Annika stepped backward, out of the candlelight, and sank into the darkness. She whistled low and then said, "There's only one person on this planet who was close enough to my grandfather to do something like that, Gemma."

"Who?"

"You're sitting right next to her."

At my side, the housekeeper jerked in her seat.

A wave of vertigo washed over me and I gripped the edges of the island.

I had been so stupid, for so long. The answers were right in front of us the whole time.

Hannah Watkins had been watching over the family for years, Ellen Bellington had said to us that day at their house.

I had watched Hannah tend to a broken coffee cup and noticed she knew her way around broken things.

Hannah herself had said that family was everything.

"Aunt Hannah?" Annika said. "You're the Woodsman, aren't you?"

Another flash of lightning and a second roll of thunder shook the house and showed Mrs. Watkins nodding jerkily, a marionette in the spotlight.

Tears ran down her face.

"I was twenty-three, not much older than you, Annika. I had finished college and was living at home, working at the mall, trying to figure out what I wanted to do with my life. I came home on a lunch break and my dad was in the garage, crying. He was in a panic. There was a woman in the backseat of his pickup truck and I thought she was sleeping. Dad said it had been an accident. He said he'd go to jail for the rest of his life if anyone found out," Mrs. Watkins said.

She wiped at her face and drew a hand down to her chest and left it there, as though she was trying to hold back a lifetime of secret grief and lost innocence.

"You were the passenger in his truck, in the woods that day, weren't you?" I asked. A deep sadness came over me; I knew what it was like to try to hold that grief inside you, how it ate away at your sense of identity, how it stole the wonder out of life.

Mrs. Watkins nodded. "I don't know why I went with him, he didn't ask me to. He seemed so broken and somehow, I thought if I went with him, bore witness to what he was going to do with her body, that I could take some of the burden off his shoulders."

"And the McKenzie boys?"

"I never meant to hurt those kids. I thought if we scared them, they'd stay quiet. We cornered them up on the trail. I had a hunting rifle from the truck. They came easily enough. Then Dad dropped me off at home, and told me to forget the whole thing. He said he would figure out what to do with them. I trusted him, don't you see? He was my father. He was larger than life," Mrs. Watkins said as her voice broke. Tears and phlegm choked her words.

"But he killed them, didn't he, Aunt Hannah?" Annika asked. She'd crept forward again, into the candlelight. "And then he waited to dump the woman's body, didn't he?"

Her expression chilled me to the core. She was curious, rapt.

Hannah Watkins nodded. "I believe he killed them that same afternoon, although we never spoke of it again. I asked him, just once, that next day when I saw the reports on television of the missing boys. He slapped me and told me that they were safe, and that he wanted to wait a few days before letting them go. He also said this could ruin our entire future, that our family's lives would never be the same. As the days passed, I grew more and more certain that he had in fact hurt them."

"Jesus. They were just kids, Hannah. Why didn't you say anything?"

She looked at me with a face that seemed melted with tears and grief.

"Don't you understand? He would have blamed the whole thing on me. He ruled this town like he ruled our house. I was a stupid girl. No one would have believed me. And once the boys were dead, what did it matter? They weren't coming back. I couldn't save them."

"What about their parents? Can you imagine for one second, if it had been your children, not knowing where they were, if they were cold? Hungry? Scared? And then multiply that feeling by a thousand and then another thousand, for every day since that those poor parents lived with that pain. Oh, God, I'm going to be sick."

Hannah wiped the tears from her face and straightened her shoulders. Her face was white and at her throat I saw her pulse beat very fast.

"I've been punished every moment of my life since by myself, my God, and my family. I'm barren. My husband wanted children more than he wanted me. I've raised my brother's kids. I've lived the last few years under the same roof as a killer. My entire existence is madness, Gemma. I would give every ounce of happiness that I might have touched in this lifetime to take back what we did. I poured my soul into trying to right my wrongs, by being here, for this one family, for the only family I can still help."

On the counter, another candle blew itself out. I pushed back from the island and stood up.

"Where do you think you're going, Gemma?" Annika asked.

She came around the side of the island and stood next to her aunt.

I took a deep breath. "I'm going to see if I can reach my police chief. He'll come to the house with a few officers and an ambulance. Hannah, we need to get you to a hospital, I'm worried you're going into shock. And if you've already got known heart problems . . . Annika, you'll need to come to the station, where I'll book you on murder charges. It's over."

Annika shook her head. "No, I don't think so. I'm taking my money and leaving. Aunt Hannah said my plan would work."

Mrs. Watkins slid off her stool and stood. She put her arm around Annika.

"Sweetheart, Gemma is right. It's over. I'm sorry, so, so terribly sorry. I wanted a better life for you, away from here. I never dreamed it was too late. If I knew you'd been corrupted, sickened the same way your grandfather was . . ."

Annika struggled against her aunt and in the candlelight I saw the silver object she held more clearly. It was a short, stubby hunting knife, the kind that folds easily.

"Aunt Hannah, let me go!" Annika said, her voice catching. She was crying and I stepped back from the women, wary of the knife and the emotions at play.

Mrs. Watkins grabbed Annika by the arm and shook her, violently. Anger flashed across her face and I saw for the first time how quickly the Furies struck in this family. "Stop it this minute, Annika. You spoiled little child. You could have had everything. I see now that you deserve nothing."

Annika tried to pull her arm free but Mrs. Watkins was strong, and tall, taller than Annika, and her grip was fueled by a deep rage.

I pulled my cell phone from my back pocket and stole a second from watching them to dial dispatch. I whispered the address and the situation into the phone but I needn't have bothered trying to be quiet. The two women were completely distracted by their own tragedies.

"Let me go!" Annika screamed. She shoved at Mrs. Watkins with her free hand, the hand that held the knife. I heard something tear, and then Mrs. Watkins cried out.

The older woman gasped and stepped back from Annika. She sank to the floor and held up hands slick with a black wetness. I dropped to the ground beside her and felt her body. Her chest was warm and damp and I pushed down, trying to stem the flow of blood. So much blood, an artery near her heart must have been sliced.

"Annika! Get me that towel, quickly."

Above me, Annika stared down with horror. "Aunt Hannah? I didn't mean to hurt you. I just . . . you were holding me so tight."

Mrs. Watkins shook in my grasp and tried to say something but her words were swept away in the stream of blood that poured from her lips. She would die before any paramedic ever reached us.

Annika seemed to realize that, too. She fell to her knees and took her aunt's head in her hands and gently, softly, brushed the hair away from the older woman's forehead. Mrs. Watkins closed her eyes and her body grew still. The lines fell from her face and a quiet peace descended over her features.

Annika carefully laid her dead aunt's head on the ground and looked at me. All the fight seemed to have left her body. She suddenly looked on the outside like the lost little girl she was on the inside. Incredibly, I felt sorry for her, for I saw for the first time how lonely living such an evil life must be.

She asked, "What happens now?"

I sat back and held my hands up, unsure what to do with the blood that coated them as thick as paint. In the distance, I heard sirens begin to make their way up the mountain, past the Swiss-Miss chalets and the more moderate log cabins, higher and higher up the road, toward a cold house, with dark secrets, that was full of old blood and now, new blood.

Annika heard the sirens, too. The knife slid out of her hands. "I'm going to prison, aren't I? All I ever tried to do was be a good girl. The best girl, in the best family."

I remembered Nicky's blood, the pattern it made in the dirt at the fairgrounds.

I remembered the skull I found in the woods, the way it gleamed like a small treasure waiting to be found.

I remembered a girl with turquoise eyes who flirted with a boy at a bar, a boy who'd lose his leg, and an old woman, ready to die, who'd kept a terrible secret to protect her only son.

"Yes, Annika. You're going to prison for a very, very long time."

# Chapter Fifty

The last time I saw Annika Bellington was on the stairs outside the old courthouse, across the street from City Hall. An early frost had come overnight and the stairs were slippery, so I walked down them slowly, one hand gripping the rail. I had dropped off the last of my files on the Bellington case and was about to head into an early maternity leave.

Things were, for the most part, wrapped up.

Chief Chavez released our findings in a press conference the day after the events at the Bellington house. On the steps of City Hall, before a crowd of hungry reporters and curious townspeople, Chavez announced the arrest of Annika Bellington for the murders of Nicky Bellington and Hannah Bellington Watkins, and the attempted murder of Sam Birdshead. Chavez took no questions. He instead ended his announcement with the news that the Woodsman had been identified, and that further information would be forthcoming.

Mayor Terry Bellington threatened to sue the department for libel, slander, and a whole host of other things, but when he saw the evidence, he shut up pretty quick. I have a feeling this will be the mayor's last term in office. If he does run again, he'll do so alone: Ellen Bellington bought a one-way ticket to Norway, and the last I heard, she was living in Oslo, trying to make a move back into show business.

When I saw Annika, she was ten feet away, surrounded by a group of older men in expensive suits. Mayor Bellington lawyered her up an hour after her arrest, and today, Annika was to be formally charged with the murders.

I must have known that, but somehow, I'd forgotten.

Or maybe I hadn't.

Maybe I needed to see her again, one last time.

"Annika. You look well."

Her hair was styled up off her face in a bun, and she wore a navy pantsuit, and looked rested and innocent of anything and everything.

"Thank you. You look ready to pop," Annika said. She smiled at me.

One of the lawyers, a small, fussy-looking man, tried to hustle her up the stairs. In return, she whispered something to him that made his face go white and his hand drop from her elbow.

"I have to thank you, you know," she continued.

"For what?"

I shouldn't have asked.

I should have lowered my head and made my way down those slippery steps and kept right on moving into the next chapter of my life, a chapter that hopefully didn't include death, so much death.

"For not killing me when you had the chance. I'll never be found guilty. These dicks make more in a day than you make in a month. And clearly," she said, "clearly I'm insane. If anything I'll spend a few months at Clear Water Lodge, attending group sessions and bumming cigarettes off the night nurses."

I looked at her and decided she might be right.

Annika waited for a response that I didn't have.

Instead, I did what I should have done a moment before. I put my head down and made my way slowly toward the street.

Three days later, at midnight, I stood at the bedroom window and watched as the first big storm of the season blew in. Behind me, Brody threw clothes, toothbrushes, and a paperback into an old gym bag. As another contraction hit, I leaned forward and rested my head against the cold glass. A single snowflake, larger than the others, caught my eye. I watched it slowly float down. The flake lost its specialness the instant it hit the ground, though, becoming just a tiny speck joining with a billion other tiny specks to blanket the world in this strange phenomenon we know as snow.

In the end, life is a series of snowflakes, isn't it? Each moment is unique and completely separate from the next, with the power to change everything and nothing all at the same time. If you're lucky, over time those billions of moments add up to a life.

Or they don't. Some people spend their entire lives seeing the snow without ever seeing the magic in the existence of one snow-flake.

"What are you thinking about?" Brody asked as he zipped up the gym bag and motioned for me to follow him. It would be a slow drive down the mountain in this weather, but I stood still another minute.

"Honey?"

I pushed off the window and turned and looked at him. "I was pondering the mortality of the humble snowflake. In flight but for a moment . . ."

Brody rubbed his chin. I saw the geologist gaze creep into his eyes. "Well, that's not entirely true. Remember the water cycle? You probably learned about it in middle school. All water molecules . . ."

He launched into the scientific explanation of why, in fact, snowflakes are immortal and I felt sorry for the Peanut. She was going to grow up with a father who replaced poetry with logic and a mother who spent her days in very dark places.

The roads were slick and visibility poor. Brody drove carefully, with the radio off and the high beams on. The road ahead came in glimpses as the windshield wipers worked overtime, and I wished I had windshield wipers of my own, to flip on when my road, my path, was not so clear.

I watched Brody in profile. He had a five o'clock shadow, bed-head hair, and a look of pure concentration. I watched him, and wondered what this child was going to bring to our lives. There were three of us now, and I hoped he felt as I did, that our choices were no longer our own. With Brody, I had known joy and pain, happiness and sorrow, laughter and love.

I trusted him with my life.

I still didn't know if I could trust him with my heart.

It was almost worse that it wasn't, in the end, Celeste Takashima in Alaska. Celeste was a known commodity, someone I could direct my anger and hate toward. If I wanted to make a voodoo doll, I could do a pretty good likeness. But now, now there was someone new out there, some faceless, nameless woman, ready to shed her bubblegum pink parka to warm his tent and polish his rocks. Brody tells me she is Canadian, married, and unattractive.

He tells me I'm paranoid and being crazy. I remind him I have reason to be.


Grace Julia Sutherland was born at 4:44 a.m., healthy, perfect, and absolutely beautiful. Ten fingers, ten toes, and eyes the color of blueberries.

Brody chose Grace, because he believes it embodies all that we hope for her, and ourselves.

I chose Julia, in honor of the woman who raised me.

# Chapter Fifty-one

In my dreams, the dead can speak. I greet them by name—Tommy, Andrew, Nicky—and watch as they run in a meadow that is soaked with afternoon sun. They play a game that involves lying still, and then jumping up with shrieks and whoops. Before the afternoon is through, the children's clothes will be stained with grass and pollen from the hundreds of wildflowers that surround them.

Before long, a little girl and a man join me. The girl takes my right hand, the man, my left. They let me whisper good-bye and then they tug, pulling me with them into the woods.

I leave the meadow.

Somehow, I don't think I'll be back again.